D0977406

COLD FRAME

ALSO BY P. T. DEUTERMANN

THE CAM RICHTER NOVELS

The Cat Dancers

Spider Mountain

The Moonpool

Nightwalkers

THRILLERS

The Last Man

The Firefly

Darkside

Hunting Season

Train Man

Zero Option

Sweepers

Official Privilege

SEA STORIES

Sentinels of Fire

Ghosts of Bungo Suido

Pacific Glory

The Edge of Honor

Scorpion in the Sea

COLD FRAME

P. T. DEUTERMANN

ST. MARTIN'S PRESS NEW YORK

This is a work of fiction. All of the characters, organizations, and events portrayed in this novel are either products of the author's imagination or are used fictitiously.

 Printed in the United States of America. For information, address St. Martin's Press, 175 Fifth Avenue, New York, NY 10010.

www.stmartins.com

The Library of Congress Cataloging-in-Publication Data is available upon request.

ISBN 978-1-250-05933-8 (hardcover)
ISBN 978-1-4668-6392-7 (e-book)

St. Martin's Press books may be purchased for educational, business, or promotional use. For information on bulk purchases, please contact the Macmillan Corporate and Premium Sales Department at 1-800-221-7945, extension 5442, or write to specialmarkets@macmillan.com.

First Edition: July 2015

10 9 8 7 6 5 4 3 2 1

This book is dedicated to the operational-level men and women of all the agencies striving to sweep back the tide of global anti-American terrorism. They work long and hard, some in offices, others out alone in the dangerous weeds, both at home and abroad, and, in the main, they have succeeded in keeping us relatively safe, often despite Washington and all of its intricate and partisan political machinations. That problem is the genesis of the well-known bureaucratic greeting formula: Hello. We're from headquarters. We're here to help you. And, universally, in reply: Hello. We're *so* glad you're here . . .

The third-largest federal agency in the entire United States government, behind the Department of Veterans Affairs and the Department of Defense, is the Department of Homeland Security (DHS). It has a $61 *billion* publicly disclosed budget, and subagencies that include the U.S. Coast Guard, Customs and Border Protection, the entire Secret Service, the Transportation Security Administration (TSA), and the Federal Emergency Management Agency (FEMA). In 2013, it counted 240,000 full-time employees plus a slightly *larger* number of contractors.

Today DHS is only *one* of eighty-five publicly acknowledged agencies of the federal government involved in America's War on Terror.

COLD FRAME

PROLOGUE

Whitestone Hall, Great Falls, Virginia, fall, three years ago

Hiram Walker pointed down at one scraggly-looking plant. "Now this little jewel, Mister Strang, discourages predation by blinding the animal temporarily the moment it takes the first few little nibbles."

"How in the world does it do that?"

"Its leaves secrete a powerful toxin the instant the plant senses predatory pressure. The first bite is free. The second one causes an ocular migraine within seconds. The animal then experiences retinal flashes that it associates with a nocturnal predator eye-flash. It backs away immediately, which is when it discovers it can't see a thing. It usually freezes in place and often defecates in mortal fright."

"So the plant stops the attack and gets some fertilizer in the bargain," Strang said, peering closer at the plant. "Nasty-looking weed. What's it called?"

"We call it Sister Dark Surprise," Hiram replied. "Its Latin name is unnecessarily complicated."

"Is the damage permanent?"

Hiram Walker had been in full lecture mode as he walked carefully among randomly placed raised beds of what looked like tangled weeds. Carefully, because he was a full seven feet, three inches tall, and also because his joints, afflicted with Marfan syndrome, were increasingly unreliable, especially when he ventured out of the big white house up on the hill. He was wearing light, woolen trousers under what looked like a nineteenth-century frock coat, complete with a small white flower in his lapel.

Hiram was fifty-two years old but looked older, with an oversized head, thinning hair, a gaunt face, deep-set, almost hooded eyes, and very large hands. Because of the Marfan, he moved in a hesitant, jerky fashion, which inevitably reminded people of Dr. Frankenstein's outsized monster.

The manor house, known as Whitestone Hall in the Great Falls neighborhood, sat on ten acres of extremely valuable riverside property that was surrounded by a fourteen-foot-high, ivy-covered brick wall on all four sides, including along the river. The house was situated high enough that there was a river view from the back terraces. There were massive wrought-iron gates at the front entrance, and solid, almost medieval wooden gates on the river side that led to more terraces cascading down to the river itself, where there was a small boathouse. The ten acres were heavily wooded except for a wide avenue of descending walks and pools edged by formal gardens that ended down by those huge wooden gates. The front drive was packed yellowish gravel, but where one might have expected more formal gardens there seemed to be a complete jungle of plants of all descriptions spreading out to the front and side walls of the property, interspersed with trees and large, strange-looking shrubs. Not visible from the road was a rooftop greenhouse that spanned the entire width of the house on the back side, facing the river. Anyone driving by on Deepstep Creek Road could catch just a momentary glimpse of the house through wrought-iron gates, but otherwise, that imposing brick wall offered complete privacy.

Hiram was the only child of the man who had invented, and then, happily, patented, the compound that kept the oil in an automatic transmission from frothing under load. Hiram was thus now a very wealthy man. His father had built the house for him, meaning that every dimensional aspect of the house and all its furnishings had been designed for a man who was just over seven feet tall and more than a little shaky on his feet. He had seldom ever left since moving onto the property twenty-six years ago. Everything he needed or wanted could be brought to him, and had been since childhood, when he had begun to inspire people to back away when they first saw him.

"Not the first time," Hiram said.

Strang smiled.

"The animal probably isn't amused," Hiram said. "But after about ten minutes its vision returns. Sometimes it tries for another bite. Not a good idea."

"Because . . . ?"

"Because Sister Dark Surprise is a rather short-tempered weed, Mister Strang. The first toxin is a precursor; if it's attacked again, a special bulb in its roots opens and pushes an alkaloid compound resembling the one in wormwood into all of its branches. A mouthful of that shuts the animal's autonomous nervous system down. It then pretty much drops dead."

"Autonomous system meaning breathing, heartbeat, stuff like that?"

"*Stuff* exactly like that," Hiram said, patiently.

"Now, alkaloids—those are always bad, yes?"

"We botanists prefer to think of them as quick," Hiram said.

"And it's the living plant that does all this, right? Not just, say, some of its dried leaves?"

"Correct."

"Hmm."

Hiram chuckled. "Let's move on, shall we? I've lots more interesting plants to show you."

They proceeded to the next cold frame. "Do Sister Dark Surprise's abilities occur in nature?" Strang asked as they were walking.

Hiram nodded. "The phase-one response does," he said. "But, no, the second response is not found in nature. Yet."

Strang gave him an arch look. "Your Phaedo Botanical Society bears watching," he said.

"You have no idea, Mister Strang."

"Well, I know a little bit," Strang said. "The society was formed to investigate the possibility that plants had brains. Its principals do research on this theory in different ways, but focus primarily on how plants defend themselves."

"That's a good, general description," Hiram said. "As far as it goes."

"And how far do this Sister Dark Surprise's abilities go?" Strang asked. "For instance, what would that badass little weed do to, say, a human being?"

Hiram stopped short and looked down at the man from the so-far-undisclosed government agency. "It sounds to me that we've come to the purpose of your visit, Mister Strang," Hiram said. "Why don't we go inside now?"

Strang smiled and nodded. Hiram thought that Strang was the plainest-looking man he'd ever seen. There was absolutely nothing remarkable about him from a physical-appearance perspective. Plain face, five-eight, brown eyes, a mild, patient expression; he would probably be just about invisible in a crowd. Hiram couldn't guess the man's age, but somewhere between mid-forties and mid-fifties. His only interesting feature was his hands, which were elongated, sinewy, with curling fingers and what looked to Hiram like heavy calluses on the edges of his palms. Karate? He had that calm and totally balanced air of physical confidence that genuine martial arts masters displayed. The whole effect told Hiram that Strang was probably affiliated with the clandestine-operations side of the agency.

They walked back to the house and went up the steps to the front doors, which were opened by the butler at just the right moment.

"Thank you, Thomas," Hiram said, stepping through the lofty entrance. "We will take coffee in the library, if you please."

"Very good, sir," Thomas Hennessy intoned as Hiram and his guest entered the main foyer. He followed them down the hallway with its thirty-foot ceilings at a respectful distance. Thomas was in his late forties, brimming with personal dignity and dressed all in black with the starched white collar and shirt befitting a proper English butler. His posture was ramrod straight and his expression reflected a watchful reserve. He spoke with a semipolished Cockney accent, smoothed out over the twenty years he had spent with an organization called the British Special Boat Service. That had been almost ten years ago, but he still carried himself with the assurance of someone who could take care of business should the need arise.

Hiram settled into a massive leather thronelike armchair in front of an equally massive fireplace, where Thomas had laid a crackling fire. He indicated a chair for Strang to sit in as Thomas pulled the library doors closed after checking the fire. Strang had to scoot back in the chair to get comfortable, which is when he discovered his feet no longer touched the ground.

"I apologize, Mister Strang," Hiram said, eyeing his visitor's discomfiture. "All the furniture in this house has been sized for me, I'm afraid. I keep meaning to get some normal-sized things put in, but then, I don't often receive visitors."

Strang nodded. He seemed to know that he looked like a kid trying out his father's desk chair for the first time. "Well, again, Mister Walker—thank *you* for seeing me. My boss said you were dealing with Marfan syndrome, which has made you something of a recluse."

"More than something, Mister Strang," Hiram said with a sigh. The half-hour tour of his special gardens had been an effort, and not for the first time he wondered how much longer he had on this earth. Marfan syndrome was a degenerative disease of the connective tissue, and the older Hiram got, the more he learned just how much connective tissue there was in the human body. If the daily pain in his joints was any indication, his prospects were not all that good. This wasn't news.

Thomas opened the doors to the library and wheeled in a coffee tray. He served them both and then withdrew again, reclosing the big white doors.

Hiram decided to get right to it. He needed to lie down, and soon. "This nameless government agency you work for, Mister Strang—is it involved in federal law enforcement? I ask because the original call came from a friend in the Bureau."

"No, sir, it is not. Or not exactly. We asked the Bureau to make the appointment for me because you've helped their lab with some forensic work in the past. Our office of course does have a name, but we try to keep our invisibility cloaks on as much as possible, given what we do."

Hiram smiled. "And what *exactly* does your office do, Mister Strang?"

"We coordinate the hunting down and execution of important foreign terrorists, Mister Walker. Men who are dedicated to the destruction of the United States."

"Ah," Hiram said. "You're involved with the sharp end of the DMX."

Strang's eyebrows rose in evident surprise.

Hiram smiled again from across the coffee tray. "I've worked with the Agency as well as the Bureau, Mister Strang," he said. "Forensically, of course, never operationally. Our little society has helped what used to be called the Clandestine Services to unravel some, ah, rather intractable mysteries from time to time. I called someone after I received the call from the Bureau about your wanting to meet. He told me you were coming at the behest of Carl Mandeville."

Strang just stared at him.

"I encourage you to speak freely to me, Mister Strang," Hiram continued. "It will save lots of time."

Strang cleared his throat. "You have the advantage of me, Mister Walker," he said. "I wasn't aware that you were read into DMX."

Hiram said nothing, waiting. Strang plunged ahead.

"The DMX committee is under political attack," he began. "There are some important members of the Senate who've taken issue with the whole concept behind DMX. There's been a proposal floated to conduct a classified policy review."

"Their objection being what, exactly? That the U.S. government is indulging in assassination of foreign nationals without any sort of due-course proceedings?"

"That's the way it's being framed," Strang said. "And, as with most Senate 'policy reviews,' the desired outcome is known well before the review even begins."

"Which is that DMX should be shut down, I presume?"

"Exactly. The CT world, that is, the federal counterterrorism bureaucracy, takes the view that DMX 'candidates' are engaged in a war against the United States. It may be an asymmetric war, but a war nonetheless. Therefore the people who end up on the Kill List are genuine enemy combatants, not just foreign nationals, as you phrased it. In wartime, enemy combatants are fair game. Especially since these same enemy combatants have no qualms about targeting innocent civilians, like they did in New York, or in Benghazi."

"You don't have to convince me, Mister Strang," Hiram said. "In my book, all terrorists, foreign or domestic, were born to die badly."

Strang nodded. "And it's not true that there's no due process," he said. "Hence the DMX committee. You know the concept, but do you know how it actually works?"

"Enlighten me," Hiram said, sipping some tea. The depth of his knowledge about the DMX was his business, not Strang's. He felt a slow warmth building in his tortured joints. Thomas, recognizing Hiram's discomfort after a rare walk around the grounds, had dosed his tea, God bless him.

"There are now eighty-plus federal agencies, offices, bureaus, task forces, operations committees, and even cabinet departments involved in the so-called War on Terror," Strang said. "The DMX is where all their efforts come together. Simply put, the DMX is where all the agencies involved in counterterrorism nominate candidates for execution. It's a tortuous process, with many iterations, but ultimately, one or two names will be approved at each meeting to go forward to the President for inclusion on something called the Kill List. The President, himself, personally must approve any such operations."

"Many are nominated, but few are chosen?"

"Exactly, Mister Walker," Strang said with a wintry smile. "The criteria for selection are both complex and time-dependent, as you can imagine. There has to be evidence presented, not just speculation, and the focus is on the terrorist leadership, not whole groups."

"Do the agencies who develop the Kill List carry out the actual executions?"

"No, sir. There is a Chinese wall between the selection process and the actual operations that follow presidential approval. The people who do the wet work have no interaction with DMX, and that is a deliberate separation."

And which side of the wall do you come from, Mr. Strang? Hiram wondered. The separation had probably been the only way they'd been able to convince the senior government officials who sat on the DMX committee to accept the assignment. I'll help to define the most valuable targets, but I will *not* be associated with any killing. Harrumph. As if that made any difference, Hiram thought, with an invisible smile.

"And what is it you want with me and our botanical society?"

"The politicians who want to see the Kill List shut down know they cannot directly come out against the counterterrorism effort, per se. They would be seen as un-American. So: they are working to shut off the assets used by the executives on the other side of that Chinese wall. The drones in particular. If they proscribe the most effective weapons, they can gut the program while still being able to claim they're in complete support of counterterrorism."

"You sound as if they might succeed."

"They very well might," Strang admitted. "There's a lot of backlash out there regarding things like, say, the NSA's domestic spying program. Snowden's drip-by-drip revelations keep fueling that fire. Ordinary citizens are becoming alarmed, to say the least. *We* feel they are more upset with the sheer scale of the CT world's scope than with the underlying concept, but—"

"Can you blame them, Mister Strang?" Hiram interrupted. "There are disturbing historical parallels with what the American federal government is doing to the citizenry these days."

Strang put up his hands in a defensive gesture. "I know, I know," he said. "But this is a vital program, Mister Walker. If nothing else, it gives potential terrorist leaders in the war against western civilization considerable pause to know that a promotion, as it were, makes one a candidate for the Kill List."

"You think they know about it?"

"Of course they do," Strang said. "We've made sure they know about it. In a way, we may have shot ourselves in the foot by doing that."

The rule of unintended consequences at work, Hiram thought. "I would think," he said, "that the size, eighty-plus agencies you said, would make this CT endeavor in general and the DMX in particular difficult to control. That it might get out of hand, somehow. Leaders of Al Qaeda-in-wherever are clearly enemies of the state and thus candidates for the list. What's to keep that mind-set from expanding?"

"Expanding?"

"To enemies of, say, the sitting administration?"

"The President must approve each name, Mister Walker."

"My point exactly."

Strang frowned. "Yes, sir, but the people who are involved in developing the list come from across the whole political spectrum. Some are appointees, but most of them are longtime senior civil servants who've lived through both parties being in power. Plus, they are completely excluded from the subsequent clandestine operations to carry out the executions. DMX is a process, a very convoluted and even controversial process, admittedly, but unlike most of the CT world's efforts, this one produces a tangible scorecard."

"Do these senators have any allies on the DMX itself?" Hiram asked.

"It's possible," Strang said. "As I said, the members of the committee are, for the most part, senior executive service bureaucrats—career civil servants, with a few political appointees thrown in at the assistant secretary level. The DMX is no place for mere deep-pocket campaign contributors. That's another reason why the senators are going after the actual means of execution—civil servants can't be touched."

"So," Hiram said. "What do you want from me and my colleagues?"

"We want your society's help," Strang said. "Actually, sir, I think we want some of your plants."

"Who's 'we,' Mister Strang? Carl Mandeville?"

"Yes, sir. He is a very—determined man. He's looking way ahead."

"To what end, may I ask?"

"To be able to continue the work of the DMX should its opponents succeed, of course."

Hiram thought about that for a moment. If Mandeville was the driving force behind Strang's visit, then someone on the DMX knew far too much about the society's research. He may have surprised Strang with his unexpected knowledge of the DMX, but Strang had just surprised him back. Then something occurred to him.

"It seems to me, Mister Strang, that there's a hole in that Chinese wall. Assuming you're on the execution side, why are you and Mister Mandeville working together?"

Strang nodded. "I know what it looks like, Mister Walker. The thing is, Carl Mandeville's in charge of the whole thing. Think of him as standing astride that wall. Once the President signs off, it's Mandeville who actually puts the name on the Kill List and designates the action agency. After that, of course, he's no longer involved."

"So you're saying that he wants some of my botanical toxins as a backup for the assassination methods in play right now."

"Yes, sir."

"Let me think about that, Mister Strang," he said. "The toxins we've discovered, or accidentally created through mutations, are merely scientific curiosities. To weaponize them, as it were, is a major departure from the realm of scientific research."

"The U.S. signed the biological weapons convention a long time ago," Strang said. "We don't want to weaponize the toxins—we want to study them so that we can develop defenses against them."

Hiram gave Strang a skeptical look. "And that's your story, and you're sticking to it, right?"

Strang gave a hint of a smile. "Yes, sir."

Hiram sighed. "Okay," he said. "I will need to consult with my colleagues in the society. On balance, and if they agree, we might be able to help you."

Thomas entered the library room bearing a tea tray along with Hiram's noontime medications.

"Thank you, Thomas," he said. "I'm going to need a video teleconference with the society tonight."

"Very good, sir," Thomas said. "I'll sort out the time zones." Then he withdrew.

Or what's left of the society, Hiram thought, once Thomas had left. Like all too many familiar things these days, the Phaedo Botanical Society was beginning to fade from view. He poured a cup of tea. He looked over the pastries and decided not to indulge, hoisted himself upright, and then went over to the tall windows overlooking the south gardens, which presented the only formally sculpted features on the estate.

God, but he loved it here. The serenity of the grounds, the security provided by that all-excluding wall and what lay just inside it, and the knowledge that anything he wanted could be summoned at his every whim. His father had been right: you were destined for a secluded life, Hiram, he'd said, but that doesn't mean you need to be imprisoned. He could indulge in every aspect of the world except travel, and, for enough money, the world would willingly come to him. He'd lived on this estate for twenty-six years, and by now he'd learned that money could indeed buy most anything except sincerity and love.

The rise of the Internet had made life even more interesting, and that had been his entrée into the Phaedo Botanical Society. He'd published one paper in the *American Journal of Botany* about his research on the genetic capabilities of weeds two years after moving onto the estate. Weeds had fascinated him since the days of exploring his father's estate gardens. Weeds: annoying, omnipresent, and yet seemingly capable of resisting every modality humans used to attack them. Spray them, they die—and then move. Root them out of the ground, they come back. They grow in the cracks of cement sidewalks and in oil-spattered railroad beds, no matter what humans do to inhibit them. That was the first time he'd broached the notion that plants, and especially weeds, might have something analogous to a brain. His paper had been well received, by and large, except for one dissenting commentary that had arrived by e-mail, along with an invitation to confer with some strangely named garden society.

Only four of the original ten left now, he thought. Besides Hiram, there was Hideki Ozawa in the Sendai prefecture of Japan, Archibald Tennyson in Kent, England, and Giancomo de Farnese in the Toscana region of Italy. Four rich old men who probably held the world's most comprehensive reservoir of knowledge on botanical toxins. Each of them had different interests, with Hiram's being on the amazing resilience of weeds and his growing conviction that so-called weeds acted as if they had brains. He had become an expert in the field of botanical mutations to see if he could replicate the natural abilities of weeds to mutate for survival. Ozawa was actually a medical doctor who researched the applicability of some of Hiram's plant toxins to cancer. Tennyson's specialty was the *natural* mutation of plants to produce useful toxins instead of man having to modify them chemically for medicinal use. De Farnese was a toxicologist who was assembling a database of the markers left behind by plant poisons in homicide cases where poisoning was suspected, a natural enough avenue of research for an Italian born in Florence.

Thomas came back with the best time to make the conference call. Hiram nodded. He began to think about how he would present Mr. Strang's request.

ONE

Francis X. McGavin, principal deputy undersecretary for interagency coordination in the U.S. Department of Homeland Security arrived at a small French restaurant on Connecticut Avenue. He was there to have lunch with the woman he was hoping to make his newest conquest. McGavin was in his mid-fifties, conservatively suited if a little on the rotund side, with the self-satisfied expression of an upper-level bureaucrat who is comfortably important but not so senior as to ever be at risk to any career-killing excursions in the world of public policy. He was married, but with no children. His wife, a Georgetown heiress eight years his senior, dismissed his peccadilloes, considering his relentless pursuit of yet another younger woman as a blank check to lead her life precisely as she wanted. They were actually pretty good friends and sometimes even discussed his latest adventures over morning coffee. For McGavin, his philandering ways were just a pleasant game. For her, they were a great relief.

McGavin drove a four-door Jaguar that he parked carefully in front of the bistro, arranging the spacing so that no oafish cabbie could get close enough to the car to mar its gleaming finish. He was not surprised to find a parking place so close—little things like that often worked out for him.

His latest quarry—it was a hunt, after all—was a thirty-something beauty with flashy legs who supposedly worked in federal law enforcement, although precisely where was still a little vague. He didn't care—he wasn't interested in her career. He'd met her while serving on one of those hush-hush government committees that seemed to be proliferating like weeds around town. They'd met for lunch twice after that, once in a group and then by themselves, but he hoped that today's date was more in the way of an assignation. She'd given him all the right signals, even to the point of casually mentioning that her apartment was on Connecticut Avenue. She'd been unspecific about the where, but, in his mind, there could only be one reason for her to have said that. He'd picked the Bistro Nord because it was small, discreet, and not on the list of places where deputy undersecretaries usually went for lunch. He'd prepaid with his Amex card so that, if things went well, there'd be no interruptions to the smooth flow of an imminent seduction.

The Bistro Nord was a dimly lit, twelve-table affair, with a small mirrored bar in one corner and batwing doors leading into a somewhat noisy kitchen. There were tall potted plants positioned strategically to give diners even more privacy. The maître d'-cum-bartender was reciting the day's lunch menu to a four-top in the middle of the room as McGavin came through the door. The maître d' concluded his spiel and approached.

"I'm meeting Ellen Whiting?" McGavin asked.

"Oui, m'sieu." He pointed to the far corner, and there she was, with those amazing legs canted diagonally out from under the tablecloth. She gave him a sly smile when he realized he'd been caught staring. Well, hell, he thought: wear a skirt like that, even a priest is going to stare. He smiled back, hoping it made him look younger, sucked in his gut, and threaded his way through the tables and into the chair opposite. She had a head start on him with a glass of white. He caught the maître d's eye and signaled he'd have the same.

At that moment, a flower vendor stepped into the restaurant. He was an odd-looking man with a white streak running through his hair from front to back. He nodded to the maître d', who frowned, as if he didn't recognize him. He began making his way around the tables, concentrating on tables for two. His flowers were wrapped in layers of green tissue paper cones, just the right size for a lunch table. When he approached their table, McGavin gave a quiet groan and started to wave him away, but Ellen smiled at the man, who then whipped out a bunch of flowers and offered it to her.

"Perfect," she said, peering into the cone of blossoms. She flashed a twenty and the deal was done before McGavin could object. The maître d' appeared magically with a vase and McGavin's glass of wine.

"There," Ellen said. "What do you think of that, Mister Very Important Principal Deputy Under-whazzit?"

"Classy," McGavin replied. "I like surprises like that."

"Try the wine," she said. "It's a white burgundy. We may need a bottle."

He sampled the wine and nodded. "Indeed we will," he said. "That's very good; you know your way around. Wines."

He gave her a look that said there were lots of ways that comment could be interpreted. She gave it right back to him, arching a little in her chair to accentuate the rest of her charms. He took another sip. She put down her glass and said she'd be right back. She then got up, being a little careless with that silky skirt, and headed for the ladies'. He loved the way her dense, blond hair swung from side to side in time with her hips. It had to be a hairpiece—she'd been a brunette before—but the effect was exciting. He made a small noise in his throat and had another sip of wine. The maître d', a roly-poly and entirely bald Frenchman, smirked when he heard that small noise and gave him a look. McGavin grinned back at him, one worldly wise man to another, fully aware that his high hopes were evident. He remembered to ask the maître d' to bring the bottle. Then he leaned forward and inhaled an appreciative draft of the exotic scent rising from the fresh flowers. He sat back in his chair, reached for his wine glass again, then stopped and frowned.

The maître d', returning with the bottle of burgundy and two small menus, was surprised by that frown. The flowers were beautiful, a small spray of vibrant color against the starched white tablecloth. The lady had overpaid, of course, but still. He stepped aside as the bistro's sole waiter, a young man dressed in black pants and shirt covered by a white apron, backed out of the batwing doors and headed for one of the tables, bearing a tray of soup in one palm.

"M'sieu?" the maître d' said.

"Cold," McGavin declared.

The maître d' was confused. It was a lovely fall day outside, not cold, not too warm, just right. The restaurant was most definitely not cold.

"Cold, m'sieu? What is cold?"

"I am," McGavin said. "My wegs are cold."

The maître d' blinked. Wegs?

McGavin suddenly looked like he was going to cry. His eyes began blinking and his lower lip was coming out like a child's. The maître d' froze, alarmed at the transformation taking place in this man's face. The flower man, who'd been working a nearby table, stopped his sales pitch and turned around.

" 'Owld," McGavin croaked, but now his lips were twisting into a weird grimace. The right side of his face began to droop and he leaned against the table for support. His eyes were abnormally bright—and, to the maître d's horror, suddenly very red. He appeared to be trying to say something, but he couldn't get it out. He made a strangling noise in his throat and began clawing at the tablecloth.

The other customers in the restaurant were staring now, aware that something serious was happening. The maître d' reached to support McGavin but he was already tilting to his right and then toppling over in slow motion like a tree, falling sideways out of his chair and collapsing in a disheveled heap on the floor, pulling the tablecloth and everything on it down on top of him in a clatter of silverware and breaking glasses. The waiter hastily abandoned his tray and rushed over. Both the maître d' and the waiter got down to prop McGavin up; he was still breathing, but only barely, and his face was now solidifying into a lopsided rictus of surprise. Then his eyes lost focus and he went very still.

The maître d' looked over at his waiter, who was slowly shaking his head. They both stood up. This man was clearly beyond help. The other diners were looking at one another, as if asking, What do we do? Do we finish our lunch? Should we leave now? Oh. My. God. That man is dead. One man announced to the dining room that he was calling 911.

The maître d' looked around, not sure of what to do next. Then he remembered the woman.

Where was the *mademoiselle*? The one with the shiny legs. Where did she go? *Mon Dieu,* does she know what has just happened? The chef was peering out over the batwing doors, his red face glistening with perspiration. The flower man approached, knelt down, and began to pick up the spilled blooms from the floor, putting them gently back into his basket and then covering them up with a napkin as if they were the real casualties. The maître d' felt for a pulse in McGavin's throat but found nothing. He picked up one of the folded napkins, unfolded it, and draped it across McGavin's face. Some of the other customers gasped when they saw that.

Others were beginning to back out of their chairs, their appetites thoroughly spoiled.

Then strobe lights began flashing through the curtained front windows. Blue ones for the police, white and red for the ambulance. The maître d' hurried to the front door. A moment later, a uniformed District policeman led two EMTs into the restaurant, muttering something incomprehensible into his shoulder mike. The uniformed medics dropped to their knees beside McGavin, already deploying equipment. One removed the cloth napkin and felt for a pulse, while the other spread the defibrillator leads. They exchanged a look that told the tale: this was probably hopeless. This guy was gone.

"Okay, everybody," the Metro cop announced in a bored voice. "I'm gonna need statements."

TWO

Detective Sergeant Ken Smith, known as Av Smith in the Metro PD, had just managed to upset a paper cup of coffee onto his desk. He was trying to get it cleaned up before anyone else in the office noticed. He'd emptied an entire box of Kleenex onto his desktop to sop up the small lake. He held his hands over the mess, waiting for the lake to stop spreading.

"Smooth move, Ex-Lax," Detective Sergeant Howie Wallace said from the adjacent cubicle. "When you gonna get a mug like the rest of us?"

"I'm not going to be here that long, partner," Av said. The lake insisted on spreading. He moved more papers and then folded his blotter to concentrate the coffee. A small brown tsunami headed for his lap. "They told me this was temporary," he said, pushing hurriedly back from the desk.

"They tell everybody it's gonna be temporary, Av," Wallace says. "We all still here, though." Howie Wallace was six-three, with an impressive set of shoulder-length dreads, glaring black eyes, and a mouthful of large teeth. His unofficial nickname was Mau-Mau, the origins of which were shrouded in mystery. He liked to wear unconventional, almost costume clothes so that the criminal element would always make him for a pimp.

Wallace started laughing. "Look at that shit go."

"Here" was officially called the Interagency Liaison Branch of the District of Columbia's Metropolitan Police Department. The branch had been established at headquarters to deal with the explosion of federal agencies involved in counterterrorism and state security matters since nine-eleven. The federal War on Terror bureaucracy had become so large that a Metro District cop could hardly work a simple street mugging without seeing some feds watching from across the streets of downtown Washington. The ILB's mission was: if what you're doing involves feds, bring it to ILB, which would then try its best to move said problem into the federal bureaucracy's ever-expanding lap. There was a second, unofficial reason for ILB's existence: this was where the department assigned detectives who had exhibited either unconventional personalities or worse, much worse, independent attitudes. If someone had been ordered to walk the plank at MPD, ILB was the plank.

Straight-up crimes in the District were handled by the MPD's District and police service area detectives. Those incidents or issues that entangled or had even the potential to entangle the MPD with the brave new world of state security were known throughout the MPD as tarbabies, as in, touch one and it gets all over you, usually forever. Hence ILB's unofficial nickname: the Briar Patch. Wrangling tarbabies was not an assignment much sought after in the ranks of MPD detectives, which meant that none of ILB's four serving detectives were volunteers.

Av Smith was one of those guys who seemed to get bigger as you got closer to him. He was five-ten and had the physique of a weight lifter up top and a runner down below. He worked out in the police gym every day of the week and usually ran ten miles before coming to work. He shaved his head every third day and favored sport coats instead of suits, mostly because he couldn't find suits off the rack that could accommodate his enlarged torso and arms. He had brown eyes and a large nose that had been broken and reset a few times, which was why he'd taken up weight lifting in the first place. He could no longer remember when someone last took a swing at him. The last guy who did probably couldn't remember it, either.

His nickname, Av, came as the result of a disagreement with his boss in the Second District. Av had had something of a personality conflict with his lieutenant. In the MPD that meant that the lieutenant had a personality, and Av had a conflict. His boss then, one Lieutenant Parsons, was apparently fed up with the amount of time Av was spending at the police gym during working hours. Av had pointed out that physical fitness was supposedly a departmental priority, in theory if not necessarily in practice. He'd then stared pointedly at the lieutenant's own prominent front porch. Parsons took immediate offense and lectured Av on how he had been chasing down bad guys while Av was still in diapers. Av retorted that the lieutenant would need a pair of Superman's diapers to chase down his own shadow. Things went downhill from there, culminating in a declaration by the lieutenant that, you, Detective Smith, are a "relentlessly average" detective. Your work's average, your closure rate is average, hell, even your name's average, for Chrissake! He'd been "Average" Smith ever since, Av to his squad room, and, then three months later, he'd become the newest member of the Briar Patch posse.

Av liked police work, if not what seemed to him like three too many layers of bosses associated with it. He actually enjoyed apprehending bad guys and building cases against them. He was known by the criminal element in his district as the skinhead white guy who showed up wearing running shoes and openly carrying an ASP in the hopes that a perp would elude and evade. He had been known to use that collapsible baton, too. One time, when Av was still a beat cop, two gangbangers were sitting in their stolen ride, its nose wrapped around a telephone pole, giving the two attending detectives an elaborate ration of crap. Av had produced the ASP and hit the windshield in the sweet spot. His theory was that it was hard to concentrate on talking proper trash when you had a lap full of broken glass. Normally an ASP couldn't do that to safety glass, but with Av behind it, the whole thing had caved in on them. The terrified bangers ultimately agreed to take the blame for the windshield, which the cops pronounced was only right. Word got around: don't mess with the skinhead five-oh with the big arms and the international orange tenny-pumps. And his ASP.

Av was actually a native of the District of Columbia, which made him one of a rare species in a city filled with political transients, military, and almost a million suburban commuters. His parents, now retired in Florida, had been federal civil servants in the Transportation Department. He'd grown up in northwest D.C., attended public schools, and then, uninterested in college, he'd done a stint in the Marines, where he developed an appetite for extreme physical fitness. He used his veteran's preference to get a slot at the police academy and had made detective in five years. At the moment, he was the only white guy in ILB.

He finally gave up on saving his desktop and dumped the entire blotter, papers and all, into the trash can. Another of the ILB inmates came in, saw Av standing over his trash can like he was going to piss in it, and just shook his head. As Av began fishing some of the paperwork back out of the trash can, Lieutenant Johnson, his new boss, approached. She was a tall, thin black woman with shiny black hair slicked into a tight bun and a face that declared for any fool to see that she was a walking, talking BS-free zone. Her first name was actually Precious, although no one in the entire department had ever had the nerve to call her that to her face, not even the chief. Av and the other ILB detectives thought she was a good boss—decisive, technically competent, and not to be messed with. She was also working on a night-school law degree and enjoyed a daily noontime run. Right now, though, she was surveying the disaster area that was Av's desktop.

"Detective Sergeant Smith," she said. Precious kept things formal in the ILB squad room; Av sometimes thought it was like being back in the corps.

"Lieutenant?"

She was carrying a folder in her right hand, but she was looking at Av's trash can. "What *are* you doing?"

"Salvage?" he said. Howie snorted in the next cubicle.

She sighed and handed him the folder. "Unexplained death in a restaurant. This is the EMS report. There are two wrinkles."

"Just two?" Av said, trying for some levity. He'd made it his mission to make Precious smile one day. So far, with not much success.

"Wrinkle number one: victim apparently was a medium mucketymuck in the SS."

SS? Av blinked. "Excuse me?"

"Sorry: the Newnited States Department of Homeland Security. You know, the federal department that's building prison camps out in the desert and buying a billion rounds of ammo for 'training'?"

Av hadn't heard anything about prison camps, but the MPD's training ammo allowance *had* been cut back recently. But: if she was saying the vic was a fed, there was an easy solution to this case.

"Great," he said brightly. "I'll get onto the Bureau, then. They handle—"

"Wrinkle number two: I've liaised with the Bureau. Apparently there is some as-yet-undefined Bureau involvement in this incident. They think it'd look better if the prelim was done by MPD. After that, well, you know . . ."

Av, realizing now that a tarbaby was materializing right there on his coffee-stained desk, sighed. And on a Friday, of course. Typical Bureau bullshit, he thought: let the MPD do the grunt work, then step in and take over the investigation for the close. More importantly, these so-called wrinkles threatened to frustrate the first law of ILB: move the case.

"Okay if I try talking to them?" he asked.

Lieutenant Johnson gave him the look that said she was not there to discuss the mechanics of the matter. He took the folder. "I'll get right on it," he said.

"Knew you would," she said. She looked again at the trash can, wrinkled her nose at the aroma of wet papers and spilled coffee, and then left the squad room, shaking her head.

Whole lotta head-shaking going on here, Av thought. Place is beginning to look like a goddamned Parkinson's ward. He heard Howie chuckling behind his newspaper.

"What?"

"I'll get right on it," Wallace echoed. "You don't sound like no temp to me, bro."

Av made sure there was no coffee on his chair, sat down, and read through the patrol report. He noted the names and places involved. He had driven by that French restaurant, but he'd never tried it. It was the kind of place you might take a special woman friend to, and Av had given up getting that involved with women for Lent, if not forever. The report said the EMS took the nonresponsive victim to MedStar Hospital Center. Av got on the phone. After some back and forth, he finally cut through all the security and privacy gatekeepers to their pathology department.

Av identified himself and asked for any available information on what had happened to one Francis Xavier McGavin, DOA.

"Don't know," the pathologist said. "EMS reported that the victim had some kind of seizure, possibly a stroke, in a restaurant. ER ordered a scan, which showed neither a bleed nor a clot, so probably not a stroke. Cardiac, maybe. Either way, you'll have to wait for the autopsy. The remains have been transferred to the OCME."

Av then called the Office of the Chief Medical Examiner, mentally kicking himself for not going there in the first place. It must have been the lack of coffee. A clerk confirmed that they'd received the DOA from MedStar, and that they were waiting for permission to conduct an autopsy.

"Who gives permission?" Av asked.

"Immediate family, an attorney, a court."

"He's supposedly a deputy under-something at DHS," Av said. "Have you guys contacted them yet?"

"Don't know anything about DHS," the clerk said. "MedStar sent him here as a John Doe. No ID onboard when he got here. You mentioned a name? You, like, got next of kin? You guys thinking this is, like, a homicide?"

"Like, it beats me," Av said, rolling his eyes. "I'm thinking we'll need, like, an autopsy report to find out, but, like, what do I know. Lemme get back to you."

Av then called back to MedStar and asked for the patient affairs office. Something wasn't adding up here. John Doe? They'd had his name from the EMS report, information indicating he worked for DHS, and the MedStar pathologist had recognized the name. So why the John Doe tag?

Patient Affairs wasn't any more forthcoming. "Francis X. McGavin? We have nobody by that name in our system," said the woman who answered. "Sure you got the right hospital?"

"Metro EMS said they brought him to your ER at 1330 yesterday. Pathology says they had him briefly, and they transferred the body to OCME. But: they recognized that name when I asked."

She sighed, asked him to wait. He could hear a keyboard clicking. "Okay, right, we did get a John Doe ER admission, possible stroke, triaged at thirteen twenty-two. White male, fifties, unresponsive. They declared him at thirteen forty-five. No name, though. Total John Doe."

Total John Doe? What the hell. "Anyone listed as accompanying?"

"No record of it. The insurance Nazis might have something on him, but probably not if he's a John Doe, especially if he was a DOA John Doe.

ER record says they did a brain scan, continued resuscitation efforts, then declared him."

"Was he carrying any ID?"

"I guess not. Otherwise he wouldn't be a John Doe, right?"

Av wanted to hit her.

"You say our pathology department had an actual name?" she asked.

"Yup."

"Give it to me again."

It was Av's turn to sigh. Like talking to a brick wall. He repeated the name, then asked if Patient Affairs had made any notifications.

"To whom?" she asked. He executed a Polish salute. It was a reasonable question. *Gotta* get some coffee. And maybe a phone book.

"He's supposedly a ranking civil serpent at Homeland Security," Av said, wondering now how Precious had known that. Feds carried badges, sometimes whole clutches of them. Building passes, scanner cards, gate cards, vault access cards. Have to check on that.

She asked him to hold again, then came back on. "My supervisor says the MPD will have to do that, since you're saying he's a federal somebody. She says government talks to government. Says you guys at the MPD have an office for that?"

And that would be ILB, Av thought. Full circle. Well done. "Yup," he said. "Thanks."

Definitely a tarbaby, Av thought. So how does a dead guy have a name at the scene, lose it at the ER, regain it at the hospital's morgue, and then lose it again on the way to the medical examiner's office? And if the guy had come to the restaurant from work he would have had both his wallet *and* his badges. Credit cards, cash, some way to pay for lunch. Where'd his wallet gone?

Okay, he thought. Back to basics here: where did that name come from originally? He reread the EMS report. There was no mention of any personal effects being bagged to go along with the victim to the ER. He looked at the beat cop's report. Restaurant waitstaff had named McGavin from the reservation, and had mentioned a woman who'd been there to meet McGavin, but who had disappeared right before the incident. The maître d' had given her name as Ellen Whiting. He had also confirmed the victim's name as Francis X. McGavin, based on the credit card McGavin had given with the reservation two days before.

Well, good, Av thought. If the restaurant has the victim's credit card info, we can get to his next of kin. That still didn't explain all this John Doe business, but the way forward was clear: contact the restaurant, get the card info, call the card company, get his file, make the notification, get the autopsy going, get a result, and presto: one more tarbaby ejected from the Briar Patch. The fact that the mystery woman had taken a powder was no longer important—she'd probably seen what happened and decided to beat feet. No reason to invite unwanted attention to the fact that she and McGavin were meeting in a trysting spot, assuming he was married. Or she was. Or they both were. Shit.

He sat back. What in hell was the MPD headquarters doing with a tawdry little case like this? Any District detective squad could do this. He asked Howie, who suggested he go ask Precious.

One minute later, ears burning, Av was back at his desk and on the phone to the restaurant.

Howie didn't say a word.

THREE

"Very well, then, we're adjourned," Mandeville announced from the head of the conference table. "Next session at my call. Thank you, everybody."

Carl Mandeville was a large, florid-faced man in his late forties. He had a commanding voice and a permanently imperious expression that declared that, no matter where he was, *he* was the man in charge. In this particular venue, a drafty but electronically secure conference room in a relatively unused section of the EEOB, he was most definitely in charge.

The EEOB, known previously throughout Washington as the Old Executive Office Building, was an 1870s marble pile that sat across the street from the White House. Its principal use was as a ceremonial office complex for the Vice President, but it also housed offices for the National Security Council staff, of which Mandeville was a senior member. In a capital where bureaucratic titles were often onerously complex, abbreviation was not only the norm but constituted a vocabulary that everyone had to master in order to be considered a Washington hand. Nobody said the words "National Security Council": it was always NSC. Nobody would refer to the deputy secretary of defense in those words: it was DepSecDef. This was not a new trend: the building where they had been meeting had originally been called the executive offices of the cabinet departments of State, War (Army), and Navy. Even in 1878, Washington bureaucrats abbreviated the building's name to State-War-Navy.

Mandeville watched the principals file out of the room. He was amused by the fact that there was none of the postmeeting chitchat that usually followed adjournment of a Washington meeting. The purpose of these particular meetings probably had something to do with that, he thought. Mandeville held the rank of special assistant to the President and senior director for counterterrorism on the National Security Council staff. He was one of twenty-two senior directors, and because the National Security Council was the most important interagency group in the capital, it followed that a senior director for its staff held tremendous bureaucratic power within the scope of his or her mandate. When Mandeville called a meeting, especially a meeting of the DMX principals committee, it was like a summons from the White House itself.

He remained in his chair at the head of the table and waited. Two staff aides came into the room, nodded deferentially, and checked the table for any papers or notes left behind. They then disabled the hummers, four small electronic machines, one for each corner of the room, which made it impossible for listening devices, either inside or outside the conference room, to hear anything being said in the room. The staffers didn't speak to him, and he didn't speak to them. When Carl Mandeville came down the hallway, people stepped aside like small boats getting out of a big steamer's way in a harbor channel.

He looked at his watch impatiently as the ancient steam radiators began to clank. Where *was* she?

As if on cue, a woman returned to the room. She carried her purse in one hand and a meeting tablet in the other. She closed the door behind her, noticed that the hummers were off, and then went around the room turning them all back on. Mandeville watched her move around the room with silent appreciation. She was a tall brunette with the body of an athlete—wide shoulders supporting lovely breasts, and beautifully sculpted legs. She had blue eyes that bordered on being violet in just the right light, and she favored clingy fabrics for her clothes. She wasn't beautiful in the traditional sense, but you wouldn't forget meeting her, either. He'd once heard one of the principals call her a slinky toy, behind her back, of course. In the same way that Mandeville projected power, she radiated a tightly controlled sexuality, assuming you were looking for it.

Her name was Ellen Whiting, and she was the Bureau's rep to the DMX. She'd replaced a much more senior Bureau assistant director, which made her the junior member of the committee. He remembered when she'd first shown up, nervous but putting on a brave face in a room full of assistant secretaries of various cabinet-level departments. He'd taken her under his wing after the first meeting, given her some pointers on how things really worked on the DMX.

She was also whip-smart, and he began to understand why the Bureau had sent her over. Three reasons: she was intelligent enough to understand the seriousness of the DMX's mission, and never hesitated when it came time for the fatal vote. Plus, if the DMX blew up politically one day, as it well might, none of the senior dragons over there in the Hoover building would have to be involved.

If she'd been some middle-aged, ultraliberal bulldagger he wouldn't have bothered, but she was somehow—memorable. He had never allowed himself to get into a relationship, much less marriage, with any of the professional women he'd met in the capital. In his view, relationships of any kind were to be carefully husbanded, and never established unless there was a clear prospect of benefit for his own career. That didn't mean he didn't keep a lookout for the possible exceptions, but after all his years in Washington watching other power players, and, in particular, watching too many truly dedicated people suffer through divorce or other marital distress, he'd decided to stay single. He'd met women over the years whom he had respected, admired, or even desired, but he felt that putting a woman in the mix was at best a distraction, and at worst a potential career liability.

Over time he'd begun to treat Ellen Whiting as if she was working directly for him as well as the Bureau, as sort of an apprentice protégée, and after a while, she'd responded. It wasn't all that hard for him to win her confidence, being a senior White House advisor and a well-known power broker, but he'd been very careful to ensure that there was nothing romantic or sexual about it. She, on the other hand, was savvy enough to understand the value of being close to someone like him, especially when one of the other members of the DMX tried to pull bureaucratic seniority on her when she spoke for the Bureau. Beyond that, he'd thought that she might be useful one day if he ever had to go through with his very close-hold plans for weeding out the weak links at DMX. From the angry set of her jaw now, though, he realized he may have been wrong about that.

She came back to the table and sat down next to Mandeville and waited for him to say something. She was definitely angry, he concluded. But there was no way she could know.

"McGavin," he said, finally. "What happened?"

"He died, that's what happened." Her fine lips were compressed into a tight line.

"You were there? You saw it?" he asked.

"Not exactly. We'd met, ordered some wine, and then I went to the powder room. When I came back out of the bathroom door, he was on the floor."

"And then you got out?"

She nodded.

"Any fallout?" he asked.

She shook her head. "Not yet. But he was DHS, so . . ."

"They know the circumstances?"

"No," she said. Monosyllabic answers. Shit, he thought. She's really pissed off. He should have expected this, he thought. She was Bureau, but had never been an operator in the CT world.

"Local authorities?" he continued.

She shrugged. It made her close-cropped, glossy dark hair shimmer as it moved in the late-afternoon light. He suddenly wanted to touch it. Down, boy, he thought. This one's too smart not to be dangerous. But it was also obvious that she was trying hard to control herself.

"Metro PD *should* treat it for exactly what it looks like," she said.

" 'Should'?"

"The incident's being handled by some low-level detectives in Metro PD's Interagency Liaison Bureau."

"What's that?"

"A channel between Metro PD and all federal LE. If a problem has the slightest link to anything federal, their job is to shop it out of MPD. Not exactly their top drawer."

"Can they make problems?"

"I doubt it," she said, after a moment's reflection. "Right now they're treating it as just another middle-aged white male getting overexcited at the thought that he might score with somebody who looks like me."

Mandeville forced a smile. "I can relate to that," he said.

"Don't," she said, looking right at him. "Look what happens."

He laughed out loud. She didn't seem to be that amused.

"We need to talk," she said.

"Oh, yes?"

She leaned forward, her eyes suddenly intense. "I think you set me up."

He did not reply.

"God-*dammit,* Mandeville!" she exclaimed. "You asked me to cozy up to him, see if I could talk him out of this policy-review business. McGavin's a known letch, you said, so show some leg, make him think that there were possibilities—your words, remember? You never said *anything* about killing him!"

"Killing him?" he said. "Calm down, Ellen. Consider the visuals: one assistant deputy under whatever-the-fuck keels over in a fancy restaurant—that's not news. Too many butter-laced lunches with vodka back."

"That's *not* what I'm talking about," she fumed. "I think you've just made me an accessory to a *fucking* murder!"

"What?" he asked. "Where the hell did murder come from? The guy died—he was overweight, mid-fifties, white—how is that murder?"

She glared at him. "It's too neat, that's how. You got me to play up to him, make him think we might get it on, I meet him in a restaurant, and he *dies*?"

"Just because you bought some flowers?" he said, his voice becoming smooth as silk.

Her eyes widened. "I don't know what you did or how you did it, or what the *fuck* flowers had to do with it, but I did *not* sign up to kill someone just because he disagrees with what the DMX is all about. Are you fucking *crazy*?"

"Calm down, Ellen," he said again. "Nobody's talking murder except you. All you were supposed to do was lure him into a faintly compromising situation and then sweet-talk him into voting against a policy review. You agreed to do that. I don't know what happened after that. I surely didn't tell anyone to kill him. What happened—happened. I'm not glad that he died, but I'm not sad, either."

"What?!"

He leaned forward. "Look," he said. "You, more than anyone else, know what our problem is these days. You know who our traitors are."

"*Traitors?* Dissent's become treason now?"

"Goddamn right," he said. "If I had my way, there'd be two more incidents just like that. The three stooges: McGavin, Logan, and Wheatley. Sitting here on the DMX and pretending to work with us, while all the time maneuvering backstage at the behest of their Senate masters to kill the DMX. Yes, two more prominent funerals would be just fine with me."

"And how do I know *you're* not behind what happened to McGavin? He had two sips of wine. I went to the ladies' room. When I came back he was crashing to the floor."

"Well, somebody better look at that wine, don't you think?" he said.

"I had had an entire glass of that wine," she said. "I didn't flop and twitch. What the fuck did you do?"

"I didn't do anything. But I'll tell you this: if either Logan or Wheatley decide to stroke out in the middle of lunch in the near future, I'm going to make sure that everybody else on the DMX makes a connection, however bogus—fuck with DMX and bad things might happen."

She sat back in her chair, staring at him, probably realizing now that he *had* in fact had the man killed. "I suspect they might manage that all on their own."

"You think?"

"Of course they will," she said. "And when they do figure it out, they will (*a*) take themselves off the committee, and (*b*) one of them will sit down with the *Washington Post* and raise the pregnant question."

"And what's the most plausible answer to that question?"

She stared at him for a moment.

He waited.

She wilted just a bit. "Someone on the Kill List."

"Bingo," he said. "Look: the people on this committee are the people who decide who goes *on* the Kill List. We're the ones who send a name to the President. Surprise, surprise, one of the 'nominees' or his black-hearted heirs entertained thoughts of payback for that singular honor."

"Seriously?"

"I've done nothing wrong, Ellen," Mandeville said. "But I will take advantage of this situation. If I can, I'll insinuate that McGavin's sudden demise just might—*might*—be related to his underhanded machinations against DMX. Washington runs on political paranoia. So: I'll throw some straws into the wind. In plain English, back off the DMX or bad things can happen. Most importantly, their puppet masters in the Senate will also get the message."

"No doubt," she said. "But they'll get the Bureau into it. Or the Secret Service. Hell, maybe both. What then?"

"Well, now, my dear coconspirator: that's the good news. If one of them gets into it, they'll *all* get into it—the Bureau, the Secret Service, the CIA, the DIA, the NSA, the DHS—I can go on for fucking ever, when you think about it. How many different federal security organs are currently grappling against global terrorism—fifty-eight? No, wait, I've got the digits right, but the order wrong, don't I. It's eighty-five, now that I think of it. Yes, eighty-five."

"So *what*?"

"Don't you see, Ellen? They'll *all* get into it, like a pack of scrabbling dogs. And because of that, they'll make a hash of it. Especially since McGavin's sudden death had nothing to do with DMX."

"You light that fuse?" she said. "You insinuate that McGavin died because he opposed DMX? Somebody will definitely come after you."

"There's nothing to find," he protested.

"You can't have it both ways," she said. "You start a rumor that McGavin died because he messed with the DMX, somebody in all those eighty-five agencies will start looking really hard at you. You're not known as a crusader for nothing."

He sat back in his chair and gave her a cold smile. "Well, if that happens, you can count on the fact that I'll have some meat ready to be thrown to the pack, won't I, Ellen Whiting. Lunch date."

"Meat?" she asked. "You mean me?"

"*You* were there, with McGavin," he said. "You picked the wine. You bought the flowers."

She just stared at him.

He held up his hands. "Let's go back to basics, here, shall we? DMX is all about taking out crazed Muslims who've spent too much time in the sun and who are bent on our destruction. DMX is not about jailing them, or prosecuting them—but *killing* them. Killing. Them. Dead. And doing so in as dramatic a fashion as possible. Like those Somali natives with their eyes out on stalks told CNN: there was a fire in the sky, then a flash on the ground, and Abdullah's car and everybody in it was just—gone. That's what the List is all about, remember?"

"But what you're saying equates legitimate dissent about DMX with the terrorists themselves."

"Guilty," he declared. "Because, in my opinion, there is *no* difference between an Al Qaeda boss ordering up an embassy bombing and some squishy liberal from the department of whatever trying to take down the one really effective weapon we have left against the terrorists: and that's the Kill List. These three political appointees—appointees, mind you, not professionals—are the main proponents of cranking up an interagency review. I've been fighting a rearguard action for almost two years now against those three worms and their sponsors in the Senate. They are especially dangerous to us because they are sitting members of the DMX committee, which gives them even more credibility. Their backers in the Senate are fully aware of that."

She put her hands up to her face, finally realizing what she was seeing.

He took a deep breath. "I am determined to purify this committee. I want no civil-liberty lawyers in this room. No doubters. No nonbelievers. People like that are contagious. What we do here ends in murder. Full stop. And, dear heart, all of us crossed that threshold a long time ago, when the first name to make the List vanished in a ball of fire."

"But he was a foreigner. A known terrorist commander, bloody up to his armpits."

"You're quibbling," he said. "Murder is murder. We vote a name onto the Kill List and he becomes proscribed—marked for death. Don't know about you, but I sleep just fine at night when we do that, because we're in a *war* with these people."

"Okay, I want to hear you say it: McGavin—did you arrange for him to be killed?"

"Of *course* not," he said. "But, like I said, I am going to take advantage of his sudden death to do some good work for Jesus. In my view, what we have here are some American bureaucrats who've joined forces with the enemy by trying to undo the DMX. Oh, I don't mean literally joined the enemy, but I'm nothing if not a net-results man. These guys are helping some shaky old barnacles in the Senate, who've lost their nerve, to take away the only surviving U.S. government entity with the power to strike our worst enemies and: Kill. Them. Dead."

"You really believe this, don't you," she said, softly. "That if someone starts to have doubts about the DMX and the Kill List, it would be convenient if they just—died? Is that what I hear you saying?"

"You *never* heard me say that, Ellen Whiting," he said. "But it's good to know you understand where I'm coming from. And just to amplify: I'd find a way to take down the entire committee if I thought that would preserve the Kill List. This town is nothing if not chock full of bureaucrats. I'm sure I could refill the DMX in about an hour."

She blinked. Then he saw understanding wash over her face: what was it he'd called her? My dear coconspirator? "What if I just go warn the other two?" she asked.

"I'll make sure your bosses in the Bureau know that you were there when McGavin suffered his unfortunate—accident."

She opened her mouth to say something, but then closed it.

"Hey?" he said. "Let's indulge in a little armed détente, why don't we? This is Washington. Let's make a deal. You agree to keep your mouth shut about my—um, sentiments. You forget I ever asked you to sweet-talk McGavin. You revert to simply being the Bureau's rep on DMX. If you hear about any sort of serious investigation into McGavin's sudden demise, you keep me informed. I, in turn, will keep my mouth shut about *your* role."

She sat back in her chair.

"All right," she said, suddenly calm. "A mutual lock, then."

"Exactly," he said, relieved. "The best kind. Now: I need to get back to my office. I believe we're done here, aren't we?"

When she had gone, Mandeville picked up the secure phone at the head of the table and called a number at FBI headquarters. He punched in four digits when the menu robot started up.

"Audiovisual support services," a man's voice answered. "Kyle Strang."

"Call me back on a secure line."

"We may have a problem," Mandeville said once Strang called back and the sync tones subsided. "Whiting's developed cold feet. Thinks I may have had something to do with the McGavin thing."

"Perish the thought," Strang said.

"Yes, really," Mandeville said. "I denied everything of course, but now she's very suspicious. I've talked her out of doing anything. Told her to go back to simply doing her day job on the DMX."

"Then there's no problem," Strang said.

"You're probably right, now that I think about it," Mandeville said. "Plus, there is a bright side. At some point, we might need a patsy."

There was a long moment of silence on the phone. "You mean if somebody *outside* of DMX starts looking into the, um, coincidences?" Strang said.

"Yes, exactly."

"Like?"

"Some office in Metro PD called ILB."

"Lemme pull the string on that," Strang said. "I'll get back to you."

An hour later Strang called back. "Metro PD sent McGavin's body to MedStar, who sent it along to OCME," he reported. "My sources tell me that OCME pathologists are holding both the cause *and* the manner of death open."

"Why do we care?"

"Cause of death should be damned near impossible to determine, but manner of death might turn out to be more important."

"I'm confused."

"Manner of death: natural, accidental, physiological incident, suicide, or homicide."

"Oh," Mandeville said. He thought for a moment. "Okay," he said. "Who's involved at MPD?"

"Like you said, Metro PD has an office called the ILB—they're—"

"Yes, Whiting told me. So?"

"One of their detectives has taken an interest."

"Again, why should we care? As I understand it, in the great scheme of things, ILB is nobody-minus."

"OCME's pushing for disposition instructions. This ILB detective told them to wait. Apparently he's on the hunt for the mysterious girlfriend who disappeared right after McGavin checked out."

"Does he have her name?"

"Apparently he does."

"Ah," Mandeville said. "That we do *not* need."

"Want to calibrate him?"

"Gently," Mandeville said. "Find a way to let him know that he's playing above his pay grade. If he's any sort of cop at all he'll get the message, but do keep it subtle. For now."

"I know some people who can do subtle," Strang said. "I think."

"Get me his name and where he lives," Mandeville said, and then hung up.

He sat back to think, as the Washington workweek began to dissolve into intractable traffic outside the EEOB. He could hear office doors down the cavernous marble-floored hallways closing and the sounds of staffers trying not to break into an unseemly trot down the halls in search of the weekend.

A Metro cop. A nobody. On the scale of important things in Washington, the Metro Police Department was somewhere down in the weeds. The distance between the National Security Council and the MPD was measured in light-years.

And yet: a presidency had been brought down by some drone leaving a door wedged open with a piece of paper, which had been discovered by—wait for it: a building security rent-a-cop at the Watergate. For want of a nail . . .

Strang would have someone lean gently, for a start, anyway, on the cop. The cop would go tell his boss, the one in the office who could both read and write, and he would tell the cop: watchit. But: was that enough?

He knew he hadn't convinced Ellen Whiting of anything. She suspected that he'd done something to McGavin, or, at the very least, lit that fuse, which was why he'd wrapped a lock on her: you bought the flowers, you were there when he died, not me. It hadn't been subtle, and she'd caught on immediately. So: for the moment, anyway, Ellen Whiting had been neutralized. She was an up-and-comer in the Bureau, where even the whiff of any kind of screwup or, worse, scandal, would see her career go up in flames.

His phone rang, and Strang gave him the information on the Metro cop.

He hung up, thought some more, and then made a decision. He picked up the phone and dialed a twelve-digit number. There were a series of clicks, and then silence, followed by a voice-mail beep.

"Beacon twenty-three," he said. "Tonight." Then he pressed the pound key and hung up.

FOUR

Av had to penetrate Amex's version of menu hell through six iterations before he snared a human in card security, who told him to bring them a warrant. Av told the man that he wasn't looking for a data dump, just a phone number for McGavin's next of kin, now that he was unexpectedly deceased. That was news to the security guy, who said there was a hefty balance on the account. The security guy's supervisor came on, took ILB's office number, called him back, and then gave him McGavin's home phone number.

A stuffy-sounding man answered the McGavins' residence phone. Av identified himself as a Metro police detective and asked to speak to Mrs. McGavin. The man told him that Mrs. McGavin was not taking any phone calls due to the recent death of her husband. Av then asked for an appointment with Mrs. McGavin. Not likely, the man responded with an aristocratic sniff. Her attorney, possibly? Who is her attorney? You said you're a detective, the man said, and then hung up.

Everyone's a wiseass today, he thought. He was about to call back, but then realized that he no longer had to make a notification because, apparently, the widow already knew. But: they still needed an autopsy authorization. Okay, if the family wouldn't talk to him, then he'd get a court order. Use that John Doe business.

He paused. *How* had the widow already known? The hospital was calling the case a John Doe. OCME, currently holding the remains, was calling him a John Doe. So who the hell had informed the newly minted widow? His office? And who'd called *them*? Not the OCME, not Med-Star, and not ILB—so: the girlfriend? Had to be, didn't it?

Okay, he decided; tee up this Ellen Whiting, then. He looked at his watch—almost four-thirty on a Friday. That meant Monday for the mysterious lady luncheon partner. Right now, let's get a court-ordered autopsy rolling. Four-thirty. Well, he'd give it a try, but on a Friday afternoon it was very likely that their honors would have bailed at two for the golf course.

Friday. Thank God. Monday would be good enough. It wasn't like he was going to bring McGavin back to life, and, besides, he wasn't even supposed to be trying to solve this one.

Carl Mandeville paused to look for traffic coming around the Lincoln Monument. Even at midnight there was still some traffic; this was Washington, after all. He crossed the narrow lane into the trees and sidewalks flanking the reflecting pool, a custom-made Burger walking stick tapping the concrete discreetly as he walked toward the distant Capitol building. More than most, he was aware of the security patrols in the precincts of the White House. Carl Mandeville did not sleep very much, if at all. He walked the Mall just about every night unless the weather was really bad. The night security people all knew who he was, the great big guy from the White House who haunted the Mall and the monuments at midnight, walking boldly forward as if on an urgent mission of state, with that fancy walking stick, which contained a seventeen-inch Damascus steel blade, gripped firmly in his right hand. He wore his usual dark suit, a lightweight overcoat if the temperature demanded it, and a dark gray fedora which added four inches to his already imposing height. Secret Service agents sitting in darkened vehicles would whisper into their lapel mikes: Mandeville, at the Lincoln, headed east.

When he'd first started making his nightly excursions onto the Mall, there'd been night owls all over the area, couples getting some air after a big dinner at one of the downtown eateries, workaholics getting some badly needed exercise, street thieves, panhandlers, and muggers over from Anacostia, hoping to get lucky, tottering drunks trying to find their cars, furtive gays, and a few homeless people. Not anymore. After nine-eleven, this part of Washington around the White House, a teeming tourist mecca by day, had become an armed camp after dark. He knew about the gun emplacements on top of many of the federal buildings, and the real reason why the 555-foot-tall Washington Monument had been closed for so long after the earthquake. If he had stopped suddenly, got down on one knee, and aimed his walking stick at the White House, seven snipers would have dropped him in two seconds. Brave new world, he thought, as he reached the World War II Memorial, so small considering the global holocaust it was supposed to memorialize. And they were all missing the point.

The threat's not here, boys, he wanted to shout to the caffeine-jagged agents trying to stay awake in their parked cars. The real threat's offshore, where an Iranian tramp steamer would one day lay to fifty miles off Maryland, open a cargo hatch, and fire a ballistic missile into the atmosphere above Illinois and fry every tendril of the electrical system the whole country depended on. The threat's on the Mexican border, where depraved Muslim fireheads carrying a vial of Ebola-virus-infected blood in a hornet spray can would come over one night amid the flood of "homeless refugees" and take a Graypup to a football game in Dallas. It was all well and good for the TSA goons to pat down granny at the airport and dump the baby out of its airplane car seat, but the Big Deal, when it came, would come from *outside* the country, directed by seventh-century barbarians who'd finally realized that the modern world had consigned them to the dustbin of history.

In other words, the Candidates.

He sighed in frustration as he tramped across the Mall itself. The DMX was the only entity in the byzantine world of federal counterterrorism that was aiming at those shadowy maniacs who set the martyrs in motion, aided and abetted by oil money and Saudi princelings who were playing both sides just to be safe. One good thing about all those agencies involved: they cast a wide net, and the process, however unwieldy, had surfaced some real bad guys out there on the edges of the Empire. And the Muslims knew it. He could never prove it, but he'd become convinced that the legislators who were now out to undo DMX had been bought off by the same people who were determined to destroy America, that blazing glass house on the hill, whose entire nervous system ran on something so delicate as the Internet and the galactic array of electronics that made it all possible.

He reached the base of the Washington Monument and, like every tourist before him, looked up at the spotlighted obelisk. He repressed an urge to wave at the watchers up there, both human and robotic, and then looked around for Evangelino. There he was, sitting on a park bench about fifty yards away, staring at nothing.

Evangelino Francini was so named by a very misguided mother of Sicilian heritage who had hoped to invoke the protection of her family's patron saint by imposing this outrageous name on her second son when he was born in Brooklyn. Once in school, where names began to matter, he'd tried to call himself just Gino, but the word got out and he had become, out of necessity and the annoyance of daily fistfights when someone called him Evangeline, one of the toughest kids in school. From there he'd graduated to being a hanger-on with the neighborhood mob, and from there to a made man in his early twenties in the Fortunato family business. Fifteen years into his career as a mobster, he'd been given the assignment of supervising the takedown of a Brinks armored van. The operation had gone like clockwork, thanks to two drivers who'd been paid off handsomely to decamp, right to the point where Gino, standing in the back of the truck in wide-eyed amazement over a pile of cash beyond his wildest dreams, had gunned down his two accomplices and then driven the van to an abandoned warehouse in Queens sometimes used by the mob to store corpses. Leaving his erstwhile associates in the van, he'd coolly taken the subway back down to Brooklyn, loaded up his Ford Econoline van with a few personal possessions, gone back to the warehouse, loaded up the cash, set fire to the warehouse, and left for Florida that very night.

It had taken the mob two years to find him, and when they did, they set up an ambush in the little trailer park outside of Gainesville where Gino had gone to ground. He'd known from the get-go that it was a matter of when, not if, they found him, so he'd created a web of people who would alert him to strangers from New York. In the ensuing shootout, he'd killed all three of the hit squad but not without taking one in the neck. His girlfriend at the time, an exotic dancer at the local strip club, had found him a cocaine-dependent doc who made his living treating the flow of illegal immigrants, drug mules, the desperate individuals who were willing to undergo organ transplant for money, and anyone else who could never afford to surface into the regular medical system. He'd patched Gino up, but in the process had damaged some nerves that had reduced half of Gino's face to a frozen mask and left him with both a stiff-legged walk and the inability to speak. He was now rich but permanently damaged, and once again on the run, moving from trailer to trailer around town and always looking over his shoulder. He slowly got his speech back, but pretended he hadn't. He'd discovered that people were often very careless with important information around a man who couldn't speak.

Until one night outside of the strip club, where he was dozing in his van, waiting for his lady, when a big guy, seriously drunk and wearing military cammies, came out of the bar followed by two Latino hoods who were obviously planning to roll the drunk. For some strange reason, this offended Gino. Yeah, he was a mobster, but he was an American mobster, and these greasers rubbed him the wrong way, the drunk being a soldier and everything. He got out of the van just as the two guys whacked the drunk army guy on the shins with a tire iron, putting him on the ground gasping in pain with tears in his eyes. Gino produced his stainless-steel twelve-gauge coach gun, which he used as a bat to rearrange the muggers' faces on their way into unconsciousness, if not death. He loaded the wailing army guy into the van, waited for his lady, and then took him back to the trailer.

Turned out the army guy, who was seriously grateful, was connected with some kind of Special Forces outfit based in the panhandle of Florida. The next morning, one thing led to another after lots of talk over coffee, and Gino was invited to come to some place called Eglin, where there were military units without names who were looking for some stone killers. The rest, as they say, was history. Gino went out to the various Stans, still frozen-faced, but this time as a contractor. He appreciated the irony—contracts had been his stock-in-trade as a mobster, too. Mandeville now had him on a personal-services countersurveillance contract under the auspices of the DMX. *He* loved the irony of having an ex-mob hit man being paid with government funds within the overarching mission of counterterrorism.

Mandeville sat down on the bench next to the motionless Evangelino, who'd gone back to using his real name on the off chance that someone would crack a smile, thus allowing him to thrash people, something he enjoyed in his otherwise blistered existence. He laid a small envelope down on the bench between him and the motionless figure to his right.

"For now, this is a targeting task. Figure out routes, routines, daily schedule. After you've got all that down, let him see your pretty face once in a while, so he knows there's a watcher on him. I may or may not need him removed, but if I do, I'll speak his last name to the message board. Which is Smith, by the way, if you can imagine that."

Evangelino hadn't moved a muscle since Mandeville had joined him. His left eye, closest to Mandeville, stared out and down just a little. Mandeville thought he had sight in it, but just couldn't move it. He had a round, pumpkin-shaped head with lots of dark hair, except for a gray streak running from his forehead all the way back to the nape of his neck. He wasn't tall, but he was thickset to the point where Mandeville could feel his menacing bulk right next to him.

He stood up, feeling uncomfortable being right next to this—beast. He looked down on the bench. The envelope was gone.

Okay, then, he thought, and walked away, up toward the Capitol building and the Smithsonian buildings. When he finally looked back, the bench was empty. He shivered. Evangelino, the man who never spoke.

FIVE

On Sunday evening Av slid into his rooftop rocker, pulled a patio chair under his feet, and leaned back to enjoy a cold beer after a session with his Exercycle. He hadn't put much effort into the workout, the day's-end beer being more on his mind than a cardio blast. It was a gorgeous fall evening in the capital. The city's atmosphere was beginning to thin out a little after the summer's endless heat, humidity, and the hordes of sweaty tourists. He was up on the roof of his three-story brick building in the southern precincts of Georgetown, supposedly Washington's toniest neighborhood. He was probably the only Washington Metro cop with a Georgetown address.

The building had begun life in the early 1840s as a warehouse, morphed into a general store, and then finally a tavern with rooms above. Av's uncle Warren, his father's brother, had bequeathed the building to him after succumbing to HIV. Uncle Warren had been ostracized by the entire Smith family after declaring one day that he was gay and that he was leaving his horrified wife. Av had been the lone exception, especially once into his teenage years. He'd refused to join in the familial shunning effort, having developed a better relationship with his uncle than with his own father. When he got back to D.C. after the Marines, he discovered that he was now the proud owner of a very valuable corner property overlooking the remaining vestiges of the C & O Canal and its narrow towpath in downtown Georgetown. His neighbors in the block included several law offices, restaurants, Cannon's fish market, and three embassies within walking distance. A stand of old oaks behind the building helped damp out the perpetual traffic roar of M Street, just two blocks north.

The bottom floor along Thirty-third Street was now occupied by an import-export company, run by a fussy little Iranian man named Bayamad Kardashian, who was quick to tell you that he was, regrettably, no relation to the young lady who was famous for being famous. Av was not exactly sure what Kardashian imported and exported, but it appeared to involve the usual Middle Eastern display of lamps, rugs, and lots of brass objects. More importantly, the Iranian paid his rent on time every month.

The second floor was a two-bedroom rental apartment unit, recently occupied by a young woman who had listed her occupation as an attorney. His rental manager had handled the details and he'd only seen her a couple of times, usually heading off to work, but she appeared to be quite attractive. The income from the lower two floors allowed him to pay the city's hefty taxes on the building and bank almost his entire monthly salary. Besides that, the neighborhood was a delightful place to live, with all the bars and fancy restaurants up on M Street offering every kind of company a choosy bachelor might want on any given boring night.

He reviewed Friday's events. The court order for his John Doe autopsy was "in process." Even though he actually had a name, he'd left the paperwork as a John Doe, hoping that would add impetus for the duty hizzoner to order it up. Unlike in the cop shows on TV, getting a court order for an autopsy took at least a day, often longer, as did any other emergent requests placed respectfully before their honors of the U.S. District Court for the District of Columbia. Budget cuts had reduced the number of judges and magistrates to the point where almost nothing happened on a same-day or even second-day basis. Either way, Av had no intentions of attending the autopsy. He'd done enough of those as a homicide detective and now he'd be entirely satisfied by the report from the slicers and dicers.

He still couldn't figure out how the victim had lost his name in the process of being processed by the ER and then regained it when he showed up in the hospital's morgue. And where the hell had the girlfriend run off to? Scared off by all the commotion? Knew there'd be cops and EMS there? Had *she* possibly done something to McGavin? And then it hit him: Precious had said the Bureau was keeping its distance because of some as-yet-undefined federal involvement— Holy crap! Was Ellen Whiting working for the FBI? He let out a low whistle. The chief medical examiner would love that.

"Knock, knock."

Av turned around to see the pretty blonde from the apartment clambering over the low parapet wall from the building's fire escape behind him.

"Hi, there," he said, enjoying the view as she straightened up. She was wearing what looked like a one-piece bathing suit covered with a sleeveless tee and a pair of clingy nylon running shorts. When he'd seen her before she'd been in her go-to-work clothes. He liked this outfit better.

"I'm Rue Waltham," she said, coming across the flat tar-and-sand roof while rubbing rust off her hands.

"Av Smith," he said, getting up to shake hands.

"Mister Kardashian said you were a runner and that you had an exercise area on the roof, but I couldn't find a way up. So I—" She indicated the external fire stairs, then looked around. The roof had two metal sheds, one for utilities and another small storage hut where Av kept his workout gear. A third, outhouse-shaped protrusion contained the stairwell that came up from his loft apartment just below.

"Oops," she said, when she saw the open stairwell door. "This isn't part of the apartment deal, is it."

" 'Fraid not," he said. "I'm your landlord, actually. I have a loft on the third floor, right below, and that's how *I* get to the roof. I'd never thought about the fire stairs."

"I'm *so* sorry," she said, obviously embarrassed.

He shrugged. "Yeah, well."

She hesitated. "I was really looking for a running partner," she said. "I'm new to the city and I'm not sure where the safe areas are."

"The towpath is a great place for recreational running," he said. "It's a pain right along here—too narrow—but once it opens up, it's great. You just have to watch out for kamikaze cyclists. Rock Creek Park's another good venue but you'd need to drive there." He eyed her slim frame. "What's your level?"

"Five to eight miles, three times a week," she said. "I've done two half Ironmans."

"Have fun?"

"Damned near died," she confessed with a grin. "But I did finish the second one."

"Well, good for you," he said. "Finishing is everything. I do two easy miles or so for a warm-up, turn it on for three, then turn it back off for an easy jog home. Mornings before work, May until the first snow. Walk-jog in the real winter."

"And you're a police officer?"

"Right."

"Well, I'd love to give it a try if you're willing. I'd just feel more secure until I get to know the area."

"Trick is to find and then stay with a crowd if you do decide to go on your own," he said. "D.C.'s a nice town, but we have our share of predators who especially like to hunt Rock Creek Park. And you're pretty enough to attract attention."

"Thank you, kind sir," she said. "And there's no one who'd, um, object to your having me for a running partner?"

"You mean a girlfriend?"

"Or a wife?"

He smiled. "Not a problem. I've made it a life rule not to get into permanent relationships with women. You guys are uniformly dangerous."

She gave him a look that said he had to be kidding. She was maybe five-seven in her tennies, with blue-gray eyes, an athletic figure, and superfine, platinum-blond hair.

"No, actually, I'm serious," he said. "My last squad had eight detectives—six male, two female. Every damned one of them except me was either divorced or about to be divorced. When it came to women, they were universally miserable. Wait, let me rephrase: the *men* were universally miserable. The two women detectives were too busy plotting revenge to be miserable, but they were working on it."

"So this is some kind of a cop thing?" she asked.

"All I know is that as long as I keep women at a professional arm's length, everything in my life seems to go smoother. I think the term of art is 'confirmed bachelor.'"

"As opposed to, say, misogynist?" she said, skeptically.

"No," he said. "I don't hate women. I simply value my freedom more than the so-called benefits of conventional boy-girl relationships."

"Wow," she said. "I really am intruding, aren't I."

"You did ask," he reminded her. "I'll be warming up on the towpath at seven. In the meantime . . ." He glanced toward the fire escape.

"In the meantime, I know my way down," she said. "See you in the morning. I think."

"I'll be there, either way," he said, as pleasantly as possible.

He smiled to himself as he sat back down. The pretty ones were all alike, he thought: they assumed any man would want to be in their company just because they were beautiful. She'd been embarrassed about intruding, and really surprised when he hadn't asked her to sit down, have a beer, talk. Dude: you turning *me* down?

Yup. Nothing personal, darling.

She wasn't there the next morning as Av went out front and began his stretching exercises. It was a gorgeous morning, with bright sunshine spreading across the eastern horizon and temps in the sixties. Even the water pouring from the canal lock looked like actual water for once. The trees were beginning to turn and the air smelled of fresh-roasted coffee beans from the shop across Thirty-third Street. Several other runners trotted by as he warmed up in the parklike wide spot created by the lock. He closed his wrought-iron gate and fell into the flow along the narrow towpath. A cyclist came by, thoughtfully ringing a bell to warn runners ahead. He'd never understood why there were cyclists on this segment of the canal. They had to dismount and then hump their bikes up and over the streets crossing the canal just about every block until they got out of Georgetown.

He set what the Marines had called a route pace, a gentle jog they used to settle out their packs, belts, and other gear. It was designed to cover the ground but not exhaust the troops. He loved his morning runs, but did not miss humping all that gear. The only things he carried now were his badge, pinned to the waistband of his running shorts under the overlong football jersey, and a .38 special S & W Ladysmith wheel gun in a cross-groin fabric holster. He still could hear the lines of doggerel the gunnies would chant, turning words into a nasal invocation to the running gods. Le-o-w-f-t, le-o-w-f-t, le-o-w-f-t right l-e-o-f-t, beedle l-e-o-w-f-t . . .

He became aware of two runners who'd fallen in behind him as if using him as the pace car. He kicked it up to full cardio speed and they appeared to follow suit. He didn't bother to turn around; some runners just did better with someone in front of them.

He turned around when he reached lock No. 5 and saw that his "pursuers" were two military-looking guys, with high and tight haircuts and typical runner's physiques. They were wearing reflective sunglasses, floppy camo hats, dark green tees over black nylon running shorts. He nodded to them as he retraced his steps. They nodded back.

Two minutes later he became aware of them again as they rejoined him for the jog home. Ten, maybe fifteen feet back, keeping perfect time with him. He wondered about it for a moment, thought briefly about doubling back to see what they'd do, and then dismissed them. This town was full of military people; he'd read somewhere that there were twenty-five thousand in the Pentagon alone. Add to that the Secret Service guys, the Bureau guys, who were rumored to run in place at their desks if they couldn't get outside, other cops, probably even some spooks from across the river. Having two guys who looked like that following behind you was hardly an uncommon sight. If he'd had that blonde as his running partner there'd probably be a small army behind them by now.

About a mile from his building, as he closed in on the passage under Key Bridge, he became aware that the two runners had closed it up. He could hear them breathing now, and their footfalls seemed to be no more than six or eight feet away. He assessed his speed, wondering if he'd slacked off, but he could run this pace all day if he had to. Just like people in a crowded room, every runner had his own sense of personal space, and they were just outside of his. He began to wonder if it was his cop sense that was getting worried. Cops were cops twenty-four/seven, and every cop he knew listened to the hairs on the back of his neck if he knew what was good for him. He slowed his pace fractionally, and the two guys behind him drew closer, now definitely inside his personal space, maybe four feet back.

They ran like that for another hundred yards or so, and then Av raised his right hand, palm out, and dropped into a walk. The two guys behind him kept coming, passing on either side, so close he could smell them. They didn't touch him, but if he'd swayed a few inches in either direction, they'd have bumped shoulders.

That was truly odd behavior, he thought, wondering if they'd been deliberately following him or were just screwing around. They trotted off ahead of him while he walked, never breaking pace or looking back. When they were fifty yards ahead, he went back up into his own jog pace to see what they might do, like maybe slow down to a walk until he passed them. They didn't, but then he became aware of a second pair of runners behind him, back about twenty feet, from the sound of them. Same deal: matching his pace, their footfalls distinct but not closing in.

His cop sense was definitely aroused now. Two guys ahead of him, two more behind him, and all of a sudden no other runners around in either direction. He was approaching Georgetown proper so he decided to fake a cramp where the canal bridged a stream that tumbled down to the river. As he came abreast of the bridge wall, he cursed and grabbed at his left hamstring, then stopped and hobbled over to the stone wall, where he sat down. This gave him a good look at the two runners behind him.

Two large black men this time, dressed a lot like the first two runners: floppy cloth hats, the same sunglasses, different-colored shirts and shorts. Av pretended not to look at them as they trotted by, but once they passed, he saw one thing different about these two: they were carrying, their weapons clearly outlined in kidney-bean-shaped black fabric pouches down low just above their hips. He wondered if they'd spotted his own groin pouch when he sat down, but his tee should have covered it pretty well. His weapon was half the size of what they were carrying. They didn't look at him as they went by, their legs keeping perfect time with each other. Definitely military, he thought. Into that left-right-left shit.

He waited until they were out of sight and two more runners, both attractive young women, had come by, and then he got up and walked the rest of the way back to his building.

So what was all that about? he wondered.

Absolutely nothing. But when he came out later to go to work, he found a pair of cheap reflective sunglasses that looked a lot like his folded over the waist-high cast-iron picket fence that fronted his building. They'd been bent in half—for a better purchase on the iron picket?

He looked at them for a moment. A message? Or someone found glasses and hung them on the fence for whoever might come back for them? No—they'd been mangled. Once again he felt his Spidey sense tingling.

Hiram settled back in his chair and watched the screens come to life with his partners in science, if not, occasionally, crime. Giancomo had called for the teleconference. He announced in his mangled English that he'd made a breakthrough regarding signal transmission paths in a monkshood plant. Then, mercifully, he turned it over to one of his assistants, a very pretty young Italian lady whose English was very good indeed. She gave them a highly technical PowerPoint presentation on what they'd come up with, and Hiram was impressed. So was Archie Tennyson, who commented that if this was true, it might now be possible to manipulate these chemical signals to affect the flow and strength of the plant's infamous toxin, aconite, or aconitine as it was sometimes called. Hiram observed that the monkshood alkaloid toxin hardly needed amplification. As they all knew, just touching the plant put an animal or a human in jeopardy of death.

"Yes, of course," Archie said. "But remember, there are circumstances where one *would* want to concentrate it—because a concentrate takes up much less volume."

And, Hiram thought, that makes it a much better agent for use as, say, a directed poison. He immediately thought of Kyle Strang and his fanatical boss, Carl Mandeville. Giancomo had also recognized the potential for deadly mischief, and commented that this discovery would be better kept "in the book," as they called it.

"But that's a major breakthrough, Giancomo," Archie said.

"We know, we know," Giancomo said. "So maybe now we reproduce the experiment, okay? In something not so bad as monkshood. See if some of the other plants can do the same thing, yes?"

They kicked that idea around, but Hiram thought it was wishful thinking. It was the deadly plants—monkshood, belladonna, death cap mushrooms, castor bean pulp—that had the most sophisticated behaviors when threatened by predation, as viewed from the plant's perspective. At the same time, the discovery excited him, because it reinforced the notion that, at some level within the plant's physiology, it was reacting to external stimuli, just as if—it had a brain.

They took a vote, and all agreed to bury Giancomo's findings in their book of experimental data for now. Interesting stuff, but not for publication until one of them could find a way to render the process harmless, or, at least, controllable. And, he hoped to God that no one else had discovered the same thing. Not for the first time, he'd been having second and even third thoughts about what he'd given to the National Security Council.

Thomas, who'd been watching the conference, remarked that the society's fixation with the world's most dangerous plants might backfire one day.

Hiram acknowledged the point. "I know," he said. "We could be viewed as master poisoners in some circles, I suppose, but then, some of our medical contributions would balance that out. Look at what we did with atropine, for instance."

"Yes, sir," Thomas said. "Didn't mean to criticize, of course. Shall we proceed with the vine-pool experiment this morning?"

"I still think it should be called the snake pool," Hiram said.

Thomas gave him a there-you-go-again look, but Hiram just grinned back at him.

SIX

Two days later, not one, Av was able to get the court order and have it sent to OCME by messenger. He called them later that morning and was told by the Forensic Toxicology Lab that it might be sometime next week before the actual autopsy would take place. Av asked why so long. The secretary asked if Av's case was an active and urgent homicide investigation. Av said not yet, but that of course would depend on the results of the autopsy, wouldn't it? She told him to go get a book called *Catch-22* and then invited him to get in line.

Av went to Precious to bitch and moan. She promptly showed him the door. This is the Briar Patch. *Move* the tarbaby, Detective.

He went to complain to Howie Wallace, who offered slightly more sympathy and said, since he didn't have anything special to do, why didn't they go out to that French restaurant and do some interviews. Av couldn't really see the point of that, the EMS reports being fairly complete. Howie said he wanted something different for lunch. Av hadn't told Howie about the four runners or the little memento he'd found on his front-yard fence. He still thought he might be imagining the whole episode, or at least the notion that someone was trying to threaten or scare him. But if so, over what?

They checked out an unmarked and went up Connecticut Avenue through the usual lunchtime traffic. Av wondered aloud about the wisdom of eating at a restaurant after they'd questioned the staff about an unexplained death.

When they arrived at the bistro, however, they got a surprise.

"Closed?" Howie said. Av double-parked, got out, and went up to read the sign.

"This is a health department sign," Av pointed out. "Food Safety. City shut 'em down."

"Just because some guy croaked? Way I read it, he hadn't eaten anything."

A taxi, pinned behind their slick-back by traffic, started laying on the horn. Av badged him and told him to shut up. The Lebanese driver threw up his hands in disgust and darted back into traffic, provoking even more horn blowing. Av got back into their Crown Vic.

"Let's go around back," he said. "I thought I saw a light on in there."

"We can do that," Howie said. "But it ain't gonna get me any snails."

"Tragedy," Av muttered. As far as he was concerned, snails were something he dug out of his running-shoe treads after a run on the towpath.

He steered the car around the corner and found what he was looking for, a service alley behind the row of buildings that included the bistro. When they got to the back of the restaurant, they found a door open. Two men dressed in kitchen white utilities were sitting on trash cans, having a cup of coffee and a cigarette. The open door revealed a brightly lighted kitchen. They got out and approached the two men. Av identified himself as Metro police.

"Now what?" one of the men said, belligerently. He was the younger of the two. Superskinny, an international orange blaze in his spiky hair, earrings in both ears. The older guy was giving Howie's outfit the once-over. Howie was sporting what he called his official middle-aged Mau-Mau look: an untucked white shirt shaped like a sixties dashiki, mirrored shades, the dreads, of course, all worn over jeans and sandals. Av thought he looked like any well-dressed bank robber.

" 'Now what?' " he said. "Not sure I understand your question."

"You people have already shut us down for no good reason. So, like, yeah, now what: you back to rub it in or something?"

"You've got us confused with someone else," Howie said. "We're detectives. We're investigating an unexplained death in this restaurant a few days ago. We're the police, brother, not the health department."

"You're the District government," the older sniffed. "What's the difference? Place is shut down and we're out of work."

"We'd like to speak to the proprietor of the Bistro Nord," Av said. "Is he here?"

"Jacques? Hell, no. You people took him away."

Av and Howie looked at each other. "Sorry, man," Howie said. "We don't know what you're goin' on about. Sign out front says Food Safety shut you down for some kinda violation. They don't take anybody anywhere."

The younger man pitched the remains of his coffee into the alley. "Tell that to Jacques," he said. "These four guys come in, buncha suits wearing, like, Matrix sunglasses? Took Jacques out front to a black SUV and then slapped that fuckin' sign on the door. Told us to shut it down and go on vacation for a while."

"When was this?" Av asked.

"Day after it happened," the man said. "Came in here like the fuckin' gestapo, man. Front and back, like it was some kinda roust. This is a respectable restaurant here. Been in business for, like, eight years, no problems with nobody, and sure as hell no health department violations. Never had a score under ninety-eight."

Av knew that eight years was a lifetime in the restaurant business. He was completely baffled. "Either of you guys here the day the dude croaked?" he asked.

The younger guy nodded. "Yeah," he said. "We catch that scene on a regular basis—middle-aged paper pusher chasin' some hottie. We all figured her for bein' something special on the side, older dude like that. She was new, but he was a regular. Nice people, you know? He was a good tipper, knew his French cuisine, too."

"But he hadn't eaten anything yet, right?" Av asked. "He sat down, said he was cold, and then, boom, he's on the deck?"

"Yeah, dude, that's exactly what happened," the younger man said. "So, like, why the fuck *we* bein' shut down?"

"Guys in suits?" Howie asked. "They show ID? Badges?"

"No, they did not," the older man said. "Nor have you, for that matter."

Av and Howie fished out their badges, and Av let the older guy look at his credentials. He asked him if they could go into the dining room.

"You want to search the place?"

"No, no, we just want to see where it happened, that's all."

"So, like, what did kill that dude?" the younger man asked.

"We don't know, yet," Av responded. "That's why we're looking into the incident. Did the guy usually pay with a credit card?"

"Yeah," the younger man said. "Amex."

Av nodded. That matched what the proprietor had said.

"Where you guys keeping Jacques, anyway?" the older man asked.

"We're not keeping Jacques anywhere," Av said. "You got a phone number for him? Home, cell, anything?"

The older guy recited two phone numbers. "Hope you have better luck than we did," he said. "You find him, ask him what we should do now, would you?"

Av promised them he would. The older man, who turned out to be the chef, then took them into the dining room and to the table where it had all gone down. Everything had long since been cleaned up. The place looked like every other small French restaurant Av had ever been in. Av automatically looked for the chalked figure on the floor, but then remembered that he wasn't homicide anymore, and that this might not even be a homicide.

They thanked the employees and went back to their unmarked. "Like, this fucker's turning into a stone-cold, like, mystery," Howie said. "Hate that 'like' shit. But: we gotta move this bitch down the road."

Av agreed. "Four guys show up, escort the owner to a black SUV, and close the place down?"

"That ain't no Food Safety shit right there," Howie said. "Let's go get that notice off the door, run it by their office, see if it's legit."

"Just what I was thinking," Av said. "You wanna try those numbers?"

They settled for Burger King on the way to the public health department. Howie innocently asked the drive-through box if they had snails today, producing an indignant squawk. Jacques's cell number had come up with a helpful voice-mail announcement that the mailbox was full; the other number just rang.

At the health department a Food Safety clerk told them that the closure notice was a legitimate form, but, after a quick search, that there was no record of any of their people writing the citation and closing the Bistro Nord. He checked the restaurant's file and found no problems, leaving another dead end and even more mystery. They went back to

ILB. As they were approaching the office Av heard a rhythmic thumping sound coming from the squad room down the hall.

"Uh-oh," Howie said, staring at the closed squad room door.

"What?"

"Wong Daddy's back," Howie said. "We don't wanna go in there right now."

Sergeant Wong Daddy Bento was the larger half of the other pair of detectives in ILB. Av had been introduced when he was first assigned to ILB and he still remembered shaking hands with Wong's viselike paws. Wong Daddy was maybe five-six if he stood up really straight, and that measurement seemed to apply to height, width, and thickness in about equal proportions. He was of mixed Asian race, predominantly Korean, with a bullet-shaped head, a wide and rather threatening face that reminded Av of some of the samurai caricatures he'd seen at the Freer Gallery, and the overall physique of a sumo wrestler minus the pendulous belly rolls. Howie had explained that when something upset Wong, he'd begin stomping one foot and then the other on the floor, much like a sumo, and growling epithets in some unknown Asian dialect. Everyone had learned to just leave the squad room whenever Wong Daddy started cranking up. Av saw Precious looking out from the doorway to her office before quickly closing her door.

"How long does this go on?" Av asked as they backed down the hall. The stomping was getting louder and so were the epithets.

"Till somebody finds Miz Brown," Howie said. "He can usually get Wong to quit with all that shit."

" 'He'?"

"You haven't met him yet; been on some kinda special tasking up on the fifth floor. He's Wong's partner. Real name's Willy, but everyone calls him Miz Brown. Black dude, real tall, skinny, and fussy, like an old schoolteacher. Everything's gotta be just so, or he'll start nagging and shit. Can't stop talking once he starts. Drives people crazy, but amazing during an interrogation."

"And they keep him, why?"

"For two reasons, but mostly because he flat *moves* those tarbabies. He gets it into that pointy little head to push a tarbaby your way, you might as well give up and take it on. He will wheedle and whine and bug your ass to death. Ask anyone in federal LE—they all know him. Plus: between him and Wong Daddy, they a force of nature when it comes to making perps sing. They are absolutely the very best interview team in the MPD. One of the districts gets a sphinx? They send for those two. You ever get the chance, you need to go watch that shit."

Av remembered now that he had heard something about this team. The wild man in the squad room had begun yelling out kiyais and slamming something on the desks. Howie said that was probably his hand. They had backed their way into the break room where, by now, the ILB secretaries were already cowering. Howie pushed the door shut with his foot.

"Anybody findin' Miz Brown?" Howie asked.

One of the ladies nodded. "He comin'."

"What set him off?"

"Bill collector, probably," one of the other girls said. Howie explained that Wong Daddy was known for his expensive womanizing and was often the target of collection agencies. Av was rapidly concluding that he'd been assigned to the department's loony bin. Wong was audibly kicking a trash can around the squad room now. Then a tall shadow flitted by in the hallway headed in the direction of the squad room.

"That him?" Av asked.

"Yeah. Everything be cool in a minute or so."

The stomping and the crashing stopped. It was replaced by a loud tirade in that same unknown dialect that went on for thirty seconds before stopping abruptly.

"Miz Brown's talkin' him down," Howie said. "And he will talk and talk and *talk* until Wong puts his hands over his ears and then that's the end of it. Then Brown will talk some more."

"We need to go see Precious," Av said. "Tell her what we found out up on Connecticut Avenue."

"Not quite yet, pardner," Howie said, helping himself to some coffee from the machine. "We got way too many loose ends. That lady has a hate-on for loose ends."

"This whole thing is a loose end," Av pointed out. It was still quiet in the squad room. The secretaries were tiptoeing back to the admin office.

"Exactly," Howie said. "Ain't no point in going in there and bothering

Precious when we can't answer a single one of all the questions you *know* she's gonna ask. We gotta do some more detecting and shit."

They went down to the squad room. Detective Brown was sitting on the corner of Wong Daddy's desk, talking urgently in a low voice. Wong Daddy was in his chair, staring at nothing but still making low growling sounds in his throat. A badly dented metal trash can lay against one wall and Wong Daddy's in-basket was flattened into a metal pancake. Av wondered again what he'd gotten himself into.

"This has federal LE all over it, you know," Av said the next morning. "Black SUVs, the Bistro's owner going for a ride . . ."

"*If* any of that's true," Howie pointed out.

"There is that," Av said, having been lied to by witnesses only about a million times.

He went to see if he could push OCME on the autopsy while Howie tried the two phone numbers again. He then ran a reverse directory to see where the home number was located. A secretary came in and announced that Precious wanted to see them. He gave Howie the high sign and they went to her office. Av told her what they had so far, which didn't take very long. He finished up by beginning to lay out what he proposed to do next, but Precious interrupted him.

"You keep talking about this incident like it's a case that needs solving," she said. "That's not what we do here, Detective. You're forgetting the mission of ILB."

Av frowned. "But—"

"No buts, Detective," she said. "You're not homicide police anymore, remember? Our mission is to move a hairball like this somewhere else. You and Mau-Mau go figure out the logical destination, and then we'll go from there. Now, out."

Outside her office, Howie and Av tried to figure out what to do next. Av was getting tired of being told to *not* do his job.

"If we can find out who took brother Jacques and where," Howie said, "then I'd say that's where this case needs to go. Maybe there's some connection between black SUVs and what happened to that civil serpent."

"We still don't know what, if anything, killed that guy," Av pointed out. "If he just up and died, then there's no 'case' to begin with."

"Who takes it from there, then?" Howie asked.

"Who's got the remains?" Av said.

"OCME."

"Sounds like OCME's problem, then," Av said.

Howie grinned. "Now you talkin' like an old hand at the Briar Patch," he said, proudly.

"Hell with this goat-rope," Av said. "I'm going to the gym, burn off that greaseburger I ate yesterday."

When Av got back from his workout there was a call-me from OCME. He called. Apparently they had gone ahead with the autopsy after all.

"On your John Doe," the pathologist said. "We got nothing specific for a cause of death. Heart stopped, lungs stopped, brain stopped. If he'd had a big burn mark anywhere I'd postulate that he'd been electrocuted. He was overweight, had Lucky Strike lungs, a fatty heart, and a lumpy liver, but: there are no indications that any of those organs precipitated death. Did he eat anything at the scene?"

"According to the restaurant people, he sat down, had one little sip of wine, said he felt cold, then went down. And it wasn't the wine because apparently his lady friend had a glass with no ill effects."

"Oka-a-y," the doctor said. "We've sent a bunch of blood and other bodily fluids off for further analysis. Now: we don't have a cause of death, but for *manner* of death, I want to keep this one open. This may not have been death by natural causes."

"Whoa—really?"

"I asked for one test right away once I examined all the major organs. It's a test for sodium levels in the brain cells. Came back abnormally high. If the brain-blood barrier is letting sodium through at those levels, it's symptomatic of poisoning. We'll know more in a week or three. Now, back to disposition of remains?"

"Don't you have to wait for all your tests?"

"Nope. We have all the tissue we need, and this is D.C.: we're short for space. The court order said John Doe, and I get that, but I seem to remember a name?"

"I was gonna ask *you* about that, Doc," Av said. "How—"

"Detective?" the pathologist said. "I won't ask you why the court order said John Doe and you won't ask me why the name went astray, okay? Trust me, it'll be better for everybody that way. Now: any family?"

"There is, and they've been notified," Av said. "But that's kind of our problem—that's as far as we can take it." He gave the doc a short description of ILB and its function within MPD. As in, this isn't our problem anymore. He waited. It was worth a try.

"Lovely," the doc said, patiently. "But I still need disposition orders."

"Well, he was DHS—maybe dump the remains on their doorstep?"

"There are days I'd like to do just that," the doc laughed. "But, look, you're the guys who got the court order; help us out here."

"Lemme see if I can get the Second District homicide people into it," Av said, with a lot more confidence than he felt. He hung up and told Howie what was going on. Howie pointed out that they were supposed to move cases *out* of Metro PD, not sideways. On the other hand, he admitted, if they had a possible homicide in the Second's patch, then maybe they had no choice here.

"We'd better clear that with Precious," Howie said.

Av's desk intercom buzzed. "Lieutenant on one for you, Detective," the secretary said.

Av mouthed the word "Precious" to Howie and poised his finger over the line one button. Howie did the same on his desk and they punched in and picked up together.

"Yes, ma'am?" Av said.

"Where are we on that Connecticut Avenue mystery?"

Av relayed what the OCME pathologist had had to say, and that he was about to contact the homicide desk in Second District. He explained why.

"They're gonna push back on that noise, Detective, especially when they hear the victim was DHS. That would imply Bureau responsibility."

There's an echo in here, Av thought: that's what I wanted to do in the first place. "Sounds good to me, Lieutenant. Guy's a federal SES in the homeland security business. The Feebs just about have to take it."

"The Bureau is the G, Detective. The G doesn't *have* to do anything, less it wants to. But, yeah, I guess it's about time I try again with the Hooverites. If they agree, I'll send you two over there for some face time with the first team."

Both detectives rolled their eyes.

"Mau-Mau, you eavesdropping?"

"Yes, ma'am," Howie said, with a grin.

"You get a proper suit on before you go consorting with Bureau people," she ordered. "They get one look at you, they'll be calling up their reaction force."

"Yes, ma'am," Howie said.

"I'll get back to you," Precious said.

When they'd hung up, Av noted that Precious didn't miss much. Howie laughed.

"You don't know the half of it," he said. "She stops in the secretaries' office coupla times a day and reads through all the message forms. She already knew we'd had a call-me from OCME."

"You gonna ditch the wig?" Av asked. "Look funny with a suit."

"*Hell,* no," Howie said.

Precious called them back into her office ten minutes later. "Bureau Metro Liaison desk says they don't know what we're talking about, refused to confirm that Ellen Whiting is a special agent or even a Bureau employee, whose black SUVs went where, or why they should care about yet another dead John Doe in the District."

"You told them John Doe?" Av asked. "But we know his name. And we know where he worked."

"First call," Precious said. "You never give everything away on the first call, Detective. Now: the ME says it's possibly poisoning?"

"Inconclusive, awaiting further tests," Av said. "But: gut feel? It's hinky and that doc knew McGavin's name, but would not tell me why he'd been posted as a John Doe. So: what the hell's going on here, please, ma'am?"

"One of those vast right-wing conspiracies is what this is," Precious said. "Okay: we're gonna do what any good bureaucrat does in this situation: we're gonna sit on this one for now. I think I need to talk to somebody upstairs."

"Sit on it?"

"Best thing is for us to go into a holding pattern here until the ME pronounces, one way or another. He says natural causes, we're done. Release the remains to the wife. He says homicide . . ."

"Yeah?"

"Shit, I don't know," she said. "In the meantime, you guys leave it alone." Her phone rang. She pointed them to the door. They went back to the squad room.

"This is so bogus," Av muttered.

"No, it isn't," Howie said. "This is ILB. We in the tarbaby biz. This is what they look like."

"Yeah, okay," Av said. "But some other agency has to be mixed up in this." Then he remembered the four guys he'd encountered on his morning run. He told Howie about that.

Howie stopped short in the hallway. "And this happened, when? *Partner?*" he said.

"Yeah, yeah, I should have said something. But: it was so out-there, you know? Like my imagination kinda thing."

" 'Cept for those sunglasses," Howie pointed out. "You keep 'em, by any chance?"

Av went to his desk and pulled out the glasses.

"Piece'a shit Chinese knockoffs," Howie said, eyeing the offending glasses. "Low-end Walmart, at best. Nobody in federal LE would actually wear this shit."

"Exactly," Av said. "So why should I take this seriously?"

"Who spikes a pair of sunglasses on somebody's fence, huh? Tell me that, my man."

"Somebody who found them on the path. My fence was the closest place to put 'em," Av said.

"Except," Howie said.

"Yeah, well, they are kinda bent in half."

"Uh-huh," Howie said. "How'd you feel, those guys blowin' past you close enough for you to smell 'em?"

"Well," Av said.

"There you go," Howie said. "Your Spidey sense ticklin' the back of your neck when those dudes were closing in on you?"

Av nodded.

"Okay, then," Howie said. "Crew gotta do something about this. You runnin' again tomorrow morning?"

"Well, yeah." Av knew very well what Howie thought about running for exercise, or, for that matter, any other form of exercise. The only exercise Howie was into involved getting lunch. "You wanna come along?" he asked, innocently.

"*Hell* no," Howie said. "But I got me a plan. Those dudes like four on one, we'll let 'em see what that feels like. Get Wong into it. He loves this kinda shit."

Gee, Av thought, remembering the scene this morning. What could possibly go wrong with that idea?

The next morning, Av warmed up outside the building just before sunrise. It was another cool, clear morning, Washington at its very best in the early fall. There was already a grunch of devoted runners headed up the narrow towpath toward the next up-and-over.

"Knock, knock," a female voice chirped. He looked around. It was Rue Waltham, the lovely rooftop visitor from the other day. She was decked out in running gear, practical and yet just the least bit sexy. It was those filmy white running shorts, he decided. Looked more like panties. She had a small fanny pack Velcro'ed to the small of her back. She grinned when she caught him checking her out.

"Hey, there," he said. "Ready to try out for the C & O relays?"

She gave him a brilliant smile, and, for just a moment, his rule about getting close to the ladies wobbled a bit. "Try's the operative word," she said. "If I hold you back, let me know and get on down the road."

"It's not a race," he said. "Let's just enjoy the morning. You warm up already?"

"No, but it won't take a minute," she said. She then proceeded to stretch and bend, and then bend and twist some more. Av continued through his own warm-up motions while trying not to stare. Had to admit: the young lady had developed a lovely procedure. He grinned when a passing runner bounced into a hedge as he trotted by, gawking. Yeah, dude, he thought. She *is* pretty, isn't she.

"Okay," she said a few minutes later. "Ready if you are."

They headed up the towpath at a leisurely jog. She ran alongside to his left and appeared to be going at an enjoyable pace. She was fit, he decided after five minutes, with no visible breathing problems. He relaxed. He'd been afraid she might be trying for something she couldn't really do, but it was evident that she actually was a runner. The morning was glorious, the air clear and smog-free, the towpath traffic light as they jogged in place while waiting to cross the streets. While they were waiting at the second bridge, he heard Rue squeak in surprise. He looked over, saw her staring at something in front of them, and then he saw it, too. "It" was a man's face looking back at them through the driver's-side window of a black Mercedes that was stuck in traffic across from them. He was wearing a red ball cap, and there was something really wrong with his face, and with his left eye in particular, which made it impossible to tell how old he was, but that left eye reminded Av of a snake's eyes. Rue looked away, aware that she was being rude, and then the traffic edged forward, creating a gap through which they quickly crossed the street and then went back down to the towpath.

"Jeez," he heard her say, and he grunted something in reply. Some weirdo wearing a Halloween mask, right there in broad daylight. They finally jogged out of the urban part of Georgetown and into the park. It was shaping up to be a glorious day; even the canal water still looked better than usual, with no visible floating bodies. He'd decided not to talk: he could maintain this pace for miles and hold a conversation, but he wasn't yet sure about her.

Once they cleared the downtown area he asked if she was ready to kick it up a bit. She nodded, and they went to work. For the next three miles he concentrated on his own pace and breathing while not paying much attention to her. She'd told him to keep on going if she faltered, but she didn't. At four miles, near Chain Bridge, he slacked off. He looked over at Rue. She was breathing much harder now, and her face and skin were flushed. She looked back at him and nodded, but obviously had no breath for conversation. He slowed to the jog pace for the next half-mile, watching her out of the corner of his eye as her color faded and she regained her breath. He looked at his watch.

"Turnaround time," he announced. "Slow jog back, okay?"

She nodded. As they turned around he caught her scent: a touch of perfume, some serious sweat, and a bare frisson of something else. Female exertion, he decided, or some of those lethal female pheromones. Shields up!

As they headed back he became aware of two runners closing in behind them. He wanted to look back but held himself in check. There were lots of runners out by then. Two more behind him meant nothing. Except: they were gaining, running harder than he and Rue were, their feet pounding harder on the towpath than seemed necessary. A moment later they passed him.

Military again. Those same sunglasses, cropped hair, extreme fitness, and passing a little closer than necessary. He'd felt Rue move in closer to him when they'd gone by. Then he realized the runners were slowing their pace a bit now that they were in front. Extra-long black tees, red shorts today, military-style ball caps. Familiar, he thought. Coincidence? Not fucking likely.

Footsteps behind them again. This time he really did want to look over his shoulder, but his cop sense told him everything he needed to know. It was another box. He touched his right hand to his gun pouch, and then remembered he wasn't alone this time. He glanced at Rue: she was oblivious, head down, putting one foot in front of the other. He had no idea what these guys intended, if anything, but he wished she wasn't in the mix just now.

He saw the bridge he'd stopped at with the fake cramp coming up ahead. There was a thick stand of scraggly trees on the river side of the towpath. Now there was no one else around, and that in itself was strange—ten minutes ago there'd been all sorts of foot traffic. All of a sudden it was just the six of them, running almost in formation, at a jog pace. He had the clear sense that both pairs of runners were subtly shortening the box. He casually draped his right hand over the groin pouch, ready to draw. And then from up ahead, at the bridge itself, came a loud: *Kiyai!*

"Walking now," he murmured to Rue. "Stay close to me."

"Wha-at?" she said, looking around.

As they dropped down into a walk, Av took her by the arm and veered to the left, walking over to the side of the towpath closest to the canal. The two guys behind, surprised by his sudden turn, trotted by and then slowed down, while the two up ahead had stopped. Then all four turned to stare at the apparition rising on the towpath.

Wong Daddy stood there just on the other side of the bridge like an ambulatory oak tree, beginning his foot-stomping routine and carrying on in the unknown Asian dialect. He was wearing a size fifty-something judo gi pants, a tent-sized Metro PD sweatshirt, and a black band around his forehead. His fists were clenched and he was amping up the volume while staring wild-eyed at the four runners. Each time he raised his arms to balance the next stomp, his gold shield and holstered gun became visible. The four runners backed up a few steps as they realized Wong Daddy was approaching them with each stomp. He had coarsened his voice and was now sounding like the senior samurai in a Kurosawa movie.

"What *is* that?" Rue asked, pointing at Wong while sticking to Av like glue. "And who are those guys?"

"'Bout to find out, I think," Av said, pulling up his T-shirt to expose his own gold shield, and drawing his snub-nose. "Go sit on that bench over there, and if there's shooting, get into the water."

"Shooting? *What?!*"

The four runners were in a close group now, and two of them had their hands under the right side of their own extra-long tees. Then, from behind the approaching madman, came the growl of a siren as a Metro black-and-white came crunching slowly up the towpath, blue lights strobing. When it reached the approaches to the arched bridge, the engine shut down and Miz Brown unlimbered his lanky frame from inside the Crown Vic. He was dressed in a suit and tie, with his gold shield pinned to his left breast pocket.

There was nowhere for the four runners to go except back the way they'd come, and by now Av was standing on the towpath in their way. Miz Brown gave Wong Daddy a tender little pat on his bald pate as he walked by, opening his credentials and asking the four men to identify themselves. Wong Daddy stopped his performance and then joined Miz Brown. When he got to within six feet of the four nervous-looking individuals, he growled something, hunched forward, and then began to sidestep around the group of four, his fingers opening and closing as if they were independently seeking something to squeeze the life out of. Miz Brown stepped into the magic circle, and displayed his credentials more prominently.

"Metro PD, gentlemen," he said. "ID, please? Preferably *before* I lose control of my troll here?"

Av could see that the four were considering a bolt, either by rushing

Brown, four on one, and taking their chances with Av's .38, or even executing a scrambling detour down the heavily wooded hillside toward the banks of the Potomac. He heard a noise behind him and turned to find Howie, also in a suit and minus the dreads wig, standing with his coat back and his right hand on his hip-holstered weapon. Traffic up on Canal Street was slowing as people caught sight of the weird tableau down on the towpath. The four guys looked positively worried now, and then two more black-and-whites hove into view behind Miz Brown's car. Four uniforms got out and spread themselves along the towpath.

That seemed to do it for the four unsubs. The oldest-looking one of them reached down and lifted the hem of his tee, revealing his own gold badge pinned to his waistband. The other three followed suit. Their tees were plenty big enough to accommodate holstered weapons, but no one appeared to be reaching.

"We're FPS," the man said. "Our creds are in the office."

"FPS?" Miz Brown asked, looking puzzled. "What you doin' out here in a national park, harassing a Metro police detective?"

"We're exercising," the man said. "We're not harassing anyone."

Av put away his weapon. "You lose these the other day, FPS?" he called, and pitched the cheap wraparounds at the man's feet.

The man looked down, then shrugged. Miz Brown took a deep breath and launched into what Howie called one of his waterfall monologues. Howie had eased up on his shooting stance and was now lighting up a cigarette while watching Brown envelop the four guys in a perfect cloud of bullshit. He winked at Av.

Av, realizing Miz Brown was in full cry, backed away and walked over to where Rue Waltham was huddled on a park bench. To his surprise, she was looking more interested in the little drama than scared.

"Relax," he told her, quietly. "They're federal cops, not muggers; some kind of misunderstanding here, apparently. We can go now."

He took her arm gently and they walked by the four runners, bookended now by Wong Daddy, who was deep-breathing while still muttering and staring fixedly at the smallest of the runners, and Miz Brown, who was lecturing the four men on the rules of interagency procedure within the District of Columbia. Once they cleared the scene on the other side of the bridge, Av suggested they jog back from here. Rue seemed only too willing. The uniforms stared curiously at the two of them as they trotted by.

"Who were all those people?" she asked.

"The four guys say they're Federal Protective Service. You know, the uniforms you see on federal properties, working front-gate security and the X-ray machines inside the lobby?"

"And they were interested in you?"

"Seemed to be," Av said. "Saw them days ago. Same deal; they boxed me in while I was running. Didn't do or say anything, just let me know they were there, and that they could have done something if they'd wanted to."

"Did you do something to a federal building?"

"Not that I know of, but, trust me, those four guys will soon be just dying to tell Detective Sergeant Brown what they were out there for."

SEVEN

"Bogus," Miz Brown declared. "I mean, c'mon, Federal Protective Service? They're a buncha building guards."

The Briar Patch crew were sitting around the conference table, drinking coffee and rehashing the towpath incident. Av asked Brown if the FPS badges looked real.

"Yeah, they did, but so what? You have to see creds and then run a check, you know? They were packing, or at least two of them were. But WTF? What were they doing out there, screwin' with Brother Av's morning run?"

"They have an answer for that?"

"Nope," Brown said. "Stone effing wall. Just out for a run, like everyone else. Didn't know nothing about nothing. One of them did want to know the last time anybody fed Wong."

"Well, I appreciate the assist," Av said. "They did it twice, and they had me a little spooked."

"Spooked," Wong Daddy said. "Shoulda let me spool it on up a little, you wanna see spooked."

Av laughed. "It was pretty good as was," he said. "Those four guys did *not* know what to do next, you started in with that Toshiro Mifune samurai shit. Wonderful."

"Yeah," Wong said, proudly. "Got that bad boy down cold."

It was the first time Av had heard Wong speak normally. He realized that Wong was a righteous piece of work, and he wanted to know him better.

"So," Brown said. "We had some fun, entertained the commuters on Canal Street a little, got to see Mau-Mau in a suit, and ran off some rent-a-cops. Can anybody tell me what started all this shit?"

"*You* talked to them," Av said. "You really didn't get anything?"

Brown shook his head. "But," he pointed out, proudly, "I wasn't listening all that much. Not my style, right?"

"I've been running the towpath for years," Av said. "Never had anyone do what those guys were doing. I keep trying to think of what I've been into lately that might have lit a fuse somewhere."

"That business up on Connecticut Avenue is the only thing I can think of," Howie said. "And I see no possible connection between that mess, strange as it is, and the Federal Protective Service."

"Strange is what we do here," Brown reminded them.

"Okay," Av said. "You want strange? Lemme recap: we initially tried to move the sudden unexplained death of one Francis X. McGavin to the Bureau, because he was working for the DHS. They said, thanks, but no thanks. MedStar ER classifies the dead guy as a John Doe. Their pathology people, however, said his name was McGavin. The FBI won't say one way or another if this Ellen Whiting works for them. OCME says they can't figure out the cause of death, other than that every important organ suddenly stopped. The ME has a theory, but he isn't willing to commit to it yet. Then he hinted at poison. But: the guy didn't eat anything at the frog restaurant. Owner of said frog restaurant was observed by his crew being taken away in a black SUV, ostensibly driven by the Food Safety Division of the District government, who supposedly shut the place down with a suspension notice that *is* written on a proper form but was never issued by the District food police. And now I've got federal building guards hassling my ass on the C & O Canal towpath?"

"Who's the hottie?" Howie asked.

"A tenant in my building, wanted somebody to run with 'cause she's new in town."

Wong Daddy looked interested. "She in play?" he asked.

"Absolutely," Av said. "I can fix you right up. I think. She may be a lawyer, though."

Wong grunted, his sudden distaste evident. He had his standards, after all.

"Gentlemen," Precious announced from the doorway. "I've just had an interesting phone call."

The fearless foursome turned as one to hear what she had to say. She came in and sat down at the head of their conference table. "From the FPS, of all people?"

The four of them looked at each other and then executed a unanimous: oooooh. Precious did not appear to be amused.

"One deputy director for management named Stein called Assistant Chief Taylor, he of the unswervingly happy demeanor?"

There were groans at the table. Assistant Chief Taylor, known unofficially at MPD headquarters as Happy, of the Seven Dwarfs fame, was one of those aging white men who desperately need about a daily quart or so of serotonin reuptake inhibitor medication. Taylor manifested a notoriously perpetual red ass; a broken shoelace was sufficient to trigger a towering rage. They could only imagine what a bitch call from the FPS might provoke.

"Four of Mister Stein's special agents were ambushed—Stein's word—on the C & O Canal towpath this morning while conducting daily physical fitness training, by an equal number of Metro PD detectives, one of whom was acting like Godzilla on crystal meth and who put them in fear for their personal safety."

"Damn straight," Wong muttered proudly.

"The description given was sufficient to identify the inmates of the Briar Patch as the guilty bastards. There were also black-and-whites involved? So: WTF, over? Inquiring minds want to know."

Av took the question and gave her the background. "It was the sunglasses that did it," he finished up. "Same thing they were wearing, but a Walmart version. Looked like a threatening message."

"Why would four FPS special agents want to threaten you?" she asked.

"Great question," Av said. "Sergeant Brown talked to them."

"And did they enlighten you, Sergeant Brown?"

"Um, I may have done most of the talking," Brown said. "They didn't say much of anything."

"No surprise there," Howie observed. "And since when did federal building guards get special-agent status?"

"Since nine-eleven," Precious said. "They're no longer just a bunch of rent-a-cops dozing at the front doors of federal buildings. Think counter-terrorism. Homeland Security. Like that."

"Well," Av said, "for what it's worth, the only weirdness I've been rolling around in the past week has to do with a former Homeland Security ass-bandit."

Precious started to ask the obvious question, but then stopped, chewing her lower lip for a moment. The detectives watched. Apparently, one did not interrupt Precious when she was thinking.

"Okay," she said. "Back to basics here: we're the ILB. Our mission is to move tarbabies out of the Metro PD. Detective Smith: can you explain how this FPS drama is related to the McGavin case?"

"No, ma'am," he said. "I can't make a connection. Right now I think these are probably four ex-rent-a-cops who've been issued gold badges, a new title, and who've been watching too many movies."

"But why *you*?" she asked.

Av shook his head.

"And it happened twice?"

"Yes, ma'am," he said. "And the second time I thought we were going to get down to some kind of business, till they got a good look at Wong Daddy cranking up his monster mash."

Precious eyed the offending monster, who grinned back at her and burped.

"Okay," she said, getting up. "I'm gonna try to go on the offense here. I'll tell the assistant chief what you told me and that I think MPD should initiate a formal interagency investigation into the actions of the four FPS people. Emphasis on the formal. Make them explain why they were following you on the towpath. In the meantime, Detective Sergeant Smith, I want a full written statement as to what happened out there. What are we waiting for in the McGavin matter, again?"

"Cause of death, manner of death," Av said. "Some kind of reliable ID on the girlfriend. Really like to talk to her."

"You gone and got yourself wrapped around a goddamned mystery, haven't you."

Av threw up his hands.

"Do you have history with the assistant chief by any chance?"

"It's possible," Av said uncomfortably.

"Super," she said. "In the meantime, mysteries are not our remit here, Detective Sergeants. This is ILB. You four nutcases put your thinking caps on and make this thing go away. And quit picking on feds. They're fragile these days, with that sequester bullshit and all."

Thirty minutes later Av and Howie pulled into the physicians-only parking area at the MedStar hospital complex on Irving Street. Howie was back in character as Mau-Mau, the dreads wig in place and casual clothes instead of the morning's suit. They'd stopped for mid-morning coffee near the hospital.

"There's the ER entrance," Av said. "EMTs oughta be hanging out around the meat wagons somewhere."

They were on a mission to talk to the EMTs who had responded to the call at the Bistro. Their names were on the incident report, and the two individuals, Castro and Baynes, were supposed to have come on-shift thirty minutes ago. They walked over to where four boxy ambulances were backed into their parking spots near the ER entrance. There was a group of white-coated, mostly young men standing just outside the ER's glass doors, smoking cigarettes. Nobody seemed especially interested when two cops walked up. EMTs and cops got along.

Av introduced himself and asked if they could talk to EMTs Castro and Baynes. Two guys stepped forward, said hey, and asked what was up.

"You guys respond to a man-down at the French restaurant called the Bistro Nord, a week ago, maybe Thursday last?"

Castro looked at Baynes. "Nope," they said in unison.

Av frowned. He pulled out the EMS report, showed it to the two EMTs. They studied it for a minute, then shook their heads. "Looks right," Castro said. "And I see our names there. But those are not our signatures, and we never did a run to any restaurant."

"You telling me somebody arrived at that place in a MedStar ambulance, accompanied by a street patrol cop, and took this guy to MedStar, who does have a record of him, and faked the names on the report?"

"Man, I don't know what to say." He turned to some of the other EMTs. "Any of you guys do a call at a French restaurant called—what was it?"

"Bistro Nord. Connecticut Avenue. Last Thursday. Guy did a flop and twitch at a table, owner called 911. He was nonresponsive upon arrival. Supposedly MedStar EMS transported him here. ER docs pronounced him a half hour after arrival."

Blank looks and head-shaking all around. "Another EMS, maybe?" one of them asked.

"But that's our form," Castro said. "Our names. Just not my signature."

Av looked at Howie. The next step was obvious: get to the patrol cop who'd come in with them. They looked again at the form. The cop's report was attached, but the block for responding officer's name was blank.

"Fuck," muttered Howie.

"So what've we got here?" Av asked when they got back in their car. "Are we saying that the Bistro deal is entirely bogus?"

"Sure looks like it," Howie said. "The meat-wagon guys—why would they lie?"

"Right," Av said. "Why *would* they lie. You know what? I'm beginning to think this whole thing took some serious organization and planning. Maybe the ME's right: this *is* a fucking homicide."

"You got a problem, right there, partner," Howie said. "You still thinkin' like a homicide cop. Ain't our job, remember? We're not detectives anymore—we the tarbaby po-lice now."

"Yeah, yeah, I get it," Av said.

One of the secretaries intercepted them when they got back to the office. "Lieutenant wants a word," she said. "But first, Mau-Mau, honey? You need to go get some Sunday go-to-meetin' clothes on. Word is Chief Sweetness and Light is inbound."

Ten minutes later they were summoned into Precious's office. Assistant Chief Taylor was sitting behind Precious's desk; she was standing to one side, her face indicating that she was not too happy to be bumped from her desk.

"Right," Taylor said, staring at Av. "That's the one."

One what? Av wondered with a sinking feeling.

Taylor was a large but not very tall man in an ill-fitting uniform. Av's mother would have called him a black Irishman: dense black hair, dark eyes, prominent five o'clock shadow, big, unpleasant face, and a loud voice.

He was staring at the two of them as if they were notorious criminals. Av had put on a sport coat, and Howie had removed the dreads and changed his shirt. Both of us have shaved heads, Av thought; maybe that's it.

"The assistant chief has been in touch with his counterpart in the Federal Protective Service," Precious announced. "There have been—developments."

"Developments." Taylor snorted. "That's one way of putting it." He pointed at Howie. "Smith I know by reputation," he said. "Who are you?"

"Detective Sergeant Wallace," Howie said.

"Where's motormouth and the freak?" Taylor asked.

"Detective Sergeants Brown and Bento are assisting with a homicide interview in the Fourth District," Precious said.

"I said I wanted to see all *four* individuals involved in that altercation on the C & O Canal," Taylor said.

"They went out before your office called down," Precious said. "We can reschedule, if you'd like."

"I don't like," Taylor said. "You—Smith. What started this crap?"

Av told him what little he knew.

"Well, maybe if you spent more time on the job and less on the tow-path this kind of shit wouldn't be happening."

"My runs are on my time, Assistant Chief," Av said. "Before or after working hours."

"Don't give me lip, Detective. The FPS people are saying you pulled a weapon on them. And I understand that you improperly diverted street patrol units for backup? Were they there on *your* time?"

"I had four individuals who appeared to be trying to corner me out there," Av said. "For all I knew this was some kind of get-back deal going down from my time at homicide. I had no idea they were FPS, nor did they identify themselves as such until I got reinforcements." He turned to Precious. "Do I need my rep here, Lieutenant?"

Precious looked down at the floor.

"You're his boss," Taylor said to Precious. "You tell him."

"For right now, you are suspended, Detective Sergeant," she announced. "Pending a review by Internal Affairs. I must ask you for your badge and your weapon, please."

Av stared at the two of them for a moment. Then he produced his shield and his Glock and put them down on Precious's desk. Taylor stood up.

"Just so you know, Smith, the suspension's a stopgap measure. Call your rep if you want to, but you're actually going to be terminated. As in: fired. This has been coming for a while, and happily you just handed me the pinch bar I needed to force your average ass out. Lieutenant Parsons sends his regards, by the way."

He turned to Precious. "Lieutenant, let me remind you of your principal mission in this department. Take no further action on that so-called John Doe until his own agency makes an inquiry. Then ask them to close their eyes for just a moment while you drop it in their laps. In the meantime, call building security and get this *civilian* out of my building."

He waggled three fingers in Av's direction as he walked out. "Buh-bye," he chirped.

Av walked back into the squad room and sat down at his desk. Well, he thought, looking around, this gig had certainly been short and sweet. He heard Precious talking to the assistant chief as he was leaving, and then she and Howie came back to the squad room.

"Detective Sergeant," she said. "I am very sorry to have to have done that. And no matter what the assistant chief says, you will get a hearing and you will have a chance to fight this termination. With my support, I might add."

"Thanks, Lieutenant," Av said. "It does seem a little extreme."

"Plain bullshit, is what it is," Howie said. "That fat asshole, Parsons? He been layin' for you, and now he's talked Happy Taylor into doing his dirty work for him."

"Actually," Precious said. "Taylor had to promise the deputy director at FPS that the officer responsible would be fired in order to get the complaint to go away."

"All that's good to know," Av said. "But the fact remains: those guys were putting some kind of move on me. I don't care which federal alphabet they belong to—I still want to know why. Lieutenant, you want me to leave right now?"

"Hell, no," she said. "Take your time. Leave your stuff if you want to.

You can't act officially until this is resolved, one way or another, but there's no need for you to do some kind of perp walk out the front door. Call your rep. Schedule a meeting. Tell him I support you."

"Thanks again, Lieutenant," he said. Precious nodded and went back to her office. Couldn't have a better boss than that, he thought.

Howie reversed the chair at his own desk and sat down. "I'll fill in Wong and Miz Brown," he said. "They were there. They saw what was going on. Come hearing time, three of us can help you with this one. Happy makin' this out like you some kinda loose cannon, but those dudes were definitely fuckin' with you."

"I sure thought they were," Av said. "Look: I think I'm just going to go home for the day."

"Call your rep, first, man."

"Yeah, I will. But before I do, I want to see some paperwork, see what the actual charges are. And in the meantime, I'm gonna do a little detecting."

"No badge, no gun," Howie pointed out. "Means no detecting."

"But that's just the point, bro," Av said. "No badge, no gun, I can do whatever the hell I want to, just like any other civilian out there. Right?"

Howie's expression reflected a certain lack of confidence in that theory.

Fuck it, Av thought. I *will* go running tomorrow morning. Those fucks show up, I will show them what *I'm* famous for. See how far they can swim with broken arms.

EIGHT

Midnight on the Mall. Mandeville slowed his pace. What would the watchers think? he wondered as he walked over toward the bench. A couple of aging, maybe closeted gay guys meeting after dark on a park bench? Was there a directional mike being trained on the man on the bench? Infrared spotlights coming on in their direction? The monument was lit up by bright white spotlights, but what was looking back at the ground? He didn't care. He and Strang had a well-rehearsed procedure.

He walked past the bench but then slowed his pace. A minute later, Strang got up and began to follow him. Mandeville deliberately changed course toward the perimeter road and the nearest parked vehicle, one of those now ubiquitous Expedition SUVs. As he walked past, the right front window slid down and an agent started to warn him that he was being followed.

"A source," Mandeville replied. "It's okay."

The agent nodded and rolled up his window. Mandeville sat down suddenly on the next park bench. A minute later, in full view of the watchers, Strang sat down beside him. He was wearing a pair of those square-lensed eyeglasses popular in European fashion circles and sported a black mustache to boot.

"A mustache?" Mandeville said. "Seriously?"

"It has an RF antenna embedded in it which can detect an audiobounce listening beam device and warn me through an earbud in these stupid glasses."

"Really?"

"No."

Mandeville grunted. Strang being funny. "What's happening with the McGavin thing?" he asked.

"The case," Strang said, "such as it is, is being handled by a foursome of exiles in something the Metro PD calls the Briar Patch."

"Enlighten me."

"Well, their mission within the MPD is to move any cases which might involve federal-anything *out* of the MPD. Such cases are known as tar-babies, hence the Briar Patch allusion."

"You're shitting me."

"Not one pound," Strang said. "This is the ILB Whiting told you about."

"Oh," Mandeville said, remembering now. "And did you lean on someone?"

"I had a team try to scare off the lead detective, a Detective Sergeant Ken Smith. As it turned out, that didn't work. Smith got up a posse and ran my guys off."

Mandeville grunted but didn't say anything.

"I covered it by pretending to be a senior guy at the FPS. Bitched to some assistant chief, demanded that they fire the guy behind what happened out on the towpath. The chief seemed happy to oblige, so I think that problem is over."

"Just like that?" Mandeville said, eyeing the man next to him.

"Well, apparently, anybody sent to the Briar Patch is already teed up for some kind of disciplinary action or even termination. Since the MPD bosses're just looking for any excuse to fire them anyway, now they have one. I'll confirm and let you know."

"Just like that," Mandeville said again.

"It's what I do for love of country and a good apple pie."

Mandeville snorted. "What if he beats it? Keeps nosing around? I do *not* need a bunch of air-mail cleared Metro cops peeking in the windows at the DMX."

"Well, that's why I wanted to meet. You have a way to set a rendition in motion?"

Mandeville took a deep breath and then nodded. "That comes with its own problems," he said. "Metro cop just disappears? Because that's what happens in a rendition. Gone from the face of the earth."

"He's single, no family, no girlfriend, and a happy loner. I can guarantee nobody at a high level at MPD will ask any questions. And, it doesn't have to be abroad."

"The quiet room?"

Strang nodded.

"Let's wait and see what happens," Mandeville said. "It's an option, but not a risk-free option."

"Sorry to hear about McGavin," Strang said, turning his head to survey the Mall and all those parked cars.

"A little too well fed, I suspect," Mandeville said, getting up. "Keep in touch, please."

"Count on it," Strang said to Mandeville's departing back.

After a weekend of general moping around, Av decided to go up to Jeff's market on Sixteenth Street to pick up a large steak and a premade salad. He bought two bottles of decent red from the wine shop across the street, thought about some French bread and maybe a baking potato, decided against all those extra carbs, and then went home. He'd felt naked out there on the street with no weapon, but he had a cure for that problem stashed in a wall safe in his loft. The old building was full of hidey-holes and odd spaces, and, like all cops everywhere, he had an ample collection of guns and ammo. As a police officer, he was required to carry at almost all times. As a civilian, he did not intend to stop that practice, confirming the old saw that cops don't carry guns to protect you—cops carry guns to protect themselves.

He turned into the cramped alley on the left side of the building and stopped to wait for a garage door, which had begun rising. The actual garage was nearly forty feet long and L-shaped at the back. There was room for his aging Ford pickup truck, a Harley, two bicycles, and a tool room, some walk-in storage bins, and a workshop. Access to the building itself was through a service door that led to a bricked-up loading bay. From there he could get to the stairwell on the right side of the building that led up to the second-floor apartment foyer and, from there, to his loft on the third floor. Only he had access to the garage. He sometimes let Mr. Kardashian store stuff in the garage, but not very often.

There was an ancient coal-fired boiler room beneath the loading bay, but all the heat and air-conditioning utilities had long since been converted to electric. Bright red fire-main piping lined the stairwell, and the exterior door out to Thirty-third Street was keycard operated. Av had often thought of installing some kind of dumbwaiter system so he wouldn't have to hump groceries up to the loft but had never gotten around to it.

His loft was what a Realtor would call an open plan: it took up the entire third floor of the old building, whose eighteenth-century interior brickwork and chestnut beams remained fully exposed. The only interior walls enclosed his bedroom, bath, closets, and a small study on the back side of the building away from any street noise. The rest of the loft included a large living room area with a working fireplace that he'd filled with a woodstove insert. There was a corner kitchen with a counter bar and a nice range, a stairway up to the roof, and all the ancient wooden structural beams, pillars, and iron framework of the original edifice. The floors were random-width oak boards, polished by decades of service. He'd put skylights in four places, so the total effect was of space and light. The woodstove in the fireplace was big enough to heat the whole place, and the fifteen-foot-high ceilings and three-course thick brick walls made air-conditioning a matter of a few window units. His uncle had done most of the engineering work when he first built the loft, and, other than to remove some of his uncle's somewhat disturbing artwork, Av had seen fit to make very few changes.

It was a great place to live and one more reason for Av to never let a woman encumber his life. They could visit, but they could not stay for more than one night. His main attraction for the opposite sex was entirely physical. That suited him just fine. He was content to live alone and enjoyed being able to do whatever he felt like doing when he felt like doing it without having to consider anyone else's feelings or needs. Whenever he felt a little bit lonely in the evening he only had to walk four blocks to find a dozen bars and nightclubs packed to capacity with good-looking women, many of whom were totally in synch with his own feelings about long-term relationships or marriage. He'd kept himself fit and healthy, had zero debt, and had an interesting line of work—well, maybe not anymore. Even so, he still had one of the most interesting cities in the whole world right there at his feet. Maybe he'd just take a year off, see the sights, something that people who lived in Washington often failed to do, and then see what was what.

Sundown found Av on the roof, enjoying the first bottle of red. He was pleasantly blitzed, thinking hard about opening the second bottle, well satisfied with the way the steak had turned out, and wondering what he was going to do with the rest of his life. He could play out the suspension beef, the inevitable hearings, and then get a union lawyer to fight the termination action, but if the MPD really wanted someone gone, he or she would get gone, one way or another. If the bosses lost through the PBA process, they'd assign him as an assistant clerk in the evidence locker and simply wait for him to get bored to death and just leave.

Or: he could just up and leave now, and save everybody the headaches. Quit instead of getting fired. Money wasn't a problem, nor was a place to live. He had no sad-eyed dependents wringing their hands and wondering aloud where the next mortgage payment was coming from. He was thirty-five years old, in excellent health, debt-free, with over ten years' worth of savings, half of them in precrash 8 percent Treasuries. His suspension wasn't the result of anything criminal, such as lying on an expense report, sexual harassment in the office, or excessive violence toward suspects in custody. He and the MPD were no longer getting along, and he wasn't ever going to win that one.

And then what? A federal LE job? A county job in nearby Virginia or Maryland? He didn't have a college degree and still didn't think he needed one. Careers required degrees, and his idea of work was that it was just that, no more, no less. Do your day job, get paid. Go home. Do what you like. Be happy.

He'd tried one semester at UMD and found the whole thing ridiculous. "Classes" of up to three hundred freshmen sitting in a smelly auditorium, listening to some foreigner, posing as a professor, read from his dissertation in English, his third language. Or, better yet, watching some of his fellow freshmen dress up like Marxist revolutionaries so that they could protest about lesbian, bisexual, gay, and transgender oppression. The bullshit of academia had convinced him to go home to talk to his parents about not wasting any more of their money. His mother had urged him to stick with it, ignore the silliness, and do what it took to just get the piece of paper. Show up, she said. Pretend you respect the professors. You'll stand out, and you will graduate. His father, ever Mr. Practical, told him to go talk to the military recruiters down at the local shopping center.

Of the four, the Marine recruiter had promised him travel to exotic places, the best physical-fitness training on the planet, and the prospect of shooting people and blowing up their shit. It had been no contest, and, of course, most of it hadn't been true, either. He'd done three years in the Pacific Fleet Marine Force, stationed variously at Marine garrisons in Guam or Okinawa, with the rest of the time floating around in a big old gator-freighter, helping his fellow marines to drive the ship's-company sailors nuts.

The physical-fitness part had been true—with nothing much to do aboard ship, the marines spent literally hours on the ship's weather decks, doing every imaginable PT regimen. He'd then rotated back to a stateside Marine base, where, older and just a wee bit wiser, he took enough local and online courses to qualify for an associate's degree in criminal justice. That, plus his veteran's preference, had made a slot at the police academy his for the asking.

He heard his cell phone chirping from where he'd left it next to the grill. Reluctantly he retrieved it and stared at the screen, which had become a bit fuzzy. Red wine, he thought. He was much more of a beer guy than a wino. He looked at the caller ID: Howie?

"Dee-tective Sergeant," Av said. "What's shakin', Mau-Mau?"

"Need to talk," Howie said. "Can we come up?"

"Come up?" Av said. This was a first. And who was "we"? "As in you're *here,* at my pad?"

"At the door," Howie said. "Getting some heavy looks from some Eye-ranian mope in the store. Wong Daddy's fixin' to start, dude don't quit with the stink-eye."

"That's Mister Kardashian," Av said, heading down the stairs. "Don't hurt him—he's cool. Buzzing you in now. Come up two floors."

He went down to the door and let them in. Off-duty Howie was in full scary regalia, dreads, hoodie, sweatpants, and Air Jordans. Wong was wearing an all-black shiny suit, complete with tie and bowler, what he called his Odd Job look. Howie accepted a beer, as did Wong.

"Slick digs, partner," Howie said, looking around at the loft.

"Generous uncle," Av said. He explained how he'd acquired the building. He had the beginnings of a headache; *damned* red wine.

"I'll say," Howie said. "All this, no rent, no mortgage, *and* paying tenants?"

"No wife, either," Wong said, admiringly. "Smart mofo standing right here in front of God and everybody."

Howie shook his head. He'd been married and had tried suburban life with four fractious children and a nagging wife. He now lived in Southwest D.C. in a one-bedroom apartment, where he could look out the windows at night and see Washington's rich gang life in full color. The homies all thought he was a harmless nut because he'd told them he was an undercover cop and also a secret agent when he moved in. They laughed that off and since then he'd been left alone.

"Listen," he said. "Two reasons we here. One, OCME called over, after you left? Said McGavin's body had been claimed."

"Oh, yeah? By whom?"

"The family lawyer," Howie said.

"Gee whiz," Av said. "Am I starting to sense some closure here, please, God?"

Howie grinned. "OCME apparently didn't resist. Shyster shows up with ID, a Georgetown accent, tweeds and brogues, and positively identifies the remains as McGavin, via televideo. He then provides a funeral home contact, signs the appropriate papers, goes back behind the Ivory Curtain. Funeral-home ghouls show up an hour later to remove the remains. For cremation."

"And they just let him go?"

"No one in MPD ever put a hold on the body as evidence, so, yeah, they let him go. Probably blowing in the wind as we speak."

Av's headache began to assert itself. They should have filed a request to the district attorney to keep the body once the ME had declared cause and manner undetermined. "Shit," he muttered. Then he remembered: they didn't work cases in ILB.

Howie shrugged. "C'mon," he said. "We didn't really have any grounds. The doc we spoke to personally asked the lawyer if the grieving widow wanted to know more about what had happened. Shyster said no, she did not, overcome with grief as she was and her cruise-planning. And that was that."

Av realized that OCME was fully within its rights. The District's lively drug trade and gang rivalries kept the ME's chop shop amply busy. An unexplained death with no such criminal attributes and no complainant, say, like one of the Metro District's homicide squads, was sufficient justification to move a body into the capable hands of a crematorium, especially when a family rep showed up and requested just that.

"Okay," Av said. "I guess that *is* that. Besides, what do I care, huh? Wait, you said two reasons?"

"Yeah. Tell him, Wong."

"I had to go see Precious for my monthly behavioral sciences lecture," Wong said.

Howie saw Av's blank look. "Once a month," he said. "Wong, here, gets to go see the lieutenant to be reminded not to conduct himself in the manner of a uniformed monster. No yelling at suspects in unknown Asian dialects, stomping episodes restricted to concrete floors, and a little more effort on paying his bills out in town."

"Once a month?"

Wong shrugged. The gesture made his black suit coat look like there were small animals running back and forth across his shoulders under the fabric. "Counseling sessions," he said. "It's possible that I'm on some kinda probation, time to time."

"But that's not the interesting bit," Howie prompted. Wong frowned, but then nodded.

"Yeah, well, I had to wait outside. She was on the phone. Had her door cracked. Sounded like she was talking to her rabbi. She was pissed off, and I mean not in her normal I'm-so-fierce way. This was different. Said somebody had told her that if she didn't play ball in getting rid of you, by name, they were gonna fire *her*."

"Who was gonna fire her?"

"*Them,*" Wong said, impatiently, as if that explained everything. "She was asking about how to deal with that shit, what'd she call it, undue command influence. Said she was gonna go to the EEOC, file a complaint, blah-blah-blah, then she got interrupted. Said no several times, then said, 'I see. All right. I will. Thank you.' That was it."

"Who's her rabbi?" Av asked.

"No one knows, least not in the Briar Patch," Howie said. "Miz Brown thinks it's one of the lady lawyers in the general counsel's office. Thing is, that's a lotta heat for what happened out there on the towpath, don't you think?"

"Well, yes, I do, but—so what? I mean, who cares what *I* think now? I've just about decided to fold my tents and walk away. I mean, I appreciate the insight, guys, but whatever this is all about, I'm not sure I care anymore."

Howie gave him a look. "I was afraid of that," he said. "How mucha that red shit you had tonight?"

"Too much," Av admitted. "Seemed like a good idea at the time. But: back to my point: since I'm history, why should you guys care?"

The two of them stared at him until he got it. His temples were really pounding now. Then the light came on. "Oh," he said. "If it can happen to me . . ."

They nodded, almost in unison.

"And what do you want me to do?"

"Fight it, dude," Wong said.

"Yeah, homes," Howie said. "Get your rep to raise some hell. Insist on a hearing. Ask a buncha embarrassing questions, drag the McGavin tarbaby into it, see if that's what's driving the train. Don't just walk out. They see it's that easy, we're *all* out on our asses, and the rest of us don't have something like this to fall back on, know what I'm sayin'?"

Av nodded. His head told him not to do that again. "Okay, my fellow inmates. I'm cool with that. But you realize: if I succeed, we may lose Precious as a boss."

"She's a big lieutenant now," Wong said. "Going to law school and all. She'll bite 'em all in the ass, and I'll hold 'em down. And *then* I'll stomp their asses. Believe it."

They got up to leave, but then Howie stopped. "What kinda neighborhood is this?" he asked.

"Busy during the day," Av said. "It's Georgetown, so we've got shops, restaurants, the canal. But at night? M Street is a happening place, but here? Sleepy Hollow. Why?"

"Saw a really strange dude out on the street," Howie said. "Sitting in some rice-burning POS out on Thirty-third Street. Like he was on a stake-out."

"Strange how?" Av asked.

"His face," Howie said. "Something really wrong with his face. Looked like a mask."

Av looked over at Wong, who nodded his agreement with Howie's observation.

"Got one eye that looks at you like a snake?" he asked.

"Yeah, he did."

Av thought about it. "I've seen him once before, out on my morning run. He scared my blondie running partner. Just a guy in traffic, except—"

"Except what?"

"He was definitely looking at me. Not like some kinda surveillance dick. He made sure I saw him, seeing me."

"Want us to roust his ass?" Howie said. "I can sic Wong here on him, maybe turn his car over, then have a little chat?"

Av blew out a long breath. "I will bet you," he said, "that that dude is long gone when you get out there."

"Let's go see," Wong said, suddenly interested in the prospect of flipping a car on its back.

They called back two minutes later. "Gone," Howie said. "Keep some heat handy, bro."

"Count on it," Av said, worried now. What the hell had he done to invite this kind of shit?

At two-thirty in the morning, Av awoke. He sat up in bed, tasted his cotton-dry mouth, and groaned. The headache had subsided, but his body was not yet in any sort of forgiving mood.

He got up, went to the fridge, got himself three good glugs of OJ from the bottle, and then cracked a soda for some carbonated relief. He looked out the windows. There were no more passenger jets sliding down the Potomac River gorge at this hour. Upriver he could just barely see the lights on Chain Bridge now that the leaves had begun to fall. He shivered. He slept with the windows open, pretty much year round, as his sleeping costume consisted of a pair of tartan flannel boxer shorts and a T-shirt. At the height of summer, the heat broke by midnight. Now that it was September, the outside air was in the low sixties. Wonderful.

He turned to go back to bed, which is when he saw someone sitting in the big recliner in his living room area. He stopped in his tracks.

"Good evening, Detective Sergeant Smith," a woman's voice said. "Please forgive the intrusion, but we need to talk."

"I've got a gun," he said.

"No you don't," she said. "You had to hand it over today, along with your badge and creds. Please. I'm here to apologize for all that and to explain a few things. It's late, and I've got a long day tomorrow. Today, I guess. Please. Come over here, sit down, and give me ten minutes of your time."

She was right—he didn't have a gun. In his tango with the red wine, he'd forgotten to extract a replacement weapon. He walked over to the living room area and stood facing her.

"Good grief," she said. "You're huge. What do you press?" He just looked down at her. She was older than he was, maybe even forty, which made her almost ancient. Dark hair, Italian or Greek face, dark eyed, aquiline nose, prominent cheekbones, slightly parted lips, strong chin. She was wearing one of those Washington power pantsuits that revealed absolutely nothing about her figure, and yet, she was certainly of the female persuasion.

Dangerous, he thought. Definitely dangerous. He sat down without answering her.

"Okay," she said. "Again, I apologize for breaking and entering."

"Who are you," he asked.

"Call me Ellen Whiting."

"Really?" he said. "*The* Ellen Whiting? Francis X. McGavin's lunch partner right up to the moment he did the big jump at the Bistro? That Ellen Whiting? You're right—I don't have a gun. On me. But I can get to one pretty quick."

"Relax, Detective Sergeant. I'm no threat to you. If I were, you'd never have made it out of that bed back there. It's not like you knew I was here."

"Shit." He sighed, acknowledging her point. "I gotta get me a dog."

"Not a bad idea," she said. "First, let me explain something. I'm from the wonderful world of federal counterterrorism, which we all know and love as CT."

"And you're here to help, right?" he said. "Like all government agencies."

She smiled. "Of course," she said. "We're always here to help and local LE is always glad to see us. But, actually, I *am* here to help—you. This suspension bullshit? That's gonna go away. That was initiated by a mistake on our part, amplified by some cowboying on the part of four support personnel. Contractors, actually."

"Yeah," he said. "What *was* up with all that? Those guys scared one of my tenants."

"The skinny blond number? She'll survive. Those guys were supposed to provoke you, get you to do something so they could apprehend you. Then we could have had our little talk in private. They failed to anticipate you'd involve the inmates of the Briar Patch."

"You in one of those cars stopped up on Canal Street?" Av asked, wondering how she knew about the Briar Patch.

"It's possible," she said.

"And those runners were not FPS, were they."

"Like I said, contractors."

"Whose contractors?"

"Contractors," she said. "Town's full of 'em, as you certainly must know. Anyway, there's no suspension paper, you haven't called your rep, IA hasn't been called, so I believe you can go back to work this morning as if nothing happened, because, officially, nothing did happen."

"Just like that," he said.

"Yep, just like that."

"And you know this—how?"

"Because my boss called Happy's boss, the chief, herself, and shared his thinking with her. Cooled the whole deal."

He thought about that for a moment. Was she DHS? Bureau? Spooking around like this, she might even be someone in Agency clandestine ops. In this town, you never knew. "The McGavin deal," he asked. "What's the story on that?"

"Who's McGavin?"

"Oh, c'mon." He snorted. "All my problems started with the McGavin deal."

She leaned forward. "Look," she said. "McGavin's death doesn't involve you, or MPD, for that matter. That's the whole point of my visit, actually. McGavin's demise was something that slipped out from under the federal invisibility cloak momentarily, and, trust me, that will *not* happen again."

"You know he didn't just die of natural causes in that restaurant, right?"

She blinked. "Meaning?"

"OCME's leaning toward poison."

This time she definitely reacted. Then she changed the subject. "Do you know how many federal counterterrorism offices there are here in D.C.?"

"I'm guessing more than one?"

"Eighty-five in the public domain, by which I mean the ones funded and authorized by the best Congress money can buy. There are some others that are neither funded nor authorized by any agency that'll admit to it. Ever since nine-eleven, counterterrorism has come a long way from just a few offices in the Bureau, the Agency, and the Pentagon. Now every federal agency in town has a CT office. The Social Security Administration, Health and Human Services, Labor, Agriculture, the Treasury, the fucking Post Office—you name it, they're all into the CT game, and, all of a sudden, even the meter maids are carrying."

"You guys must be tripping over each other," he said.

"Hourly," she said.

"Is the country that much safer?"

"Depends on what you think the threat is," she said. "I work for people who think the real threat has morphed."

"What's that mean?"

"Instead of bearded hajjis wearing bedsheet bombs, think American Muslim converts scheming on Twitter. Think a whole generation of kids who've been diagnosed as ADD, ADHD, OCD, LD, and chugging down Ritalin and other mind-altering substances since they were five. Kids who've spent more time staring at an electronic device than they have sleeping and eating. Or, on the other side of the spectrum, think strong, extremely fit and aggressive young men who have spent three tours on the moon called Afghanistan, killing men, women, and children, with robots as accomplices. Now they're back, can't find a job, and they're a little twitchy. Or, try pizza-faced, gated-community nerds who stay up all night hacking into nuclear power stations and turning off the reactor-cooling water pumps—for fun, giggles, and bragging rights."

"I didn't hear Al Qaeda in all that."

"Oh, they're still out there and they're still blowing shit up, but they've dispersed their cells to make themselves smaller targets. Makes them even more dangerous, in some people's opinion, kind of like a cancer that's metastasizing. They are absolutely *not* defeated, as some of our more disingenuous politicians would have you believe. But: they are at least being engaged by the folks at JSOC and other unconventional agencies. This new breed, the homegrown breed? We're still circling that problem, and what we're seeing is not comforting. Not to mention the bleeding open sore that we call our border with Mexico."

"Okay," he said. "Gotta ask: who's 'we'?"

She didn't answer.

"R-i-i-ght," he said. "And you're telling *me* all this, why, again?"

"Basically, so that you'll forget all about the past week. Go back to being a Weird Harold down in the Briar Patch. Do what the computer geeks call a system-restore to, oh, I don't know, ten days ago? Resume your workouts and your dedication to not getting involved with women because they are so very dangerous."

"Your being in my house at two in the morning kinda proves my point, don't you think?"

"Your life must be very boring, Detective Sergeant, although the deeper I get into the world of CT, I can see where boring could have its appeal."

"Somehow I doubt that," Av said. "Ellen Whiting. I think you're either Bureau or Agency."

She gave him a speculative smile. "I'll be going now," she said. "We won't meet again."

"Fine by me," he said. "Leave the key, would you?"

She fished in her pocket and put a key down on the coffee table. Then she got up and headed for the front door.

"Hey?" he said. "What do I do with the autopsy report that OCME's gonna send us?"

"Nothing, because they'll be sending it to me," she said, as she went out the door and closed it behind her.

He waited for a minute, then picked up the key and went to the door. He opened it and tried the key. It didn't work. It didn't even go into the lock.

On Monday he got up, put on his running gear, and went out front. He'd decided to walk today. Maybe jog a little, but mostly just get some fresh air into his system and squeeze the residual alcohol out.

The platinum blonde wasn't in evidence. Can't imagine why, he thought, although he was already missing her stretching routine. He warmed up as usual and then just started walking. Bored in fifteen minutes he took it up into route pace. Much better. The serious runners still went by him with sympathetic expressions. He must be leaving an alcohol vapor trail, he thought. He kept a wary eye out for cowboy contractors in sunglasses. At one point he passed Rue Waltham, who waved delicate fingers at him as she ran by in the company of two military guys, who seemed to be competing for her attention.

He got back an hour later. The most exciting thing he'd seen was a sideswipe collision between a marine runner and a cycling Nazi, which had resulted in the trash-talking cyclist being thrown into the canal, along with his bike. Av, who'd had his own share of near misses with tunnel-visioned cyclists coming up behind him like they owned the towpath, had thought that only fair. He showered and shaved, and then made coffee. He took it up to the roof to enjoy late sunrise and to look down with sympathy at all the commuters. At nine-thirty his cell went off. It was Precious.

"Where are you, Detective Sergeant?"

"Suspended, last I heard," he said.

"Not anymore. Right now you're late for work. Make my day: get your average ass back in here."

His badge and creds were waiting for him when he got to MPD headquarters. The officers gave him a funny look when he scooped them up and then presented them so he could then go through the X-ray machine. Up in the office, Howie greeted him with undisguised glee and handed over Av's Glock and the spare mags.

"Welcome back, partner," he said. "All us snuffies want to know: how'd you manage this?"

Wong and Miz Brown were having coffee at the conference table, so Av grabbed his usual three-paper-cup rig and sat down with the rest of the crew. He told them about his midnight visitor.

"Golly gee," Howie declared. "Your own personal fairy godmother, complete with a happy ending."

"Nice and neat, isn't it," Av agreed. "Yesterday I was as good as fired. Today, everything's cool; welcome back, Kotter. No hard feelings, we hope."

"All this from some B & E artist claiming to be a fed?" Wong said. "She good-looking?"

They all laughed.

"Detective Sergeant Smith?" Precious called from the doorway. "It seems we have an appointment with Assistant Chief Taylor."

"*We* do?" Av said.

"Now would be nice," she said. "Do *not* bring that coffee."

They went upstairs to the assistant chief's office. Three civilian aides and one uniform occupied desks in the outer office. None of the aides would even look at them. Happy Taylor made them wait for fifteen minutes before admitting them into his presence, where he proceeded to ignore Precious and tell Av that he remained firmly on the assistant chief's notorious list, and that no matter how he had managed to evade suspension, it was only a matter of time, et cetera, et cetera. Av took the opportunity to remain silent, especially after a gentle kick in the ankle from Precious.

As they were leaving, Taylor put two fingers to his eyes and then pointed them at Av, which he assumed was Hollywood for: I'm watching you. Once in the outer office, with Precious walking ahead, one of the aides actually did make eye contact with Av, who put two fingers to his eyes and then pointed one of them at his own temple and made a circular motion. The aide seemed to be having trouble keeping his composure as they left the office.

Back downstairs, Precious told him that Wong and Miz Brown had a homicide-related interview over at the Sixth and suggested that Av go along to watch. Av figured this had more to do with getting him out of the building for a few hours than furthering his professional education. He was curious, though.

Carl Mandeville was fuming at his desk in the EEOB. On Saturday morning he'd been tipped off by a committee staffer friend in the Senate that three members of the DMX had gone to a meeting with Senator Harris, the chairman of the select committee on intelligence and counterterrorism. Subject unknown, principals only, no horse-holders in the room. Mandeville could guess the subject, but the surprise had been that there were more traitors on the committee than he had suspected. McGavin, Logan, and Wheatley were the three weaklings he'd known about. He'd taken care of McGavin, so why had *three* members of the DMX shown up to meet with his nemesis? The third man was Howard West, deputy undersecretary for counterterrorism at the Energy Department. Why the hell was Energy even on the DMX? he wondered, then remembered: DOE was responsible for the safe operation of all the nuclear power plants. The target's rep, Mandeville thought caustically. One would think that, of anybody on the committee, the guy responsible for protecting *the* prime terrorist targets in the country would be in support of DMX, and yet here he was, consorting with the enemy.

He'd always assumed he had three bad apples on the DMX, senior government officials who went through the motions and then scurried around, behind his back, trying to take down the program. Now he wondered how many more two-faced bastards there were, and, more importantly, was Senator Harris about to make a move? There were twelve statutory members of the DMX. They could not vote themselves out of existence, so a procedural mutiny wasn't his problem. But if a third of them, or more, appeared before Harris's committee in some prestaged hearing and declared a vote of no confidence in the entire concept, that would be fatal.

This latest betrayal posed another problem: he had already planned out something for Hilary Logan that would be even more unconventional than McGavin. His strategy had been to take out two of them and then let the others seize upon the notion that people who screwed with the DMX could face grave consequences. He'd take care of Wheatley, too, if necessary, although knowing the man, he was pretty sure it would not be necessary. But four of them? That would be too much. That was serial-killer territory.

He swiveled around in his chair and looked out the large window at his view down Independence Avenue. There was only one other alternative: take them *all* out, and then start over. He felt a rush of excitement. It could be done. Whenever the DMX met the entire floor was almost hermetically sealed for security purposes to keep everything and everybody out. Those same arrangements could be made to hold everybody in, too.

Blame it on the terrorists. Proclaim that the DMX had been so effective and such a deterrent to the bad guys that they'd attacked it. That would neutralize Harris and his allies, and then allow him to repopulate the DMX with people he could trust to carry this mortal fight to the enemy as only the program could.

He smiled. He amazed himself sometimes. The scale of it! Why the hell not?

Av and Howie took their seats in the darkened room behind a one-way glass pane. The interview room had a single, rectangular table and four chairs. One for the perp, one for his lawyer on one side, and two for the detectives on the other side. There was audiovisual equipment high up on a shelf overlooking the entire room. The interviewee in question was a gangbanger from an Anacostia neighborhood so riven with drug and gang violence that it had once been one of the unofficial no-go zones within the MPD. Anacostia had become a lot safer since those days, but the area, just east of the Anacostia River, could not shake its rep as an urban free-fire zone. The banger's name was Lavon Jerome Tiles, otherwise known as "Gooey" Tiles. He'd been found, gun in hand, stoned out of his mind in an alley, where he was sitting on the still-warm corpse of another gangbanger. When asked why he was sitting on a dead body, Gooey stated that he'd been cold. No longer in the loving grip of his opiate of choice, Gooey now refused to say anything and was demanding his public defender.

Said public defender had come and gone. He'd told Gooey in no uncertain terms that he was to pay strict attention to that "remain silent" part of the Miranda warning, and since he wasn't going to say anything, the lawyer could then leave to tend to his three other charges, who were actually going to be in court. Gooey responded that he was down with that, no problem. That's when the Seventh District guys had asked for Miz Brown.

Wong Daddy and Miz Brown came into the interview room and shut the door behind them. Brown was wearing a sport coat, white shirt with tie, and dark slacks. Wong had a tent of some kind over his upper half, shiny black nylon warm-up suit pants, and size twenty-something sandals. Brown carried a leather folder filled with forms. Wong carried a yard-long piece of what looked like a two-by-six pine board. Gooey, maintaining his supercool pose, refused to look at either of them, and even yawned. He was wearing an orange jumpsuit and his wrists were handcuffed through a ring under the table. If he'd noticed the board, he gave no sign of it.

Brown introduced himself, pointed out that the conversation was being filmed and recorded, and proceeded to read Gooey his Miranda, after which he attempted to get the suspect to sign forms acknowledging his Miranda and the bit about the filming.

"Ain't sayin' shit, ain't signin' shit," Gooey pronounced. "Thass it, yo."

Brown then spoke to the camera, asking that the record show the suspect refused to sign the admin forms. Back in the viewing room, two of the Seventh District detectives had come in to watch. Av asked one of them what the "Gooey" was all about. He was told he really didn't want to know the answer to that. Av didn't press it.

"Will you please state your full name?" Brown asked.

The suspect stared at the wall and said nothing, his expression saying, what part of shit don't you understand?

"Do you understand why you're here for questioning?"

No response. Brown stood up and began to pace on his side of the table. He cleared his throat and looked down at the floor for a moment.

"Here we go," Howie said in the darkroom. By now, two more guys had come in to watch.

Brown turned to the camera and began to lecture it. "The problem here," Brown began, "seems to be that the suspect does not appear to understand the significance of his current refusal to engage the police authorities in a meaningful discussion about the modalities of what certainly appears to be a murder committed by the suspect who stated that the reason he was found with and actually on top of the victim was that he was suffering from thermal exposure to cold, which, in all truth, wasn't that extreme but which, admittedly, might induce a person of limited intellect to establish close physical proximity in order to make himself more comfortable following what was obviously a serious altercation, which, from the evidence at hand, probably involved the subject in the role of shooter, seeing as the gun used in the shooting was within physical proximity of the subject, who . . ."

"Jesus," Av whispered. "When's he come up for air?"

Howie just grinned. "He just getting started. Keep an eye on Gooey and Wong."

Gooey had been trying hard to pretend that nothing was going on, but the waterfall of sincerely concerned words coming from Miz Brown was making his eyes water.

". . . for the purposes of establishing a logical reconstruction of the events in question, it is of course necessary to have input from all parties to the incident whenever that is possible, however, with one party to the incident deceased, and the other indulging in a display of puerile intransigence because he believes that if he talks to the police, he will be branded as a snitch, even though there is no way anyone can know that he spoke with the police, unless, of course, the police decide to put that word out onto the street, in which case . . ."

That last bit made Gooey turn his head, showing the observers that, despite his seeming nonchalant attitude, he had been listening to Brown's barrage. Then Wong put the board down on the table with an audible clack and began to stare at it. As Brown droned on in sentences lasting five minutes each, Wong swiveled his massive head to look at Gooey, and then back to the board. Gooey was sitting up a little straighter in his chair, his professional slouch being undermined by whatever his own imagination was telling him about Wong and the possibilities presented by that board.

". . . evidence which includes but is not limited to the gun itself, fingerprints on the gun, gunshot residue on the hands of the subject here present, a ballistics match between the bullets that killed the deceased individual and the bullets in said gun, the time of day, the attendant meteorological conditions, and . . ."

In the background, just below the threshold of Brown's monologue, Av could now hear a keening sound. It wasn't especially threatening, although he had heard a dog once make that sound just before a dogfight started. Wong was stroking the board now, inspecting it inch by inch and then looking over at Gooey for just a second before resuming his intense study of the board, its grain structure, its weight and heft, how well his hand could span it, how heavy it was, and then back at Gooey.

That worthy had now picked up on the keening sound and deduced that it was coming from Wong's direction. Miz Brown never once let up, not even to take a deep breath, but kept the torrent of words coming, one after another, all somewhat relevant to the issue at hand, but not necessarily following in any sort of logical order. The guys behind Av and Howie in the darkroom were laughing quietly as they watched the show through the one-way and saw Gooey's increasing concern over Wong and his board.

"I got a ten-spot sez Gooey sings within five minutes," one of the detectives announced quietly.

"I'll cover that," his partner said. "I say four minutes."

". . . past behaviors are an important indication of the suspect's predilection for violence and an even better indicator for future antisocial behaviors that fall into the category of extreme violence such as the case at hand, and . . ."

"Yo," Gooey said, raising his hand.

Miz Brown fell silent. He put his left hand in his coat pocket. Av saw the little red lights go out on the recorders. Brown raised his eyebrows at Gooey.

"'Sup with de slope and dat board?" Gooey asked.

Wong stopped his ministrations and fixed Gooey with a baleful glare. "Slope?" he asked, in full Kurosawa samurai voice. *"Slope?"*

Gooey started waving his right hand as if trying to make Wong vanish. "Want my shap, man," he demanded, speaking to Miz Brown. He looked sideways at Wong. "Dis fucker's crazy, yo."

"'Shap'?" Av asked.

"As in Shapiro—O.J.'s lawyer," Howie said. "Homeboy wants his lawyer *in* there."

Wong sat up straight and started to inflate his torso. Gooey tried to be brave but his enlarging eyes betrayed him. Wong slowly picked up the pine board, made some more of the keening noises, and then, using just his hands, twisted the board in half, lengthwise, and slammed the two pieces triumphantly down on the table with a sound like a gunshot. Gooey jumped. Everyone in the darkroom also jumped.

Gooey was trying to back up in his chair, but it was bolted to the floor and his hands were still chained to that ring in the table.

Wong began speaking in the unknown dialect, growling out the words with lots of facial emphasis.

"Hey-hey-hey-hey-hey!" Gooey shouted. "Muh-fucah's losing it here. Gimme me outa here."

Wong stopped his growling, took in a long breath, let it out, and then brought one of the pieces of the board up to his mouth like an ear of corn, opened his mouth wide to give Gooey a good look at all those teeth, and then took a huge, splintering bite. He started chewing it, staring at Gooey the whole time. The detective behind Av in the darkroom did lose it, covering his mouth as he bent double with laughter.

Gooey, however, was not amused. Gooey was scared shitless.

Wong spat out an entire mouthful of pine pulp, growled some more, and looked over at Miz Brown.

"Yes, Detective?" Brown said, in a so-very-sincere voice.

"Dry," Wong said, spitting out some more splinters and wiping his mouth. "Needs blood."

"What?!" Gooey yelled. He started pulling on his cuffs, frantically trying to leave the scene. As best Av could tell, if he had to leave his hands behind, that was going to be okay with Gooey.

Wong took another bite out of the board and chewed dramatically, growling and spitting at the same time, splinters and spittle flying everywhere, while never taking his eyes off Gooey, who was visibly about to piss his pants.

"Blood?" Miz Brown said. "Really? *Blood* would help? How much blood?"

The detective behind Av got up and left the darkroom, unable to contain himself any longer. Av heard him tell someone outside in the hall how much he loved this job.

Wong Daddy sprayed an entire mouthful of pine pulp and splinters in Gooey's direction, licked his lips, and then turned to Brown and pointed at Gooey. "Blood?" he asked. Then he clacked his huge teeth in Gooey's direction. Av saw the little red lights come back on.

The teeth-clacking apparently did it. Gooey started babbling: "Aw-right, *aw-right*! Yeah, I whacked de mothafucka, he be dissin' my lady, yo? Had it comin', nine ways, aw-right? God-*damn*! Y'all get dat crazy muh-fucka outa here, I'll talk to y'all. God-*damn*! He gonna bite? Yeah—lookat dat mothafucka—he gonna bite!"

Wong, moving just out of the camera's view, began foaming at the mouth and making barking sounds. Miz Brown encouraged Wong to take a break, go get some water, forget about blood, it being salty and no help for a mouthful of splinters. Wong hesitated, got up, made some truly ghastly noises, faked one last move toward Gooey that made him squeak, and then left the room.

Miz Brown removed his hand from his coat pocket and asked Gooey if they could start over. Gooey nodded enthusiastically as Wong slunk out of the room, still spitting splinters and making growling noises. Av saw money changing hands out in the hallway.

Fucking beautiful.

Back at headquarters, Av asked Wong how he managed chewing a mouthful of pine splinters.

"It's not pine," Wong explained, "it's balsa, duded up to look like pine. Presplit, coated in a little olive oil, so I didn't really need any blood."

Av grinned. "And the foaming at the mouth?"

"Oh, that?" Wong said. "I can do that shit on demand." He proceeded to demonstrate that ability just as a messenger came into the room with a priority intradepartment envelope. The messenger, a probationer, took one look at foaming Wong, dropped the envelope, and backed hurriedly out of the room in absolute horror.

"Wong, for Chrissake," Howie protested. He retrieved the envelope, looked at the addressee block, and gave it to Av. He opened it, looked at it, and then pronounced: "OCME speaks."

Av remembered the fairy godmother's assurances that the medical examiner would *not,* in fact, speak—to them. He scanned the results, looking for the conclusions block. "Hoo-aah," he said quietly. Second District's got themselves a possible homicide.

"Yeah?" Howie said.

"Victim died from aconitine poisoning, based on preliminary analysis."

"What's that shit?" Wong asked, wiping the foam off his mouth.

"Prolly what you been eatin'," Howie observed. "Foamin' like that."

"According to this," Av said, "it's a toxin produced by a plant called the *Aconitum,* or monkshood, which makes aconitine by terpenoid biosynthesis from mevalonic acid that polymerizes subsequent to phosphorylation."

"Everyone knows that," Wong said. "So then what happens?"

Av read some more of the pharmacological report, hoping to encounter some recognizable English. "Here it is," he said, finally. "It stops the big muscles of the body by attacking the neuron channels that make 'em expand and contract. We're talking heart, lungs, skeletal muscle paralysis, here. Floods the brain with calcium and sodium, which is apparently not good, either. They're sending some samples to the Bureau's lab, because some of what happened didn't quite make sense, such as, how fast it killed him."

"But he didn't eat anything," Howie reminded everyone.

"Didn't eat anything *in* the restaurant," Av said. "But before he got there? Had himself a veggie fit, maybe? Munched on a monkshood plant by the sidewalk?"

"Now what?" Wong said. "What do we do with that report?"

"What report?" Precious asked from the doorway.

"Dum-te-dum-dum, *dum,*" Howie intoned, to the tune of the old *Dragnet* show. Precious frowned. She gave really good frown.

Av briefed her on what he had managed to glean from the report. Precious nodded and then announced that this was actually good news, inasmuch as they could now do what ILB was supposed to do and drop that tarbaby on the Second District's homicide squad. "I want this thing gone. Outa here. Over and done with. Any questions?"

"Doesn't fit with the mission," Av said.

"Say what?"

"Our mission here at ILB, as I'm constantly being reminded, is to shop the tarbabies all the way *out* of MPD. How's about give me a day to see if I can get the Bureau to eat this one?"

"How do you propose to manage that, Detective Sergeant?" Precious asked.

"Same way as my suspension managed to disappear?" Av said.

Precious gave him a look, shook her head, and then went back to her office.

"Ooooh," Howie said. "You got the Look."

"So?"

"Means you better be right, partner," he said. "Precious not keen on being shut down like that."

NINE

That night Av picked up Chinese on the way home. He considered giving the remains of the second bottle of red a second chance and decided to go with beer instead. It was dropping into the lower fifties, so after a standup dinner at the kitchen counter, he lit up the woodstove with the remnants of last year's wood, reminding himself to lay in a supply for the coming winter. He'd shifted into jeans and a real shirt in deference to the cooler weather. As he watched the sunset from the loft, he wondered about that OCME report. His night visitor had promised that there would be no report, and yet . . .

Moreover, she'd known all about his suspension and the Briar Patch. *And* his aversion to getting deeply involved with women. How had she known that? He'd said it to—his curvy blond tenant, Rue Waltham. Was *she* a player? With that hair? No way. So maybe the Feebs had bugged his place?

You're getting paranoid, he told himself. But, then again, he reminded himself, even paranoids have enemies. Well: why not find out?

"Hey," he said, speaking to the ceiling in a louder than usual voice. "Fairy Godmother: I think we need to talk again. We *did* get a report from the medical examiner. He's implying somebody poisoned McGavin with a plant. We're thinking we have to call in the Bureau lab. That what you want?"

He waited for the phone to ring. Nothing happened. He sat down and flipped on the TV.

"Knock-knock," a female voice called from the rooftop stairway. "Sergeant Smith?"

He muted the wide-screen, got up and looked up the stairwell. Speak of the devil. Rue Waltham was tiptoeing down the stairs in her stocking feet, a pair of fancy party shoes in one hand. She looked as if she'd been out somewhere besides the office.

"I'm so sorry to bother you again," she said. "I've locked myself out. Can you get me into my apartment?"

"Sure," he said. "I have master keys somewhere. You do the fire escape again?"

"'Fraid so," she said, showing rust-colored palms. "I looked for an intercom or something . . ."

"Yeah, I had one of those until the salesmen found it. Hang on a minute."

He went to his bedroom to the gun safe, opened it, and removed the master key collection, found the one for the apartment on the second floor, and came back out to the living room. Rue was standing there taking it all in.

"This is lovely," she said. "You kept the original walls exposed and everything."

"My uncle did all that before he left it to me," Av said. "Here. This should do it. Drop it in my mailbox in the lobby when you go out tomorrow."

"Thanks so much," she said, slipping her shoes back on while holding on to the telephone stand near the couch. "I found a running group by the way."

"No more adventures on the towpath, then?"

She grinned. "That was something," she said. "And that one guy—is he Samoan?"

"Nobody knows," Av said, walking her to his front door. "And nobody asks."

She thanked him again, and he locked the door behind her, leaving a faint hint of perfume in the air. She was pretty, he thought, even if she was a lawyer. He wondered where she worked. Then he switched on the wide-screen, cracked another beer, and started channel surfing. He turned in at eleven, half expecting another visitation from his fairy godmother. It didn't happen. For some reason, he was mildly disappointed. He compared Rue to Ellen Whiting. No comparison, he thought. None whatsoever.

The next morning he did his usual warm-up out front. Rue Waltham was not in evidence. Still a little Wong-averse, probably. He took off on his usual route up the towpath, gearing up to some serious running sooner than he usually did, having screwed off for the past few days. He put some effort into it, and, golly gee, it hurt. He put some more effort into it and finally achieved that endorphin-saturated state where it hurt but it didn't. The Marines always said that pain is the sign of weakness leaving the body. Sure it is, along with the ability to walk afterward. Then it did start to hurt, no shit, and he slowed, having covered, based on the surroundings, four clean, hot miles. He dropped down into a jog, and then reversed course back toward Georgetown.

He'd gone half a mile when he heard what sounded like a whole squad of runners behind him, a lot of feet pounding flat-footed on the hard dirt of the towpath. Pretty much in unison.

Aw, shit, he thought. They're back.

They were, but not in the way he imagined. Two guys passed him, two more fell in beside him, and then a familiar voice said from right behind him: "You wanted to talk?"

He looked over his shoulder. Gone was the unisex business suit from the previous evening. Now she was wearing one of those iron-cupped halter tops that full-breasted female runners wore to keep from breaking their collarbones. A taut and well-muscled abdomen topped some tasteful white nylon running shorts and two exceptional legs.

"Damn," he said. "It's a girl."

She rolled her eyes. She was matching his pace with ease, not even breaking a flush. Probably hadn't just done four miles, though, he thought.

"You look a little winded," she said. "Why don't we slow it to a fast walk and you can tell me what's on your mind."

He said okay. They slowed, and the platoon of escorts backed away. He then told her that ILB was going to turn the OCME report over to the Second District homicide squad. He suggested that she run a little interference with the Bureau instead, and then he'd convince Precious to hand it over to them instead of opening a case within MPD.

She looked sideways at him. "And you're suggesting we do this why, exactly?"

"I owe you one," he said. "You are Bureau, right?"

She looked away and then nodded.

"Then I would think you'd want to keep this particular tarbaby in federal channels," he pointed out.

"What exactly did the ME come up with?" she asked.

"*Aconitine* poisoning," Av said. "Some evil mung that's synthesized by the monkshood plant. Does a number on brain and large muscle cells; floods 'em with calcium and sodium. All natural substances, but apparently bad shit."

"Does the report say how he came to consume *aconitine*?"

"Nope," Av said. "But it did say they were sending some more tissue samples to the Big Lab in the sky, which might give you the opening you need to get the Bureau to take my tarbaby. Please."

She smiled. "I hardly need an opening to the Bureau, Detective," she said. "But I'll consider what you're suggesting. Can you stall the report in-house for a day or so?"

"I can, as long as there is a definite prospect of shopping it *out* of the house," he said. "Means I may have to tell my boss about you and your squad of special agents here."

"We'll survive," she said.

"And I'd appreciate the bugs coming out of my loft," he said. "Seeing as this whole deal will soon be over, right?"

"But then how will you summon your fairy godmother?" she asked, lightly.

"Turn in place three times in my special slippers and clap my hands?"

She laughed out loud at that, and then took off at a respectable pace, followed immediately by her posse of athletic specials. Yeah, he thought, watching her go. If the platinum blonde downstairs was streetable, this one was downright sexy. And dangerous, he reminded himself, sternly. Still, he appreciated the eye candy.

By the time he got to the office and grabbed his first cup of coffee, there were two men in severe-looking suits with visitors' badges waiting in the conference room to speak to him. Beauroids, he thought immediately.

Howie asked him what he'd done now. Av dug out the OCME report from the pile of papers on his desk and asked Howie if he could make a quick copy of it, and then bring the original into the conference room.

"You shoppin' this to the Bureau?" Howie asked.

"If they're willing to take it and the creeks don't rise," Av said. "Remember the mission."

"Those hoods are downright ugly," Wong commented.

"They get paid extra for that," Howie said, as he unstapled the OCME report. Then he pointed his chin at Av. "Newbie's playin' with fire in there."

"I can stomp if it would help," Wong offered. Av grinned and went to the conference room. The two special agents introduced themselves as being from the violent crime division of the Washington Field Office. "I'm Special Agent Jim Walker," the taller one said. "This is Special Agent Mike Freer."

Av asked if they needed coffee. Both demurred. Av sat down and asked how he could help them.

"We're investigating the death of one Francis X. McGavin of the DHS at a French restaurant up on Connecticut Avenue called Bistro Nord. We understand from Lieutenant Johnson that you did a preliminary investigation into the circumstances?"

"You're shitting me, right?" Av asked.

The two agents appeared to be taken aback. "Why, um, no," Walker said. "Why would you say that?"

"Sorry," Av said. "We handle a lot of cases that seem to straddle the MPD-federal LE divide here." He recounted Precious's initial efforts to move the case to the Bureau, and that they had rejected it due to some unspecified Bureau involvement. "I've probably confused this with something else. Why don't you tell me what you got, and how I can help you?"

The agents relaxed a bit. Special Agent Freer laid it out. "We got a call from the Patient Affairs office at MedStar," he said. "Claiming they had a John Doe DOA who might be from the DHS. They said OCME had been in touch and had asked about notification. They were notifying us because the DOA might have worked for a federal agency. When we pulled the string at Pathology, they said the DOA had been moved to the District's OCME. We followed up on that, where we discovered the John Doe's identity was McGavin and that ILB was running the case."

Av followed the alphabet soup carefully. He told them that OCME had performed an autopsy and that McGavin's family lawyer had claimed the body. He hesitated for a moment, and then said he had something odd to share with them, but he wasn't sure what it meant. He described his interaction with the towpath cowboys, his midnight visitation from the fairy godmother, and their subsequent meeting this morning out on the towpath.

"This woman says she's *Bureau* CT?"

"No, not exactly."

"What's her name?" Freer asked.

"Ellen Whiting?" Av said.

"Aw, fuck." Walker sighed.

Av had to laugh. "My sentiments exactly, Special Agents. Look: I'm just a lowly Metro homicide dick, recently demoted to what we fondly call the Briar Patch. I'm beginning to think I've stumbled into something way above my pay grade, and I would be most appreciative if my Bureau would take this tarbaby off my hands." He paused, as if looking for the report. "To which purpose, I happen to have the OCME report on what it was that killed said Francis McGavin. That report constitutes just about the entirety of our case file, which, like I said, I would be more than happy to hand over to the loving arms of *any* interested federal LE organization, actually."

"What did kill him?" Walker asked.

"Aconitine?" Av said.

The two agents looked at each other blankly.

"It's a plant, or it comes from a plant. Bad shit, stops all the major organs that do their jobs by expanding and contracting, like the lungs or the heart."

Freer and Walker looked at each other meaningfully. Then Howie showed up in the doorway to the conference room with folder in hand.

"Can I take that as a yes, Special Agents?" Av asked hopefully, indicating to Howie that he should hand over the folder.

"Is your lieutenant available, Detective?" Walker asked, finally.

Dammit, Av thought. They hadn't said yes.

Howie and Wong Daddy treated Av to lunch at one of the local cop bars near the Indiana Avenue headquarters building. They were celebrating the new guy's first successful tarbaby launch. Miz Brown hadn't come along. Howie said Brown was getting into religion and no longer approved of going to bars. The two special agents had closeted with Precious, and then the three of them had gone to see the people in the MPD's Criminal Investigations Division, OCME folder in hand.

"But is it really gone?" Av asked. "I mean, I now understand why you call them tarbabies—that mess just kept sticking to one part of me or another."

The other two laughed. "Happens all the time, bro," Howie said. "But you heard what Precious said: that matter has gone to its well-deserved reward—at the Bureau."

"Her saying it's over and done with didn't have much effect the first coupla times," Av pointed out.

"This time the Beauroids left paper," Howie said. "An official mezmorandum, no less. I quote: 'All materials relevant to the case of the John Doe slash McGavin death at Bistro Nord are to be turned over to the Federal Bureau of Investigation forthwith.' No further action on our part is desired or required. Here endeth the lesson."

"Interesting that they seemed to recognize my fairy godmother and her connection to counterterrorism," Av said. "And yet, they didn't seem to know anything about aconitine."

"Did you?" Howie said. "Besides, who cares? We got three more tarbabies in this morning while you were pasting that one onto the Bureau."

"Three?" Av said.

"Endless supply out there," Wong said. "You gonna eat those fries?"

Av changed when he got home that afternoon, went up to the roof, and worked out with his home weight set for a while. He'd decided he was going to enjoy the Briar Patch, if only for the eccentric company. With any luck, unknown federal authorities were no longer bugging his loft and he wouldn't have to consort with his fairy godmother anymore. Dragon lady was more like it, he thought. That said, she certainly did exude that certain something, especially when going in the away direction. But: what the fuck? Ellen Whiting. Nobody by that name works here, they'd said. No, wait—they'd simply ducked the question, hadn't they? And yet, the two special agents had practically winced when they heard the name.

He went down to the loft after his workout and took a shower. He was thinking about what to do about dinner when the phone rang. His landline number was listed and he got an average number of telemarketer calls right about this time of the evening. He looked at the caller ID, which read: fairy godmother.

Oka-a-y, he thought; that's pretty clever. He picked up the phone. "Do you know that the Federal Bureau of really serious Investigation calls you: oh, fuck?" he asked.

"In their dreams," she said.

"Well, yeah, I get that," he said.

"I feel like some serious red meat for dinner," she said. "Interested in joining me?"

"That would be a yes," he said. "Just as long as I'm not the red meat in question."

"Poor baby," she said. "Going through life like that. But, no, I was thinking a nice rare steak at Henninger's up on M Street."

"Hope you're buying, Fairy Godmother."

"I am and I'll make it worth your while, too. The reservation is for seven. In your name. I'll be there about seven-thirty, so I can make an entrance."

"Can't hardly wait," he said.

"And let's have done with the 'fairy godmother' bullshit. How about just plain CT?"

" 'Fairy godmother' sounded less dangerous," he said.

"Listen to you."

She did indeed make an entrance. The restaurant was getting noisy as it filled with the typical mix of Washington young professionals, twice as many women as men, and absolutely everyone on the make in one way or another. Av had arrived as instructed and was working on one of the craft beers made right there on the premises. She'd scored a corner four-top that allowed him to take the gunfighter's seat and observe the show. The young women were all trying to look bored and interested at the same time, while the men postured with each other, dropping acronyms and famous Capitol Hill names. There were a few White House staffers at the bar, identifiable by the tops of their security badges, which were adroitly positioned in suit coat pockets to just barely show the White House logo. All part of the game, he thought. A White House badge beat a Justice Department badge, hands down. Like that.

CT arrived at seven-thirty, decked out in a knee-length, shimmering white dress clingingly cut to flatter her athletic figure while not being starlet ridiculous. Her hair was done in a Grecian curl and she was now a blonde. She wore what looked like a single emerald pendant at her throat. She looked straight at him as she moved confidently past the crowd near the bar, which parted like the proverbial Red Sea, men losing their trains of thought and suspending conversation, the ladies shooting daggers at this beauty who cut through them like a hot knife through butter. The fact that she was probably twice their age probably made it hurt even more. Av stood up as she approached the table.

He, himself, had cleaned up a bit for the occasion, wearing a navy blue sport jacket over khakis and a white, long-sleeved shirt. The coat had been custom cut to make room for both his enlarged shoulders and the .40 caliber Glock model 27 holstered just above his left hip. He discovered that she actually had green, not blue eyes, matching that softly glowing stone at her throat. He smiled as she approached the table, letting his eyes roam freely, as she had undoubtedly intended.

"Entrance definitely achieved," he said, as a waiter hurried over to pull back her chair.

"But still dangerous?" she asked teasingly as she sat down.

"Upgraded to lethal, I think," he said. "Have I got the appropriate deer-in-the-headlights look?"

"Not yet," she said, "but you will." She turned to the waiter. "Stoli Elit, double, straight up, and ice-wrapped, please."

Av was shaking his head. "If I tried one of those I'd be babbling on the floor about halfway through," he said.

She shrugged delicately. "Comes with age," she said, her eyes twinkling. "The tolerance for alcohol, that is. I don't often drink, but when I do, I want to feel the hit."

"I have at least one beer every night," he said. "Probably just habit. Did a whole bottle of red the other night, which schooled me not to ever do that again."

The waiter arrived with her cocktail, which was served in a double-walled martini glass that surrounded the liquor with an ice collar. He presented menus, but she waved them off. "Bring me a three-inch-thick, certified Angus rib eye," she said. "Apache rare, with half a baked potato, fully loaded, and a small Caesar on the side."

The waiter looked to Av. "What she said," Av told him. He thanked them and hurried off. "I like my beef rare," he said. "But what's Apache rare?"

"They keep a small charcoal grill going back there," she said. "They take a room-temperature steak, small but cut really thick, and slather it with herbed garlic oil and then pound rock salt onto both sides. They take a bellows to the coals, blow off all the ash, and then drop the steak directly onto the coals. Sear it for three minutes, take it off, bellows again, then flip it for three more minutes. Repeat—six minutes a side total. Comes out with a black, crunchy, salty, and garlicky crust and warm rare inside. Wonderful."

"Reminds me of the Texas definition of rare," he said. "Cut off its horns, wipe its ass, and bring it to the table."

She failed to smile, which is when he realized she was busy doing the Washington room scan, sipping her vodka and looking around the crowded dining room to see if there was anyone truly important here.

Av exhaled. In a game of wits, he was probably way out of his league with this one. That didn't bother him too much; the eye candy was compensation enough. He also knew this wasn't really a social occasion. He had the sense to let her reveal the purpose of the evening in her own sweet time. He did wonder how old she was, but then thought, if she looks like that, what could it matter?

The steaks were indeed amazing. She attacked hers with gusto and there was no more conversation until they both were finished. He'd ordered a glass of red with his; she'd opted for another Elit.

When the plates were cleared she sat back and gave him an appraising look.

"What do you think should be done with an American who goes over to the dark side and gives aid and comfort to Islamic terrorists?" she asked, out of nowhere.

"I'm a sworn police officer," he said. "So, for the record and any pocket recorders: you find him, apprehend him along with a boatload of solid evidence, try him, and put him away for life."

"That's it?"

"Well," he said, "there is always the death penalty, but I happen to think that an injection that makes you sleepy and another one that makes you dead is too easy. I prefer the notion of a slow death by incarceration. You know, living forever behind the razor wire among animals who walk upright, and knowing you will never, *ever* leave except in a prison body bag which you might have actually sewed together, bound for a grave in the weeds of a prison cemetery, and that, when you do leave, you will have experienced the serial joys of every conceivable sexual orientation, human, bestial, or otherwise."

She nodded, acknowledging his point. "The problem with that is there is always the chance the bad guy might get off. Look at all those Al Qaeda homeboys still down in Gitmo, and it's been, what, twelve, thirteen years? And they're still enjoying their afternoons in the Caribbean sunshine, reading their holy comic book?"

"Sounds like you believe in the vengeance theory of crime and punishment," he said.

"I lost my brand-new husband in the north tower," she said. "That's absolutely what I believe in."

He wiped the faintly patronizing expression off his face and tried to think of something appropriate to say. He drew a complete blank—what *could* you say to that?

Then he thought he understood.

"You and your Ray-Ban posse wanted to talk to me about the McGavin case," he said. "Because you *wanted* MPD to back out. Because—why? You're running some kind of a federal vendetta hit squad?"

Her eyebrows rose. "What*ever* are you talking about, Detective?" she said with a bright smile, but her eyes were approving. Call me CT, she'd said. But she'd also said her name was Ellen Whiting, which had drawn a sharp reaction from the Bureau agents who'd come to get the OCME report. Different offices? Or was Ellen Whiting a bogus name? He decided to try something.

"*That's* why the Bureau guys recognized the name CT," he said.

Her smile faded. "CT is an acronym, no more, no less," she said. "Just one more in a town drowning in alphabet soup. CT: counterterrorism. OC: organized crime. C4ISAR: Command, Control, Communications, Computers, Intelligence, Surveillance and Reconnaissance. Now: what the hell is *aconitine*?"

"Trimethoxy-4-(methoxymethyl) aconitanyl-14-benzoate. It has the chemical formula $C_{34}H_{47}NO_{11}$."

She stared at him.

"You asked," he said, with a grin. "It took me a half hour to memorize that shit, courtesy of Wikipedia. Basically, it's one plant's very special way of telling you: I'm not edible. Really, I'm not."

The restaurant bar scene was going full blast now, and it was getting hard to hear. She'd totally ducked his implied question. "Want to get a coffee somewhere?" he asked.

"No, thanks," she said. "My turn: you want to get lucky with me?"

His face must have shown his total surprise because she was laughing at him now. Once again he didn't know what to say. From a physical point of view the answer was clear, but this lady was, well, he wasn't quite sure what she was. After all, he had rules.

"I apologize for shocking you, Detective," she said. "I just wanted to see if this all-women-are-dangerous business of yours was just a mildly sophisticated line. I know some women who would immediately make it a project to convince you otherwise, with you smiling all the way to the bedroom."

"I think all women *are* dangerous," he said.

"Why?"

"Because they all come with conditions and, usually, a lot of hidden costs. I'm talking about permanent or semipermanent relationships, Special Agent. Not just a hookup."

"So marriage, family, children—not on your personal horizon?"

He hesitated. "Not sure, but I tend to think not. For one, I'm a cop. I *like* being a cop, but being a married cop means you eventually have to choose—being a cop, or being a devoted husband and father. You must know how that usually works out, right?"

"Never got the chance, I guess," she said. "But, yeah, I've seen a fair number of Bureau marriages break up, but by no means all."

"I figure, why take the chance? I enjoy the company of women, okay? But the cop in me is always wary. I guess I like to see the back of them as much as I like to see the front. That's just me."

She nodded her head and raised her glass in a *salud.* "Know thyself," she said. "But you're young and fit. Don't you ever find yourself experiencing certain—needs?"

"Sure," he said, and then waited.

"And?"

"I'm not a man who's ruled by his needs," he said.

"So let me get this straight," she said. "If I pushed back my chair a little and discreetly removed all of the various impedimenta I have on underneath this dress, slipped my shoulder straps off, got up and came around the table to straddle you in your chair and pressed my boobs into your face, you'd, what? Call for the check?"

"One way to find out, I suppose," he said, innocently. "But: they'll never let us in this restaurant again, and that was a really good steak. Besides, as I remember, *you've* got check duty."

She laughed out loud. It was a pretty sound, and he saw a couple of men looking his way with unmistakably jealous expressions. Best of all, he hadn't really answered her question. On the other hand, neither had she. Who the *hell* was this lady?

They walked outside to the sidewalk on M Street, which was almost as crowded as the restaurant. She told him she'd enjoyed dinner. Then she looked around, almost as if she was checking for surveillance or eavesdroppers.

"Do me a favor?" she said. "In the event that there are any more, um, developments in the McGavin matter, would you give me a call?"

"Sure," he said. "Except I don't have your number."

"Just pick up the phone, dial three 'fours' and then your own number. I'll get back to you."

"So my place is still bugged? Or at least my phone?"

"*Every*body's phone is bugged these days, Detective," she said with a smile. "Don't you read the papers?"

She then flagged down a cab. She got in with a flash of those gorgeous legs, waved good-bye, and then drove away. As the cab merged into traffic he wondered if he'd screwed that up, but then his better sense intervened. If nothing else, she was probably one of the wild ones, and those were precisely the ones to stay away from. The agents this afternoon *had* recognized her name, and not that CT bullshit, either. Ellen Whiting. Oh, fuck, they'd said. That had to mean something.

He started walking along M Street to get back to his building. Most people on the sidewalk were obviously out for a party night, so he was surprised when he saw two large men in suits get out of a parked black Crown Vic with tinted windows and fairly bristling with antennae to stand right in front of him. They both discreetly opened credentials cases where the letters FBI were clearly displayed. The taller man asked if he'd mind getting in the car.

"That depends," Av said. "What's the beef?"

"No beef, Detective Smith," the agent said. "Man in back wants to have a short conversation."

Av looked into the backseat, where an older-looking black man, also in a suit, was looking at him expectantly. When he saw Av hesitating, he made a come-on gesture. Av glanced behind him, where two more guys in suits were standing next to yet another government car that hadn't been there a minute ago. The agent had called him Detective Smith, so, he figured, what the hell. He got into the backseat.

One of the agents outside closed the back door and got into the front. The other went around and got in on the driver's side. The car pulled out into traffic and went exactly nowhere, evening traffic on Georgetown's M Street being what it was.

The black man to his left turned in his seat and extended a hand. "I'm Supervisory Special Agent Tyree Miller of the FBI," he said, pleasantly. "And I'm hoping you and I can have a brief conversation without our having to resort to some kind of, um, official proceedings."

"I'm Detective Sergeant Ken Smith, Metro PD," he said. "And if official proceedings are in the offing, we're not going to have a conversation about anything at all."

"I understand, Detective," Tyree said. "Truth be told, we're not all that interested in you. It's the woman you just had dinner with who's attracted our attention. Can you tell me her name?"

"CT," Av said. Ellen Whiting had paid for a terrific steak. CT would do for now.

"CT?" Miller said. "CT what?"

"That's it," Av said. The car was moving now, but still only at about two miles per hour. "She paid me a visit in the middle of the night. I found her sitting in my living room when I got up to tend to a red wine hangover. We talked, well, actually, *she* talked about a case I was working on. Then she left."

Miller blinked once, like a large frog. "What case was that, Detective?"

"The case of a Homeland Security civil serpent dying under mysterious circumstances in a French restaurant up on Connecticut Avenue. Name of Francis X. McGavin."

Tyree sat back and looked out the window for a moment. He didn't seem all that surprised. "And what was the outcome of your midnight discussion? Or was there a point?"

Av nodded. He told Tyree about the canal towpath incident, the supposed FPS connection, and how he'd been suspended for organizing that, even though one of the other Briar Patch detectives had done the real organizing. The following day all had apparently been forgiven.

"Then two of *your* people showed up, picked up our case files on the McGavin matter, told us they'd take it from there, and that was that."

"And when you talked to those two agents, did the name Ellen Whiting come up?"

Aw, shit, Av thought. He nodded.

"Had you heard that name, Ellen Whiting, before, Detective?" Tyree asked.

"Yes," Av said. "Supposedly she was the woman with McGavin at the restaurant when he died. When we initially tried to shop the case to the Bureau, they declined, saying there was a Bureau angle to the case. We naturally assumed this Ellen Whiting was Bureau."

The car made a left turn across a lot of traffic, evoking some horns of protest. Neither of the agents up front so much as glanced at the other cars.

"But then this woman who identifies herself as, what was it—CT?—appears in your home in the middle of the night."

"Right. She says she's in the counterterrorism business, but did not mention the Bureau. Or the FPS, either."

"So we've supposedly got the Bureau, the Federal Protective Service, and now some eponymous counterterrorism agency as her employer of record. Hence the CT?"

"I suppose," Av said. "When she called earlier today, that's what she wanted me to call her—CT. My partners and I'd been calling her my fairy godmother, because of the way all the top-floor heat suddenly evaporated."

"May I ask what you two talked about tonight?" Tyree asked. "Over steaks, beer, and fancy vodka, very cold?"

So they'd had someone in the restaurant, Av thought. That meant a lot of agents were out tonight on this matter. "Nothing of great significance," he replied. "She wanted to know my thoughts on what ought to happen to Americans who joined forces with terrorists. She also told me that her brand-new husband had died in the World Trade Center on nine-eleven."

That seemed to pique Tyree's interest, and Av thought the agent in the right front seat was writing something in a notebook. "Did you get the impression she was trying to recruit you for something, Detective?" Tyree asked.

Av, surprised, hesitated. Then he thought, what the hell, tell 'em the truth. "I don't know what to think, Supervisory Special Agent," he said. "That's possible. In fact, I asked her if she was running some kind of government hit squad, but she blew that off."

"So how did the dinner date end?"

"She gave me the impression that she was ready to go somewhere and put a fine finish on the evening," Av said. "But I declined."

"She cuts a pretty impressive figure," Tyree said. "Why'd you decline?"

"She's a little scary, maybe?" Av said. He wasn't inclined to share his own personal rules of engagement with these guys just now. "What's the Bureau's interest in this woman, if I may ask?"

"If I told you, I'd have to quarantine you, Detective," Tyree said, but then he smiled. "That was my feeble attempt at a joke."

"A joke," Av said. "Fancy that."

One of the agents up front stifled a snort. Miller ignored it. "I think you can guess from the nature of my questions that we're very interested in talking to this individual, for a variety of reasons, including her penchant for even hinting that she works for us."

Av nodded. Impersonating a Bureau special agent was a major crime in the eyes of everyone at the Hoover building. "She never did actually claim that," he pointed out. "So I guess she probably does *not* work for the Bureau?"

"We, on the other hand, are worried that she does. Not directly, perhaps, but in some capacity."

Av was confused. They'd obviously had someone in the restaurant close enough to hear their dinner order. So why hadn't they just grabbed her up? And this guy was implying that they could not identify this woman as one of their own employees? His BS detector started to hum. Those two agents had surely known that name.

"What directorate do you work for, Mr. Miller?" Av asked.

"Professional Standards."

Ah, Av thought. That was the Bureau's name for their internal affairs people. That would explain some of this ambiguity. Or did it?

"So, if she calls me again, you guys want, what, a heads-up?" he asked.

"We'll probably know before you will, Detective," Tyree said, pleasantly. "But we would surely appreciate a debrief of whatever happens after that. Here's my card. Anyone who answers that number can take your report. I believe this is your residence?"

Av looked out the window and saw his building. He nodded. "It is and I will," he said. "Always glad to help my Bureau."

"That's the spirit," Tyree said as the rear door was opened. "The Bureau is a good friend to have."

"And the converse is also true," Av observed.

Tyree smiled again. "Just so, Detective Smith. Good night now."

Av laughed quietly as the car drove away. Message received, he thought. In a way, he liked the FBI. They came right to the point most of the time. If they said it, fucking believe it. F.B.I.

TEN

Carl Mandeville pasted as pleasant a smile as he could manage onto his face as he listened to Assistant Secretary Hilary Logan bang on about his growing concerns over the Kill List and the need for a full review of the DMX committee's whole operation. They were having dinner at a tony restaurant in residential Georgetown called 1789. They were seated in the Wickets Room, one of six dining areas in the restaurant.

Hilary, one l, thank you, as he would say, not two like that Gorgon, considered himself to be a respected gourmand. He was one of those men who really did live to eat, and, not surprisingly, it showed. Three chins presided over an acre or so of worsted wool vest, and the high color in his face told Mandeville that Logan had maybe about three more years before his coronary arteries finally put him in the ground. The problem was that Mandeville didn't have three years. Logan, a staunch advocate of killing off the DMX program, was a clear and present danger. Unfortunately he was also the scion of a wealthy Boston family with titanium-strong ties to the Massachusetts congressional delegation. His father owned a bank in Boston, and thus it was that Hilary was the Treasury Department's rep to DMX.

"My *dear* Mandeville," Hilary puffed, between mouthfuls of a fourteen-ounce filet smothered in bordelaise sauce. "You simply *must* understand that this DMX business is becoming an increasingly dangerous liability to America's foreign policy. Murder will out and all that, yes? And we *are* talking murder. It's simply un-American to send operatives out into the third world to murder these demented Muslims. Un-American."

"Those same demented Muslims of whom you are so fond feel that they are engaged in a war with the West, not just an energetic discussion," Mandeville said. "They think it's okay to fly hijacked airliners into buildings. To park dump trucks full of explosives in front of American embassies. To drive a motorboat full of explosives into the side of an American warship parked peacefully in a harbor. To mail envelopes full of anthrax to American government buildings. You think these things are, what, okay?"

"Of course not," Hilary said, pursuing the final roast potato around his plate with a fork. "But there are rules, Mandeville. Rules of *civilized* behavior. DMX is basically uncivilized. Some of us feel that we'd be much better off if we captured them, brought them to trial for the murderers that they are. Make them face the consequences of their actions in a court of law. Prove to them time and again that the civilized world does not condone their barbarous tactics. But we do *not* sink to their level and shoot them in the head while they're parking their car in front of the mosque."

He reached for his wineglass, which was half full. "Oh, dear," he said. "We seem to have expended this bottle—another one, perhaps?"

"Yes, why not," Mandeville said, signaling the hovering waiter. They had been indulging in a really good 1999 Châteaux Margaux and it suited his purposes to have another bottle presented, especially since Hilary, with one l, was buying.

Mandeville's left hand gently massaged the tiny, clear gel cap in his coat pocket. Just squeeze it, his contact at the army labs had told him. Pop it like a pimple. And the best part was that it would take about an hour before its effects came on. He waited for the waiter to bring a second bottle, open it, and then let it breathe on the table for a few minutes.

"I understand your concerns, Hilary," Mandeville continued. "But the American people will *not* abide it. Ordinary citizens know that our judicial system bends over backward to give lawbreakers in this country every protection, but when they see buildings falling down at the hands of foreigners bent on killing America, itself, people here at home want those bastards dead, not pulling off some kind of O.J. on them."

"Not *everybody* wants them dead, my dear fellow," Hilary said. "In fact, I want them captured, tried very publicly so that the whole world knows what they did and why they did it, and then caged for life. As you know, I don't approve of the death penalty."

"Funny, the terrorists have no such qualms about killing," Mandeville said. "They even like to film it these days—like the journalist they captured and then beheaded on television a year ago."

"Hear me out, Mandeville. I believe it's worse to be caged up for the rest of your life than put to sleep like a surgery patient. We get enough of them in cages, maybe that will make some of these turd world countries reconsider their visa policies, rather than allow these thugs to run free under their noses."

"They let them run free because they have been *coerced* into doing so, Hilary," Mandeville replied. "Why? Because the thugs are better organized, armed, and funded than the local governments. No, this won't do. DMX fulfills a pressing need: to reflect terror right back at these Islamist maniacs who hate us and all we stand for. If you expose the DMX to a political review in today's supercharged political climate, we lose a very effective, if not the only effective weapon against the terrorists."

Logan just shook his head, started to say something but then a crumb caught in his throat and he reached for his water glass. His sleeve knocked his steak knife off the table. As Logan reached down to retrieve it, Mandeville saw his chance. In one swift motion he passed his left palm over Logan's almost empty wineglass as if to steady it while the fat man was struggling to bend down. He glanced at his watch as Logan straightened up and reached for the breadbasket. Now all he had to do was get Logan back out onto the street in no more than about forty-five minutes, tops.

"Let's see if this bottle's as good as the last," Mandeville said, expansively, pouring a splash into his own glass. He pointed to Logan's glass. "Finish that." Logan gulped down the last of his wine and smacked his lips in obvious anticipation of another bottle. Mandeville signaled the waiter to bring fresh glasses, in honor of the excellent wine—and to make sure any residue ended up in the dishwasher.

Av had spent the early evening at Georgetown University attending a lecture on forensic toxicology, courtesy of the MPD's continuing education program. Even though he was no longer assigned to a homicide bureau, he was determined to keep up with the science end of the city's too many murders. He'd halfway expected Precious to nix his request, but since she, herself, was attending night school, she was all for it. He thought the little interlude with Happy might have influenced her thinking, as well. He thought she was still embarrassed about all that.

He left the east campus and walked down Thirty-fifth Street toward the canal area, enjoying the gentle evening breezes coming off the river below and how the streetlights seemed to polish up the million-dollar town houses of the university neighborhood. Another block brought him to Canal Street, where the M Street bar and restaurant rush hour was building. As he waited for the light to cross Canal Street, he saw a yellow cab slow and then stop in the intersection, as if getting ready for a left turn—except there was no left turn possible there. Then he saw a rather large man open the left rear door of the cab, heave himself unsteadily out of the vehicle, and then walk straight into the heavy flow of traffic going the other way through the intersection toward the Georgetown nightlife. There wasn't even time for horns—two vehicles hit the man, the first a Mercedes sedan that spun him off its left front bumper. The man bounced off the side of the yellow cab, back into the road, and then was struck by a SUV, which hit him head-on and smashed his body under the front end. The driver of the SUV slammed on the brakes, causing the following car to rear-end it, sending the SUV lurching forward another ten feet in a hail of glass.

The man from the cab was no longer visible. Av knew he was probably pinned under that Suburban. He hoped he was dead because otherwise they'd be sewing on him for a year. The yellow cab was still stopped right where the man had gotten out. The driver, who looked to be Middle Eastern, was standing next to the driver's-side door with both hands held to his face. The driver of the third car, a woman, was leaning against the remains of her steering wheel airbag. She appeared to be crying

Amazingly, the traffic began to part around the three stopped vehicles and the cab, with only the two cars right behind the wreck coming to a stop. Av wanted to go out into the intersection but the westbound traffic coming out of Georgetown was barely slowing—if they hadn't seen the man get hit, they'd assume it was just another fender-bender.

The man in the Mercedes, however, knew better. He gingerly got out of the car and walked back toward the Suburban, his right hand held in front of his mouth as if he was about to be sick. At that moment a patrol car rolled up, its blue strobes flashing. They must have been in traffic, Av thought. He thought about going out into the intersection now that traffic was being forced to stop in both directions, but hesitated. The two cops had their hands full right now, and soon there'd be more cruisers and an ambulance on scene. He decided to check the incident board in the morning and then call the District people working the incident to give a witness statement. What in the world had prompted that guy to get out of the cab like that? He'd never looked—he just got out and walked like some kind of zombie right into the stream of traffic. He made a mental note to emphasize that point when he gave his statement. Then he resumed his walk home, thoughts of dinner somewhat muted now.

Carl Mandeville had the White House staff car drop him off at the Lincoln Monument after dinner. He told the driver he needed to walk off all that rich food, and asked him to pick him up in an hour at the reflecting pool behind the Capitol building. As he started up the walkway toward the World War II Memorial, he reflected on his discussion with Logan at dinner. That idiot's worldview was all too typical of the so-called progressive intelligentsia in Washington, insulated as they were by inherited money, an affluent lifestyle, and a certain group-think smugness that seemed to warp their approach to everything, from Georgetown dinner parties to public policy.

Strang would be alarmed by what he'd done tonight, but he'd needed to show Strang not only who was in charge but also what could happen to anyone who crossed him. Normally he did not indulge in direct action, taking care always to have a layer or two between his masterminding and any actual wet work. He sensed, however, that Strang had been taking him a wee bit too much for granted lately, with all his let-me-take-care-of-it suggestions, as if he was the one driving the train. What would happen to Logan tonight, no, probably what had *already* happened, would snatch him up nicely.

One of his former subordinates in the Agency, now a division chief, had told him about Strang and how it might be useful to Mandeville to have someone "sleeping" in the Bureau headquarters. Mandeville had jumped at the offer, if only to have eyes and ears at the Hoover building, and, if necessary, another hired hand. His first major tasking had been to talk the strange millionaire botanist out in Great Falls out of some of his rarer toxins, and he'd opened that door that handsomely. But: given how easily that Metro PD cop had been able to deflect Strang's "subtle" efforts at intimidation, perhaps he'd overestimated the old spook's abilities. One thing was for sure—Strang knew nothing about Evangelino, and he was determined to keep it that way.

On the other hand, he'd have to be extra careful in dealing with the third one, Wheatley. He smiled in the glow of the faux gas lamps throughout the Mall area. It would be interesting to see how pompous Mr. Wheatley reacted to a second member of their little committee going to meet his maker. Hell, it'd be interesting to see if Wheatley even showed up for their next meeting once he heard the news. And Ellen? He had to be careful there, he thought: she was on ready alert, and Logan's sudden demise might trigger her into doing something awkward.

Patterns, he reminded himself, as he walked briskly by the inconspicuous bronze statue honoring John Paul Jones. Be careful about establishing patterns. He needed to let Wheatley stew for a while. See what the Metro PD cops did with the Logan matter. See if that same Metro cop got involved again. Figure out what to do with him if that happened. Well, hell, he knew what he would do: switch Evangelino into second gear, that's what.

He raised his walking stick in greeting as he passed a Secret Service vehicle. He saw a flash of a hand wave back. Good to know someone was on the job, he thought, as he strengthened his stride toward the big white building up on the Hill. No meetings tonight. Evangelino would report tomorrow by text as to whether or not he knew enough about that detective's daily routine to take him out at short notice. Evangelino was all about preparation, but when he moved, the target simply disappeared off the face of the earth, sometimes, he'd heard, literally.

ELEVEN

At nine-thirty the next morning, Av called the Second District station and asked for the desk sergeant. He identified himself and then asked for whoever was handling the fatal pedestrian incident in Georgetown last night. A second sergeant picked up, listened to what Av had to say, and asked if he'd come to the district office. Apparently there was some federal interest in the victim, and Av being from ILB and all . . .

"Aw, shit," Av announced to the squad room when he hung up. "I think I just grabbed a tarbaby."

"Good work, my man," Mau-Mau said, brightly. "That's what hands're for, right?"

Av checked out on the board for the Second District. He bummed a ride from street patrol and arrived fifteen minutes later. He went through security and then discovered that he was not the only visitor that morning. The reception area was sporting a contingent of federal agents, along with some suits that Av learned were from the Treasury Department, of all places. The feds were standing around looking annoyed. The two cops at the reception desk were looking worried. Av walked up, handed over his ID, and said he was here to give a witness statement on the pedestrian incident in Georgetown last night, which, according to the morning's *Washington Post,* had been a fatality.

The room suddenly went silent. While one of the cops made a hushed call, Av turned around to find every one of the feds staring at him.

"What?" he said.

"You saw it?" one of the suits asked. He looked older than the rest and had an air of authority about him.

"I did," Av said. "Who are you?"

"You first, Sergeant," the man said with a demeaning tone of voice.

Av reacted. "I'll give my statement to the MPD investigator who's working the incident," Av said. "You can talk to him when I'm done."

The man began to get red in the face and Av wondered if maybe he'd been the least bit tactless. Again.

"You listen to me," the man began, but he was interrupted when the station captain, a large and totally bald black man, came through the doors behind the desk and called for Detective Sergeant Smith.

"Right here," Av said. The captain nodded and then indicated that Av was to come through the counter doors. He looked around the room at the assembled feds, sniffed, and led Av back into the inner offices.

Av had many questions, but the captain's bearing indicated that he was probably not in a sharing mood, so he just followed. They went into a conference room, where some station cops, a sergeant in civvies, and a secretary were sitting around a table. There was a TV screen up on the wall, which displayed the reception area. The captain indicated where Av was to sit. He then went to the head of the table.

"I'm Captain Wright," he said. "I understand you're ILB?"

"Yes, sir, I am. But I'm not here in that capacity. I witnessed the accident last night."

"Why didn't you identify yourself to the officers on the scene?" the captain asked. The other cops were studying their yellow pads.

"They had their hands full with uncooperative traffic, then EMTs, and what looked like a pretty messy scene. I waited until this morning to call and give my statement."

"Okay," the captain said. "That's hardly standard procedure. You should have identified yourself and given your statement right there and then."

"Yes, sir," Av said.

"Okay. So: what happened?"

Av described what he'd seen.

"You're saying this guy got out of the cab and deliberately walked into oncoming traffic?"

Av hesitated. The captain caught it. "What?" he said.

"'Deliberately' might be the wrong word. He got out of the cab, which had stopped in the intersection. It took some effort. He was—really fat. He didn't appear to be scared, just determined. He got out, straightened up, and then walked straight ahead, like—I'm sorry, but some kind of zombie."

"Zombie."

"Hands at his sides. Staring straight ahead. Walking like his joints were freezing up. Small steps, but determined. Right until that car hit him. So: what's the crowd out front all about?"

The captain sat back in his chair. "Your 'zombie' was the assistant secretary of the treasury for international trade."

My zombie, Av thought. Then a sneaky little thought crept up in the back of his mind—the Bistro case. The captain looked as if he was reading Av's mind. "Isn't Precious Johnson your boss?" he asked, finally.

Av nodded.

"Guess what?"

"This is going to the Briar Patch?"

The captain smiled, but it was not a warm smile. "You better fucking believe it, Detective Sergeant," he said. "We don't do zombies here in the Second."

"Wow," Av said. "Can't wait. Especially with all those happy campers out front."

The captain smiled again, but it was mostly teeth this time. "*Your* happy campers now, Sergeant," he said. "I'm gonna call Precious. My people will show you out the back door. With any luck you can beat that pack of suits back to HQ."

"I'll need a ride, then," Av said. "Sir."

"You ever seen Al Pacino doing some directing?" Precious asked, looking at the Gang of Four seated in front of her. "You know, where he goes: Cut! Cut! Cut! What the *fock* was that? What the *focking fock* was that? You *focking* fock. How did this dumb *fock* get onto my set, will somebody focking tell me *that*?"

Mau-Mau nodded appreciatively. "Thass it—that's his voice."

Av was more apprehensive than appreciative. Precious had been looking right at him the whole time. She was still looking at him.

"Um," he said. He had made it back before the federal posse showed up at HQ, but he had not, apparently, been able to outrun the telephone. Precious had been waiting for his return in the squad room, with the other three inmates already mustered uncomfortably at the conference table.

"Um?" she said, back to her normal voice. "You witnessed a fatal accident last night involving an assistant secretary of the *focking* treasury, and you went where? Home?"

"It was medium chaos cranking up out there, boss," Av said. "Cars trying to get around the wreck, intersection traffic going every which way, street cops trying not to puke. They had their hands full. The vic didn't have an assistant secretary sign on him, and patrol didn't need a witness right then, they needed a coupla snow shovels for a serious wet cleanup."

Precious glared at him. Wong Daddy chose that moment to intervene in Av's defense. "No way Sergeant Smith here coulda known that the blood bag under the Merc was an assistant whatever," he pointed out.

Mau-Mau lost it when he heard the word "blood bag." Precious almost was able to control her face but then she snorted.

"Jesus, Wong," Av said. *"Blood bag?"*

Wong shrugged. "Big Merc like that, coupla tons, then a Suburban? You're gonna have hair, teeth, eyeballs, and—"

Precious slammed her hand on the table and yelled something in the unknown dialect. Wong winced and said he was sorry.

"Okay," Precious said. "Needless to say we have a new and exciting tarbaby to handle. I got a call from Captain Wright in the Second and he said this one was tailor-made for ILB. Especially after he heard Sergeant Smith's description of the incident. Tell me you didn't say something about a zombie?"

Av went through it again, and then asked the question that had been bothering him all the way back to the office: this was the second senior government official to die in a bizarre manner in just a couple days. Related?

Precious started shaking her head. "No, not related. Definitely *not* related. I do not, I repeat, *not,* need any goddamned conspiracy theory raising its ugly head here in the Briar Patch."

"But—" Av began.

"No," Precious interrupted. "Trust me on this: that kinda shit turns tarbabies into tar pits, from which no one ever emerges alive, got it, gang?"

Four heads nodded in unison.

"Good. Now: we've got four *federales* on their way over here as we speak. Bureau, Homeland Security, Treasury, and, for some strange reason, someone from the State Department. Don't ask—I don't know. Now: they'll want an update of whatever MPD can kludge together in one hour. And we, boys and germs, are *eager* for them to take over the investigation, right? So, get on to the Second, get what you can, and stand by."

An hour later Av and Mau-Mau escorted the four feds to the visitors' conference room, where Precious was already standing at the head of the table. Introductions were made all around and then everybody sat down. Precious led off with a quick overview of what ILB was all about, and then handed over to Av, whom she described as a senior detective and an eyewitness to the incident. Mau-Mau smothered a smile at that.

Av described what he'd seen and then added some details from the Second District's preliminary report. The cabdriver had been questioned and his story pretty much bore out what Av had told them. His passenger suddenly yelled stop, opened the rear door, heaved himself out of the cab, and then proceeded to walk in front of a car.

"Did the driver describe the man's state prior to the incident?" the Bureau rep asked.

"He did. He said the guy was half in the bag, but not so drunk that he couldn't tell the driver where he wanted to go, which was to his town house in Foxhall Village, and to comment on what a lovely evening it was. Driver said the guy was no drunker than most of the people he picks up around there. When he yelled stop, the driver thought the guy needed to vomit, so stop he did."

"Did the driver see any physical indications that he was experiencing some sort of vascular accident?" the Treasury rep asked. "Slurred words, tremors, unsteadiness? I ask because of your comment that he looked like a zombie before he took the final step into traffic?"

"Wish I'd never used that word," Av said. "But: that's what he looked like to me. And the driver didn't mention anything like that."

"You run into lots of zombies in your work, Sergeant?" the State

Department rep asked. He was a large, obviously fit and muscular man in his late forties with a shaved head and a commanding presence about him that fairly shouted military special operations. Av figured him for either CIA or maybe even the Pentagon, but never State Department. And: he didn't care for the guy's attitude.

"No," he said. "Not normally. Although, sometimes, after midnight, you—"

"Sergeant," Precious barked.

"Right. It's just possible I was speaking metaphorically?"

The big guy put up his hands in mock surrender.

"Look," Av continued. "The guy became rigid once he hoisted himself out of the cab, which, by the way, took some effort. When he walked out into traffic it was like he was an automaton: one leg in front of the other, his upper body ramrod straight. He never looked to either side, almost as if he either expected the impact that was coming or had no peripheral vision. It was—horrific. Think small, fat dog rolling around under the back wheels of a bus."

That image produced a moment of silence. The guy from State then apologized. "I take your point, Sergeant," he said. "Sorry about the wisecrack. We've checked with the restaurant—1789. They confirm he was there with one other person."

"Expensive place," Av said.

"Indeed it is," the State rep said. Av thought for a moment that the guy looked familiar. "The staff said he had dinner with someone called Carl Mandeville, according to the reservation list. They had two bottles of very expensive—$250 a pop—wine, and seemed to have been talking business. No arguments, no sort of scene. Logan asked the restaurant to call him a cab, and then they left together."

"And who is this Mandeville?" Av asked.

"One of us," the Homeland Security rep said. Av waited for further explanation, but apparently "us" was all he was going to get.

"We've told you what we know, which is pretty basic traffic accident stuff," Precious said. "You guys gonna take it from here?"

"Absolutely, Lieutenant," the Bureau rep said. "Consider this matter to be off your radar."

"Terrific," Precious said, beaming.

The meeting broke up. Precious closeted with the DHS and the Treasury reps. The State rep approached Av. "Where's the freak show today?" he asked with just a trace of a smile. That's when Av recognized him—one of the runners on the towpath.

"Sergeant Bento is in the basement, sharpening his dentures," Av replied.

The man grinned. "On a grinding wheel, no doubt," he said. "Appreciate the briefing."

As he and Av shook hands Av felt a card being palmed into his hand. Once back in the squad room he looked at it. Colonel James Steele, U.S. Marine Corps. Joint Special Operations Command, Fort Bragg, North Carolina. On the back was a handwritten note, done in tiny but precise printing: "Seventy-five. Beer on me. Bring crew. 1730. Tonight if possible. If not, call."

The Seventy-five was a Marine Corps hangout bar right across the street from the Marine Barracks at Eighth and I Streets in southeast D.C. Av led the way in because he looked most like a marine among the group. Mau-Mau was in his usual terrorist gear, Wong wore a Hawaiian shirt over judo gi and sandals. He had a 16d nail sticking out of the corner of his mouth like a cigarette. Miz Brown was dressed all in black like a funeral director, complete with a homburg and round granny glasses. He hadn't wanted to come along; he'd claimed that marines made him nervous. Av had told him that that was their job.

Steele waved from the back of the room. They walked through the tables while being watched by every jungle bunny in the room. It felt like there were range finders swiveling around to track them, but when they sat down with Steele, the bar's noise level resumed and nobody seemed to care anymore.

Steele chuckled when he saw the nail in Wong's mouth. Wong eyed the colonel, reversed the nail in his mouth with his tongue and then spat it down in front of one of the chairs, where it stood, quivering in the wood.

"I sit here," he announced, to a chorus of quietly approving animal noises from nearby marines.

"Absolutely," Steele said, grinning.

Av introduced his team to the colonel, who had two pitchers of beer arriving in about one minute.

"Gentlemen," he said after everyone had damaged the first glass. "I'm not from the State Department, although I do have an office there. I'm from the Joint Special Operations Command at Fort Bragg, North Carolina, commonly known as Jay-SOC."

"Snake-eater," Wong said.

"I've never actually had that pleasure," Steele said. "But I did put a spectacled cobra into the front seat of a cab once in Somalia. The driver was not taking me where I needed to go."

"What happened?" Mau-Mau asked.

"He died, we crashed. I had to get out and walk. Two guys with AKs came running up to me and started raising hell about something, so I handed one of them the snake. He freaked, tried to shoot it, shot his buddy instead. Then the snake bit the shooter. Serendipity, you know? I walked away. Nobody bothered me."

"With the snake?" Wong asked.

"Hell, yes," the colonel said with a grin. "All the way back to camp."

Wong nodded appreciatively. He would have kept the snake, too. For dinner.

"But enough about me," the colonel continued. "I wanted to talk about Mister Hilary Logan, late of the U.S. Treasury Department. Sergeant Smith, you said he was acting like a zombie when he got out of that cab. I made a wiseass remark without first engaging my brain. I'm kinda famous for that. But here's the thing: we know *how* he died. What we don't know is what made him get out of a cab in the middle of a busy intersection, at night, and then step into oncoming traffic."

"Sounds like maybe suicide," Mau-Mau said. "Tough way to do it, but, still . . . ?"

"I can't imagine anyone committing suicide like that," Steele said.

"I can," said Miz Brown, speaking for the first time. "We see it all the time in Metro PD: people jumping down in front of an oncoming Metro train or stepping in front of a bus."

Steele shook his head slowly. "I've asked the Bureau to call for an autopsy," he announced. "They'd been drinking, two whole bottles of wine, in fact. But the driver's description of his passenger doesn't match the actions of a totally wasted drunk. They stagger, weave, throw up. They don't put on a thousand-meter stare and start robot-walking."

"I have to remind you, Colonel," Av said. "That ILB is no longer involved in this. The Bureau guy made that clear today, and my boss said amen. In fact, that's our job in ILB: move the cases that come *to* ILB *out* of ILB. You've got yourself a mystery, I admit, but we no longer care."

"You should, Detective," the colonel said. "Carl Mandeville, Logan's dinner date? He's the executive director of the DMX committee. Logan was the Treasury rep to the DMX committee. Francis X. McGavin of Bistro Nord fame was the DHS rep to the DMX committee. And the one thing that links those two guys, beside being dead and being members of the DMX committee? Is you guys."

"Seriously?" Mau-Mau exclaimed. "You think *we* had something—"

The colonel raised a hand. "No, no, no. Of course not," he said. "But once it gets out within the CT world that two members of the DMX have died within days of each other, inquiring minds are going to start asking questions—and doing pattern analysis. I understand you guys want nothing to do with this, but I wanted to warn you that ILB may get swept up if a shitstorm starts."

"Ain't nothin' to that," Mau-Mau said. "We'll just do what we're paid to do in dear ole ILB, and that's bounce said shitstorm right back on the first federal agency comes makin' trouble for us. Now, I got one for you—what's a DMX?"

"Kick-*ass* black rapper," Wong offered.

"Hardly," the colonel said. "It's just one of a hundred classified committees related to counterterrorism. What makes it different is that members are relatively senior officials."

"What's it do?" Av asked.

"It's a Washington committee, Detective Sergeant," the colonel said. "It doesn't *do* anything but talk. I'll bet you've got some committees in MPD just like it."

Av wasn't entirely satisfied with this answer. The way the colonel had uttered the word "DMX" earlier was now being papered over as if DMX was no big deal. Then he suddenly understood: the whole purpose of this little beer muster had been for the colonel to find out if they knew what they'd bumped up against. "We surely do," Av said. "So: what would you want us to do if somebody does comes knocking?"

"Call me?" the colonel said. "I can get the heat off you mosh skosh. In return, I get a leg up on the pack of hounds that's probably going to get into these two deaths."

That's two, Av thought. First the Professional Standards guy from the Bureau, now this colonel from Jay-something, wanting to be "kept informed." Or was it three? His fairy godmother had said something along the same lines, hadn't she?

"Sounds reasonable," he said. "Right, guys?"

The other three nodded. Miz Brown hadn't said anything else, which was good, because if he got going they'd be here all night. That did not mean he hadn't been listening, though. Mau-Mau had told him that Brown had a tape recorder in his head, which was probably where he got all those words once one of his verbal waterfalls started. Right now, though, there was more important business: the colonel had just ordered a third pitcher of beer. Wong fielded a phone call, smiled, and then had some more beer.

"So how's the War on Terror going these days?" Av asked, just to be sociable.

They sat there drinking beer and indulging in general-purpose BS for the next half hour, and then Wong's current main squeeze made her entrance. She was Chinese, highly made-up, wearing a clingy, gold lamé dress with slits in all the appropriate places, shiny red heels, and a hairdo that looked to be made of black lacquer. Has to be a joke, Av thought—she looked like something out of a Charlie Chan movie. Wong beamed.

It being a Marine bar, the denizens didn't embarrass themselves by making rude noises, as would have been the case in any army bar. Instead, a wave of appreciative silence moved with her as she approached their table and smiled down at Wong. He made a noise that sounded to Av suspiciously like a whimper, which made perfect sense to Av. There was a quick exchange in an unknown dialect, and then Wong rose, excused himself, bowed to the colonel, thanked him for the drinks, and then followed his dragon lady out of the bar, while two dozen grown marines tried not to cry.

Wong's departure seemed to be the signal for the beer muster to close up. Miz Brown said he had to get ready for night school. Mau-Mau followed, saying he had a really hot date lined up.

"What's her name?" Av asked.

Mau-Mau actually looked sheepish. "Her name is takeout," he said. "Haven't decided what kind yet, but the Knicks are on tonight, and, well . . . that's gonna have to do."

Av and the colonel laughed, saluted with their beer glasses, and watched him go.

The colonel poured out the last of the pitcher and then sat back in his chair. "So, Detective, whad'da you think about the situation in general?"

Av considered the question for a moment before answering.

"With all due respect, Colonel," he said, finally, "I think you've been blowing a fair amount of smoke. That in turn makes me think that there is some kind of serious shit going on here in River City."

The colonel's face settled into a disturbingly stark stare. His mouth flattened into a straight line, and his eyes seemed to almost freeze over. Av recognized a game face when he saw one. He thought he heard a marine at a nearby table give out a low "whoa."

"Great minds think alike, Detective Smith," the colonel said, quietly. "Washington is full of people playing games, almost always for personal, financial, or professional advantage. You guys have bumped up against the DMX, which is the sharp end of the counterterrorism spear. Think black widow, okay? Multiple eyes and venom as powerful as a cobra. DMX produces the Kill List, which goes to the President. Once he approves it, the big gray drones leave the Midwest for faraway places and people incandesce in the night. Yes, it's just a committee, but it's unlike ninety-nine point nine percent of Washington committees. This one kills people."

"You said a moment ago that it was just another committee, that they talk but don't actually do anything."

"You're not cleared to know *any* of this, Detective," the colonel said. "So appreciate it and then forget I ever said anything. You were right about being careful, though. Guys like Mandeville take no prisoners. You get the slightest indication that Mandeville or anyone on the DMX for that matter is taking an interest in you, personally, put your papers in and get the fuck outa Dodge."

"Just like that?"

"No, Sergeant. Faster than that."

An hour later Av was ensconced on the rooftop of his building, enjoying a beer and the beginnings of another lovely sunset. Their little séance with the colonel was much on his mind. He couldn't decide if all these encounters—the runners on the towpath, the mysterious Ellen Whiting, the Bureau rat-squad supervisor, and now this cold-eyed colonel—represented nothing more than a bunch of self-serving federal officials trying to protect their respective turfs. Or: perhaps it was something more sinister?

He considered calling each of his brand-new best friends and telling them about the other two. Throw some shit in the game, and maybe that way they'd all get their cloaks and daggers out and go after each other. The Briar Patch solution—move the tarbaby. He decided to pitch that idea at the morning meeting; see what Precious thought of that. He grinned when he imagined her response: what the *fock* are you thinking, you *focking fock*?

The phone rang. The caller ID read "out front now." When he picked up, there was only a dial tone. He went to a front window and looked down at the street. There he saw a white Harley Low Rider parked in front of his gate, and a woman, her helmet in her lap, looking up at him and beckoning. He recognized that face: Ellen Whiting. She was talking to Rue Waltham, of all people. He grabbed his wallet, creds, and his off-duty Glock and then headed downstairs.

Rue passed him on the stairs and gave him a nice smile. Once out front, Ellen complimented him on his choice of tenants and then handed him a white helmet. She waited while he fit it, put it on, and fixed the strap. She was wearing black leather pants, a white T-shirt under a sleeveless leather vest, and black gloves with steel antiroadrash buttons. The Harley's engine was running at idle, encouraged by an occasional throttle bump to let everyone know what brand of bike was present for duty, and then he climbed onto the backseat. She slapped her visor down and he did the same. He looked for handles, thought briefly about her waist, and then found the two grips just in time. He was surprised to hear her voice in the helmet telling him to hang on tight as she U-turned and then goosed the bike up Thirty-third Street, and then right on M Street.

When they got to Wisconsin she turned left and they rumbled up through the residual evening traffic to the National Cathedral. They parked in the almost empty public lot out front since the parking garage was closed. She extracted two coffee smoothies from a saddlebag and handed one to Av. They then walked back into an area called the Bishop's Garden, taking their helmets with them.

She looked different from the other night. No more glam makeup and seductive lips. In fact, she looked scared. And, this evening, no more mass of blond hair. She had close-cropped dark hair. She'd been a platinum blonde the other night. Hairpieces?

"I had a Harley when I was in the Marines," he said. "Didn't get to ride it much, so I finally sold it, for just about as much as I'd paid for it. Got another one a few years after I joined the force. Still have it. Gotta love that sound."

"Foreign travel get in the way?" she asked.

"It was like the recruiters said: Join the Marines. See the world. Meet lots of interesting people. And kill them."

She smiled and sipped her smoothie, but he noticed that her hands were clasped together and her knuckles were medium white. Lady *was* scared of something. He gave the gardens a quick scan, looking for guys in running gear and mirrored glasses.

"So what's the occasion, godmother?" he asked. "Not that I'm complaining. But you look—worried?"

She didn't reply for a moment. "You read about the guy who played bullfighter with the Mercedes over in Georgetown the other night?" she said, finally.

"Happened right in front of me," he said. "Wish I'd been elsewhere."

She stared at him. "You're shitting me."

"Not one pound," he said. "What about him?"

She sighed. "His name was Hilary Logan. He was the assistant secretary of the treasury for international trade. He was also Treasury's rep to the DMX. Do you know what that stands for?"

"In fact, I do," Av said. "Got a tutorial just this afternoon from some guy calling himself Colonel Steele. You know him by any chance? Says he's from Jay-shit or something like that. Fort Bragg, North Carolina."

"Jay-SOC," she said. "Joint Special Operations Command. Military.

Operational headquarters for the snake-eaters. And no, I don't know him, but I'll bet I could describe him to you."

Av smiled. "Yeah," he said. "They do all look kinda alike, don't they. Anyway, he invited all four of us for beer at a Marine dive down near Eighth and I. Then he warned me to watch our collective asses, because whatever's going on involves this darkside committee called DMX. Is that for real, by the way? They order up assassinations and shit?"

"Not exactly," she said. "We—they—"

"Whoa," Av interrupted. "'We'?"

She sighed. "Truth in lending time, I guess," she said. "I am also a member of the DMX. I represent the Bureau."

"Which Bureau?"

She gave him an impatient look. "*The* Bureau, smartass."

"Okay, so not Bureau of Indian Affairs, then. Right. You know a guy named Tyree Miller by any chance?"

She stared at him again. "You do get around, don't you," she said. "Tyree Miller? Not willingly. A tap on the shoulder from Tyree Miller means your day is about to turn to shit. Why?"

"Well," he said. "We had a chat after you took off in that cab." He told her about his little séance in the Bureau car, emphasizing the fact that Miller had implied that she, Ellen Whiting, did *not* work for The Bureau.

She leaned back on the bench and stretched her legs straight out, as if trying to straighten out a cramp. "And you agreed to call him and tell him about any further contact you and I might have?"

"I did," Av said. "What the hell, Ellen Whiting: who am I to tell some senior-looking dude in the Bureau's Professional Standards Division to fuck off? And, oh-by-the-way, ever since our brave little band touched the McGavin tarbaby, I've had encounters with three people claiming to be federal high-poobahs, all either warning me to be careful or wanting to be filled in on any 'developments,' whatever that means."

"Claiming."

"Yeah, claiming—you and Colonel Steele. Miller at least showed me creds, as did the agents with him. Colonel Steele first claimed to be working for State. And you? I have no idea who you work for."

She unzipped a pocket in her leather jacket and produced a credential folder, which she opened for him. Senior Supervisory Special Agent Ellen

Whiting. Shitty picture, but the creds and badge looked real. He also was pretty sure he was seeing the bulge of a compact semiauto outlined in the other pocket of her biker jacket.

"Okay," he said. "So why would Miller even imply that he didn't know who you worked for? And why didn't the guys he had watching us inside the restaurant that night just grab you up and take *you* to see Miller?"

"Because he was being careful, Detective Sergeant," she said. "And, of course he knows who I am and where I stand in the headquarters hierarchy. But you're right about the mystery: why didn't he just call me in if he wanted to know something."

"If they asked about what you're doing at DMX, could you tell them?"

She shook her head. "My boss's boss could," she said. "Whether or not she would is another question altogether. Don't get me wrong: Miller holds a powerful position at Bureau headquarters, but these days, because of the counterterrorism mission, the Bureau is getting more and more compartmented in terms of who knows what. Damn, this *is* getting complicated."

"Complicated makes me thirsty," he said. "Let's go get a drink. Then you can tell me what's going on, or not."

"A public bar is not the place for what I need to tell you," she said.

"This bar is," he said.

Fifteen minutes later they were ensconced in a corner booth of the Ye Olde Fairy Queene, a fern bar on Connecticut Avenue, complete with real ferns and a truly sweet-mannered bartender named Eli. Av had a beer; Ellen Whiting had ordered a ginger ale. When he raised an eyebrow, she told him that Elit vodka and Harleys don't play well together.

Ellen looked around. "This is a—"

"Yes, it is," Av said with a mischievous grin. "It's an old murder police tactic. If you're sensing a tail or some other complication, chances are he or she is going to stand out in a gay bar, right? And Eli over there knows a lot of the gay feds in town, so he'd give me a high sign if you just happen to be part of a tag-team program tonight. So, now—what the *fock* is going on here, please?"

"*'Fock'?*"

"Inside joke. Stop stalling."

She nodded. "Okay. I'm the Bureau's rep on the DMX. I represent the assistant executive director of the Bureau for counterterrorism. The DMX is part of the National Security Council interagency system. Are you familiar with what people call the interagency?"

"Nope," he said. "Sounds like a tarbaby factory, though."

She smiled. "One way of looking at it," she said. "But basically, since national security involves issues which cross many different agencies' remit, the National Security interagency system is a series of groups which meet to sort out courses of action and jurisdictional issues."

"Series?"

"Yeah. 'Layers' is maybe a better word, like in a parfait. It's based on seniority. Say you get two agencies facing a common issue. First the worker bees try to solve it. If that doesn't work, the issue rises through a series of meetings between more senior layers of the bureaucracy until it gets to a level, say deputy secretary, where they get tired of messing with it and make a decision."

"Okay. And if they don't?"

"Then *the* National Security Council itself meets, first without the President, and then, if necessary, with the President."

"And all this takes how long?"

"An entire career can be made and spent working one issue through the NSC Interagency process."

"And this is what you do at this DMX thing?"

"No. DMX *starts* at the principals level. Each agency represented on the DMX committee comes to the meeting with a single name, which that agency is proposing for something called the Kill List. Each rep makes the case for why their 'candidate' merits being elevated to the status of enemy combatant and killed without notice or even due process, say, like the case of an American who's gone over to Al Qaeda."

"Wow," Av said. "And does this committee reach a decision?"

"Sort of. DMX is technically an advisory committee, not an executive committee. They can only nominate candidates for the Kill List to the President, usually one per meeting. The chairman is Carl Mandeville, whose title is special assistant to the President and senior director for counterterrorism on the National Security Council staff."

"Damn," Av said. "Can he say all that in one breath?"

"He makes the final decision on whether or not to put a name forward, based on what he hears at that meeting. If there's any serious push-back on a name, then he'll usually tell the agency that nominated that individual to go back and bolster their arguments for taking him out. If we all agree, yeah, that's a true badass who needs to die, then that's usually how it goes."

Av remembered the name from his conversation with Colonel Steele. "So these meetings aren't usually about turf issues?" he asked.

"Not visibly," she said. "Deciding which agencies were going to get to play on the DMX took a year and a half. Now that was all about turf. No, this is serious shit, and turf wars aren't allowed in the room, although sometimes it feels to me as if agencies are competing to see who can get a name onto the list. We're all professional bureaucrats, so I guess we can't help it even when we're making decisions like this. But it's Mandeville who makes the final call on putting someone in America's crosshairs."

"Colonel Steele said the DMX decides, the President signs, and then the big gray drones leave for faraway places. How do you feel about being part of something like this?"

"When you hear the briefings, say, like when the CIA rep comes in and describes how a certain Paki colonel enjoys capturing Western journalists and personally sawing their heads off with a dull hacksaw while they're tied to a chair? It gets easier with time."

"I can see that," he said. "But the cop in me is so ingrained with defendant protection procedure, you know, Miranda stuff, that I'm not sure *I* could do that. So: why tell me?"

She nodded, then looked around the bar. There were more people there now, but no one seemed to be paying them the slightest bit of attention, not even Eli.

She sighed. "I probably shouldn't have, but you remember I talked about Americans who go over to Al Qaeda or ISIS, guys like Anwar al-Awlaki?"

"Yeah?"

"Cases like that are one of the most sensitive aspects of DMX, because the guy we were looking at is an American. Our Constitution doesn't allow our government to kill its own citizens, at least not without due process."

"Your meetings sound like due process, of a sort, anyway."

"And Awlaki was duly nominated, approved, found, and executed by a drone," she said. "It wasn't that hard a call, really: he looked like Bin Laden, lived in a cave very far from home, and helped the nine-eleven attackers. He fit the profile like a glove. But: lemme give you a what-if."

"Okay."

"What if an American citizen goes over to the enemy, and then comes back to the States clandestinely, for the purposes of conducting terrorist attacks here at home, say, starting forest fires, derailing oil trains, or causing explosions on a gas pipeline? Seen any news stories like that?"

"All of the above," Av said. "But I haven't heard that these were terrorist attacks, just—bad shit happening. What's your real question?"

"If we knew where he was, using whatever assets which are available to the DMX agencies, and they are substantial, could we put his name on the list? And then have a sniper kill him in downtown Cleveland one day?"

"I'd say no. You'd get your Cleveland field office to snatch him up, read him his rights, appoint him a shyster, haul his ass into federal court, and then prosecute him in a death penalty case. You're obviously in a gray area killing people overseas, but here? Talk about some seriously bad optics."

She nodded. "I agree," she said. Then she paused to sweep the barroom again. Av had the clear impression that there was another, even more interesting shoe about to drop.

"Frankly, Detective Sergeant," she said. "I'm getting scared." She took a big breath and blew it out. "There. I've said it. I'm scared."

Av tried to make light of it for a moment. "You? A senior supervisory special agent at the FBI—scared?"

"Listen carefully, Detective Sergeant: I think McGavin and Logan were not random events. I believe they were murdered."

Whoa, Av thought. Time the fuck out. Yes, McGavin's death was possibly poison of some kind—the ME had implied as much. Logan? How could that be a homicide? Suicide, maybe, but—he'd witnessed it. Nobody pushed the dude in front of that car. He stepped out, all on his own.

He studied her face. She was staring down at her ginger ale, her lips tight and her hands even tighter on that glass. He reached out and touched the back of her left hand. She started and then relaxed her grip on the glass.

"Before you break that thing," he said. "So: I'm listening. I assume you have a prime suspect?"

"Yes, I do."

"Before you reveal that to me, understand that I'm duty bound to run with it. Sure that's what you want?"

"I don't know what I want," she said. "Because I'm tangentially involved. I simply don't know what to do, and I *always* know what to do."

"Okay," he said gently. "Start from the beginning. You've told me about the DMX, and I appreciate that that information is highly privileged and needs to be protected. You say you think McGavin and Logan were murdered. By whom?"

"Carl Mandeville, executive director of the DMX."

Av was shocked. This was the guy Steele had warned Av about—leave town if you think he's interested in you. "Holy shit" was all he could manage.

"Amen to that," she said. "I believe that the people he's killing have privately come to the conclusion that the whole concept of the DMX is legally wrong and morally repugnant. There are—were—three of them: McGavin, Logan, and Wheatley. Maybe others, I don't know. Apparently at the behest of certain U.S. senators, they'd begun within their respective agencies to lobby secretly for an internal review of the entire process. Basically, they want to kill the DMX, and they're confident that such a review would do that. Why? Because nobody would be willing to get out on point defending it."

"Okay, and?"

"And, Carl Mandeville is determined to prevent that. Now two of those three persons are dead."

Aw, shit, Av thought, again. Here it is: the mother of all tarbabies, sitting right across the table from him. Suddenly some of this recent hugger-mugger he'd been encountering was starting to make sense. That guy in the mask, for instance.

She sighed again. "And you want to know why I'm telling *you* all this, right?"

"I'm guessing it's because you don't have a rabbi in the Bureau?"

"Did," she replied. "I replaced him on the DMX. He got out on early retirement."

"From the *Bureau*?"

"Let's just say he was encouraged to pack it in."

"Ah," Av said. "Didn't care for the DMX, did he?"

"I wasn't privy to all that. He had a séance with the director one day and the next day we were doing his hail and farewell. I was selected as his successor to the DMX, probably because wiser heads ran like hell when they were asked to do it. I was called in the next morning to the executive deputy director's office, read into the program, and that's all I know. In terms of rank, I'm the least senior rep at the table."

"Are you qualified to be there?"

"I have some credentials in the CT world, Detective," she said stiffly. "I've been around, okay? Mandeville says he actually asked for me, which is bullshit, I suspect. But, yeah, it was a surprise. And now, I just had to talk to somebody."

"Jesus, Ellen," Av said. "I'm not somebody, I'm a fucking nobody. I'm a has-been homicide dick. My previous lieutenant exiled me to the Briar Patch and since then he's been trying to get me fired, as I think you will remember."

She rubbed her left temple with her left hand, as if her head hurt. "I think I'm going crazy," she said.

"Oh, gosh, I wonder why," he said. "Given this alternative universe you work in, where eighty-five different government agencies compete to consign some crazed Muslim bastard to death-by-robot, for bragging rights? Let's see, now: who the hell *would* you talk to?"

"Okay, okay," she said. "Obviously I've strayed a little too far off my reservation. I'll take you back to your man cave now."

He smiled. "In your dreams, Supervisory Special Agent Ellen Whiting," he said, leaning forward. "I'm speaking as the senior representative of the Briar Patch, now, and I must insist: tell me more."

"Senior?"

"Okay, maybe as the *only* representative, present and accounted for? You need some help with a homicide? Maybe the four horsemen of the Briar Patch are just the guys to call."

"You're kidding, right?"

"Not at all," Av said. "That's the good news, Ellen Whiting: no one takes us seriously."

"Clearly. And?"

"Who would see *us* coming."

"Oh."

"Yeah, oh. And congratulations: you've just achieved formal tarbaby status."

"Ducky," she said. "Why don't you get brother Eli over there to fix me a real one."

"No," he said. "Remember your Harley. In the meantime, I'll gather the Briar Patch posse together and we'll kick this around. Putting all the supersecret spooky shit aside, it's a possible homicide. We don't need to know anything about your precious DMX. Give me a contact phone number, then take me back to my place. Then you go home. *Then* get that drink."

She cocked her head. "I must be losing my touch," she said. "Most guys would have said: take me back to my place, come on up, and I'll get you whatever you need. In the way of booze."

He grinned at her. "I'm not most guys," he said. "And, besides, you're still scary. Even scarier, now that I think about it. Jesus, Special Agent."

"Jesus isn't cleared for DMX," she said.

Av rolled his eyes. They finished their drinks and went back outside, both of them looking around for watchers. Seeing nobody obvious, they climbed aboard the bike and headed back down Wisconsin. They'd gone two blocks when a black Mercedes S500 in front of them slowed down for no apparent reason. Ellen slipped the Harley into the next lane to pass, but then had to brake for a red light. The Merc slid alongside a moment later and stopped for the light. Av glanced casually to the right and saw the Halloween mask looking right back at him.

"Hey?" he said into his helmet mike. "Guy on the right is a tail."

Ellen didn't hesitate for a second. She gunned the Harley into the intersection and right across it so fast that Av nearly fell off. She then went down to the next intersection, turned left in front of oncoming traffic and a cacophony of blaring horns, and then sped into a residential area with narrow streets made even narrower by parked cars. She went around several blocks until suddenly they were slanting down a winding road toward the bottom of Rock Creek Park. She pulled into a creekside parking lot and shut the bike down.

"Okay?" she said as she took off her helmet.

"Chee-rist, what a ride," he said, grinning.

"What'd you see?"

He told her about the Halloween mask and the times he'd seen this guy before.

She pursed her lips for a moment and then asked him to describe the man in as much detail as possible. Av did.

She shook her head. "Guy who looks like that?" she said. "Not likely to be a professional surveillance operator—the face is too distinctive."

"I'm thinking that's the point," Av said.

"He wants you to know you're being stalked?"

"Yeah."

"Oka-a-a-y," she said. "And who might want you to think that?"

"You tell me, Special Agent," he said.

"*Supervisory* Special Agent," she reminded him. "And, yes, I think I know who might be doing this." She looked over her shoulder and then screamed: *"Down!"*

Av didn't hesitate—he dropped and rolled as fast as he could down toward the creek as an autoloading shotgun opened up, blasting tree branches and leaves all over him. As soon as he dropped off the bank and into the edges of the creek he pulled his Glock and pointed it up the hill at—nothing. He thought he could hear a powerful V-8 gunning it back up the hill, but there was no sign of a shooter except for a haze of gun smoke drifting down toward the creek.

He looked around for Ellen Whiting. He couldn't see her, but then he heard her cursing from around a sharp bend in the creek. He stood up, wet from the waist down but alive, and crawled up the bank. Ellen stood up some fifteen feet away, looking like a bedraggled wet hen. When the leather vest flopped open he was treated to a spectacular wet T-shirt. She saw him looking and gave him an annoyed look, but he noticed that she didn't close up the vest.

"Friend of yours?" he asked, wiping off the leaves and other debris.

"Friend of *yours,*" she said. "God: what a face."

"So how the fuck did he follow us down here?" Av asked.

"Give me your cell phone," she said. He handed it over.

She punched more buttons than Av knew existed on the phone, then listened.

"Yup," she said. "There's a GPS tracker on your phone. Whither thou goest, he goeth, if he wants to."

Av sat down on a flat boulder and watched the creek flowing by so peacefully it was almost hard to remember the feel of hot steel shot passing far too close to his head as he'd dived over the bank. Then he thought about it: that car had been no more than twenty feet away in the brief, very brief glance he'd had. The guy had had an autoloader, and yet hadn't hit him? He looked over at Ellen, who was watching him work it out.

"That was a warning, I think," he said. "*I* wouldn't have missed at that distance."

"Me, neither," she said.

"Is this Mandeville?" he asked quietly.

"God, I hope not," she said. "Either way, we've gotta get out of here before the cops show up."

"I am the cops," he said.

"Not for this you're not."

TWELVE

Av had been noodling on his brand-new personal tarbaby all morning. Friday had turned into a perfect cluster, with Precious on a tear from the very first hour over some new and preposterous budgetary edict from "upstairs," Wong Daddy getting served with a paternity suit, Mau-Mau getting called into the internal affairs office over an off-duty altercation that had resulted in a civilian being thrown into the Potomac, and Miz Brown announcing that he had truly found Jesus Christ and was going to put his papers in and go to divinity college.

He told Howie that he needed to talk to Precious.

"What about?"

"The mother of all tarbabies?" Av said.

"You right. Don't wanna hear nothin' about it. It's Friday, so, when you get done, we'll be havin' lunch in Chinatown at the Dragon."

Av was waiting when Wong came out, looking appropriately contrite. He knocked on her door and stepped in before she had time to sink her teeth into the next problem.

"Lemme guess," she said, looking up at him over her reading glasses. "Dog ate your homework."

"I wish," Av said. He closed the office door, prompting Precious to give him a look. "That bad, Sergeant?"

"This'll take a few minutes," he began.

When he'd finished, Precious, visibly at a loss for words, began to shake her head.

"And this all goes back to that business with the FPS?" she said.

He nodded. "Apparently they weren't FPS, either. Truth be told, I'm not sure who any of these people are."

"And you probably don't want to know, either," she said. *"Damn!"*

She swung her chair around to look out the window for a minute. Her office had a magnificent view of several large white courthouse buildings across the congested street, which appeared to be littered with cop cars, lawyers conferring in little knots while cadging a quick smoke, and bewildered witnesses trying to figure out which court was theirs.

"Does this alleged supervisory special agent have any *evidence* that this Mandeville dude killed those two people?"

"Evidence?" Av asked. "As in go-to-a-grand-jury evidence? I don't think so. She's convinced that he used her somehow to ice McGavin, and the second one, Logan, is just too much of a coincidence in her mind."

"Dear God, Sergeant. The National Security Council? That is so far above our pay grade as to lack breathable oxygen. Why did she come to you?"

"Metro caught the McGavin incident," he reminded her. "Second District handed it off to ILB. Mau-Mau and I zigged instead of zagging, thereby planting both feet in it. Ultimately, we succeeded in handing it off to the Bureau, or so I thought."

She nodded her head vigorously. "And that's what we're gonna do again," she declared. "And right now, too."

She reached for the phone, then hesitated.

"Yeah, that's the problem, isn't it," Av said. "Who you gonna call . . . ?"

She chewed on her lower lip as she thought about that. "And this shooter down in Rock Creek?" she asked.

"A messenger," Av said. "As in, somebody with assets wants me, or more likely MPD, out of this business."

"What'd your special agent friend think?"

"*Supervisory* special agent," Av said. "She's scared. She thinks Mandeville is the boogeyman here. But—"

Then he had an idea. Tyree Miller. He told Precious. She wasn't so sure. "Professional Standards is the rat squad on steroids," she said. "You reach out to them and you are reaching into a basket of serious snakes."

"Yeah," Av replied. "But he asked me to call him if there were any developments regarding Ellen Whiting. I believe this shit qualifies."

"If he's Bureau and she's Bureau, why doesn't he just call *her* in?"

"Funny you should ask that," he said. "He said that he wasn't positive that she *was* Bureau."

"Oh, c'mon," Precious said. "That has to be bullshit."

"Or—she's not, really," Av pointed out.

Precious threw up her hands. "Too many mysteries here, Sergeant," she said. "Much too murky for me, and much too federal. The bureaucrat in me is inclined to just do the armadillo."

"And if the third 'traitor' dies under ambiguous circumstances while we were busy pretending we knew nothing about what's going on?"

"How could we prevent *anything* that's going on behind the federal iron curtain in this town?" she asked. "That's why Upstairs stood up ILB in the first place, because everyday cops can't do business with all these CT people. How could we even start to mess with this?"

"Simple," he said. "First, warn the third guy that he's in someone's crosshairs. Anonymously, if we have to. Then get Second District to open a homicide investigation on McGavin. OCME thinks aconitine, and that's a poison. Verify that's what killed him at that restaurant. Determine that it was a homicide, and then, you know, we run it."

"As I've explained countless times, Sergeant, we do not—"

"Yeah, yeah, I know," he said, cutting her off. "Not ILB 'we.' You take it to the Investigative Services Division chief. Let our bosses talk to Bureau bosses. Encourage them to reaffirm that this does *not* involve Metro PD, or, regrettably, we'll have to direct one of the districts to open a homicide case. That should move it, right there."

"Let me ask you something," Precious said. "You personally involved with this Ellen Whiting person?"

"Not on your life," he said. "She's very attractive but more than a little scary for my tastes. How many senior FBI agents ride a damn Harley?"

"Okay, but she seems to keep appearing in your life, doesn't she."

"I know, but last night in the bar? She seemed genuinely scared. She doesn't have a rabbi anymore—guy retired—and she wanted help."

"And you agreed?"

"I told her I'd think about it. She's gotta know I'd bring it to my boss. Maybe that's what she really wanted. I don't know. But if any of this is true, and we do have two dead guys now, this has to go uptown to the Bureau."

"Got that right," she muttered. She looked out the window again. "What you gonna do, you see this Halloween guy again?"

"Open fire?" he said.

"Assuming you see him the next time," she said.

"Gonna be looking now, boss," he said.

"Okay. Keep this to yourself, and that includes the inmates out there. I'm gonna think, then I'm gonna make some calls. You may be right about how to approach this."

"Wonders never cease," he said.

"Don't push it," she said. "Now: out."

Av caught up with the other inmates at the Dragon Palace twenty minutes later. The Dragon was a four-story brownstone in Washington's diminutive Chinatown, decorated fantastically with all the requisite good-luck symbology. The first floor was a typical tourist-trap Chinese buffet, with identifiable foods swimming in aromatic if greasy steam pans. The second floor was for regulars, mostly cops and the working stiffs from the courthouses, with the occasional judge sometimes gracing the premises. The center of the second-floor room was the food service area, while private booths with ornate but discreet screens surrounded the room on three sides. A carpeted stairway led from the tourist buffet area to the second floor. A bright red door led to another stairway to the upper floors. The kitchens were down in the basement. Av had heard that the third and fourth floors offered even more privacy if the customers' objectives went beyond lunch, although he had never verified that rumor with Wong, who would know.

Miz Brown stuck his head out of one of the screened booths and waved him over.

"My man," declared Mau-Mau. "Give it up."

"Can I get some chow first?"

"No," Wong said.

"Mercy, yo," Av said. "At least a beer?"

Mau-Mau stuck his hand out of the screen and waved an empty beer bottle. A cold one appeared in fifteen seconds. Av asked for some food. The young Chinese waiter smiled, bowed, and darted away. Av thought maybe he should have specified what kind of food he wanted.

"Well," he said. "Like I told brother Mau-Mau, here, this thing is a potential motherfucker. Even got Precious upset."

"You know what you are?" Mau-Mau asked. "You are a genu-wine shit-magnet. You been here, what, two weeks? And we all got this bad feeling that the big black bird of Upstairs is about to lift its tail feathers on our heads."

"That's certainly possible," Av said, deciding to ignore Precious's orders. "I guess I need to fill you in."

Ten minutes later, there was a profound silence at the table. The waiter had returned with a plate of fragrant *things* for Av, who fell to with enthusiasm while the others digested his story. Finally Mau-Mau spoke.

"The National fucking Security Council?" he began.

"That a big deal?" Wong asked, spearing an entire egg roll.

"Oh, yeah, brother Wong, that's a big deal," Mau-Mau said. "Talkin' serious federal juice, okay? Miz Brown, how's that retirement package shapin' up? Is it hard? Can maybe I do it, too?"

Miz Brown beamed and said it wasn't hard at all. He offered to explain, but all three of them immediately put up their hands. At that moment, the screen was pulled aside by a different waiter. The inmates turned as one. A striking woman was standing there, displaying her Bureau credentials. "May I join this conversation?" she said. "Before you guys get any deeper into a certain minefield?"

"Gentlemen," Av said. "Let me introduce Supervisory Special Agent Ellen Whiting, of the First Team."

"You married?" Wong asked.

Everybody grinned, including Ellen as she sat down. "Would it matter, Detective?" she said with a smile. "But no, I'm not. Thank you for asking."

"Are we in some kinda trouble?" Mau-Mau asked.

"I'm not sure," she said. "Sergeant Smith, you said you had met Tyree Miller?"

"Right," Av said. "After you and I had our dinner date. He blew some serious smoke up my ass. Said he wasn't sure you even worked for them. Did he lie?"

"Oh, yes, he did," Ellen said. "His office called me this morning. Said we needed to talk. Made an appointment for noon. Can you imagine why?"

"Yes, I can," Av said. "I went to my boss this morning. Told her what you told me. Mentioned Mister Miller by name. I'm guessing she took it up the line, and somebody Upstairs dropped a dime." He paused for a moment. "But, wait—that just happened. Like twenty minutes ago."

"Which should mean that that's *not* why they want to see me," she said.

Av looked pointedly at his watch. "Since you're here and not there, I take it you blew them off?" he asked. They all looked at her approvingly.

"I called Miller's office at ten, told them something had come up and I needed to reschedule to two o'clock. They said fine. I asked what the meeting was about. The guy I talked to told me it concerned my clandestine meetings with a Metro PD cop in odd places, such as his pad in the middle of the night and then at a gay bar down the street from the National Cathedral."

Aw, shit, Av thought. They had *both* had tails on them. "And what'd you say to that?" he asked.

"That we were in lu-u-v," she said brightly. "What else?"

"You went to a gay bar?" Wong asked, looking at Av. "With *her*?"

"What's this minefield you're talkin' about?" Mau-Mau asked. "Me and my pension want to know."

"One thing at a time, guys," Ellen said. "Sergeant Smith, what do you think your boss will do with what you told her?"

Av told her what he'd recommended.

Ellen closed her eyes for a moment. "Okay," she said. "Today's Friday. How fast will your chief of investigative services react to this situation?"

"*Our* chief of D's?" Wong said. "Fast?"

Av grinned. "I don't know," he said. "I don't think Lieutenant Johnson knows, either. Upstairs might just try to hush the thing up—wait to see what, if anything, happens. Or, more likely, he'll go wailing to the chief, herself, and get her to call someone in the Bureau. How did you find us here?"

"I called ILB, asked one of the secretaries. She said you guys usually came here on Fridays, so I gave it a try."

"Bring your watchers with you?" Av asked.

Ellen sighed. "Probably," she said. "But it's not like they had to try very hard."

"Uh-oh." Mau-Mau groaned.

"Meaning, if we are interested in someone's whereabouts, we have the means to track that someone right down to a gnat's ass." She turned to Av. "Remember to bring your phone today? Or, how'd you guys pay for lunch? Credit card, by any chance?"

Three worried nods.

Ellen shrugged. "There you go," she said. "But, look: despite what happened yesterday, I think there's a much bigger problem here in River City."

"And what is that?" Mau-Mau asked.

"As I told Sergeant Smith, I believe that some officials who disagree with the whole concept of the DMX committee are being killed to shut them up."

The other three inmates looked at Av with expressions that said: so it was true, what he'd been telling them.

"You still believe that Mandeville is behind those two deaths?" Av asked.

"Yes, I do."

"So the minefield you're talking about is the fact that we now know what you know. And that could be some dangerous knowledge."

"Oh, Lord," Howie said. "We're all going down."

Nobody had an answer to that dire prediction. Finally, Ellen spoke up. "There's someone I think can help us," she said. "A civilian. I think I need to go see him."

At that moment two tiny hands pulled aside the privacy screen. An elderly Chinese lady stood there, her face a study in wrinkle-art. "Black Suburbans," she announced to the four cops. "Suits. Matrix sunglasses. Looking for missy, here, I think."

"Oh, shit," Ellen said. "I need to avoid this."

"Mary Soo," Mau-Mau said. "This lady needs a way out. Third floor open?"

"Red door, right over there," she said. "Missy come with me."

Miz Brown and Mau-Mau stood up when Ellen did. "Want some company?" Mau-Mau asked. "He's about to retire and I'm thinking hard on it."

"Yeah, you guys get gone," Av said. "Wong, you should probably go, too. I think I can handle this by myself."

"Fuck that noise," Wong said. "Not done with these egg rolls."

Mary Soo rattled off some lightning-fast Chinese to the waitstaff, and then led the three escapees through the red door. Av heard the lock click when it closed. Two waiters hurried over and cleared the two empty place settings from the table, and then drew the screens closed down to just a crack. A minute later, Av watched three large men come up the big stairway from the buffet room below. One of them conferred with the waitstaff and then they approached Av's booth. A waiter ran over, bowed, and drew the screens open. Wong cocked his head to one side.

"You guys like egg rolls?" he asked. "We got extra."

THIRTEEN

Hiram Walker got up out of his "throne" chair when the young lady was shown into the library. He smiled inwardly at her efforts to control her expression: he was almost a foot and half taller than she was. He positively loomed over her as they shook hands. He hoped his joints weren't creaking too loud.

"Special Agent Whiting," he said. "I'm Hiram Walker. Please, do sit down."

The call had come two hours ago. According to Thomas, a Special Agent Ellen Whiting had wanted to speak to Hiram Walker concerning an ongoing project in the Bureau laboratory regarding obscure botanical toxins. Thomas had asked for her number and said he would forward her request. Then he had spoken with Hiram's friend in the Bureau's lab, who'd checked the building directory and phone book, and confirmed that she was a supervisory special agent in the counterterrorism division. He had then called the lab and asked for her by name. They drew a blank. So she was an FBI agent, but evidently did not work in the laboratory division. Interesting.

Thomas briefed Hiram, who now, armed with this knowledge, watched her arrive in front of the house on the library's closed-circuit television. She was driving what looked like an official government car, complete with several antennae and the requisite tinted windows. Thomas had gone out to meet her and opened her door. As she went up the stairs, he'd nodded discreetly at the unobtrusive camera mounted near a downspout: the car's interior also looked correct.

She shook his hand firmly and then backed down into a chair. Hiram still hadn't done anything about the furniture, so only her medium-high heels touched the rug. Hiram realized that he was probably never going to adjust the furniture. As long as people looked at him as if he was some kind of freak, then they could endure freak-sized furniture. After all, he told himself, he hadn't called her. She had called him.

"Mister Walker, I don't actually work in the Bureau's laboratory," she said straightaway, presenting her FBI credentials. "I work in one of the Bureau's counterterrorism offices. I reached out to someone I know in the lab to see if they had any properly cleared experts here in the Washington area who might be able to help us with a problem. Your name came up, along with something called the Phaedo Society?"

"What kind of problem?" Hiram asked, casually studying her. She was wearing a conservative pantsuit, practical shoes, minimal makeup, and a businesslike hairdo, and, yet, she still managed to convey an aura of latent sexuality. She had gray-green-blue—he couldn't quite tell—eyes, which she was hiding behind some birth-control glasses. His experience with women was sparse, but for some reason, this one excited him, even though, right now, anyway, she was all business.

"Do you—" She stopped and took a breath. "Do you know anything about the program that the U.S. government uses to attrite the leadership of the major terrorist groups around the world?"

He smiled. "You're in luck, Special Agent. May I assume we're talking about the DMX?"

He'd surprised her; he was certain of it—her widening eyes gave it away. "Yes," she said. "But—"

He put up a hand. "Let's just stipulate that I know enough about the DMX to guess that you're not here to talk about a Bureau lab project. You're here because of two recent and fairly puzzling deaths down in the city. From what I've read in the press, those two officials were senior enough to have been appointed to the DMX, especially since people in their respective agencies were rather vague about what Logan and McGavin did—or did not do—within their respective agencies. And, from further reading and perhaps a few discreet inquiries to some people *I* know in the government, how and why these two gentlemen died is perplexing some of the best forensic pathologists in town. How'm I doing, Special Agent?"

"Holy crap," she said. "Much too well."

The antique clock up on the fireplace mantel chimed five times. Hiram beamed.

"Five o'clock," he said. "I usually have a wee dram of single-malt at five o'clock. Not supposed to, of course, but I find it's just plain necessary. May I offer you something, even if you are on duty?"

"Yes, please," she said. "I'm partial to the Macallan, straight up."

"I'm sure we can oblige," Hiram said, as he pushed the call bell under the chair's arm. A moment later Thomas appeared.

"Two Macallans, please, Thomas. Straight up, as usual. And perhaps a footstool?"

"Right away, sir," Thomas said.

He returned in three minutes with the drinks and a small, carpeted footstool for Ellen's aching legs.

"My friend at the lab said you had Marfan syndrome," she said. "Didn't they think Abraham Lincoln was afflicted with that, too?"

"Not anymore," Hiram said. "But yes, I've looked like this since about sixteen. It's a genetically driven disease of the connective tissue—joints, principally, but it also compromises the aorta, leading to an aneurysm or a simple dissection. I'm fifty-five, which is a long life for Marfan. Hence my secluded lifestyle."

"And you're from the Washington area?"

"Heavens, no. Delaware. My father's estate borders the old DuPont place. My mother had me somewhat late in life. They are both gone now. The Delaware estate is part of the conservancy now, because of the gardens."

"Did you go to public—no, I guess private schools, growing up?"

"No, I'm afraid not," he said. "The unusual height came on pretty early, along with difficulties in walking and general getting around. My father let me go out for Halloween just once. We drove to the nearest suburban neighborhood. Unfortunately my appearance cleared the streets of both children and adults."

She grinned at the thought. "Full monster gear? Stitches and everything?"

"Dr. Frankenstein would have been so proud," he said with a smile. "But the police came, and after that, I became something of a permanent recluse. Fortunately I was born into a rich family, so I could be 'hidden away,' as it were, in high style."

"This *is* a beautiful house," she said, looking around at the library furnishings. Everything gleamed softly, indicating real walnut paneling, solid brass accouterments, and the kind of oriental rugs that belonged on the wall, not the floors. "But don't you ever get, I don't know, lonely?" She raised a hand to her mouth. "I'm sorry—that's—"

He waved it off and smiled at her. "Of course," he said, quietly. "But ever since I entered my gold-plated cloister, I've had everything I wanted brought to me. If you have enough wealth behind you, that's not very hard to accomplish, when you think about it."

He went on to tell her about his education at the hands of a small army of tutors over the years, from secondary school right through to what would have qualified him for a graduate degree had he chosen to pursue the piece of paper.

"I'm a bit of a ghost," he said. "I don't drive, I don't have a social security number, I don't have a listed telephone number, and I don't file tax returns, because I have no income. I'm the sole ward of an enormous trust fund whose only purpose is to provide for whatever I need. Or want. My father invented the compound that keeps automatic transmissions from frothing their oil at high speeds, you see, and licensed that patent for one dollar—for every automatic automobile transmission ever made, anywhere."

"Good God," she said. "That *would* be huge. And yet you seem to know what's going on downtown, as if you like to keep your hand in."

He nodded. "Washington is the most fascinating city in the world, in my opinion, so I watch. Given the resources I have at hand, I can really watch. I think I've discovered the underlying theory of a capital city."

"What's that?"

"That the people with power have a basic, unquenchable need to make it known that they, indeed, have power. So they talk. They boast. They posture. They whisper into unreliable ears at Georgetown dinner parties. Given today's technology, none of that remains a secret for more than, oh, about two minutes."

"So," she said. "You're a watcher, but not a player?"

Her eyes had become appraising. He realized she obviously thought that *she* was a player.

"Um, not always," he said. "I hear things. I make inquiries. Then I know things. People find that out, I can sometimes be a player. God knows, I have the time. Fact is, though, my time is really devoted to the study of plants."

She smiled, and those chameleon eyes lit up. Hiram thought it was a delight to see. "Tell me," she said, quietly, enjoying her Scotch.

"I took up the study of plants thirty years ago, when I became sort of a houseplant myself. The family estate was not huge, much as Delaware isn't huge. But the gardens were amazing. Even as a child, I understood that an afternoon walk among all that was a special privilege. Since the estate's walls were my horizon, I got involved. Nowadays, my personal research is focused on the way plants defend themselves from predation, which can include animals, herbicides, machines, or even other plants. Do you own a home, Special Agent?"

"Not me," she said. "I'm an urban cave dweller. But my father was a serious hobby gardener, so I know all about his war on weeds."

"Just so," Hiram said. "So-called weeds, in particular, fascinate me."

"So-called?"

"Weeds," he said. "The gardener's name for those plants that he did not intend to grow. But they're plants, just like the ones your father *was* trying to grow. They're amazing. They're masters of symbiosis. They've learned how to take advantage of all that watering and fertilizing just as much as the desirable plants do, and: guess what? They've evolved the ability to hitch a ride on that unnatural gravy train, some of them in quite amazing ways, such as sending out side roots for surprising distances in order to steal nutrients. A clump of weeds five feet away from your father's prized row of tomatoes might be feeding on what he was feeding the tomatoes."

He stopped. He'd been lecturing. That wasn't why she was here. "Forgive me, I find all of this fascinating. You probably do not. You're here to inquire about toxins, aren't you?"

"I'm not sure," she said. "'Poison' was the word I had in mind. But here's the thing: I was present for the death of Frank McGavin."

That surprised him. At the same time he felt a sudden jolt of recognition. Strang, he thought. That fucking Strang. He'd eventually told Strang no, but then Strang had sicced his boss on him, and Carl Mandeville was nothing if not persuasive. Now he definitely wanted to hear this. "Do you know a man named Kyle Strang?" he asked. "He supposedly works at the Bureau."

"No," she said. "I don't know the name, but let me check." She pulled a tablet computer out of her oversized bag, clicked some keys, and then shook her head. "If I were on my secure computer in the office I could probably find him, but the government phone directory for the Bureau doesn't show a Kyle Strang."

It was getting dark outside. He wanted her to stay, but that was impossible. In an hour or so, he would turn into a limp and very weary human replicant.

"Look," he said. "I think I have much to tell you, depending on the answer to one final question, if you will be so kind. Then you must come back."

"Of course," she said, visibly intrigued. "What?"

"Did what happened to Mister McGavin involve flowers, by any chance?"

Her face paled. "Yes, it might have," she said. "A vendor came in, selling flowers for the tables. I bought a bouquet for our table right before McGavin went down," she said.

He nodded. "Let's make a deal, my dear. I'll tell you how, if you'll tell me who."

"No problem," she said. "I think I already know who. But I am desperate to hear how."

Thomas had appeared in the doorway with a tray of what looked like meds. Ellen understood and stood up.

"Tomorrow?" she asked. "Or whenever you're able? This is important, Mister Walker. I think there's another—incident—planned. I'd like to stop it."

"Tomorrow, then," he said. "Nine, if you can. Mornings are better for me, as you can probably see."

"Nine it is," she said. "And thank you, sir."

"Don't thank me yet, Special Agent," Hiram said. "I may have had an unwitting hand in that 'how.' "

"Trust me, Mister Walker," she said. "I know the feeling."

Mandeville had Strang on a secure call. "Jungle drums," he said. "Are telling me the Bureau has taken on the Logan accident?"

"I'll check that out," Strang said. "But why?"

"Where is Ellen Whiting?"

"I have no idea," Strang said. "I can probably find that out, too, but—"

"No," Mandeville interrupted. "No. I'm going with your idea. I've set in motion a domestic rendition for that Metro cop. Petersburg. What I need to know from you is whether or not the Bureau's involvement in Logan was precipitated by Ellen Whiting. Can you do that?"

"It's Friday night," Strang said. "I can sniff around over the weekend, but the major players won't be there."

"Do what you can," Mandeville said. "This is important. And if it helps, I've got the Bureau's Professional Standards people doing the grab."

"Tyree Miller?"

"Yes."

"That's a pretty closed-mouth group," Strang said. "But I'll work it. I can't be too obvious about it, though, given my cover."

"I understand," Mandeville said. "For what it's worth, I've set in motion a real rendition for this cop, but for right now, I need him sanitized."

"I understand," Strang said. "I'll work it."

"Yes, please do."

Mandeville broke the secure connection. Ellen, he thought, his fingertips drumming lightly on his desk. I was going to make you my protégée. Have you joined them? That was why he was going to snatch the Metro cop. If everything quieted down, he would have his answer about whether or not Ellen Whiting was keeping her part of their bargain. If everything did *not* quiet down, then his next course of action would become clear. And necessary, too.

Then he remembered: he needed to switch off Evangelino, for the moment, anyway. That was the good thing about having someone like that at your beck and call—you never needed to explain anything to him. And, best of all, he never argued with you.

FOURTEEN

It was definitely a Friday night in Georgetown, as evidenced by the rumble of traffic up on M Street. Av sat in his deck chair up on the roof and savored the beautiful fall evening. He could just barely hear the splash of the small waterfall coming out of the canal lock out front. The canal was running high after thunderstorms the night before. He'd gone for a run, showered, and then changed into formal rooftop attire: jeans and a long-sleeved T-shirt.

The restaurant encounter with the feds had been of the short but not-so-sweet variety. They'd asked where Ellen Whiting was. Av and Wong had played dumb. One of the agents said that they'd seen her come into the Dragon Palace. Av had said, good for you, but what's that got to do with us? The lead agent asked Av to confirm that he was indeed Sergeant Smith of the MPD's ILB. Av had nodded. The three feds stared at him for a moment, as if trying to decide whether or not to apprehend him in place of Ellen Whiting.

"So it's your statement that Supervisory Special Agent Whiting is *not* here somewhere in this restaurant?" the lead agent said.

Av shrugged, as did Wong, who now looked like a giant chipmunk with an entire egg roll sideways in his mouth.

"What's upstairs?" another of the agents asked.

"Don't know," Av said. "Downstairs is for tourists, this floor for regulars, who are mostly courthouse snuffies or LE. Upstairs they probably don't speak English. Can we see some creds?"

The lead agent produced Bureau credentials while the other two continued to stare down at the two cops.

"Thank you," Av had said. "Are we done here?"

"For now," the lead agent said. "We'll probably meet again."

"Hot damn," Wong had said, sucking loudly on his cup of tea, and staring meaningfully at the smallest of the agents.

When the dynamic duo had gone back to the office, Mau-Mau and Miz Brown were not in evidence, and neither was Precious. The two detectives were reportedly up in the personnel office. The usually omniscient secretaries had no idea where Precious was. Av thought that maybe she'd sensibly just taken the rest of the day off, promising herself to climb the bureaucratic mountain on Monday with the tarbaby from hell. That would be a much better day than a Friday, when all conscientious civil servants turned off their phones by three o'clock at the very latest.

He'd stopped by the wine store on the way home and bought some more of that expensive red. He was determined not to be defeated this time. The trick with red was to go slow, he told himself, and now that he'd had two glasses, he was much less worried about headaches.

Ellen Whiting, however, had the makings of a headache. Supervisory special agent. Senior enough and sufficiently connected to have been sent to the DMX in place of an assistant director. Where was she now? Had she gone back to the Hoover building for that meeting with Tyree Miller's boss? Did FBI agents ever take it on the lam? And then there was Precious, out of the office on undisclosed business. Mau-Mau and Miz Brown, the two retirement-eligible members of ILB, were worried about their pensions and starting paperwork.

So why am I worried? he thought. If some superspook's gone rogue and taken some extreme, unilateral action, that has to be a problem for federal LE, not Metro PD, which was, as Precious kept reminding him, well out of it. Except: the thirty-something hottie possibly masquerading as a special agent kept trying to involve him in this mess. Was any of this shit even true? Or was he worried because the two most experienced inmates at ILB were alarmed enough to put their papers in?

As he considered having a third glass of red, he thought he heard car doors opening and then closing out on Thirty-third Street, and then the same sounds from the back of his building, down in the narrow alley. When he realized he could no longer hear traffic on Thirty-third Street, he got up from his chair to take a look. He saw blue strobe lights reflected on building façades across the street. He wanted to look over the rooftop parapet wall, but something made him hesitate.

What. The. Phuque, over? The sounds and lights had all the earmarks of a building being surrounded by a tactical team. Not a building—*his* building. He hurried down the stairs into his loft apartment and went over to the curtained windows. Sure enough, the street below was filled with SUVs and other federal-looking vehicles. There was even an MPD squad car up at the corner of Thirty-third and Cady's Alley, blocking the right lane. There was another one on the other side of the arched bridge over the canal. Then he heard heavy footsteps coming up the interior stairs. Uh-oh, he thought. Goon squad, inbound.

They did have the courtesy to knock, as opposed to breaking down the door with a SWAT master key. He went to the door and opened it. The stairwell was filled with federal agents, all wearing windbreakers with their agency logos and identifying letters stitched into the fabric. It was an eclectic group: FBI, DHS, and ATF, of all people, and lots of guns, of course.

"Detective Sergeant Kenneth Smith?" asked the man standing in the doorway. He was huge, sumo-huge, and he was standing there with his hand on a holstered Glock.

"That's me," Av said. "How can I help you?"

"We have a warrant for your apprehension," the big guy said. "Will you come quietly?"

"Do I have a choice?" Av said. "And can I see the warrant?"

"In the car you can," the FBI agent standing behind the big man said. Av recognized him from the Dragon Palace. The agent gave him a cold smile when he saw recognition dawn in Av's eyes.

"Okay," Av said. "Perp-walk or just a come-along?"

"Just a come-along," said yet another voice standing farther down the stairwell. Av recognized Tyree Miller. "We also have a search warrant for your premises here. Are there any explosives or other dangerous materials in this building?"

"Not in my apartment," Av said, as the realization that he was about to be taken away by federal agents sank in. "Can't speak for the renters on the second floor or Mr. Kardashian's store, though."

"You have any weapons on you?" the big man asked, eyeing Av's wine-time outfit.

"Nope. I don't carry in the peace and security of my own home."

"Okay, let's go," said the big man, stepping in and putting a huge paw on Av's upper left arm. Av knew better than to offer resistance. Guys like this went through life hoping and praying that someone would resist so they could throw them down the stairs.

Tyree Miller fell in behind Av as they went down the stairwell. "You could have just called," Av said over his shoulder to Tyree.

"Yeah, but we like our drama," Tyree said. "Shows the taxpayers that their Bureau is on the job."

"So what's the beef?" Av asked as they approached the front door.

"Later, in my office," Tyree said. "For now just be nice, okay?"

The initial interview was held in Tyree Miller's office, with Tyree presiding and with three other agents present, one of whom Mirandized Av and then had him sign a form indicating that he understood his rights under the law. Av thought that Tyree's office was rather small, but then realized that the office reflected Tyree's mission more than his importance. Nobody liked the rat squad.

"As a serving police officer, I do understand my rights," Av said, as he signed his name. "But not why I'm here. Anyone going to clarify that for me?"

"Yes," Tyree said, handing Av a second piece of paper. "Here's the warrant, signed by Judge Ellerton-Smith. She sits on the FISA court. Know what that is, Sergeant?"

"I do," Av said. "That's the federal court that doesn't have to abide by the Constitution."

Tyree frowned. "And you went to law school where, Sergeant?"

"University of Snowden?" Av answered. Tyree grunted. The other agents studied their yellow legal pads, their faces uniformly devoid of expression.

"Be that as it may, Detective Sergeant," Tyree said, slowly, "that warrant specifies that you are suspected of obstructing justice and possibly aiding and abetting the prime suspect in two different homicides, each involving a senior administration official."

"Did someone just allege that?" Av asked. "Or is evidence required before this secret court issues a secret warrant?"

Tyree sat back in his chair. "The government has to present evidence to support probable cause," he said. He slipped on a pair of reading glasses and held up the warrant. "You were involved with both incidents, first as an investigating officer, in the case of McGavin, and, second, as a witness, in the case of Logan. These 'coincidences,' coupled with your association with Special Agent Ellen Whiting, *and* your felonious lying to federal officers when they asked you if she had been present in that restaurant, were sufficient for the court to sign out a warrant for your apprehension and a search warrant for your premises."

"Your people find her in that restaurant, Mister Miller?" Av asked. "Because if you didn't, you're gonna have a tough time making your so-called felony stick."

Tyree looked over his reading glasses at him, his expression clearly hostile.

"We know she went into that restaurant, Sergeant," Tyree said. "My people *watched* her go into that restaurant."

"And your superstar agent asked me if it was my statement that she was not in that restaurant," Av said. "I didn't actually say anything. I just shrugged. Sergeant Bento nodded, too, as I remember. Thinking back on it, I'm willing to bet that she was *not* in that restaurant by the time your ace investigators made it upstairs. That means I was telling the truth. Now: how is that a felony?"

"You deliberately deceived a federal agent, Sergeant. That is a felony."

"Not me," Av said. "Lemme repeat the question—did your people find her in that restaurant?"

There was a full minute of silence in the office. Tyree Miller appeared to be having trouble controlling his temper. He sighed and took off his reading glasses.

When Miller didn't answer, Av asked another question. "And who is this prime suspect I'm supposed to be aiding and abetting? Special Agent Whiting?"

"We're not here to answer your questions, Detective Sergeant Smith,"

Miller said, ignoring said questions. "I personally find it hard to believe that you, as an experienced homicide detective, were directly or even indirectly involved in what happened to those two officials. I do think, however, that you are being used by someone who is far more experienced and cunning than you are. When you deceived my agents in the restaurant, and that's still a felony, Detective Sergeant, I took the opportunity to bring you in for questioning, mostly so you would understand that we are extremely concerned about these two incidents. We, just like most Metro homicide detectives, do not believe in coincidences."

"Or, apparently," Av said, "in due process, the right to be represented by an attorney, and the right to face my accusers in a court of law that conducts its sessions in the light of day and not in some white-tiled basement with blood drains in the floor. I think you have two options: you either charge me or you let me go."

Tyree shook his head. "We don't have to charge you, Sergeant," he said softly. "Or let you go. You have intruded into the world of federal counterterrorism. The CT community plays by very different rules." He leaned forward. "If we want to, we can rendition you to a foreign country, where the rules of evidence and procedure have more to do with vise grips and batteries than lawyers."

"Well, whoopee-goddamn-do," Av said. "Given that threat, from now on you can just call me Mister Miranda."

"You refusing to cooperate with us, Sergeant?" Tyree asked.

"Hell, no, Mister Miller. I'm just gonna remain silent, like that man over there suggested just a few minutes ago."

Tyree said nothing. Then he directed one of the agents to get him a detention order. He then spun his chair to face the windows and closed his eyes.

"Don't be a dumbass," said one of the other agents while they waited. "If you won't *help* us, he's going to put you into a federal prison where you can't *hurt* us. Think about it, Sergeant: who knows where you went tonight? Your loving wife? Your kids? Your parents? Your tenants? Your boss? Those clowns you call your partners?"

Av stared straight ahead. It was full dark outside now. He could see the line of federal buildings out along Pennsylvania Avenue, their granite and marble façades illuminated by spotlights. Somehow the lights made them look bigger, more formidable, like bastions of overwhelming federal power, and these days, too many of them had shooters on the roof, twenty-four seven.

The other agent came back into the office with a form. "Petersburg?" he asked Tyree, who turned his chair back around and nodded.

The agent sat down at the conference table and began to fill out the form. When he was done, he passed it over to Tyree Miller, who read it and signed it.

"You sure, Detective Sergeant?" Tyree asked. "Really, really sure you want to dummy up? For the last time, what were you and Ellen Whiting meeting about?"

"Why don't you ask her?" Av said quietly. "She does work here, doesn't she?"

"Call the marshals," Tyree said. "One for Petersburg."

FIFTEEN

It took three hours to get down to the federal prison complex at Petersburg, Virginia. Av was taken to something called Annex Fourteen, which appeared to be a low-security installation within the outer perimeter of the higher security complex. It was almost midnight by the time he was processed in. The guards who did the in-processing didn't look to Av like the typical corrections officers he was used to seeing. These guys appeared to be fit, young, with buzz-cut haircuts and a military air about them. They were surprisingly polite, always referring to Av as Sergeant Smith. They had him fill out some forms, undergo a more detailed body search, swap his clothes for an orange jumpsuit that actually fit, see a medical technician to answer questions about any medications he was taking or any other medical issues they might need to know about.

Then they escorted him to an office where he was turned over to an older but still military-looking guard, who greeted him politely and told him where to sit. He introduced himself as Master Sergeant Lawson and offered Av a cup of coffee. Av accepted, somewhat confused by the admissions process. He noticed the man had a globe and anchor tattoo on his upper right arm with the motto Semper Fi underneath, just like the one Av had.

"This is not a jail," the master sergeant said. "This is a holding facility. I don't know why the Bureau wants you held and I don't need to know. But I do need to fill you in on how things work here."

"I'm a homicide detective assigned to the Interagency Liaison Bureau of the Metro PD in Washington," Av said. "And *I* don't know why the

Bureau wants me held, either. So I guess we're even. And, yeah, I'd appreciate any gouge."

The master sergeant smiled at the term "gouge." "Saw your ball and crow. Where'd you serve?"

"PacFleet," Av said. "Nothing exciting. Missed Iraq and Afghanistan."

"Good timing," the master sergeant said. "You familiar with the story of Uncle Remus?" he asked.

Av laughed. "Lemme guess: as in, tarbaby?"

"As in tarbaby," the master sergeant said, nodding. "You have managed to grab, and with both hands apparently, the federal counterterrorism tarbaby known as person of interest. That's what your form says, anyway."

"That form signed by a guy named Tyree Miller, in the Bureau's Professional Standards Division?"

The master sergeant glanced down at the form. "No," he said. "The form signed by Assistant Director William Edrington, who runs the counterterrorism division of the Effa-B-Eye. Assistant director—that's pretty high up. Wait—yeah, Miller signed *before* Edrington. So who's Tyree Miller?"

Av blinked. He didn't know what to say. The sergeant saw his confused expression.

"Look, it's late. One of the guards will take you to your room. I think you'll be pleasantly surprised. But first, I need to tell you what the important rules are, what you can do, what you cannot do, where you can go, all that good shit."

"Room?" Av asked.

"Yeah, room. This is the Petersburg Federal Correctional 'campus.' Don't you love that—campus? Anyway, there's everything here from a Camp Fed for white-collar crooks like Bernie Madoff, to a supermax annex for some Hannibal the Cannibal wannabes. After nine-eleven, the government, in its federal wisdom, foresaw the need for a facility where they could detain people who were not yet convicted of any crime, but who were simply 'of interest' to some federal LE outfit, somewhere. Like you."

"Without a whole lot of regard for the Constitution, either."

"Ah, the Constitution. Not much in vogue these days, is it. Anyway, they had one of the motel chains come down here and build one of their motels right here on the 'campus.' Your room is a typical nonsmoking motel room. No sexually deprived roommates, a private bath, television, small refrigerator, windows, curtains, air-conditioning, and heat—the standard-issue cheap motel room. There's a dining room, which is open from 0630 to 1930 daily. It's catered by one of those geezer-heaven cafeterias downtown. You can go to meals or not as you please. They only ask that you tell them in the morning whether or not you're coming for lunch and dinner. There's no reveille. You can sleep in every day except Saturday, which is field day. You remember field day, right?"

"Absolutely."

"Good. Field day here means everyone's up at 0730 and ready to clean their rooms. Otherwise, there's a library room, a weight room, even a small indoor lap pool. You can use what you want, when you want. If you're a smoker, there's a smoking area out behind the building. You a runner?"

"I'm not sure," Av said.

The master sergeant laughed. "Yeah, I guess that can be taken two ways. No, I mean a regular runner, because if you are, you can run with the guard force. They go out every day except Sundays at 0630, rain or shine. Otherwise, like I said, your day is your own. You have to be in your room by 1930 every evening, but you will not be locked in. All exterior doors except mine open to an electrified fence, so, really, there's nowhere to go, thus no need for you to be locked in.

"Now," he said, pausing for emphasis. "There's one hard-and-fast rule, and it's kinda the price of all this easy living while you're in federal custody: you may not speak to any of the other detainees. You can speak to the guards all you want, and they may or may not reply. You can speak to the service staff. But. You. May. Not. Speak. To. Any. Detainee. Is that clear?"

"I guess it is."

"No, no, I need to know that I've made myself clear. Because if you do speak to any other detainee, your living accommodations will change in a heartbeat and not for the better. Trust me on that, okay? Think of yourself as a Benedictine. You will observe the Rule of Silence, and that includes signing, wall-tapping after hours, eyelid-blinking, note-passing—you name it, we know about it. You will be under audio and video surveillance at all times in this facility, even in your own room, even in the head—there are no women here, so that's not a problem. It's kinda like the Garden of Eden, Sergeant: God only gave 'em one rule: don't touch the fucking apple tree. Look what happened. So: do not communicate with any other detainee. Not good morning, good night, or go to hell. Nothing, got it?"

"Got it," Av said. "How about calls or visitors?"

"No calls out; no calls in," the master sergeant said. "No Internet access, either. The only visitors you can expect will be LE."

"How long will I be here?"

"Beats me, Sergeant Smith. Your detention order says indefinite. The record is three years and two months, but that was an unusual case, I'm told. Some detainees are retrieved and taken somewhere else for questioning. They either come back or they don't. Some have gone overseas, for reasons I don't *want* to know about. The population right now is forty-two. You'll make forty-three. Okay—that's enough for tonight. We'll see you at breakfast."

Once in his assigned room Av took a quick tour and then a shower. There was a laundry basket on the bed with clean towels, military-issue underwear, socks, and a second jumpsuit. He'd been wearing sneakers when they picked him up. At the initial in-briefing, he'd been fitted with a pair of desert boots and given a military-style baseball cap. His name had been stenciled on all the linens and both his jumpsuits. They were efficient, he thought.

Or, he realized, they'd known he was coming. How was that possible?

WTF.

He began to wonder if Tyree Miller had been right: Was he being used? And, if so, for what? And the overarching question of the day: by whom?

His marine training took over. When in doubt, get some sleep. He decided to turn in.

SIXTEEN

Ellen Whiting was nothing if not timely. Thomas brought her to the library the next morning at five minutes after nine. Hiram greeted her pleasantly, looking much better than he had the night before. He was wearing wool trousers and a tweed jacket over a plain white shirt, a burgundy ascot, and sporting a small white flower in his lapel. After a quick coffee, he took her out to the gardens. The day was cool and bright, and many of the plants were showing signs that their season was ending. She was wearing a businesslike pantsuit and low-heeled shoes. The air was filled with the scent of vegetation and some of the plants were still bravely trying to bloom. She realized she couldn't identify a single one of them.

Hiram explained that the gardens were laid out concentrically, with the house at the center of all of them.

"It's a bit like what they do at Disney World," he said. "The tourists walk all over the place, unaware that most of the engineering is beneath their feet, like some kind of iceberg. Down there are miles of tunnels big enough for electric golf cars, pumping stations, utility lines, filtration systems, and feeding matrices beneath all the gardens."

"I didn't know that," she said. "But I do remember that all the gardens there were perfect."

"Right," he said. "These don't look perfect, of course, except behind the house, because these are technically weed gardens. They don't know they're weeds, of course, but we do, and between here and the lab is where we do our most interesting business."

"Why weeds?" she asked.

"As I said before, they're the ultimate survivors in the plant kingdom. You're walking in the realm of pure Darwinism out here, Special Agent."

"You said 'we'?"

"I have a gardening staff of twenty-five people, which Thomas oversees for the most part. My research involves three lines of effort: the first is to see what the plants do on their own, the second is to steer their development out here in the gardens through chemistry, basically, and the third is the mutation program, which is restricted to my lab."

"And this is all about toxins and poisons?"

"Not directly," he said. "More like proteins, carbohydrates, sugars, pollen, and some substances which rather defy classification. Lots of biochemistry, but then anything living is all about chemistry, isn't it."

"I was a liberal arts major," she said. "Bio-anything is over my head, I'm afraid. But if these are all weeds, they're the biggest weeds I've ever seen."

"Tall, perhaps, but then we have the ability to present perfect growing conditions if we choose to. You can make roses grow out through snow if you control the environment underground. The rings out closer to the walls have the really big plants, most of which are mutations. I don't let them out of the lab until I've done two things: sterilize them so they can't reproduce, and establish a continuous sampling system to each plant so I know what *they're* up to, chemically speaking."

He went on to explain about the Phaedo Botanical Society, and how they collaborated from time to time, primarily to find ways to channel some of their more interesting discoveries into the worlds of medicine and environmental science. "In our view," he said, "plants are the answer to some of the world's biggest problems, such as clean energy, food production, of course, and pure water. For example, take a Himalayan tree called *Moringa oleifera*. One seed from that tree can purify a liter of muddy water. It's a weed, really, which is just another word for a wild plant."

"What's your ultimate fascination with weeds?" she asked.

"I think that plants have brains," he said. "Not like ours of course, but in the sense that some aggregation of their cells acts like brains. At least that's my theory, and I think weeds are probably the best example of that."

"I can see that," she said. "Our brains could be called just an aggregation of specialized cells, I suppose."

"Each of us in our little botanical society has a pet theory like that," he said. "We collaborate on projects when two or more of those pet theories intersect."

"Would curare be an example of how plants can help us?"

"Yes, it would. A potent poison in some applications, and yet it's used in tiny amounts to supplement general anesthesia. It's a profound muscle relaxant whose effects can be easily reversed. The technical name is tubocurarine chloride, which is isolated from the bark and stems of a South American vine, *Chondodendron tomentosum,* and is the purified form used in medicine. In toxic concentrations, the way the Indians there make it, it brings on respiratory paralysis in wild game, or anything else hit by a curare-tipped arrow."

"Yikes," she said. "Would that grow here, say, in northern Virginia?"

He shrugged. "In an appropriate environment, say inside an environmentally capable greenhouse? Yes. But at the risk of sounding smug, what I'm working with these days has gone a long way beyond curare. Let's go see some of the other gardens."

They spent the next two hours walking through the various plantings, which ranged from what looked like totally natural patches of fairly ugly vegetation to manicured rose gardens lining the large, stepped reflecting pool that led down toward the Potomac River. Then he took her down to the basement laboratory, which looked like every other lab she'd been in. After a brief tour of the lab, they took an elevator up to the back side of the mansion's roof, where a narrow greenhouse extended the full length of the house. From the driveway this had looked like the ridgeline of the roof.

Toward the end, she noticed that he was moving slower, and suggested they go back into the house. He gratefully accepted her suggestion and they took the elevator back to the ground floor. When the elevator door opened, Thomas was standing there, as if he'd been about to set out on a rescue mission. Hiram excused himself for a few minutes, asking Thomas to take her to the sunroom for lunch. As they walked back through the house, she asked Thomas if Mister Walker needed a lot of medications.

"Do you know what Marfan syndrome does?" he asked in reply. "Besides the elongated body and the face-in-a-vise look?"

"Mister Walker mentioned something about the aorta?"

"Got it in one," Thomas said. "Main blood supply right down the middle of the body. If that lets go he'll go down like a felled tree. They've got better drugs now, and he has a cardiologist and a vascular surgeon who come once a month. We have a medical treatment room here in the mansion with whatever machines they need. But basically, he must pace himself and I must pay careful attention to medications. Here we are, miss. You sit there, if you will, please, and he'll be right along."

The sunroom was like an ornate greenhouse at one end of the expansive, column-lined porch along the back of the mansion. Everything was white—the circular table, the wrought-iron chairs, even the framework supporting the eight ornate panels of glass which arched up to a point some sixteen feet above the table. The table was set for two, and the chair she'd been shown to was, to her great relief, normal-sized. The one across from hers was throne-sized, just like the one she'd seen in the library.

She took in the view, the beautiful avenue of trees and flowers laid out alongside the reflecting pool, which descended through a series of small waterfalls almost a thousand feet to the tall trees that lined the riverbank. There was a patch of golf-green-quality grass on the exterior side of the gardens, and then a dense forest beyond that. She wondered if that huge brick wall went all the way around the estate.

"Special Agent," Hiram's voice boomed from behind her. She blinked as he slipped past her to his side of the table. Her head had been level with just above his knees, he was that tall.

"This is really beautiful," she said as he sat down, carefully, she noted.

"That is the blessing of the plant world," he said. "Nurture them, and they produce beauty to the eye and solace for the soul. They produce the air we breathe and the food we eat."

As if on cue, Thomas came through with lunch, two salad plates with more ingredients than Ellen could count. He returned with a bottle of white burgundy, poured out, and then left them alone. Outside, the noonday sky was displaying that special hazy blue that signaled the end of summer.

"To your good health," Hiram toasted, and she lifted her glass. The wine was wonderful. She glanced at the label, which listed Montrachet, among other things.

"This is spectacular," she said.

He smiled. "Wine is not my friend," he said. "But then neither is Marfan, so I tend to balance one against the other. And, of course, it comes from plants."

She smiled and tucked into the salad.

"Tell me about yourself," Hiram said. "Wait, let me rephrase. What's a nice girl like you doing in the FBI?"

She laughed. "I'm a Washingtonian," she said. "Both my parents were schoolteachers here in Fairfax County. I grew up in Herndon, which is one of the not-so-important suburbs. Went to George Mason, got a degree in business management, and then went to work for the Department of Transportation as a cubicle slave."

Hiram smiled. "Must have been pretty boring," he said.

"I didn't end up living at home like some of my classmates did," she said. "The issues were interesting, but I learned pretty quick that the bureaucracy's main focus was on nurturing itself, not solving the issues affecting transportation."

"That's universally true, from what I've observed," he said. "And then?"

"I was dating a guy who was a newbie agent at the Bureau, and he told me that they were desperately trying to recruit and integrate women agents into the major Bureau career fields. I decided to take a shot. Long story short, I ended up in the New York field office, met a young investment banker at a conference, and we got married. That ended, unfortunately, on nine-eleven."

Hiram's eyebrows went up. "And now you sit on a committee that . . ."

"Yes, exactly."

Thomas appeared and refreshed Ellen's wineglass. Hiram raised his empty glass, but Thomas ignored him and put the bottle back down on the table.

"Oh, my," Ellen said, after Thomas left. "Nanny Thomas?"

"He knows, just like I know," Hiram said.

She reached across the table and poured him a small splash. "Live a little," she said.

"That's just the problem," Hiram said with a tired smile.

"Anyway, I've made my way. A career with the Bureau is about competence and conformity, in about equal measure. Hew to the straight and narrow, do your job, do it well, and they'll unfailingly promote you. Screw something up, then things become a lot less certain."

"And you being on the DMX?" he asked. "How'd that happen?"

"My boss got across the breakers with an ADIC—that's an assistant director in charge, one rank level below *the* director. I don't know what it was about, but one day he was gone and they were looking at me to take over one of his duties, which happened to be the DMX."

"Was that a promotion?"

It was her turn to smile. "More like an assignment where the potential for screwing up was significant. DMX was—and still is—controversial. Savvier and more senior career agents probably declined the 'opportunity,' and there I was."

"What do you do when the committee actually meets? In general, I mean—I know it's all superclassified."

"For good reason, Mister Walker. The information we use to make a nomination is derived from sources and methods that need rigorous protection. But to answer your question, we brief and we talk. And talk. Some agencies are into posturing, others are trying to protect themselves, the spooks like to be spooky—it's a *government* committee, Mister Walker. But when we approve a nominee, we're writing his death warrant."

"And Carl Mandeville—what can you tell me about him?"

"He is the special assistant to the President and senior director for counterterrorism on the National Security staff. He works in the EEOB. That's the old executive office building. Nowadays it houses the ceremonial offices of the Vice President and the offices of the National Security Council staff."

"How important is he?" Hiram asked, sipping the last of his wine with visible regret.

"He's a legend in his own mind," Ellen said. "On the other hand, because no one knows exactly what his powers are, people are afraid of him, and he encourages that reaction. He's arrogant, physically imposing, overbearing, and typically about half a mile ahead of anyone trying to go up against him."

"A true mandarin, then," Hiram said.

"Precisely," she replied. "And, I'm pretty sure, a killer, or at least someone who has organized two murders. He's the 'who.' Now: your turn. Please."

Hiram nodded. "In 2011, a man called Kyle Strang approached me." He went on to tell her what Strang had talked about.

"All of that being aimed at having a backup program in case the opponents of DMX shut off the means to execute the Kill List?"

"That's what he said."

She worked on her salad and had some more wine. "The things you handed over—would they account for the way in which these two men died?"

"Can't tell," Hiram said, hedging just a bit. "I don't know how they died."

"Well, let me fill you in on the one I was present for. That was McGavin. We were in a restaurant, we had a sip of wine, I went to the powder room, and when I came back, he was dead on the floor."

"And the flowers?"

"Right, yes. I bought a bouquet of flowers from a vendor who came into the bistro."

"Recognize them?" he asked. "The flowers?"

She thought about that for a minute. "No," she said. "Very pretty, but no, I couldn't tell you what they were, but then again, I don't know anything about flowers, except—very pretty. The only technical term I've heard related to his case was 'aconitine.' "

"Ah," he said, nodding. "And Logan? I read in the papers that he got out of a taxi and just walked directly into oncoming traffic."

"That's all I know. I have a contact in the MPD who actually witnessed it. He said the man looked like a zombie."

"What in the world is a zombie?"

She giggled. "*The Zombie Revolution*? Dead guys walking around and scaring people. Rigid bodies, lurching walk, scarifying faces—oh, shit, I—"

He was laughing now. "Walked right into that one, didn't you," he said.

Ellen realized she was blushing.

"Back to business," he said. "Aconitine is a by-product of the monkshood plant. Extremely poisonous, and known to be so for centuries. The other case, Logan, is more complex. You're describing the effects of what possibly might be a saxitoxin, commonly produced by algae, which are, of course, plants, usually aquatic plants. The best-known vehicle for human attacks are the cyanobacteria, some of which have been implicated in amyotrophic lateral sclerosis/parkinsonism–dementia complex."

"That's a mouthful," she said.

"So to speak," he replied. "Sometimes people eat shellfish, which tend to act as the ocean's filtration system, and then have a reaction which mimics what you've been describing. It can range from a temporary discomfort to outright death. That's why they clear the beach when an algal bloom appears."

"Okay, here's the tough question—did you give Strang anything like that? A bucket of pond scum or something?"

"No," he said. "But I did give him one of my mutations of kelp."

"Kelp?" she said. "As in those big-ass seaweed formations off San Diego?"

"Yup," he said. "Kelp is an alga."

"Holy shit."

"Indeed, but it also means that Mister Strang or his boss has some connection with a certain army laboratory at Fort Detrick, Maryland, known as USAMRIID. It's where the army used to develop biological weapons."

"Good God!" she exclaimed. "I thought we were long out of that horrible business."

"We are," he said. "Now they work on ways to *defend* our troops against bioweapons that the other guys might use, such as our good friends in North Korea, Syria; enchanting places like that."

She sat back in her chair. "I had no idea, and, I guess, I should have."

"The world of toxins is all around us, Special Agent. Consider all those Hollywood lovelies who want fuller lips or a wrinkle-free forehead. What do they use?"

"Botox?"

"Yes, Botox. Otherwise known as botulinum toxin. Think botulism, often synonymous with death by paralysis. You see the problem here?"

"I'm starting to," she said. "Would a toxicologist be able to sniff out one of these saxitoxins?"

"I would," he said. "But not most forensic criminology labs, no. The Bureau's lab, yes, if properly cued. That said, it's not what I do here, Special Agent. These lethal compounds the plants produce are defensive mechanisms. I'm interested in how they develop them and how they mutate them to fit changing circumstances—an increase in animal predation, the onset of drought, humans and their sprays, and so on. Sometimes humans are helping—think Roundup Ready corn seed, for instance. But then there are my beloved weeds, who manage it all on their own."

"So if Mandeville gave him some substance like that, it might not even be detectable?"

"Correct," he said. "Why do you say 'gave him'?"

"Mandeville had dinner with Logan an hour or so before he did the zombie-walk into traffic."

"Hmmm," Hiram said. "Then here's what I would suggest, Special Agent: focus on Mister Strang and the nature of his relationship with Mister Mandeville, and possibly the USAMRIID. And, secondly, test Mister Logan's cellular remains for chlorophyll."

"Chlorophyll? Seriously?"

"Yes. It's basically all an alga does—turn sunlight into 'stuff,' using chlorophyll, like just about all plants. It does not belong in human cells, but a saxitoxin can put it there. In the meantime, I need to do some research of my own."

"Would these substances be something you could keep, say, at home in your refrigerator?"

"No," he said. "What I gave them was the individual toxin and the instructions on how to maintain it. That would take a biolab of some size and complexity."

"Like USAMRIID?"

"Yes, that would be perfect. And, of course, your Mister Mandeville would probably have access to the scientists at Fort Detrick. I'm not saying they're making bioweapons out there, Special Agent. It's just that the process of developing a defense against chemical and biological weapons is to, first, reproduce or at least model the weapon. See?"

She nodded as Thomas appeared on the porch, which she realized was her cue to leave. She thanked him for the tour, lunch, and the frightening education.

He smiled that rueful smile. "We'll probably be in touch, Special Agent," he said, not getting up. "And please understand something: if someone at the rank and position of a Carl Mandeville has gained access to things like an aconitine aerosol, he can do a lot more damage than one man at a time, okay? Watch yourself."

After his afternoon nap, Hiram went back to the library and reread the *Washington Post* article about the assistant secretary of the treasury's bizarre accident. He was still tired after his day with the pretty special agent. Yesterday, he'd spent the entire day trying to figure out why a very special crossbred specimen had simply "up and died," as his greenhouse helpers quaintly phrased it. He was wondering if another one of his weeds had killed it. They did that, from time to time, as if to remind him that there was a lot he didn't know. It often gave him the sense that they were watching him about as much as he was watching them.

The article reported that the police were still investigating, of course, and that there was a possibility that alcohol may have been a factor. Revealingly, the driver of the Mercedes had not been charged and nor had the cabdriver. The latter had testified that his passenger had asked him to stop the cab, then opened the door, got out of the cab, and then walked directly into traffic. Then he'd added two interesting details—that the victim was walking like "some kind of robot" and that he appeared to be grinning dramatically as he got out of the cab. Confirmation of what the pretty FBI agent had told him.

The article also mentioned that Logan was the second senior Washington bureaucrat to die in the past week under strange circumstances, the other victim being one Francis X. McGavin, who had collapsed in a restaurant from what was rumored to be poisoning, according to the District's medical examiner. The problem was that he had not eaten anything. He'd had a single sip of white wine while waiting for his lunch partner, but that had come from a bottle that had served two other people. The medical examiner's office so far had not identified the suspected poison, nor was it even confirming that poison had been involved.

Hiram put the paper down on the side table and rubbed the small bones in his aching face. No lack of eager-leakers at the Metro PD or the medical examiner's office, was there, he thought. That wasn't what was worrying him. In 2011 he'd consented to share a few of the Phaedo Botanical Society's more exotic botanical extracts with the Department of Homeland Security, supposedly in support of the DMX counterterrorism project. He'd talked to the other members before going ahead and everyone had been onboard. He'd given the spooks access to three plants, two from his own breeding program and one from Ozawa's research, and that one, a variant of algae, produced symptoms bearing a remarkable similarity to those of the Treasury man, nuchal rigidity and a prominent rictus.

Logan had also walked into a busy stream of traffic, which might indicate tunnel vision, yet another symptom involving a saxitoxin. He didn't have enough details about the McGavin case, so there were no conclusions to be drawn there. Yet. On the other hand, two of the plants he'd given the counterterrorism people could drop a human like a stone from just a passing contact with some of their volatiles. He shuddered to think about what this Mandeville fellow was contemplating. He realized he needed to talk to his colleagues in the society. He asked Thomas to set up a call that would catch most of them in daylight hours, or at least, early evening. Thomas named the time.

"It's a good thing Ozawa still has insomnia," Hiram remarked. "Thank you, Thomas."

At the appointed time he went to the communications room, located just behind a discreet door in the library. He sat down in front of a Polycom total room immersion display, consisting of an eighteen-foot wraparound media wall, with three eighty-four-inch thin-bezel HD color displays. After the initial round of greetings and the usual inquiries about health and home, Hiram got down to business.

"Gentlemen, we may have a problem, and it's one in which I may have had a hand. Do you remember the request from the U.S. government four years ago for some of our botanical toxins?"

Nods all around. "Has something gone astray?" Tennyson asked.

"It's possible," Hiram said. "I'm waiting for some medical examiner's reports to see if there's any possible match. I've heard of one incident that seems to have involved aconitine in a vapor state. The other one I haven't seen, but based on the victim's appearance, it may have been related to a cardiac glycoside from an oleander derivative, or a saxitoxin."

"Veec-tims?" Giancomo de Farnese asked. "'Ees accident?"

"I'm afraid not, Giancomo," Hiram said. "I think one of the Borgias is back."

"Santa Maria," Giancomo said.

Ozawa finally spoke up. "You give compounds to government, or plants?"

"Compounds, Hideki," Hiram said. "To my knowledge the U.S. does not have any programs to develop toxins. They stopped their biological warfare program years ago. They do defensive work, but no developmental work."

"Who died, then?" Tennyson asked.

Hiram told them. Ozawa hissed and de Farnese rolled his eyes.

"Do they know about us?" Tennyson asked.

"As of at least four years ago they did," Hiram said. "They knew about the Phaedo Society *before* coming to ask for help, but I think that was because I'd been helping our intelligence and federal law enforcement authorities with some perplexing poisoning cases. What I gave them was supposed to be used in covert operations against the terrorist world."

"So now someone's using them in Washington?" Tennyson asked.

"Yes, I think that's the case," Hiram said. "Two senior government officials have died under very strange circumstances. It was probably a mistake to ever let some of our materials loose in the government."

"Yes," Ozawa said. "Mistake."

Hiram was a bit stung. "Does the Japanese government know about you and your work, Hideki-san?"

Ozawa sat back and blinked. Then he nodded forcefully, once. *"Hai."*

"Giancomo?"

"What *governo*?" De Farnese asked. "Italia has no *governo.* Only clowns."

Smiles. Tennyson spoke up. "Her Majesty's government has used my services in much the same way yours has, Hiram," he said. "And even some of your own rather marvelous creations. What's going to happen now, do you suppose?"

Hiram hesitated. He didn't want to scare his brethren. "There are people investigating what has happened. The killer may find out about that. He may even attempt to neutralize the source of his killing agents. He may even come here."

Ozawa's face broke into an evil grin. "He comes, you make video, yes?"

"Hideki, you're a bloodthirsty bastard, aren't you?" Tennyson said.

Ozawa put on what he thought was a face of total innocence. "In interest of science," he said. "Only science."

"Hideki-san has a point, Hiram," Tennyson said. "You've gone much further along the mutation road than we have. I, myself, would be terribly interested in what happens if someone attempts to breach Whitestone."

"Very well, gentlemen," Hiram said. "I will report when it's over, assuming I'm still able to report."

"Have no fear, Hiram," Tennyson said. "Did that snake pool experiment succeed?"

"It's possible," Hiram said. The connection was supposedly secure, but still . . . one had to be careful.

"Must make video," Ozawa said. "For science."

Hiram snorted and signed off the net.

SEVENTEEN

Carl Mandeville was in the office bright and early Saturday morning. Many of the staff were in as well: a posting to the National Security Council staff meant that Sundays were yours, at least some of the time. Otherwise, you came in, too often with the word "Divorce!" ringing in your ears.

Mandeville picked up his secure phone and dialed a number. When the ringing stopped and the tone sounded, he said one word: "Beacon." Then he hung up and sent for coffee. Thirty minutes later his phone rang. The caller ID on the secure phone said, simply: Beacon.

He picked up. "New orders," he said. "I have your current subject under rendition at Petersburg. Maintain a watch there. I'll be going down there soon to talk to him, see if I can turn him. If I can't, I'll need to ramp it up a little. Actually, a lot."

Then he hung up. There was something to be said for an operator who couldn't speak.

Then he placed a call to the commanding officer at the United States Army Research Institute for Infectious Diseases at Fort Detrick, Maryland, on the secure link.

"Colonel Kreckich speaking, sir," a voice answered.

Mandeville confirmed his identity and then told the CO that he would need some of the special materials in the near future.

"Which specific materials, sir?"

"Aerosol of belladonna sap," he said. "We have an opportunity to take out a high-level meeting of AQ in Syria. I need a single canister.

No, two. I want them delivered to my office suite in the EEOB for further transport to JSOC. Armed forces courier, with hand-delivery to me, personally. I have the DMX code ready."

"I'm ready to write."

"DMX 17454312. Authentication is venom 7789."

"Stand by."

Mandeville waited while the CO verified the authentication code from the daily tables.

"Authentication accepted. We will advise delivery."

Mandeville hung up. The commanding officer of USAMRIID knew his business. Mandeville had been fascinated to learn that the CO was a veterinarian, but that actually made sense. Their research involved a whole host of primates, whom they subjected to the entire spectrum of horrible diseases that enemies of the state might choose to weaponize.

The two canisters being brought to him were early-warning devices used by the army to warn of chemical attack, which the soldiers nicknamed "sniffers." In practice, the canisters sat in a receptacle on top of a large detection-and-analysis device that monitored the air around it. If the device sensed any one of a dozen chemical agents, it fired the canisters, which blew out a mist of strongly scented mint. The rule was, smell mint, MOPP-up immediately. Get your mask on, then get your suit on. The neat part was that if the canister on the actual analyzer let go, it sent out an order by closed-loop cell phone to other canisters placed around the area being protected. Like house smoke detectors, if one went, they all went. It was that satellite spray system that Mandeville's planted biochemist had converted to an actual weapon. One cell phone call, and the sprayer would fire, but it wouldn't be mint this time.

He wondered if that weird genius out in Great Falls had any idea of what the government was doing with some of his magic potions. The canisters represented what some of the more self-important senators up on Capitol Hill liked to call the nuclear option. He had no qualms about killing off the entire DMX and starting over. He'd have to figure out how *he* was going to survive this catastrophe, and then how to pin it on someone in the terrorist world. Maybe he'd set it up so that he could arrive at the meeting room only to find everyone dead. A precursor string—that's what he needed. Gen up an intel report of a threat to the DMX, itself.

Something that they could officially ignore because of weak provenance, and then, regrettably, say: oh shit, we should have paid more attention to that.

He nodded to himself. That was definitely the way to do it. If he could turn the bothersome Metro cop, then maybe this escalation wouldn't be necessary, but the cop was clearly a potential liability. The traitors on the DMX would just love to get him in front of a Senate committee to bolster their case against the DMX. Talk about a media firestorm.

He shook his head. No. He couldn't risk it. He needed to wipe the slate clean, along with the cop, then pin it on someone on the Kill List. Or maybe blame that Walker guy. He smiled at that thought.

EIGHTEEN

On Saturday, his first day in detention, Av had experienced the surreal environment of the master sergeant's Benedictine rule. He went to breakfast with about thirty of the other inmates, being careful not to make too much eye contact or inadvertently pop out with a "good morning" to anyone. The food wasn't bad—standard hotel buffet stuff in steaming Sterno-heated trays. The rest of the inmates looked to be a pretty bland bunch—middle-aged, all white, nothing extreme. A few shaved heads, but, for the most part, they all looked entirely normal. It was unsettling to be eating breakfast in total silence, watched by four guards who seemed to be bored but who were definitely watching.

He skipped lunch, having nothing to do between breakfast and the call for the noon meal. He went to the weight room instead, waited for one of the few benches, and got as much of a workout as he could manage with other silent inmates looking on, waiting for a turn on the gear. That night he showed up in the dining room and was told that, since he'd failed to sign up for evening meal, he would have to wait to see if there were any no-shows. He was in luck and tucked into some kind of meat loaf. It didn't taste bad and it didn't taste all that good, either, and suddenly he missed his headache-bringing red wine.

He watched TV that night, after finding out where he needed to be for the morning run with the guard force. Then he remembered it would be Sunday—their day off from the regimen of a ten-mile run at dawn. Batting a thousand here, he thought.

It had begun to dawn on him that nobody knew where he was, except of course, the Bureau. Would they have told Precious that they had him in custody? On a Saturday, would she even know he was "missing"? No, she wouldn't, not until he didn't show up on Monday, which is when he assumed she was going to take the megatarbaby up the chain of command to the chief of detectives. Who would do what? Nothing, in all likelihood. Upstairs would hunker down and wait to see what, if anything, happened. Every day in Washington sprouted a crisis or two. Seasoned bureaucrats knew full well that often the best response was to do nothing at all. A surprising number of crises resolved themselves once it became clear that nobody cared all that much, or, that everyone was waiting to see what everyone else was going to do. It was a big government, and sheer inertia often won the day. Especially when she told them that the detective who'd lit this fuse was AWOL.

On Monday he got to run with the guard force. Any hopes that a morning run would present an opportunity to escape were dashed when he saw *where* they were running—between the two lines of razor-wire-topped perimeter fencing that surrounded the entire federal complex, complete with some enthusiastic German shepherds who clearly wanted to meet the new guys. The master sergeant had said that detainees could talk to guards, and so he did. They were, for the most part, young men in their twenties, physically fit, with shaved heads and an easy familiarity with both disciplined running and all the military gear draped over their bodies. Av ran in the middle of the pack; there were three other detainees running, and by some subtle maneuvering, they were all separated by at least a half-dozen guards. One of the two guys running on either side of him asked Av when he'd been in the Corps, and he told them.

"I assume you guys are all marines?" he asked.

The older of the two barked a laugh and told him never to assume. Av remembered hearing that golden rule a million times during his stint in the Corps. That comment also tied off the conversation. Av put his head down and settled into the comfortably familiar route pace, feeling a little peculiar running in a bright orange jumpsuit among all these guys in full battle-rattle. Somewhere up front one of the guards broke into one of the age-old drill chants—*I don't know but I've been told*—which was echoed by all the runners in the pack. The nice thing about a morning run was you didn't have to think about the rest of the day. He picked up the chant with the rest of them.

That night, after skipping the evening meal, Av was summoned to the guardroom and told he was going to have a visitor.

"Who is it?" he asked. The duty officer, who appeared to be a sergeant, shrugged his shoulders. They escorted him to a windowless room where there was a small, rectangular conference table, two chairs on either side, and one chair at each end of the table. Av recognized the one-way glass window in one wall and the AV camera rig surveying the table area from over the door.

"You sit here at this end of the table," the guard said. "Your visitor will sit down there. You are required to stay in your chair at all times. If you move, one of us will be in here to restrain you quicker than you can get to the other end of this table. For what it's worth, we practice that. Everything will be recorded unless your visitor requests otherwise. You're a cop—I assume you knew that."

"Never assume," Av said, sitting down. The guard chuckled and left the room.

It still felt surreal—all this between-us-professionals stuff—and yet he was a prisoner in every sense of the word. He wondered who the visitor was—Precious, maybe? He heard voices out in the hall and then the door opened. A guard came in, followed by a large and imperious-looking man wearing what looked like a really expensive suit. Everything about him was bigger than usual—his head, his upper body, his hands. Six-two, maybe three, and just big, not fat but outsized. Intense, glaring eyes, heavy brows, a steely, downturned mouth. Av had heard the term "command presence" and this man had it in spades. He resisted a sudden impulse to stand up as the man fixed his eyes on him.

"I'm Carl Mandeville," he said. "I am special assistant to the President and senior director for counterterrorism on the National Security staff. Are you Detective Sergeant Kenneth Smith of the Metro PD?"

"That's right," Av said, quenching a reflexive "sir" at the last instant.

Mandeville nodded. Then he told the guards that his conversation with

Detective Sergeant Smith was classified and that he wanted no one in the room or in the adjoining room. He also wanted the audiovideo equipment disabled.

"Sir, we have to—"

Mandeville glared at him. "Detective Sergeant Smith is not a threat to me," he said. "Go tell your commanding officer that I want total privacy, and that means *total* privacy, understand? Now: out, please."

The guards withdrew and Mandeville took a seat at the other end of the table. He didn't say anything, obviously waiting for something. Two uncomfortable minutes later there was a knock on the door and Master Sergeant Lawson came into the room.

Mandeville looked over at him and raised his eyebrows. "Problem, Colonel Lawson?"

"No, sir, none at all," Lawson said. "We tape everything for our protection, but if you want the equipment off, it's off. I'll have people outside in the passageway if you need anything."

"I need two bottles of cold water," Mandeville said.

"Yes, sir," Lawson said. "Right away, sir."

Colonel Lawson? Av thought. Here we go again.

Mandeville resumed his glaring-Buddha pose at the other end of the table until a guard came in with two bottles of water. Mandeville nodded. Once the guard closed the door, Mandeville slid one of the bottles down in Av's direction. They both cracked the tops and drank. Mandeville glanced over his shoulder at the camera above the door. The red light was not on. Av had the impression that if the light did come on, Mandeville would somehow know it.

"If I say the term 'DMX' to you," Mandeville began. "Do you know what that means?"

"I think so," Av replied. "It's a secret government committee that recommends names to the President for assassination because they are important people in the foreign terrorist organizations throughout the world. And you're the chairman."

Mandeville sighed. "The fact that you know both of those things is why you are here," he said.

"Oh, bullshit," Av said.

Mandeville raised his eyebrows. "Bullshit?" he said.

"Yeah, bullshit," Av said. "Two members of the DMX have been murdered, possibly at your behest. They were killed because they expressed significant reservations about this committee's legality, moral standing, and the constitutional implications of a secret American government assassination program. *That's* why I'm really here. Not for something I did, but for something I know."

Mandeville sat back in his chair and took a long draught of water. He put the bottle down on the table. "You don't *know* anything, Detective Sergeant," he said.

"Then why the fuck are *you* here?" Av asked.

Mandeville stared at him. People did *not* talk to him this way.

"Look, big shot," Av said. "I'm Joe Shit, the ragman, okay? I'm just a cop. I have no ambitions to be a 'player' in your wizard-world of counterterrorism. Sounds to me like you've become a crusader with this DMX shit. And, you're right—I don't *know* that you are a murderer, but if you are—if you've been directly or indirectly orchestrating homicides in the District of Columbia? Then you're gonna get caught and you're gonna go to jail. I don't care who you think you are—murder is murder, Mister Director of whatever-the-fuck."

"And who's going to do all that, Detective?" Mandeville asked, softly. "You? From here?"

"Here's something *you* don't know," Av said. "Murderers *always* fuck up. By definition, they're defective human beings, and they always fuck up. Somehow, somewhere. There's no statute of limitations on homicide, and even if you think that what you're doing is for the greater good of national security? If you're doing it in the District, it's still just murder."

"But that's just the thing," Mandeville said. "It's not. What the DMX does is to identify, evaluate, locate, and then eliminate enemies of the state, our state, the United States. Eliminate. Kill. Disappear. Strike. Vaporize. Poison. Irradiate. Electrocute. Drown. Smother. Bury, especially bury. You can call it murder, but I can call it duty, see? Nobody can touch me as long as I am wrapped in the mantle of the DMX."

"Foreigners, though, right?" Av asked. "The chief of Al Qaeda in east-bumfuck-Egypt, right? What's your DMX charter say about killing Americans right there in River City?"

"Nothing," Mandeville said, triumphantly. "Nothing at all. It is silent, and that's a silence *I* can drive a truck through."

"Ironic, isn't it," Av said. "If you were an Arab, the DMX would call *you* a terrorist. So—let's quit fucking around here. What do you want from me?"

Mandeville took a deep breath, trying to control his temper. "Here's why I came," he said. "You can't touch me, you and whoever you're working with, and I think I know who that is, actually. I have friends in very high places, which is why you're here in the quiet room at the snap of my fingers. I can see to it that you stay here forever. Or, I can have you moved every two weeks to some of the DHS's more interesting 'undisclosed locations.' Remember those?"

"Whatever," Av said, trying to look bored.

"You just don't get it, do you, Sergeant. Why don't you consider playing ball here? Because that's the only thing that can save you—you need to work with me, not against me. I'm convinced that the rot in the DMX goes even deeper than I thought. People are losing their nerve—senior people. It's an American character trait—if a war goes on long enough, the weaklings get tired of it. We Americans have become spoiled—we demand instant results."

He took another long pull on his water bottle.

"The bad guys are living back in the seventh century, for the most part. That's a cultural gap of over one thousand years. They're cunning. They're patient. They know us. They know that fat, soft America will eventually lose its nerve. The DMX stands alone as *the* most effective, *the* most surgical method of eliminating our most dangerous enemies. Our people don't do drone strikes that take out birthday parties because some Air Force stick monkey out in Arkansas got careless. We are focused. We take our time. And just when some stinking, bearded, mumbling piece of shit is beginning to enjoy the adulation of a few hundred 'martyrs,' he looks up one night and finds Death, himself, gliding through the doorway on titanium wings."

"And that makes you, what? The Crusader in Chief? The Lone Ranger? Everybody else is wilting in the heat, but there you are, standing tall, steadfast, and mighty?"

"You need to join forces with *me,* Sergeant. You're right: I *am* the DMX, and I need help. America needs help."

"Listen to you," Av said. "You're a psychopath. You know the definition of a psychopath? It's someone who believes his own bullshit. If he says it, it just *has* to be true. Somehow you've turned yourself into a jihadi—and a killer. Jihad and murder go hand in hand these days. Look what just happened in Iraq. So, no thanks. You may have me neutralized, but somebody out there, and I, too, think I know who that is, is going to put your crazy ass in jail."

Mandeville glared at him. "That your final answer, Detective Sergeant?"

"You bet," Av said. "Isn't DHS moving to the old Saint Elizabeth's Mental Hospital facilities for their new HQ? You need to drive yourself up there. Check yourself in—they'll take you as soon as they lay eyes on you. Get settled. Bounce around your rubber room for a bit. Then sing to yourself for a while in the dark. Squeeze your hands together twenty times a minute. Drool, maybe. I hear they've got some bitchin' pills for that."

Mandeville's face turned bright red with rage. He stood up, knocking his chair over backward. He started to say something, but then clamped his mouth shut and left the room, slamming the door behind him. Av heard a lot of shouting out in the hallway for a minute and then more door slamming. Man knew how to make an exit, he thought.

Av took a long drink of water and let out a prolonged sigh. Well, hotshot, he thought, you know how to break a deal, don't you. Then Colonel Lawson came in, with two of the guards. He looked down at Av, then started shaking his head. It reminded Av of the day in the office with the big coffee spill. Then the colonel picked up the chair Mandeville had upset and sat down in it. He indicated for the two guards to also sit down.

"Sergeant," he said. "Meet Captain Phillips, Marines, and Captain Walston, Army JAG."

"Officers?" Av asked.

"We're all officers here, Sergeant," the colonel explained. "This is a DOD training facility as well as a federal detention facility. We've got both Army and Marines. We rotate officers through here so they can be deployed later into situations requiring that we hold prisoners who are more than just enemy soldiers. One of the outtakes from the Abu Ghraib affair."

Av was bewildered. Every time he thought he knew who he was dealing with, they surprised him. The colonel didn't stop there.

"I listened to that guy's rant about something called the DMX. Do you really know what that is?"

"Unfortunately, I think I do," Av said. "And that probably *is* why I'm here. I thought he said he wanted no recordings?"

"I must have missed that, Sergeant Smith," the colonel said. "That often happens. I didn't like the discussion about murdering people. He seemed to think it was okay."

Av sat back in his chair. "Like I told the Grand Dragon," he said. "I'm just an ordinary homicide detective. Lately I got assigned to something Metro PD calls the Interagency Liaison Bureau." He went on to describe the Briar Patch and what its mission was. The colonel nodded.

"We have something similar at Marine Corps Headquarters," he said. "There's the Corps, and then there's the counterterrorism circus. I fully understand the concept of a tarbaby."

"Well, this all started with a tarbaby. We shopped it to the Bureau, and then went on about our business. Or so we thought. Spooks began to drop out of trees. Everybody lying about who he was or what he did or who he worked for. Then I get grabbed up by the Bureau, I think, and sent here. And, apparently, this is all legal?"

"This is all *authorized,*" the colonel said. "Personally, I suspect that none of it's legal, but then, consider the outfit that's running the show these days. Legal doesn't figure big in this administration, as you may have noticed. But: the threat is real, the bad guys *are* coming, and that seems to mean that anything goes."

"I didn't actually believe that some big kahuna at the National Security Council was dabbling in homicide," Av said. "Now that I've met him, I do."

"And you want to do something about that?"

"*Hell,* yes. And about this secret gestapo-style detention bullshit, too. I'll bet this place is another one of the DHS's bright ideas."

"This program is way above my pay grade, Sergeant Smith."

Av shook his head. "Nice try, Colonel," he said, "but you, a commissioned officer, are participating in a program that is arresting and imprisoning American citizens without even a hearing, much less a trial, access to counsel, and a conviction. There will be a day of reckoning over what's been going on here, if not a full-scale revolution, and either way, you and everyone else who's just been 'following orders' is going to face some real consequences. I'm thinking Nuremberg trials, here, Colonel. Remember those?"

The colonel stared at him for almost thirty seconds. Then he excused the two captains. Av sensed that they seemed to be really glad to get out of that room.

When the door closed, the colonel took a small remote out of his pocket and clicked the camera above the door back on. "In light of what you have disclosed to me, Detective Sergeant Kenneth Smith of the Washington Metropolitan Police Department," he announced to the otherwise empty room, "I am of the opinion that you have been wrongly detained in this facility. I am not permitted to just let you go, but I can turn you over to any law enforcement agency, federal or local, who can be held accountable for your whereabouts once you leave this facility. So: Sergeant Smith. Do you want to make a phone call?"

NINETEEN

The who-you-gonna-call decision had been a no-brainer, and Wong Daddy had ridden to Av's rescue in grand style. Somehow he'd managed to appropriate a large, black Expedition, with tinted windows and bristling with all the LE trimmings. He'd also brought along three huge black men, all outfitted in MPD SWAT gear. Even the marines were impressed when they saw the four guys who'd come to pick up the shaved-head police sergeant. Wong had signed Av out, listing his title as the principal deputy assistant manager, Interagency Liaison Bureau, Metropolitan Police Department. No one in the admin office had so much as blinked an eye.

Once out on I-95 they headed north to an interchange featuring a Holiday Inn Express, where they pulled off and let the three other guys, all members of Wong's sumo gambling club and not police at all, get out to pick up their own ride, a retired UPS truck decked out as an urban camper. Wong took the federal license plate off the Expedition and replaced it with a civilian plate. After promises of beers owed and profuse thanks from Av, the three linebackers disappeared up the interstate.

"Hungry?" Wong asked. Av knew that that was Wong-speak for: *I'm* hungry.

"Sure," he said. "A beer would be good, too."

Wong reached behind him and fished a Yuengling lager out of a slush-filled cooler parked behind the right front seat. He casually thumbed off the cap and passed the bottle to Av. Thankful for the tinted windows, Av took an appreciative pull. Wong continued north on I-95, matching his speedometer to the interstate number, along with at least a third of the cars out there.

"So WTF," Wong said. "How'd you end up in a federal pen?"

"Did anybody miss me?" Av asked.

"Precious said you were 'on assignment,' on some kinda 'special project,' at an 'undisclosed location.' "

"She actually say that shit?"

"Nah," Wong replied with a grin. "Said she had no idea where you were and to get our lazy asses back to work while she worked on that problem."

"Mau-Mau and Miz Brown get their papers in?"

Wong grinned again. "Didn't happen," he said. "Chief Happy got wind of it, called 'em both in and told them he was still waiting for an opportunity to fire their asses, so their requests were denied. So: the Petersburg pen?"

Av told him the story of getting snatched up by a bunch of feds, threatened by some high pooh-bah at the Hoover building, and then being taken to the quiet room, as Mandeville had called it. He described how the place worked, and finally, his interview with the big man himself. He concluded with the observation that he thought that Mandeville was certifiable.

Wong nodded in agreement, and then looked in his rearview mirror. There was a set of headlights pretty close in. Wong was doing ninety. This guy wanted to pass? He said something to Av, who looked in the right side mirror. The guy was practically drafting on them. Wong muttered something and turned off the cruise control. The big SUV began to slow.

Av had a sudden funny feeling about this.

"You got a gun handy?" he asked.

Wong, concentrating on the headlights behind him, did a cross-draw and handed Av his .45. Av looked again in his right side mirror. The headlights of their pursuer were so bright he almost couldn't see. He let his window down, took off his seat belt and turned sideways. He rested the muzzle of the .45 on the windowsill, holding it with both hands against the sudden blast of wind.

The car behind them finally jerked to the right and then came up alongside them on Av's side. At first Av thought he was going to roar past, but he didn't. Wong reengaged the cruise and the big SUV accelerated. The car on the right kept pace, and then Av saw the driver's side window coming down.

There he was: the man who'd sent them scrambling down the banks in Rock Creek Park. He was looking over at Av with absolutely no expression on his face. Then he saw Av's gun, at just about the same time as Av fired three shots in quick succession. A cloud of windshield glass blossomed in the slipstream between the two cars before the other man fell back. Av looked in the mirror and saw what looked like a lot of smoke and road dust as cars in the right lane hit the brakes and tried to avoid the rapidly decelerating vehicle in front of them. Finally, their pursuer drifted off the road onto the berm and then was lost from view as they went around a broad curve on the interstate.

"Get the fucker?" Wong asked calmly, back to maintaining ninety in the speed lane. There were no cars behind them, for the moment.

"Warning shot," Av said. "That was the guy who tuned us up with a twelve-gauge down in Rock Creek Park the other evening," he said. "He must have been staking out the Petersburg facility."

"Working for?"

"I'm guessing this is Mandeville's guy," Av said. "The big kahuna must really not have liked my tone of voice."

"Fuck him if he can't take a joke," Wong said. "Let's eat."

He took the next exit and headed down a typical Virginia interstate exit complex of hamburger joints, gas stations, motels, strip malls, nail salons, and a collection of other buildings whose dominant architectural feature was quivering neon.

"Where we going?" Av asked.

"Relative of mine runs a Korean barbecue joint right next door to the VHP station. Cop place. Good chow, cold beer. No civilians."

As advertised, the place was right next door to the Virginia Highway Patrol station. Wong pulled the Expedition into the VHP lot and parked. They then went next door to a place whose sign read: ROK GARDEN. If anybody in the station saw the SUV with the tinted windows and all those antennae, they paid it no attention. Wong asked what Av liked and he went for the BBQ chicken, minus any kimchi. Wong did the ordering, which for Wong included beer, rice, and several small bowls of things that Av was pretty sure were trying to make eye contact with him. It was a half hour after shift change at the VHP and there were several staties in the place. The lady running the place had greeted Wong like a long-lost child. Av asked how the place kept civilians out. Wong explained that if unwanted civilians came in, they were seated politely and then the waiter brought out a bottle of Vietnamese *nuoc mam*, or fermented fish sauce, and uncorked it at the table. That inevitably led to an immediate evacuation, sometimes in the physiological sense.

Once Wong had put away several dishes of food, he let out an extraordinary belch that made all the cops in the room jump and someone in the kitchen cheer. Wong patted his large stomach and then picked up on the discussion in the car.

"So they picked you up, did some razzle-dazzle at the Hoover building, then sent you to Petersburg, told you not to talk for a whole weekend, then some White House big dog showed his teeth at you, and then the jungle bunnies let you go? Just like that? Don't figure, partner. Need to check your shoes for a tracker button or something."

"Don't need to," Av said. "There was a microdrone hovering over your Expedition when we got out. Twenty, thirty feet up? Looked like a little red-eyed bat?"

Wong was alarmed. "No shit?"

"Yeah, shit," Av said. "Look, one thing I've learned? The federal beehive wants to see you, they can see you. Just too damned many of them for anyone to run and hide like they do in the movies. That's what I can't figure out. I feel like a fugitive, but I haven't been on the run and I haven't done anything. I need to talk to Ellen Whiting again."

"The one you took to a gay bar? She still speakin' to you after that shit?"

"I don't know," Av said. "Except she was the one who came to me for help, if you can believe that."

"What you think that heavy dude is gonna do, once he finds out the jarboons turned you loose?"

"He'll put *me* on the Kill List, probably," Av said.

"You need to crash somewhere? I've got ladies all over town who can—"

"No, thanks," Av said, cringing at the thought of crashing at the dragon lady's crib. "I'm gonna go home."

TWENTY

It was close to midnight by the time Wong dropped him off at his building. The streets were just about empty and it looked like all the bars and restaurants had closed some time ago in honor of a low-volume Monday evening. His first problem was how to get into his own pad—they had carted him off without wallet or keys. Then he remembered the slinky blonde coming up the fire escape.

Once on the roof he unearthed the spare key he'd buried in a flowerpot after one too many beers one night had led to a lockout. His loft apartment showed no signs of the search warrant, which surprised him. He'd seen places tossed by Metro PD detectives that looked like a war zone. His gun stash was untouched, and his wallet and keys were in their usual bowl in the kitchen. He checked his telephone to see if it had been altered, and then realized he didn't have the faintest idea of what a bug might look like. They probably had positioned a satellite out in space directly over his house that could tell them every time he broke wind. He dug out Ellen's phone number from his wallet and picked up the phone.

"You guys still there?" he asked the dial tone. It didn't seem to understand. He dialed the number. No one answered and there was no voice mail—the phone just rang. He knew his own phone would be transmitting his caller ID, so maybe that would show up on her phone. Or maybe not. Hell with it, he thought. I'm going to bed.

He checked that the front door was locked, which it was. He started to set his brand-new chain but then thought better of it. The last time she'd come through that lock in the middle of the night with disturbing ease. He left the chain off but then set up one more precautionary measure. He went into the kitchen and got his change bottle out. He emptied two handfuls of coins into a metal pitcher and then poised the pitcher right on the edge of a living room table. He tied some string to the pitcher and connected it to the door handle. Anyone opening the front door would bring that pitcher crashing down onto the wood floor, and that should give him time to pick up his weapon and be ready for a little home defense. He rousted a .45 out of his gun safe, loaded, chambered, decocked it, and then went to bed.

The pitcher did its job almost too well about an hour before dawn, crashing down onto the floor and apparently scaring the shit out of whoever had just come through the door. It did sound like a woman's voice, so Av turned on his bedside table light and slipped the automatic just under the covers. A moment later Ellen Whiting appeared in his bedroom doorway.

"That was dirty pool," she announced. "I think I wet my pants."

"More than I needed to know," he said with a grin. She was wearing running clothes, of all things, with an FBI ball cap and a bulging little fanny pack. "Welcome to my high-tech world."

All the chairs in his bedroom had clothes or other stuff piled on them, so she came over and sat down on the corner of his bed.

"I just heard," she said. "Late yesterday afternoon, in fact. I got a call from Mister Miller to come down for a little chat. He told me that the CT division had picked you up and that you were now being held in a 'secure location.' "

"What'd he want from you?"

"I don't actually know," she said. "He asked me what I thought of that, and since I couldn't think of anything clever to say, I asked him why and for how long. That's up to your division, he said. Claimed to just be the messenger; said he was surprised I didn't know about it, seeing as you and I had been keeping company.

"How'd you get out?"

He described his having milk and cookies with Carl Mandeville, and then the Marine colonel's decision to let him leave.

"Why'd he do that?" she asked.

He told her about the colonel eavesdropping on the conversation with Mandeville and getting what looked a lot like cold feet. He also described what he'd said to encourage said cold feet.

"And Mandeville offered you your freedom in return for—what? Helping him save the DMX?"

"That's about it, Ellen," Av said. "I told him to fuck off, in so many words, and I also told him that if he was murdering people he'd get caught. I don't know if he knows that I've been sprung, but we picked up a tail on the way up—that guy from Rock Creek Park?—so I guess he does. Assuming he works for Mandeville, tomorrow, well, I guess today, I'm gonna go up my chain in MPD and lay this whole fucking thing out to the chief, herself, including the two homicides, the one pending homicide, and who's behind them and why."

"God," she said. "That ought to do it."

"Should have done it as soon as you told me the story," he said. "I know we don't have much of a case, but I suspect the light of day will be as dangerous for Mandeville as anything *I* could do to him."

She pressed her lips together and stared out the window, where the dawn's early light was trying its best to gleam.

"He has—assets," she said, slowly. "People from the serious-business division of the Agency, and anything he wants from the Special Operations Command, I'm guessing. He's obviously gone through that Chinese wall and now has some action executives on his side. But: that means it wasn't Mandeville out there, personally killing McGavin and Logan."

"Sure about that?" Av asked. He really wanted some coffee, but also wanted to make damned sure she hadn't come around to tie off a suddenly dangerous loose end. Anyone who could get through locked doors like that had a skill set that fairly cried out previous clandestine ops service. "*He* was the one at dinner with Logan," he said. "And *you* were the one at lunch with McGavin. You're both on the DMX. You say Mandeville's gone rogue. But what if the two of *you* have gone rogue?"

She looked back at him, her face suddenly grave. "That why you have a gun under the covers there, Detective?"

"Damn straight. Until I know who you are and, more importantly, *what* you are, I'm all done taking chances. Next spook who materializes out of a storm drain is gonna take a couple for the team."

She nodded. "I think," she said, choosing her words carefully, "that you need to meet somebody, preferably before you go turning over the Mandeville anthill at MPD. His name is Hiram Walker, and he has had a role to play in these murders."

"Just give me his full name and I'll include it in the bucket list for the chief," Av said.

"No, Sergeant, that would be a mistake. Look: he's willing to help, and he has some extraordinary assets that he can make available. I spent some time with him this weekend and you have to see this to believe it."

"He a Mafia don or something?" Av asked. "What kind of assets?"

"Plants that can kill people?" she said softly. "He calls them his smart weeds."

"Now that's some creepy shit," Av said, trying to imagine what a smart weed looked like.

She looked at her watch. "Let's you and me have some breakfast, then I'll call him and we'll go out there to Great Falls. If after that you still think I'm out to get you, then, by all means, go climb the mountain. But I think it's very important that you meet Hiram Walker *before* Mandeville acts on the fact that you're out of his clutches."

"Breakfast sounds fine," Av said. "Coffee in particular. But first, take that fanny pack off and toss it over here, if you don't mind."

She smiled, reached for the snaps, and pitched the pack onto a pillow. It landed with a thump that told Av there was indeed a weapon in the pack. Then she stood up and stretched.

"Anything else you want me to take off, Detective?" she inquired, innocently. "It's still early. I do need some exercise, but it doesn't have to be outside."

"Oh, c'mon," he said. "We're supposed to, what: fall in l-u-u-v now?"

"You still seem to think I'm dangerous," she said, smoothing the flimsy fabric of her running shorts across her thighs. "Hell, I might have a stiletto strapped to my thigh for all you know."

"Not in those shorts," he said, then realized he'd just admitted to checking her out. She smiled again, then folded her arms across her stomach. In one smooth and obviously practiced move, she removed her T-shirt, halter bra, shorts, and then her underpants. She put her hands on her hips in a clear, what-do-you-think-about-this posture.

Av swallowed and then nodded in wide-eyed appreciation. "That's unfair," he said, trying to keep his voice from squeaking. "But I'm glad to see there's no stiletto down there."

"According to your rules, there is something infinitely more dangerous than a stiletto, though," she said, glancing down. "Right, Detective?"

This time he did squeak. Dammit.

The next moment she was right next to him on top of the covers, like a fast-moving snake. He felt a moment of panic—her fanny pack was now back in reach. Then he heard it hit the floor on the opposite side of the bed. "That's not the gun I want right now, Detective," she whispered. "It's this one."

He was doomed. No other word for it.

She giggled like a girl. "Why don't you let *me* take charge for a little while," she said. "What is it they say in the U.K.? Lie back, think of England, and do your damn duty."

Then she pulled the covers down, pushed his gun out of the bed, and draped herself on top of him, pressing her lips to the hollow of his neck while the rest of her body melted into every square inch of his. For some reason he recalled Mau-Mau's worried refrain: we're all going down. Apparently he muttered those exact words, because she broke contact for just a second, looked deep into his eyes, and said in a thickening voice: "Well, I sure as hell hope so. Got some serious horns to deal with here."

Sometime later she pushed the hair out of her eyes, looked down at him, and said: "Gotcha, scaredy-cat."

He opened his eyes, saw that there was real sunlight outside now. He tried to remember his name. Damn. Yup, that was it. Damn! He thought he could feel every blood vessel tingling in his body. "Amen to that," he said. "I have been well and truly got. Get enough exercise?"

She leaned forward, pulled his face into her breasts so he could listen to her heartbeat. Definitely cardio range, he thought. Had to admit, he thought—that beat the hell out of jogging. Then she slid out of the bed and headed for the bathroom. "You said something about coffee," she said over her shoulder. "And breakfast?"

"Um," he said. "Coffee for sure. Breakfast, we may have to go out."

"Typical bachelor," she said. "Beer, charcoal, coffee, ammo, but food? Never."

"What's in your pad?"

"Same," she said, turning on the shower now. "Assuming you can walk, get in here. I'm going to need my back done."

"Never assume," he mumbled as he got out of bed.

Fortunately he had a Keurig and a basketful of fully aged K-Cups. He'd been right about the food problem, but she'd fired up her phone, found a Georgetown bakery that would deliver from seven to ten in the morning, smart businessmen that they were. They ended up on the roof with warm croissants and high-test coffee. Below them the morning traffic was already up and running. It was almost eight o'clock, and Av wondered if he was going in to work today, or if he should wait for Precious to call. The Petersburg interlude now seemed to be some kind of bad dream. The sun felt good, though, and there was a tentative fall breeze hunting loose leaves through the big oaks out back.

"Who's this someone you want me to meet, again?" he asked.

"Older dude, named Hiram Walker," she said, attacking her third croissant. She'd borrowed one of his football shirts, put her panties back on, brushed her hair, and declared victory. The croissant collapsed and she ended up with a chin full of crumbs. That made her giggle, and, suddenly, Av felt a dangerous emotional twinge, upon which he instantly stomped.

"That's a whiskey," he said. "Canadian whiskey?"

"His father named him that for a reason, apparently," she said, pinching and then flopping the T-shirt to get all those crumbs off her bobbling breasts. "The original Hiram Walker was apparently some kind of genius," she said. "Famous for never giving up until he'd succeeded at whatever he was trying to do."

"That can be a dangerous philosophy," Av said. "Turns people into fanatics. Sometimes it's better to step back, look at what you're doing, and maybe regroup."

She eyed him across her coffee mug. "Fanatics," she said. "That's a loaded word. Like crusaders." The sound of a jet descending the Potomac gorge into Reagan airport floated across the breeze, its engines whining lazily at low power.

"I was face-to-face with one in Petersburg," he said. "Scary dude, Ellen, as you must know. I think you've been right all along—Mandeville's removing obstacles, all in the name of the new God called national security. Besides that, I failed to show appropriate respect."

She blew out a long breath and finished her coffee. Then she frowned.

"What?" he asked.

"Listen," she said.

Then he heard it: the faint but unmistakable sound of a helicopter, the sound of its rotors thumping almost subliminally over the traffic sounds below.

"Channel nine traffic copter," he said. "Down by the Lincoln."

"No," she said. "Closer. Much closer. And suppressed. That's a SpecOps Black Hawk, I'm sure of it."

He had no idea what she was talking about, but then he thought he heard the door down in his apartment bang open. He jumped out of his chair and looked down the rooftop's stairway, only to see Rue Waltham, dressed in a bathrobe and holding a cell phone in one hand, standing at the bottom.

"Run!" she said urgently. "NOW!" Then she turned and ran, herself.

A moment later Ellen was pushing past him and scrambling down the stairs. "That helo's coming here," she shouted over her shoulder. "Get dressed, get your cop stuff, and then get out of here. I'll be right behind you."

"Ellen, wait—what the—"

But by then both Ellen and Rue had disappeared, so he followed her down. She was already streaking down the stairs to the loft. He followed her inside. She was in the bedroom, pulling on her clothes; Rue was nowhere to be seen. Still grappling with the sudden appearance of his tenant, he went to the dresser, grabbed underwear, clean jeans, and his Redskins football T-shirt. By the time he was dressed Ellen was already headed out the front door, snapping her fanny pack back onto her waist and then checking the weapon inside. He retrieved his smartphone, wallet, badge, and .45 and followed her down the main stairs. At the side vestibule he told her to hold up.

"I've got a garage," he said. "How did you—"

"I took a cab from my apartment to the Watergate," she said, cocking an ear for that helicopter. "Then I jogged over."

"C'mon, then," he said. He led her through the service door into the garage area and locked it behind him. When she saw the Harley, she asked if it still ran.

"Should," he said. "I had it out three weeks ago. But my truck—"

"No," she said. "Not the truck. They'll have you in two minutes. You take that mountain bike over there, and I'll take the Harley. Got riding gear?"

He found the big black motorcycle helmet on a shelf while she checked out the motorcycle. He gave her his leather riding jacket and a set of chaps to cover her bare legs. She put everything on and then wheeled the bike out toward the door, the clothes billowing around her slim frame. He got the Harley's keys out of a bottle and then fired up the opener to raise the metal warehouse door. As daylight streamed in from the bottom, the sound of the approaching helicopter was unmistakable, not overhead, but definitely coming, the clatter of its rotor blades echoing against all the brickwork in the neighborhood. He handed her the keys.

"Listen carefully," she said. "I'll take off into traffic and head east, toward the center of town. You wait three minutes, then walk the bike around to the towpath and start riding west. When you get to Chain Bridge, get up on the bridge and walk it across. Then ditch the bike, call a cab, and ask him to take you to Tysons Corner mall. Once you're in the cab, tell the driver you've changed your mind, and that you really want to go to 6500 Deepstep Creek Road. That's out in Great Falls. Tell him you want him to take the Georgetown Pike. This is important: leave your phone in the cab when you get there, and leave it switched on. Get out and approach the gates and tell them I sent you."

"This that Hiram Walker guy?"

"Yes, it is," she said. Then before he could ask any more questions, she dropped the helmet visor and kicked the Harley into life. Then she accelerated out of the garage right into all the traffic on Thirty-third Street, to the accompaniment of many horns and screeching brakes. Almost immediately, a siren started up about a block away, then a second. He watched for a moment from the shadow of the garage entrance, then punched the door control to lower it. He heard the motorcycle's engine throttle down for a moment and then accelerate, probably turning onto M Street.

He went to the mountain bike and unchained it from its rack, checked the tires, and then looked at his watch. The towpath was pretty narrow right here in the Georgetown precincts, but it widened out upriver of Georgetown U. The traffic crossing the river on Chain Bridge would be heavy at this time of day, so walking the bike across would make sense. He found his bicycle helmet and put it on, which obscured his shaved head. The big football shirt would hide his holster and badge rig, and his phone and wallet could go in the bag behind the seat. He'd forgotten to bring sunglasses, but his helmet had an abbreviated sun visor, which would conceal at least the top of his face.

He rolled the bike toward the service door. Even through the three courses of old brick between him and the outside world, he thought he could still hear that helicopter, which sounded as if it was hovering right over the building now. Suppressed or not, its rotors punched a menacing staccato of pure military power down into the canal. Then the pitch changed and the noise began to diminish. The sirens became louder, and there was a lot of horn blaring out on the street, as if maybe the cop cars were trying to push through traffic and traffic was pushing back.

He waited a few more minutes for the sirens to go away, then rolled the bike through the service door, making sure it locked behind him, and, with a final deep breath, rolled it out of the building. He almost expected gunfire once out in the morning light, but there was only the usual traffic in the street. No helicopters or cop cars or Expeditions loitering in the shadows. They'd gone after the decoy, apparently. When he thought about it, he realized those vehicles had to have been there *before* the helo showed up. Had they seen her go into his building, and then made a move to get them both?

Them, again. They. Them. He shivered in the morning sunlight as he realized just how many of "them" were in this town these days.

As he pedaled up the towpath, being passed by the occasional runner and then having to stop, get off, and portage the bike up and over a street crossing and back down to the path again, he thought about the mysterious but damned exciting Ellen Whiting. Their bedroom encounter had been swift and urgent, at least the first time. Round two had been gentler but no less demanding on her part. Only afterward, when she'd rolled off into a warm ball alongside him, had he begun to wonder what the hell he'd gotten himself into. Was it as simple as what she'd said? Got some serious horns here? She probably thought he'd been gaming her a little—playing hard to get and thus arousing her interest. It had been months since he'd taken a woman to bed, and, in a way, he still hadn't—she had clearly taken *him* to bed, and she had been in control just about every time they'd met up.

A bell rang behind him and he pulled to the right just in time to let a speed bike whiz past on his left, about one foot away. He wondered what Ellen Whiting was doing right about now as she led an enraged federal posse into the red zone around the Mall, the White House, Ellipse, and all those tourist buses massing at the reflecting pool. Probably having the time of her life, he thought with a grin. He remembered what his father had called women like that: sport models. Then his grin faded as he remembered the old traffic cop refrain: you can outrun me, but you can *not* outrun my radio . . .

TWENTY-ONE

Hiram Walker looked up as Thomas came into the library to report that there was a man in a cab at the front gates asking to be admitted.

"What's his name?"

"Detective Sergeant Kenneth Smith, Washington Metro Police Department," Thomas announced.

"Yes, let him in and bring him to me. See if he wants a coffee."

Five minutes later Thomas ushered Av into the library and then went to get a coffee tray. Hiram stood up and offered an oversized hand. "Sergeant Smith," he said, "welcome to Whitestone Hall. I'll bet you're wondering why she sent you here."

"That's putting it mildly, Mister Walker. It's already been a pretty interesting morning."

Hiram pointed to a chair and then sat back down on his "throne." He was relieved to see that the policeman's feet actually did touch the ground. Av told him most of what had happened earlier, omitting the more personal activities.

"I received a brief text from Ellen," Hiram said. "Saying you were coming and that she was going. Where, I don't know."

"She's leading some federal LE on a wild-goose chase, I expect," Av said, trying not to gawk at the giant sitting across from him. "They'll eventually catch her—it's a small town, after all—and then we'll see how good a bullshitter she really is."

Hiram laughed. "A pretty good one, Sergeant," he said. "But I believe her heart's in the right place and that there is a serious problem to deal with downtown."

"That being the DMX?"

Hiram hesitated. Ellen had said that this policeman knew about the problem, but that he was absolutely *not* read into the DMX. The policeman smiled when he saw Hiram hesitate. "I know, Mister Walker, I know," he said, as Thomas came in with the coffee tray. "And now you can guess what *my* problem is."

Hiram nodded, waiting for Thomas to back out of the library. They fixed their coffees and then resumed their conversation. Hiram told Av about his having let some covert agencies use some of his more exotic plants, and that he now thought that Mandeville had really gained access to them in order to kill off his opposition on the DMX.

"Ellen told me that she was involved in the first one," Av said. "We got a lot of smoke blown our way when we looked into the McGavin death. Even the ME drew a blank, or else somebody got to them. The Bureau said it wasn't their problem, and then it *was* their problem, and then—frankly, I'm completely confused at this juncture."

Hiram said he understood. "The sheer size of the counterterrorism world down there is enough to make confusion the order of the day, I'm sure. I'd like to think that that is part of some grand strategy to confuse the enemy, but unfortunately, it's just Parkinson's Law. Ellen said you met Mister Mandeville under rather strange circumstances—do you think they were coming for you this morning?"

It was Av's turn to hesitate. He really didn't want to expose the fact that he and Ellen had gone to bed together, but if he said that they might have been after her instead of him, it would be pretty obvious. "I *think* they were coming for me," he said. "I think Ellen had come to warn me—she's aware of Mandeville's crusade to do some ethnic cleansing—and then she decided to provide a decoy so I could get away. Before the helicopter showed up, she'd been telling me about you and that you might be able to explain what had happened to those people."

Hiram put down his coffee cup and stood up. Ellen had told Av that Hiram was tall, but he'd had no idea. "I have to move around from time to time, Sergeant," Hiram said. "With my condition there will come a time when I will be unable to move much at all. Care for a tour of my gardens?"

"Is it safe to tour your gardens?" Av asked, remembering Ellen's words.

Hiram smiled. "As long as you stay on the sidewalks near the house, Sergeant," he said. "It can be a bit of a jungle out there, you know."

They'd been outside for half an hour when Ellen finally showed up at the gates. She joined them outside, dressed now in her business clothes and driving a government sedan. Hiram had been explaining how plants process sunlight, water, and CO_2 to make food, and Av was glad for the distraction. She greeted Hiram with a warm smile and a quick handshake; with Av she was more reserved, which he thought was a little amusing, considering. But then, the previous few hours of her morning may have been a wee bit stressful.

"The sergeant tells me you've been having an adventure this morning," Hiram said.

"Not for too long," she said with a grin. "I took off on the sergeant's motorcycle as a distraction, and they went for it. I pretended not to notice the helicopter or any of the blue lights stuck in rush-hour traffic behind me. By the time they realized where I was headed, the sergeant here was probably crossing the river into Virginia."

"Where'd you lead 'em?" Av asked.

"To the Hoover building, of course," she said, innocently. "That's where I work."

Av laughed. Hiram shook his massive head. "Do you know who 'they' were, Ellen?" he asked.

"Nope," she said. "Black vehicles, MPD, and the helicopter looked military but had no markings, although I didn't spend a lot of time staring at it. I did go across the Fourteenth Street Bridge to the Pentagon, circled through north parking and then up to the Arlington Cemetery boulevard, then back across the Memorial Bridge to the Hoover."

"What happened then?"

"Went in the building, down to the gym facilities, got cleaned up, changed clothes, and then up to my office. Thirty minutes later, got a summons from Mister Miller, who wanted to know where I'd been earlier this morning. I told him, and then asked why he wanted to know."

"What'd he say to that?" Av asked, wondering just how much she'd told Miller.

"Have a nice day?" she said. "As in, that's all, thank you. Then I came out here."

"So if it wasn't the Bureau who was flying helicopters around the capital center this morning, who was it?"

"Beats me," she said. "But since there were no heat-seeking missiles fired at it from the White House roof, it had to be federal *and* cleared in advance."

"Is that something Mister Mandeville could arrange?" Hiram asked.

"Not on the spur of the moment," Ellen said. "The airspace around the capital is closed to all traffic by a no-fly zone, deadly force authorized. He's senior enough to get it done, but it would be a protracted process, with lots of meetings and coordination."

"I guess I could check with Metro PD's operations center," Av said. "They'd have to be part of that process."

"I think you need to stay off the electronic grid for a while," Ellen said. "If that was Mandeville this morning, he won't quit, and he's got long arms."

"I was just showing the sergeant around some of the gardens," Hiram said, glancing up at the sky, as if looking for helicopters or other flying objects. "But perhaps we should go inside and discuss this matter further?"

Back in the house, Hiram had Thomas take them to his communications room, which was behind the library, while he tended to some medications.

"This is where he confers with the other members of the Phaedo Society," Ellen said, as Av looked around at the big screens, now dark, and all the smaller displays, which seemed to be watching a laboratory of some kind, the estate's perimeter, and three screens of separate news stations. She then had to explain what the Phaedo Society was.

"Mister Walker must be fabulously wealthy," Av commented. "This is a serious setup."

"He never leaves this place," she said. "Imagine that."

Thomas came in and told them that Mister Walker would be with them shortly. Then he went to a console in one corner of the room and made several settings, some of which changed the perimeter security cameras' angle of view.

"Expecting company?" he asked, but Thomas did not respond. He completed his settings, asked if they needed anything, and then withdrew, closing the door behind him.

"Explain something to me, if you can," Av said. "Rue Waltham?"

"Who's Rue Waltham?"

"The blond number who sounded the alarm this morning?"

Ellen shook her head. "No idea—I didn't see anyone else in the apartment." As Av was about to object, Hiram came looking somewhat better than he had earlier.

"Sergeant," he said. "Why don't you and Ellen here come with me to my laboratory," he said. "I think I can get a better handle on what killed McGavin and Logan. I've asked a friend in the Bureau lab to get me copies of the OCME results on both victims."

"They'll do that?" Ellen asked.

Hiram nodded. "I've worked with them from time to time, especially when they have an embarrassing toxicology mystery."

"Actually, I can't stay," Ellen said, looking at her watch. "I've got a pre-DMX meeting this afternoon and then I can come back. Can Sergeant Smith stay here until we can find out who that was this morning?"

Hiram nodded. "Certainly," he said. "So the Bureau *will* be looking into it?"

"Maybe, maybe not," she said. "If it was an apprehension mission coordinated by someone in the White House, then the rest of federal law enforcement might be studiously looking the other way."

"Curiouser and curiouser," Hiram said. "Well, the sergeant was closer to the McGavin investigation and autopsy than you were, so get back when you can, and, in the meantime, we'll go to the lab and see what we can see."

"Right," she said. "I'll try to get back by five. I'll call Thomas if I can *not* make it for some reason." Then she turned to Av. "I think Mandeville knows you're not in Petersburg anymore and that you know too much. If he's willing to kill members of the DMX for disagreeing with him, he'll sure as hell be willing to ice you. You're safer here than anywhere else right now, but I'll know more this evening. Okay?"

"You sure are an interesting date," Av said. She rolled her eyes.

"Do this for me," he asked. He wrote down a phone number on a notepad by his chair. "Call Sergeant Bento at this number, tell him where I am, and ask him to tell Precious."

" 'Precious'?"

"She's our boss at the Briar Patch. She can be trusted."

Ellen nodded and said she would. Then Hiram rang for Thomas, who escorted her out to her car and opened the main gates.

"What in the world have you gotten yourself into, Sergeant Smith?" Hiram asked.

"Beats the shit out me," Av said. "But I'm ready to stop anytime."

Hiram gave Av the same tour he'd given Ellen, after which he listened carefully as Av recalled the events surrounding McGavin's death and some of the things the pathologist had said. Av couldn't tell if his information was helpful or not; Hiram just listened, but with an intensity that made him think Hiram's big brain was recording every word. Then they discussed the second incident, and Hiram was most interested in Av's description of Logan looking like a zombie.

Over lunch, Hiram told Av about the Phaedo Botanical Society, how they'd begun sharing their research and how that had evolved into a study of nature's deadliest botanical substances. Av asked about the name.

"The word comes from the writings of Plato, an ancient Greek philosopher. It's the title of one of Plato's writings, but actually it's a man's name. The Phaedo describes the last hours and death of Socrates, another Greek philosopher."

"I don't have a real college education, Mister Walker," Av said. "You're talking over two thousand years ago?"

"Yes," Hiram said. "In ancient Athens, Socrates was a bit of a rabble-rouser whose philosophic teachings began to worry the Athenian upper classes. The city was struggling to find a better form of government after the defeat at the hands of the Spartans, and Socrates was not a fan of democracy. They decided to shut him up by bringing him to trial for failing to honor the city's gods and for 'corrupting' the city's youth."

"What happened?"

"Well, Socrates being Socrates, he made something of a mockery of the trial and the charges. He annoyed the jury, so they found him guilty, and the city fathers took that opportunity to sentence him to death by forcing him to drink hemlock tea."

"What would that do to you?"

"Modern medical theory differs, but what Phaedo describes was a wave of cold creeping into the core from the extremities; when it got to the heart, it was all over. Not quick, but apparently not all that unpleasant, if you can believe Phaedo. On the other hand, Phaedo hadn't been drinking hemlock tea."

Av considered this story. "Then this Phaedo Society is all about poisoning?" he asked.

Hiram smiled. "Very perceptive, Sergeant, but not entirely accurate. Our interest in botanical toxins has more to do with the theory that plants are smarter than we know. So-called weeds, in particular. Anyone who has tried to make a flower or vegetable garden from scratch would know exactly what I'm talking about."

"Never have," Av said, suddenly feeling a bit sleepy. "But I have heard some of my neighbors with yards cussing weeds."

"Well, basically, we think that the persistence of weeds has to do with some kind of botanical instinct to survive, analogous to our own human survival drive. That's why you see them in the cracks of sidewalks, for instance. Some plants have taken this instinct, if you can call it that, to a higher level by developing toxins to discourage predation, be it by animals, angry gardeners, or farmers who dump truckloads of glyphosphates on their fields."

"What's this got to do with what's going on now?" Av asked.

" 'Toxin' is another word for poison, Sergeant. It's entirely possible that whoever's doing this is using botanical toxins. Some would be easy to detect—aconitine, for instance. Others would be damned near impossible. That's why I want to see those OCME reports."

"Where the hell would a guy like Carl Mandeville get shit like that?"

"From me, unfortunately," Hiram said.

Av just looked at him. He suddenly felt that he was back in the bowl again, going round and round but undeniably headed for an unpleasant ending.

Thomas came in, cleared the plates, and then announced that he'd heard from Ms. Whiting, and that she would not be able to make it back to Whitestone Hall this afternoon.

"Did she give a reason?" Hiram asked.

"No, sir," Thomas said. "She did say to tell the sergeant here that she had been 'unavoidably detained.' "

"Detained?" Av said, suddenly alert. "That could be a code word."

Hiram raised his eyebrows. Av described how the people who had taken him to Petersburg had been very careful to distinguish between detention and arrest. Hiram frowned and then asked Thomas to follow up on expediting the OCME reports from the Bureau's lab people.

They sat in silence after Thomas left. Av was truly worried now. He rubbed his eyes, realizing he was more tired than he'd thought. Ellen had told *him* what to do when the big black helicopter showed up, but now? Was he in a safe house or was he back under a different form of detention? He had no phone, and he was pretty sure that getting out of Whitestone Hall would not be any piece of cake. And why wasn't Ellen coming back—had Mandeville figured out what had happened this morning and taken Ellen Whiting off the boards? When he opened his eyes, the giant at the head of the table was looking at him with a sympathetic expression.

"Ellen Whiting," Hiram said, "strikes me as a woman who can hold her own in just about any circumstances. I can see that you're worried, and I understand your apprehension about everything that's happened recently." He finished his coffee. "I have sources in the government," he continued. "Not appointees who come and go, but people who've been in Washington for a long time. Let me pulse those sources, see what I can find out about this Mandeville person and the problems within the DMX."

Av threw up his hands. "The National fucking Security Council?" he said. "The DMX? Black ops helicopters over Georgetown? The quiet room in the federal penitentiary at Petersburg? Mister Walker, I'm just a low-level Metro PD cop—so why do I think there's this big black dragon coming for me tonight?"

"Probably because one is," Hiram said, with a smile. "But take heart, Sergeant—we know how to handle dragons here at Whitestone Hall."

After lunch, Hiram had Thomas take Av up to one of the guest suites on the second floor. The rooms were seldom used, but beautifully appointed. Thomas suggested that Av relax, perhaps take a nap. There'd be drinks in the library at five-thirty. He said that Mister Walker would also be retiring for the afternoon, due to his condition.

Once Thomas left, Av decided that he'd been given good advice. He shucked his clothes, took a long, hot shower, and then flopped onto the large, soft bed. He thought back to his physical interlude with Senior Supervisory Special Agent Ellen Whiting earlier in the day. Special, indeed, but no longer just dangerous.

Lethal, that was the word. Then he was asleep.

Hiram Walker was not napping. He and Thomas were busy going through the security precautions that needed to be in place before darkness. From the communications room, he had Thomas start up the big emergency generator down in the basement, and then they switched the entire house and hydroponic system over to internal power. They then reviewed the switchboard settings for the house lighting systems, so that if an intrusion team arrived and cut the power from outside the perimeter, the visible lights in the house would go down—but only the lights. They then went to the lab, where they set up the grounds' hydroponic feeding system for manual control. They lined up specific chemical tanks to the plant networks that would need to be excited if someone came over the walls in the dark.

Hiram was pretty sure he knew what was going on and fully expected that some kind of government team would be coming tonight to recapture the hapless police sergeant. Av had related his conversation with Mandeville down in Petersburg, especially the part about Av telling Mandeville no, which was not a word anybody on the National Security Council staff was used to hearing. Mandeville sounded like a nut, but a nut whose sense of patriotism and self-importance had been inflamed to the point of Hitler-in-the-bunker madness.

Thomas came over and reported that the feeding systems were lined up and the same three huge screens used for teleconferencing were now switched into the estate's camera systems. He asked that Hiram recheck the settings. Hiram did so and then asked Thomas to patch the eagle's nest camera to the communications room display center. This was a trainable camera mounted at the very top of a sixty-year-old black Austrian pine tree at the southeastern corner of the property. It gave a full view of Deepstep Creek Road in both directions, with both day and night vision capability. Hiram did not expect an intrusion team to just come down the road and break down the front gates, but he did expect a fake VEPCo electric utility truck to show up before any raid began.

He smiled to himself for a moment. A man with Marfan syndrome had time to watch a lot of movies, but still, why not be on guard? The sergeant wouldn't wake up for a few more hours, thanks to the little something Thomas had added to his lunch. He was disappointed that Ellen Whiting wouldn't be here tonight. He'd been impressed with her brains and go-ahead style, not to mention her delectable physical attributes. He knew, however, that she needed to be on the outside for what was probably going to happen tonight. Perhaps after this adventure was all over he could get her to come back. Not for the first time, he regretted the stark fact of life that anything he wanted had to come to him and not the other way around.

He looked at his watch and sighed. Time for meds.

TWENTY-TWO

Carl Mandeville reached for the secure phone when it lit up. It was Strang.

"Everything in place?" he asked.

"Almost," Strang replied. "I just need to confirm a couple of things."

"All right—what?"

"This is a demonstration, correct? The team will penetrate the Walker estate and demand they hand over that cop. But deadly force is *not* authorized, and if there is real resistance, they back out. Right?"

"Yes, of course," Mandeville said. "As yet I don't have a FISA warrant, so we're going bareback here until it comes through. Still, I'm pretty sure that this Walker fella will probably just crap his pants and hand him over. He's a scientist, but he's afflicted with Marfan syndrome, so I'm not expecting some kind of martial arts dustup."

"Okay, I just needed to confirm all that. We'll have a diversion at the front gate, and a SWAT team on standby in the neighborhood. I haven't coordinated with Fairfax County, either. We hope to get in and out in under sixty minutes. Secure tactical comm. The people at the front gate will have a cover story if the locals interfere."

"And no connection to the DMX, right?"

"Perish the thought," Strang said.

"Who are you using for this?"

"Really want to know that?" Strang asked.

"No, I guess not," Mandeville said. Mostly because you're not going to get him, he thought. I am. "I'll be here until you report back. When you get him, take him back to Petersburg yourself, this time to the penitentiary side. I'll tell them what to do from there."

"Got it."

Once Strang was clear, he called the secure drop for Evangelino. When the phone picked up with its usual silent hiss, he spoke four words: "Blue Line. Fourteen hundred." Then he hung up, got his lightweight trench coat, and went down the hall. He had three secretaries, all of whom stood up when he appeared in the doorway to the executive secretariat.

"Going for a walk," he announced.

Yes, Mister Mandeville, they all chirped in unison. No "when will you be back" or "how can we reach you." They knew better.

Thirty minutes later he was seated on a wooden bench in the Metro Center underground station. It being early afternoon and not yet rush hour, the station was pretty empty. He glanced up at the lighted train board on the ceiling, which gave an ETA for the next train coming through and which line it was running. Blue Line coming through in three minutes. He looked at his watch. It was just now two o'clock. Close enough, he thought. When the train blew into the station, he got up and started walking alongside, front to back, as the cars squealed to a stop.

There.

He stepped through the next set of doors just before they chimed and slid shut. He went toward the back of the car, where the stone-faced operative sat all alone, dressed in a plain suit and a gray fedora hat, the left side of his face staring through the train and into the dark tunnel ahead. Mandeville gave a mental snort. Thinks this is occupied Berlin back in the seventies, he thought.

He took the seat behind him, the two of them facing forward as the train gathered speed and headed out toward the suburbs.

"Are you ready for tonight?" he asked.

The fedora nodded once.

"Good. They're going in sometime after sundown. They'll make a big-deal entrance at the gate while their intrusion team goes over the wall and into the mansion from the back. I'm guessing they're not going to succeed, but they might. Either way, as the commotion settles down, you know what to do."

Another nod.

"If they do manage to pick him up, I'll send instructions to Petersburg to turn him over to you when I'm ready, and you're ready. If they don't get him, once *you* capture him, terminate him and put the body in the river. I'll send you a signal when their team goes in, and another when we find out what they did or did not accomplish." He paused. "Sure you remember what he looks like?"

The ruined face turned to look directly at him, and, not for the first time, Mandeville wondered if that baleful left eye saw or not. Then the man grinned at him. A woman sitting a few benches down from them saw that grin, got up, and moved quickly to the other end of the subway car.

"Okay, then," Mandeville said. "Good hunting."

The train pulled into the next stop and Evangelino rose and got off. Mandeville remained seated until the next station stop, then got out, went up and over the bridge across the tracks and sat down to wait for the next train going back into town.

Now, he thought, that interfering prick was going to find out just how ruthless the CT world could be when someone crossed Carl Mandeville. He was betting on Evangelino. The only hole in his intelligence picture of Walker's estate was what was under all that leafy canopy out there. The walls were formidable enough, and he probably had some electronic surveillance, too, but both his operations tonight could handle all that easily.

This damn mess had gotten away from him, he realized, and it was time for some decisive action. The vials had arrived from Fort Detrick and were now in his safe. The next meeting of the DMX was in three days, and there was going to be a terrible "accident" in the meeting room. The fact that the DMX meeting room was almost hermetically sealed off in all respects would make the results even more dreadful. The whole committee extinguished in a few deep breaths. Especially his onetime protégée, Ellen bitch-kitty Whiting. He'd even figured out how to blame the whole thing on Walker and his little society. Pity the old man never left the estate, because if he did, he could become the very first civilian to ever attend a meeting of the DMX.

He smiled to himself. Wouldn't that be a nice, tidy package. He'd have to work on that.

TWENTY-THREE

Av woke up as if from some kind of trance. He blinked his eyes and then looked outside. It was just about full dark. Surprised, he looked at his watch: almost six P.M.

Damn, he thought—I slept that long? There was a soft knock at the door and the butler, Thomas, stuck his head in.

"Drinks in the communications room when you're ready, Detective Sergeant," he announced. "Have a good kip?"

"I guess so," Av said, sitting up and stretching. "Had no idea I was that tired."

Thomas beamed. "Very good, sir. Come down whenever you're ready. The room's right behind the library."

"Um," Av said. "I'm not sure I'll be dressed for the occasion."

"Not to worry sir. It is a large house, but Mister Walker much prefers to keep things informal. You'll be fine."

"Thomas," Av said. "Are you ex-military?"

Thomas smiled proudly. "Special Boat Service," he replied. "Twenty years."

"Wow—even I know what that is. I think I saw something about that outfit in a movie?"

"Lots of illusion in those movies, sir," Thomas said, and then closed the door. Av got up, stretched again, looked for his clothes. His room looked out over that strange-looking jungle covering the five acres in front of the house. In the descending darkness, the driveway showed up as a pale ribbon bisecting a mass of plants, shrubs, and trees. Beyond the wall he saw the top of a white Virginia Electric Power utility truck parked next to a telephone pole. Then the lights went out.

Hiram and Thomas sat in the communications room and scanned the electrical circuit screens to make sure all the externally visible lights had gone out. They could feel the big generator down in the basement humming along nicely. Hiram sat in a large, comfortable chair, while Thomas sat at the main communications console.

"Show me the eagle's nest, please," Hiram said.

An infrared image quivered onto the center screen. Down below the tree three VEPCo utility workers pretended to be doing something at the side of the truck, while a fourth was getting the embarked cherry-picker arm ready to come back down from a trip to the pole's crosstree.

"Those will be the operators," Hiram said. "See the backpacks?"

"Yes, sir," Thomas said. "It looks like they're carrying some kind of submachine guns on their chests. I'm thinking MP5s."

Hiram nodded.

"Who's got MP5s?" Av asked from the doorway.

"Come in, Detective Sergeant," Hiram said. "I believe we're about to have visitors."

Av came over and sat down next to Hiram in one on the armchairs and stared at the screens. "VEPCo's issuing ski masks now?" he asked.

"Not VEPCo, we're pretty sure," Hiram said. "I think this is a team of operators sent by Mister Mandeville to retrieve you."

"Wonderful," Av said. "Maybe it'd be better if I just went down to the gate and said hi. No point in bringing guys like that in here to tear up your house."

Hiram smiled. "Let's just see what they do and how far they get. You said it was U.S. Marshals who took you to Petersburg. If these people have been sent by Mandeville, they are probably not marshals."

"Yeah, but still: there's no reason for you to get involved," Av said. "This isn't your problem—it's my problem, even if I'm not sure what that problem really is. Can we contact Ellen?"

"Remember that Ellen brought you here, Detective Sergeant. She may have been expecting that Mandeville would try to scoop you up. Doing that here is going to be much harder than those people out there think. Ah, they're moving now."

The three of them watched the screen as the little camera, whose image was swaying gently in a small night breeze, tracked the team of three down past the gates and to the left front corner of the wall.

"Switching," Thomas said. The image went dark and then resumed, this time from what appeared to be a wall-mounted camera. It showed the men moving swiftly at the very base of the wall, and then stopping about halfway down to the river, just out of sight of the camera.

"Shit, it lost them," Av muttered.

"We know exactly where they are, don't we, Thomas."

Thomas switched the display to reveal a graphic outline of the estate's entire perimeter. Nothing was displayed within the walls, but there was a green band of video all along the outside of the wall. "Not all of my plants are inside the walls, Detective Sergeant," Hiram said. "There's ivy all along the outside face of the bricks. Wherever they stop to throw up a rope or something, the ivy will reveal it to a network of sensors monitoring cellular fluids within the stems. That will tell us where they are and which inside-perimeter camera we need to turn on and where to point the infrared spotlights."

"The plants are part of your security system?"

"The plants *are* the security system," Hiram said. "Some of the things growing out there are dangerous, so I can't have anyone scaling these walls and trampling through what looks like a jungle but in fact is the outside portion of my laboratory."

"Got 'em," Thomas said, pointing to a segment of the wall, where little red lines were appearing.

"Did you happen to notice if they were wearing night vision devices?" Hiram asked. Thomas hit some keys and replayed a segment of the eagle's nest camera recording. "I don't think so," Thomas said after studying the images. "I thought those were just ski masks."

"I'd say they are," Av said. "We have some like that—it's like a skull-cap with a boom mike on it, only the boom contains a monocular NVD. They can pull it down, look into the dark, then flip it back up. I think it's called a near-infrared device."

“Then it needs an IR illuminator,” Thomas said. “Mister Walker, we may not need the IR floods.”

“Good,” Hiram said. “Now let’s see if *Yucca gloriosa* does its job. That’s Spanish dagger to you, Detective Sergeant. Once they get to the top of the wall and look down they’ll see a band of Spanish dagger plants, all over six feet tall, at the base. Wouldn’t want to climb down into that.”

“So they can’t get in?”

“Yes they can, but only where I *want* them to get in. There’s a gap in the Spanish dagger planting about twenty feet down the wall toward the river from where they are now. Assuming they find it, they’ll try to get in right there.”

“They’re going the wrong way,” Thomas commented, as the little red squiggles lit up along the outline of the wall. “Now they’ve turned around. Here we go. About thirty feet.” They watched in silence as the display tracked the intruders’ progress along the top of the wall.

“No razor wire or shards of glass up top?” Av asked.

“No, it’s just a flat concrete cap so that the stems of the ivy can come up and over, along with some microfiber mesh underneath those stems. They can’t feel it, but the mesh can surely feel them. Here we go, they’re stopping.”

“Camera five coming up,” Thomas said, switching the display again. At first there was nothing on the display, and then a flash of greenish light, followed by a second, that seemed to be emanating from the operators’ shoulders. “They’re taking a look,” he said. “I’m going to bring up a low-level IR illuminator in that sector as soon as they turn off their own, see if they notice.”

Gradually, Av saw a picture beginning to emerge on the center display. One man was already on a rope, descending quickly with the rope wrapped around one leg to the inside base of the wall. Then the second, and finally, the third. Thomas saw a hand go up to flip its monocular down, and dimmed the IR floodlight to its lowest setting. The man took a quick sweep, then flipped the boom back up against the side of his head. Thomas turned up the IR flood again.

“What’s down there?” Av asked.

“They’re standing on the banks of a moat, actually,” Hiram said. “Not much of one, maybe ten feet across and not very deep. It's covered by a mat of water-hyacinth plants that have been crossbred with kudzu. The mat's about two feet thick, and right where they are, the mat has been sectioned into a float of sorts. Once one of them steps onto the mat, he'll realize that's it's not terra firma, but: it will support him until he gets out to the middle, which is when the mat is going to flip over on itself and trap him underwater."

"Uh," Av began.

"Remember, the water's only four, four and a half feet deep. All he has to do is stand up and claw his way back out."

"They're communicating with someone," Thomas announced.

"Can we eavesdrop?" Hiram said.

Thomas shook his head. "They'll be using encryption."

They saw a second man's hand reach up to drop his boom. This time Thomas left the tree-mounted IR flood on. The man took a long look, and then pushed his boom back up. One of his partners clipped a rope to his harness. Then he stepped out onto the mat as his partner paid out the rope. He stood for a moment on the spongy mat, and then began to move carefully across, until, suddenly his arms began to windmill, producing a blur of IR light as the mat rolled over. The two men back on firm ground started pulling hard, and soon the first man emerged from under the mass of wet greenery and flopped down on the banks of the water channel.

"Bubblers," Hiram said.

Thomas switched to the control panel for the wide area network of pipes and tubes that underlay the entire garden. He switched on a CO_2 source and soon there were bubbles rising invisibly through the extended mat of hyacinth. In response, the matted mass of vegetation began to move here and there, as if there was something large moving around under the matted mass of vegetation. Av grinned as he saw the men back up against the wall. One of them was gesticulating as he radioed back what they'd encountered.

"Is there a way around the hyacinth bridge?" he asked.

"There is," Hiram said. "It's just to their right. Hopefully they'll find it. Thomas, turn off the CO_2 in the moat. Leave the IR lights at their present level and warm up the UVB matrix."

Av watched the three men huddled at the base of the wall. Their images were in and out of focus. Every time they moved, things went a bit fuzzy.

"Thomas mentioned drinks," Av said, spying a liquor cart.

Hiram turned in his chair. "Quite right," he said. "The best part is yet to come. Over there, in the corner. I'll take a small Scotch. You have one, too, but not too much. You may still have to run for it."

Av went across the room to the small bar on wheels. There were three decanters. He sniffed the first one: bourbon. The second one smelled like a peat bog. He fixed two glasses of that and brought one to Hiram. Run for it?

"Good," Hiram said. "Now, watch this."

The three men were on the move again up on the big screen, easing their way along the hard ground at the base of the brick wall. Without the stimulation of the CO_2 matrix, the hyacinth beds had settled down. They finally encountered a wall of Spanish dagger and stopped. One of them pointed into the jungle: a large tree had come down across the moat, its trunk almost three feet thick. Its upper branches were smashed all along the base of the wall, but the trunk was intact. A bridge. Clearly a bridge.

"That's convenient," Av commented.

"That's planned," Thomas replied from the console. "It's not a real tree."

"Damn," Av said. "Looks real."

"The intent, Detective Sergeant," Hiram said, "is to nudge intruders into areas where they will encounter some of my more interesting creations. The whole idea is to scare any intruders so badly that they leave."

"What's coming?" Av asked.

"Know what a Venus flytrap is?" Hiram asked.

"Yes, sir," Av said. "A plant with teeth, a big mouth, and some strong digestive juices. Insects land, the flaps close, and then the juices go to work."

"Quite so," Hiram said. "I've created a mutation, using a plant whose popular name is elephant ears. Watch."

The first of the operators was edging sideways across the tree trunk, roped up to one of the men waiting at the base of the wall. He stepped off, tested the footing, then took off the rope and flung it back to the second man. Once they got across, all three activated their night vision devices. From what Av could make out on the screen, they were standing in a grove of what looked like small, blurry Christmas trees all along the inner edge of the moat. The plants were about man-high, but Av could not make out individual branches, only the dark green mass of the plants themselves.

"UVA spot to full power on that plant nearest to the group," Hiram ordered.

The men were huddled together, consulting what might have been a map or diagram of the estate. They could probably see the wall across the moat, but behind them there was just an undifferentiated mass of dark vegetation. Thomas entered some control information and Av waited for something to happen.

"You can't see the ultraviolet light on this IR screen," Hiram said. "But that plant can definitely see it. Think of it as an artificial sunrise."

Suddenly, one of the men turned around. Right behind him one of those "Christmas" trees was opening to reveal two vertical, kidney-bean-shaped lobes, as tall as the plant and hinged at the middle. The edges of the lobes were spiked, and apparently, the inside of the plant was much warmer than the outside, because those spikes were clearly visible on the screen.

The man stepped back and nudged his partners. All three backed away from this sudden apparition.

"UV spot to low," Hiram said.

As the three men stared at this thing that was gaping at them, the two lobes slowly began to fold inward until it once again looked like a fat Christmas tree on the screen. The men talked some more, consulted the map again, and turned to head into the jungle. The camera lost sight of them, displaying only faint blobs of warmth when there was enough contrast with the vegetation they were pushing into.

"Full UV matrix," Hiram said.

Again, nothing seemed to happen. Then there appeared to be a commotion off to one side of the screen, as IR blobs came in and out of focus. Only then Av realized that a lot of that vegetation consisted of the giant flytraps, which were now all opening wide. One man pushing through all the vegetation inadvertently stuck his arm into one of the lobes, causing the plant to close on his arm. He tugged frantically but could not get it loose. A second man pushed closer, wielding a large knife, and began to cut into one of the lobes. After a few seconds of hacking away, the trapped man was able to pull his arm out of the plant, but then he frantically began to wipe some substance off his arm as if it was burning his skin.

The man who had cut him out backed into another set of gaping lobes, which snapped shut, trapping the backpack he was wearing.

"Where's the third guy?" Av asked, as the two intruders struggled in jerky motions on the green screen. The man trapped by his backpack shrugged out of the straps and stepped away from the plant and turned around to yank it out of the plant's grasp. The first man was pouring water out of his canteen all along his forearm, which was showing up as being much warmer than the rest of him.

"Strong stuff, digestive juices," Hiram noted. "Dissolved his shirt sleeve and probably burns like hell right now. Ah, there's number three."

The third man came into the frame, dragging a lobe of one of the plants behind him that was attached to his right foot. The second man had taken his knife out again and was hacking his way into the plant to release his backpack.

"Gotta say," Av said. "I'd be shittin' and gittin' right about now."

Hiram smiled. "We'll let them get clear of their personal flytraps," he said. "If this doesn't persuade them, we'll stimulate the spider plants."

"Aw, shit," Av said. "*Spider* plants?"

"Well, they're not spiders of course, but if we stimulate their root systems with a sudden dose of electrolytes, they begin to flex their branches. The branches hang down from a central trunk, like a weeping cherry. From a distance, they look like a big spider standing up and getting ready to come at you."

"In the dark?"

"It's not dark to the plants right now, Detective Sergeant. Remember the UV light. And those guys are all on night vision devices, which distorts the real picture even more."

The three intruders were once again huddled together, with the leader appearing to be back on the radio. The flytraps around them waited like baby birds, lobes agape and weaving slightly. The leader was gesticulating now, clearly arguing with whoever was on the other end of that comm link. The other two were still dealing with patches of the sticky fluid from the flytraps.

"How far are they from the spider plants?" Hiram asked.

Thomas switched to a new, diagrammatic screen. Av saw now that the estate's defenses were in concentric rings, beginning with the wall and the Spanish dagger, then the moat, then the flytrap band, and a band inside of that showing trees and small, star-shaped objects between the larger trees. "Ring four," he said. "Hydroponics are ready to go."

"Let's see if they're ready to call it off," Hiram said. "What's eagle's nest showing?"

Thomas switched screens again. The utility truck was still there, but now there were four other vehicles parked along the road. "There's plan B," Av said. "If the stealth crew can't get in, they'll break down the main gates and stage a frontal assault of some kind. See that big one? That's the federal version of a SWAT command vehicle. They *will* get in."

Thomas had gone back to the camera watching the three operators, who apparently had been told to press on despite all the alien things snatching at them.

"Okay," Hiram said, wearily. "Send the electrolytes and restart the CO_2 bubblers in the vicinity of the fake tree crossing. Add some pure oxygen."

The leader took a swig out of his canteen and passed it around, as the other two had exhausted theirs. They started forward, spread out now, pushing through vegetation and keeping a respectful distance from the flytraps.

"Electrolytes are going in. Do we want sound?"

"Not yet," Hiram said, finishing his Scotch. "If they run from the spiders, then activate the approaching-crowd sounds behind them." He glanced over at Av, whose face was a study in amazement. "I've had years to build all this," Hiram said. "The really important stuff is in the main laboratory and up in the greenhouse. These mutations were mostly for fun, up until I realized what I had achieved in the lab."

"Audio?" Av asked.

"Sure. Remote speakers, programmed to play a variety of digitally produced sounds. Remember the movie *2001, A Space Odyssey*? They had an organ playing a single note in the background just to spook things up a little. We can do that. Or, we can generate the noises made by a distant crowd of men pushing through brush and calling to one another. The screech of a bobcat from a tree right above you. The hiss of a king cobra from directly behind you. Combine things like that with darkness and the phantoms of night vision, plants that seem to be moving on you—most humans will just bolt."

"This human would have bolted a long time ago," Av said, finishing his whisky as he studied the screen. And then he saw them: green blobs rising from the forest floor and swaying back and forth like drunks. At the top of each blob there were eight "eyes" reflecting back at the IR light from the floods. The three men saw them at just about the same moment and stopped cold.

"Eyes?" Av asked.

Hiram grinned. "Reflectors. Tape. As everyone knows, spiders have lots of eyes. Pretty cool, huh?"

The three intruders didn't think so. One unlimbered his MP5 and got ready to fire. The other two called him off, consulted briefly, and then all three turned back in the direction of the wall. As they entered the area of the flytraps, the plants near them began to close and then open again. That apparently did it. The man who'd been ready to start shooting did just that as he backed up in the direction of the wall. The muzzle blasts were brilliant in the IR image as he shot some flytraps to pieces and blew up one spider plant for good measure. They could just barely hear the stutter of the rifle outside.

"Eagle's nest!" Hiram ordered, leaning forward.

Thomas switched cameras and they saw men tumbling out of the SWAT vehicles and start moving toward the main gates at the sound of gunfire. The command vehicle backed up in a cloud of diesel smoke to allow the vehicle that looked like a cross between a tank and a small bulldozer through on the lane.

"Thomas—time to get him to the river."

Thomas switched to the screen that covered the estate's main gate. Then he got up and beckoned for Av to follow him. Av didn't hesitate: that SWAT team or whatever they called themselves would be in the house in less than two minutes.

Thomas and Av trotted down the house's main central hall and then turned into a stairwell. Taking the steps two at a time, they raced down to the basement level. As they passed a coatrack Thomas grabbed some raingear and threw it in Av's direction.

"Where we going?" Av asked.

"To the river. There's a tunnel from the house down to the boathouse. Chop-chop!"

They went through two steel doors, which Thomas locked behind him. When they came to a third door, Thomas entered a code and opened the door to reveal what looked like a concrete utility tunnel: there were insulated pipes, electrical cables, and water lines running along the ceiling and on both walls. The steel door shut itself behind them as they trotted down a gradual slope, their passage lit by glass-enclosed lightbulbs at twenty-foot intervals. Av saw some branch tunnels headed off the main passage, also filled with a great deal of plumbing.

After a five-minute downward-sloping jog they came to another steel door. Thomas again punched in a code that opened the door, admitting a wave of cool air. They were looking at a boathouse. Outside, Av could see the wide expanse of the Potomac River shimmering in the darkness, almost a half-mile wide at this point. Thomas took him to the U-shaped dock, where Av saw a small motorboat hanging on a lift frame. Thomas activated the lift. A winch began to grind away and the boat lowered down to the water's surface.

"Put that stuff on," Thomas said, indicating the raingear. As Av got into the light vinyl pants-and-coat combination, Thomas clipped a strobe light to the coat's collar. Then he handed Av an inflatable life jacket and a set of diving gloves. Av put the jacket on and then the gloves. Thomas handed him a diver's knife, encased in a rubber sheath. He indicated that Av should attach it to his right leg, using the Velcro straps on the pants.

"Okay, sunshine: listen up and listen carefully. That's the Potomac River out there."

"Got it," Av said, half jokingly.

"Good," Thomas said. "Because it's a man-killer. Most blokes have no idea how many people this river has killed along here, but it's a surprisingly large number. We are two miles upstream of the Great Falls of the Potomac. You must *not* go through that cataract under any circumstances. You cannot survive that in a boat. So: take this boat out across the river and head toward the Maryland side and stay there until you're past the Great Falls."

"It's dark," Av said. "How will I know?"

"Once you're out on the river and about two thirds of the way across, turn off the engine. Let the current carry you downstream. The big roaring noise to your right will be the cataract."

He told Av to get into the small boat and then handed him an eight-foot-long pole.

"The Maryland side is full of rocky channels, but nothing like the big cataract. With the engine off the current should carry you through the open channels, but you'll need that pole to fend off the bigger snags. Once you hear the cataract behind you, your next challenge is the Little Falls Dam. There's a patch of quiet water between the Great Falls and the Little Falls. Once you hit that, start the engine again, turn left, and then beach the boat on the Maryland side. After that you're on your own, mate."

"Oka-a-a-y," Av said, not at all confident about his navigating skills on the darkened, man-eating Potomac.

"One more thing: make that turn earlier rather than later. If you hit the Little Falls, no one will ever find you. As soon as you think the Great Falls are behind you, turn left toward the Maryland side and get out of the river. Crank it up, now."

Av turned to the little outboard engine as Thomas instructed him on how to start it. The engine caught after two pulls. As Av was wondering whether he needed to warm it up, Thomas cast him off and shoved the boat with his right foot out into the current. Av pointed the little boat across the black mass of streaming water. He saw flashes of light up on the grounds of the big house. He wondered if Hiram had any idea of what a SWAT team did when it broke into a house. On the other hand, he wondered if the SWAT team had any idea of what Dr. Frankenstein might have waiting for them when they tried it.

While Thomas was seeing to their guest's getaway, Hiram took over the main console and upped the magnification on the main gate area. That team was definitely getting ready to do something. The street tank had arrived in front of the main gates and was pointed at the house. Several other figures were deploying on either side of the gates, while a smaller team was headed down the wall in the direction of the intrusion team.

Hiram switched the cameras again to find the terrified threesome climbing back over the wall, with two of them on the rope and the third man covering their rear with his submachine gun while standing on the end of the rope.

Back to the treetop camera. The assault team, for that's what it looked like, were all in position, but, for some reason they weren't moving. He searched the scene for a command vehicle, and thought he saw one back up the lane.

What were they waiting for? Orders? Or did they want to debrief their intrusion team first to see what the shooting had been all about.

He was relieved when Thomas came back into the room.

Once clear of the boathouse and the Virginia bank of the Potomac, Av pointed his little boat on a diagonal across the big river, already feeling the strength of the current. The engine was small but it sounded like it was happy. He was glad for the raingear. His jeans and T-shirt outfit weren't meant for a fall night on the big river.

Av's knowledge of the Potomac was limited to MPD barbecue outings down on Haines Point, where the river was a silvery lake, with no hint of violence. If someone fell in at Haines Point, the immediate worry was what he might be covered in when they got him back on the bank. This was very different and he could feel the current's strength. It made him wonder what would happen if he tried to go back upstream and if the little engine was big enough.

Av knew that several miles upstream at Harper's Ferry, the entire Shenandoah River added its stream to what was coming down from the eastern slopes of the Alleghenys. As it approached the palisades along Great Falls, that huge volume of water was funneled into rocky gorges some sixty to eighty feet high. Moving water confined becomes fast water, and, with the bottom made of slate, shattered over the eons into rows of underwater crevasses, the river there was no place for swimmers or, for that matter, small boats.

AV could sense that his boat seemed to be going faster, if the lights along the Virginia shore were any indication. He pointed the bow of the boat to the left to compensate for what felt like an out-of-control surge in the current. Then he heard the low rumble of the Great Falls cataracts to his right. He recalled taking a young lady out to Great Falls Park for a picnic date. He remembered the sign on the rocks above the booming cataract: if you go into the water, you will die. He'd never seen such a stark sign at any park, but one look at the rocky gorge confirmed the message.

He pointed the bow of the little motorboat farther to the left to make sure he wasn't being swept into the deceptively calm open channel above the cataract. Then he remembered his instructions: get left of the center channel, kill the engine, let the river take you through the fast-moving channels until that menacing rumble was *behind* you. Then, light the engine back off and run for the Maryland shore.

Okay, he thought. He reached over and switched off the outboard. The first thing he realized was that the rumble of water going down the Great Falls gorge was louder than he'd thought. Too soon? he wondered. But no, it was to his right and sliding behind him. Loud, powerful, threatening, but passing behind him. Ahead was a wide expanse of river, spattered with small white ripples as the current ran over rock snags. He grabbed the pole and prepared to fend off obstacles, but then realized he couldn't see anything that resembled obstacles. Then he learned that the obstacles had a purpose of their own as the boat banged off a rock, and then another one, swerving in the current and jinking in different directions as if totally out of control. He felt ridiculous holding the pole. What good was it if he couldn't see the rock coming?

Then the boat stopped suddenly, pinned by the muscular current against a rock ledge. The water began to rise up on the upstream side of the boat, certain to swamp it. He lunged with the pole and, when it hit solid rock, he pushed. The boat swirled in place, dropping him into the middle of the boat, and then it whirled again and swept downstream. He got back on the single gunwale, trying to get his bearings, and then the boat hit the next snag, again dumping him onto the aluminum bottom. The pole sailed out of his grip with the impact. He tried to regain his footing, but the boat was nothing but a cork now as the big river's current flung it downstream, banking from snag to snag, sometimes hard enough to make him wonder if the small craft could take much more.

Little Falls Dam. In his effort to stay upright, he'd forgotten all about the Little Falls Dam.

He scrambled to the back of the boat and set the ignition switch. The boat hit something really solid and almost backed up in the current for a moment before shooting through a chute of white water. He felt a swirl of icy water on his feet. The hull was punctured; he was sure of it. Regaining his footing, he started pulling on the rope as hard as he could.

Choke. You have to choke it.

He set the choke and tried again. He smelled gasoline. Dammit! Flooded it.

The boat went sideways and stopped suddenly, heeling over at an alarming angle. Water began to sweep in as he kept yanking on the cord. Then the engine caught. He grabbed the handle and gunned the engine. More water came in, so he turned the handle, urging the boat across the current and out of the narrow chute of white water. It made it, but he felt that the boat was getting logy and unresponsive. Too much water onboard.

Where was Maryland? Which way? He had no idea.

Then the sky above him exploded into white light as a helicopter swooped down over his position, its rotors punishing the air over his head and blowing huge clouds of spray everywhere. Blinded by the spray, he pushed the handle hard over, trying to get out from under the roaring machine that seemed to be right over his head. He could smell the acrid stink of JP-5 from the turbine exhaust. Then a rope or wire slapped him in the chest before flying off to one side of the boat.

Rope? He realized the situation was totally out of control. He had no idea of what to do next. The downwash from the hovering helicopter continued to blind him and he was still going downriver. How far was that dam?

Then a man dropped into the boat, almost capsizing it in the rushing current. He was wearing a dark jumpsuit and a compact helmet with a wraparound face shield. The weight of two large men in the boat began to sink it. A second man appeared, still on the rope, dangling just above the boat and pointing some kind of weapon at Av's face. A second wire appeared, with a horseshoe-shaped collar dangling from the end. The man in the boat braced himself and slipped the collar over Av's head and under his armpits, and then made a signal. Before Av had a moment to realize what was happening, the wire tightened and he was dangling over the boat and the river, and then being hauled up toward a black, rectangular hole in the side of the hovering helicopter. He felt himself slipping out of the wet horseshoe collar and quickly grabbed the sides.

He looked down through all the downwash spray blowing in the harsh white light and thought he saw the rolling curl of the Little Falls Dam just fifty feet from the now twirling boat. The water going over the low dam was deceptively calm as it dropped over the eighteenth-century rock abutment into a dark coil of white water. The man who had dropped into the boat was beneath him, riding a second wire back up.

He looked up. The wire was being stabilized by another man who was leaning out of a side hatch in the aircraft. In the clouds of downdraft spray under the helo he saw the little boat pop over the falls, drop straight down into that roiling black water, and then disappear without a trace. He bumped up against the side of the aircraft, and then someone pulled him in, removed the horse collar, dropped a cloth hood over his face, and pushed him away from the hatch until he bumped up against a bulkhead. The helicopter continued to hover for a few more seconds until the man below him was hauled in. Then it lifted urgently away from the river's surface, banked hard, dipped its nose, and accelerated.

Hiram watched the crowd of menacing vehicles converging at the front gates, their strobe lights flashing a whole spectrum of color. Nobody was moving, yet.

"Thomas," he said. "I think we should go ahead and open the gates. Not sure we could find any more like those."

Thomas flicked on the main entrance lights and then commanded the gates to open. Hiram reached over to a side table and picked up a telephone.

"Nine-one-one, what is your emergency?"

"Home invasion," Hiram stated, matter-of-factly. He gave the address for Whitestone Hall, and then added: "Shots fired."

Thomas raised his eyebrows. "Always wanted to say that," Hiram said, his hand over the telephone's microphone. The operator wanted to know how many people were in the house and where they were located. Hiram told them two and that they were in the library. She asked how many intruders were at the scene. "About thirty," Hiram said, and then hung up. "Now get me the news-tip hotline number at WTOP," he told Thomas, who punched the station's name into a computer.

"877-222-1035," Thomas said. Hiram dialed the number as he watched the screen. The crowd at the front gate didn't seem to know what to do now that the big gates were open and they were all standing under floodlights.

"WTOP: news hotline," a young woman's voice announced.

Hiram told her that one of the mansions out in Great Falls was being assaulted by a government SWAT team, and gave her the address. "There are reports of gunfire," he concluded and then hung up.

Out front a line of armed men in bulky defensive gear had started through the gates and were spreading out on either side of the driveway.

"Not too far, boys," Hiram muttered. "Stay on the road."

Then one of the unarmed vehicles turned in and headed for the house. The rest of the vehicles remained clustered around the front gates, while one SUV, bristling with antennae, crawled slowly down the lane toward where the intrusion team had first climbed the wall. The tank had backed out of the scene when the gates opened.

"Showtime," Hiram said, getting out of his chair. Thomas got up as well but Hiram waved him back down. "Stay on the consoles, watch the walls. They may try again."

Thomas reached under his cable-knit sweater and produced a handgun.

Hiram smiled and shook his head. "That would be all they'd need," he said. "No, I'm going to do a little monster Kabuki. See how they like that. Unlock the front doors."

The screen showed the SUV had reached the area of the front portico. Three men were getting out of the vehicle, two in defensive tactical gear with weapons, and one in just a suit, a small portable radio visible in one hand. Hiram walked through the library and down the main hall of the house, pausing only to pick a pretty pink flower from a vase. He squeezed the flower and then applied the resulting fluid to his closed eyes. He felt a mild stinging sensation, and then the surface of his eyes went numb. He glanced in a mirror as he walked toward the front doors. His eyes were now bright red.

He stopped halfway to the door and waited. There was a tentative knock on the front doors, and then, after a long minute, someone tried the right-hand door and swung it open. The three men stepped into the darkened hallway, and that's when Hiram drew himself to his full height and began to walk toward them, affecting just the slightest limp.

"Holy shit!" one of the armed men said when he saw Hiram approaching. All three of them stopped in their tracks. The two armed men adjusted their grips on their weapons and moved away from the man in the suit. Hiram focused on that man: he had to be the boss. He walked up to within three feet of the suit, leaned forward, and opened his eyes wide.

The suit made a noise and stepped back away from this glaring, red-eyed apparition leaning over him.

"What do you want?" Hiram asked in his best imitation of a sepulchral voice. He resisted the temptation to put a Boris Karloff accent in play, something he had mastered a long time ago.

"We—um—we want Detective Sergeant Kenneth Smith of the Metro Washington Police Department," the suit said. He was about forty, pasty-faced, and incongruously out of shape considering the company he was keeping.

"Where is he?" the man asked.

One of the armed men pressed a hand to his head and listened to a message from the front gate. Then he spoke up. "Fairfax County cops are on scene?" he announced.

The suit hesitated, and then asked Hiram again: where was the detective sergeant?

"He was here and now he is not," Hiram said, inching closer to this obviously frightened civil servant. "He came by boat, he left by boat. He's on the river. How is your intrusion team?"

"Wha-a-t?" the man answered. "What intrusion team?"

"The ones who fired automatic weapons in my gardens," Hiram said, leaning forward. The man practically quailed. "They are lucky to be alive.

Did you know that? That is a *venom* garden. The plants out there can eat and *digest* humans. I suggest you leave now."

"I must search this house," the man said in a weak voice.

"Show me your search warrant," Hiram replied.

"I don't have one," the man said. "Actually, I don't need one. This is a matter of national security. The FISA court can backdate—"

At that moment the sounds of a helicopter could be heard coming through the open front doors. It made a waspish sound, not military at all. The guard who'd received the first radio message again pressed the side of his helmet to his ear.

"News chopper," he said, looking worried for the first time.

Hiram chose this moment to step forward and get so close to the suit that the man had to literally bend his neck back to look into Hiram's massive face. "Do you wish to become immortal?" Hiram whispered, baring his huge teeth just a little.

"Wha-a-t?" the man squeaked.

"Whoever sent you would want you to leave now, before all of you become national news. Think of *me* appearing on national television and telling the world what your people did tonight. Without a warrant. Without informing the local police forces. Climbing a wall and invading a private residence. Firing automatic weapons—against plants." Hiram straightened up. "Go now, while you still can."

He then turned his back on them and walked back down the hall into the gloom at the other end. To his immense satisfaction he heard them scampering out the front doors.

He glanced up at the surveillance camera at the end of the hall. "Oscar, yes?" he asked the watching Thomas. "At least an Emmy."

He could hear Thomas laughing all the way from the comm center.

Back in the communications room Thomas had been watching the scene unfold at the front gates as the Fairfax County police argued with all the unmarked federals. Hiram wished he had an audio feed from the gates. Then a second news chopper appeared, this one a bit more bold than the first one. The aircraft swooped down over the trees along the river and then came slowly up the wall with its landing lights on. The first helicopter immediately maneuvered to take advantage of the lighting to film the entire cluster-fuck going on out on the lane. They'll all be bailing out pretty soon, Hiram thought. The black world of counterterrorism feared nothing so much as the sudden arrival of the media.

"Boss?" Thomas said.

Hiram turned around and looked at the screen. A ghostly green figure was moving up the western side of the defensive garden.

"Well, well," Hiram said. "All the Hollywood out front was, what—a diversion?"

"Apparently so," Thomas said. "But look where he's headed."

"Ah," Hiram said. "You know what, Thomas? These people are beginning to annoy me."

"God help them, then," Thomas muttered.

Av felt the aircraft settling in altitude as it flew in what seemed like pretty much a straight line. His back was against a bulkhead, and he was still hooded. No one had done anything to restrain him, but he felt the presence of large men in tactical gear sitting on either side of him. The inside of the helicopter smelled of sweat, gun oil, hydraulic oil, and ozone in about equal proportions. That side hatch was still partially open, which helped.

He forced himself to relax. They were waiting for me, he thought. As soon as he'd made it halfway across the river, there they were, and probably a good thing, too. He'd been a lot closer to that dam Thomas had warned him about than he'd known. He could still see the little boat going over what looked like a nothing waterfall and just disappearing in a roil of shiny black water.

So: who were "they"? Mandeville's people? Tactically trained operators from the other side of that mythical Chinese wall between the DMX and the real work?

He felt the men on either side of him move away from the bulkhead.

"We're going to land now," one of them said, leaning in to speak through the hood. "Then we're going to get out. Do we need to restrain you?"

Av said no. The hood was secured by tight elastic around his throat. Where was he going to go?

"Be cool," the man said. "Don't make me break one of your legs." As if to emphasize the point, the invisible man tapped what felt like an iron rod on his shinbone. Av resisted the impulse to cry out. That really hurt.

The helicopter did some banking and turning and then pitched up slightly, the rotors gaining power as the machine flared out to make its approach. A moment of sideslipping, lots more noise from the rotors, and then he felt the aircraft bump gently down onto the ground. Almost immediately the engines began to whine down. The rotors followed suit, spinning down from full RPM to an almost gentle whop-whop as they shed lift and airspeed. Av could almost see them starting to droop.

He heard doors sliding fully open on both sides of the aircraft and then he was hoisted upright. Someone removed his sheath knife.

"Steps," the man said. "Wire handrails on either side. Go down, slowly."

Av stepped out and down onto the first step. He reached for the wires and found them.

Once on the ground, both of his escorts moved in and walked him up what felt like a grassy slope. He could still smell the jet engine exhaust through the rough cloth of the hood. Then he stumbled when his right foot hit concrete. The men kept him from falling and then told him to stop.

"Bench," one of them said, turning him around and then pushing him down onto what felt like a wooden park bench. The other one took hold of Av's right forearm and pressed it down onto the bench. Av felt some kind of restraint slip over his hand and then click down onto the bench. Then he sensed he was alone, although the two men made no sound as they walked away.

It was cool, wherever he was. The helicopter was silent now, although not very far away. He could hear its engines clicking in the night air as the turbines cooled down. He thought he could hear another, lower-register sound in the distance. The river? Yes, that's what it was. So they were somewhere along the Potomac, probably on the Virginia side since the river noise seemed to be coming from way below where he was sitting.

Nothing happened for about fifteen minutes, but then he heard the sound of a heavy automobile crunching its way over gravel and coming in his direction. The vehicle stopped not too far away. He waited for the sounds of doors opening, but now there was just the sound of the river pushing through the palisades. He heard some radio communications chattering from a speaker in the direction of the helicopter. He caught a whiff of cigarette smoke, which told him that whoever was nearby, they weren't exactly excited by what they were doing.

He surreptitiously tried the arm restraint, which seemed to be working just fine. The bench was rock solid and probably bolted to the ground. Not going anywhere soon, he thought. Still no noises from the vehicle, but definitely more cigarette smoke. They were obviously all waiting for someone. He thought he knew who that someone was going to be.

TWENTY-FOUR

Hiram picked up the phone and dialed a number. While it rang he asked Thomas if he'd managed to put the tracking button somewhere in Av's clothing. Thomas nodded.

"This is Ellen Whiting."

"We got him out onto the river and we've dealt with the clowns they sent to grab him here," Hiram said.

"The HRT has him," she said. "With any luck it'll be going down in about fifteen, maybe twenty minutes."

"Where?"

"Fort Marcy Park," she said. "Off the GW Parkway. You know, where that Clinton lawyer supposedly shot himself."

"Do you have any kind of support?"

"Couldn't reach out to anybody federal beyond the HRT, not for this, but the sergeant's partners are with me. If he comes, he won't come alone, but I think we can handle it."

"Very well," Hiram said. "I've got one loose end to deal with here, and then we'll be right along."

"Loose end?" she said.

"I think the first intrusion was a diversion. The real deal's here now. One guy."

"Watch yourself," she said. "But hurry."

"This won't take long, Special Agent. He's about to enter the snake pool garden."

"Jesus, Hiram," she said. "*Snake* pool?"

"Just a figure of speech, my dear," Hiram said and then hung up.

He turned back to the big screen, while keeping one eye out for any activity on the front-gate display, visible on the right-hand screen. The figure creeping through the woods was clearly visible. Adrenaline, Hiram thought. Warms you up. Who are you?

"How far from the edge?" he asked.

"Thirty yards, maybe less. Looks like he's checking a weapon of some kind."

"Close in."

The telephoto function revealed the man checking a semiautomatic handgun with a bulb of some kind at the end of the barrel. "Silencer," Thomas said. "Start the warm-water matrix?"

"Yes. Add ten percent nitrogen and UV lights as well. Stir those things up. That's a killer out there."

Thomas punched control orders into his console, and eighty-degree water began to push out to what they called the snake garden. There were no snakes, of course, or at least none of theirs. Surrounded by strategically placed Spanish dagger plantings was an Olympic-sized pool with what looked like a narrow, grass-covered footbridge across the midpoint. Based on where the intruder had gained access to the grounds, there was really no other covert way to go if someone was trying to get near the house from the direction of the river without a lot of backtracking, other than taking a very exposed walk up the gravel walk between the cascading pools.

It was what was inside this pool that made it a wholly different proposition than the scary monsters on the landward side of the estate. The pool was roughly rectangular and twenty feet deep, and filled with a species of African water vine that had evolved to trap and feed on animal proteins. They grew just below the surface of still water and created a great mass of vines, tubes, and tendrils, all rooted in three feet of muck. They fed during the daytime, hence the injection of warm water into the pool and the rise of the UV radiation would stimulate their tendrils to secrete a water-impervious sticky substance all along the vines. Hiram had nurtured this particular specimen because it, of all his plants, acted most like it had a brain of some kind.

The figure stopped when he encountered the pool and the footbridge. He turned to his left but then saw the wall of Spanish dagger.

He was wearing night vision gear with its own illuminator, which made it easy for the estate's IR video system to track him. The man then went to his right and found the second stand of Spanish dagger plants. He came back to the footbridge across the pool.

He clearly did not want to cross that pool.

"This one senses the trap," Hiram observed.

"Then we need to motivate him," Thomas said.

"Right, do it."

Thomas activated the line of small speakers that had been mounted in trees down near the river. He selected the program that would make the sounds of a group of men starting to spread out in the woods and then come forward on the trail of the intruder. The sounds were started at a very low level, barely audible behind where the intruder was now, unless he was listening very carefully. They'd continue, gaining slightly in volume, then stop suddenly for a couple of minutes as the search team "froze" for some reason. Then they'd resume, getting louder now but still barely audible. If that didn't do it, Thomas could add the whining of eager but still restrained search dogs to the mix.

The posse program, as they called it, had run only for about sixty seconds when the intruder made his decision.

Hurry up and wait, Av thought. Just like being back in the Marines. He felt himself getting sleepy. He yawned. He was bushed.

A part of his brain reminded him that he'd just been plucked out of the river by some kind of military team, blinded by a black hood, and then deposited on the ground, only to be handcuffed to a park bench. He tried to recall how all this had started.

The McGavin thing. Then he tried to make sense of it. He couldn't. He mentally recited his mantra of protest: I'm just a drone in the Metro PD's Briar Patch. So why the hell am I sitting here, waiting to be reintroduced to some maniac on the National Security Council?

A cold sensation settled over him. You know exactly why, he realized.

The intruder pulled a length of white rope out of his backpack, fastened a loop around his chest under his arms, and then tied one end off to a tree near the edge of the pool.

"Good thinking," Thomas said.

"That won't save him," Hiram said. "Look at the IR signature from the pool."

"Oh, boy," Thomas said. "I must say, boss, that I've never quite been able to get my head around the concept of a plant having a brain, but this one . . ."

"Is hungry, unless I miss my guess," Hiram finished for him. "Ah—showtime."

The intruder advanced across the footbridge, which had been built with a slight arch. His weapon was no longer in evidence, and he had both hands on that rope as it uncoiled behind him. He stopped a few feet from the top of the gentle arch in the bridge.

Hiram's eyes gleamed as he watched. One sentient being—on the bridge—had just sensed another sentient being—under the bridge. He was convinced of it.

Then the bridge broke in half and dropped him into the water.

The man disappeared for a moment but then surfaced in a froth of water between the two segments of the bridge, which were sagging out of sight in the water. The piece of the bridge nearest the intruder's start point snagged his rope, broke it, and pulled it underwater.

The man frantically tried to clear it, but not before the bridge had pulled him almost underwater. Then the rope snapped clear, but it was too late. The great mass of vines, sensing prey, had uncoiled a sponge of sticky tendrils.

The green man struggled in the water, pulling hard on his rope, but the mass of vines beneath him far outweighed his efforts to escape. He pulled harder, and then, taking a deep breath, dropped beneath the surface to get some leverage on whatever had his legs and then resurface and pull himself out.

He did not reappear. The two of them watched, waiting for the tell. Finally it came—a mass of bubbles surfaced on the pool. After that, nothing moved.

"Okay," Hiram said. "Another bad guy returned to the biomass. Let's go."

Hiram checked the front-gate cameras before going down to the lab. The circus out by the gates had wound down to the point where only two Fairfax County cruisers were parked out front, and the cops appeared to be doing paperwork. The federal posse had decamped when the second news chopper showed up, and now both helicopters were also gone. Thomas had done one final perimeter scan and found no more intruders. One of the hydroponic lines was losing pressure, possibly from that burst of gunfire out in the defensive gardens.

Down in the lab Hiram went to one of the glass-fronted refrigerators and pulled out a short-stemmed white carnation that was standing in a solitary test tube. There was a clear plastic bulb at the base of the stem, filled with an amber fluid. He picked up the test tube and then he took the elevator back up to the main floor, where he went to the hall closet. There he shed his tweed jacket for a black frock coat that had been tailored for his towering frame. Steadying his hands, he extracted the flower and slid that stem into the boutonniere slit in the coat's lapel He picked up a walking stick and a black homburg and then walked down to the front doors.

Out front was what they called the Batmobile—a specially configured Class B recreational vehicle made by Mercedes that could accommodate Hiram's extra-tall frame just behind the two captain's chairs in front. The roof was raised and there was an electric sliding door on the side that he could use to enter the vehicle, as well as handrails so he could position himself in the oversized middle seat without too much discomfort. All the windows except the front windshield were tinted. The living quarters furnishings in the back of the vehicle had been removed; that area now contained communications equipment that fed a small television screen set, facing aft, between the two captain's chairs up front. The vehicle was painted a shiny black, hence its nickname. Two finlike communications antennae on the back of the roof added to the image.

Hiram carefully pulled himself into the center of the vehicle and then Thomas closed the electric sliding doors. He got into the driver's chair and punched some data into the navigation device on the console.

"Drive the indicated route," the robot finally said.

"How long?" Hiram asked.

"Thirty minutes," Thomas said. "Assuming the Beltway is moving."

"Very well," Hiram said. "Let's go."

They drove down the big front drive out the gates past the two cop cars, and headed out onto Deepstep Creek Road toward the Georgetown Pike.

"Your meds are in the cup holder on the console."

"And thank God for that," Hiram said.

"Thank Thomas, too."

Av had started to fall asleep when suddenly he heard another vehicle approaching. The cigarette smoke seemed to disappear, and he now could hear people around him, gathering themselves.

Showtime, he thought.

Someone approached and removed his hood. He took a deep breath and looked around. He was indeed sitting on a wooden park bench. It wasn't any kind of large park, but more of a scenic overlook pull-off. The helicopter was sitting quietly to his left, its blades drooping over the grassy spot where it had landed. There were three crewmen in flight suits and helmets standing under it, looking at him. The vehicle he'd heard approaching was a black Expedition, stopped now in the small parking lot. All of its doors were open and there were armed men getting out. A hundred feet beyond, another vehicle was coming down the lane with only its parking lights on.

The approaching vehicle appeared to be an armored sedan, if the heavy crunching noise of the gravel was any indication. It pulled into the spot next to the Expedition and shut down. A man jumped out of the driver's seat, hurried around to the right rear door, and opened it respectfully. The imposing figure of Carl Mandeville materialized and then headed toward the bench. He stopped about three feet away, looking down at Av like an eagle looks at a fat rabbit.

Av resisted an impulse to shout out a, Hey, Carl, what's shakin', dude. Instead, he cleared his throat, hawked up a presentable goober and spat it at Mandeville's shoes. All the men around him looked at him as if he was insane. Somehow Av found that satisfying.

Carl Mandeville did not. He came closer, leaned down, and slapped Av in the face.

"Big, brave man," Av said through stinging lips. "Pretty good when your target is handcuffed to a bench. They call that Chicago style up there at the White House?"

Mandeville straightened up. He pulled a handkerchief out of his trousers pocket and wiped his hand, as if to remove any contamination. "I hear they call you 'average' Smith," he said. "Average asshole would be more like it, I think."

"Better than average murderer," Av said.

Mandeville stared down at him for a moment. "Well," he said quietly, "in for a penny, in for a pound." He turned to the operators standing near the Expedition. "Where did they pick him up?" he asked.

"Out on the river," one of them replied. "Just above Little Falls Dam."

"Good," Mandeville said. "I don't want him anymore. Tell the pilots to go put him back, right where they found him." Then he turned to Av. "You know about the Little Falls Dam of the Potomac?" he asked.

Av shrugged. "Great Falls, Little Falls, all waterfalls look alike to me," he said. Some of the men behind Mandeville seemed to have disappeared. Didn't want to watch this? Or hear it?

"Well, this one's different. It's called Little Falls Dam because it only drops about five feet. Man-made, a long time ago, to divert water to the Washington city reservoirs. But here's the thing, Detective. There's a rotor on the downstream side. That means that anything, or any*one* who goes over those little falls ends up underneath them, rolling and rolling for just about forever. The rotor never lets go once it takes somebody, and there have been dozens of people lost there. Dozens. You're going to be next."

Av didn't say anything. What could he say to this lunatic? Please?

Mandeville stepped back and looked at Av with a satisfied smile. "My specialty, Detective. Loose ends."

Then Av saw one of the pilots walking toward them. He called out to Mandeville by name.

"What do you want?" Mandeville said, obviously annoyed. "My instructions should have been perfectly clear."

"Not going to do that, Mister Mandeville," the pilot said.

"*What* did you say?"

The second pilot walked up. "He said we're not gonna drop a guy into the river just above Little Falls Dam," he announced. He was older than the first pilot and had the air of command about him. "In fact, we're leaving now. You want us, you can find us over at Bolling. Good night." A pause. "Sir."

Mandeville was obviously stunned by this development. Then he realized that the people who had come with him were also leaving. The Expedition was backing up as the helicopter's turbines began to turn. The man who had driven Mandeville here was walking toward the Expedition, which was now waiting for him, the right rear door held open.

Hey, what about me, Av wanted to shout out, but the only one who could hear him now was Carl Mandeville, who was becoming almost apoplectic. The Expedition made a wide turn and then went up the lane toward the parkway, its taillights flickering through the shrubbery that lined the lane. The helicopter spooled up to full power, lifted off, turned in place, blowing a whirlwind of leaves everywhere, and then dipped down into the river gorge.

Then it was just Av and his tormentor.

"What's going on, big shot?" Av asked. "Rats abandoning the sinking ship?"

Mandeville glared at him, then looked around again to make sure that everyone had indeed left. The armored sedan was still there.

"Do you know where *you* are, Detective?" he asked, seeming to get himself under control.

Av lifted his tethered arm, yanking gently on the cord that held him to the bench. "Right here on this bench," he said.

"This is Fort Marcy Park," Mandeville said. "This is where the Clintons' lawyer killed himself. Right on that bench, in fact. Shot himself in the head. Right side, as I recall, even though he was supposedly left-handed. I think he was also a man who knew too much."

"So I'm going to be a suicide?" Av asked.

"An 'apparent' suicide," Mandeville said. "Know the difference?"

"No."

"An apparent suicide is one which doesn't get investigated too closely. If it looks like a suicide, then, well, it probably was. Lots of cops eat their guns. You were suspended, accused of all sorts of strange behavior, detained in a federal penitentiary, from which you managed to escape. But then the authorities tracked you down, went to your home again, but you did a runner. And now here you are, alone, in the dark, obviously distraught at how your life has gone right off the tracks."

"Is this what's called spin?"

"Oh, yes, Detective. That's exactly what it's called. And people who work at the White House are masters of it. Trust me on that."

"You really kill those guys, those two assistant secretaries?"

"Me?" Mandeville said. "Absolutely not. They were terminated by a professional, for the crime of treason. I simply lit the fuse, so to speak."

"Treason? For what, disagreeing with you?"

"*Hell,* no," Mandeville said, vehemently. "I am a servant of the state. I am the keeper of the DMX, which is one of the few remaining *sharp* arrows in the quiver of national security that can actually do some good. Those men were determined to take it all apart. Two of them have been dealt with, and the third, I am told, has gone, let me see, on *vacation.* As if that will make any difference."

"You're going to get him, too?"

"I am going to purify the DMX," Mandeville said, the gleam of certain madness in his eyes. "The whole DMX, if necessary. Whatever that takes. But first, I need to take care of the insolent loose end sitting in front of me."

Mandeville took a deep breath and looked around again. The park was quiet and dark. The river made its eternal rushing sounds down below in the gorge. The hum of traffic up on the parkway competed with the night breeze lifting up the rock walls of the Potomac gorge, annoying the trees.

"Good-bye, Detective," Mandeville said. Then he pulled out a pistol from his suit coat pocket, approached Av from the right side, and lifted the gun to point at Av's temple.

Av took a deep breath, tried to think of something really clever to say, and drew a panicked blank.

Then there was a loud snap, followed by a yelp from Mandeville as the gun went flying out of his hand, which was now spurting blood. The big man whirled away, clutching his bleeding hand, but looking for the gun. He saw it and bent down to pick it up with his other hand. He raised it, weaving a little from the pain in his right hand, and turned back toward Av.

Snap!

This time the gun itself was hit, along with one of Mandeville's fingers.

He screamed this time, trying to hold one bleeding hand with the other. He bent over at the waist, grunting in pain. Av watched in amazement as the big man finally sat down on the ground, almost weeping, his two bloodied hands held tight to his stomach, his breath getting ragged. The gun and one finger were on the ground right in front of him.

Then Av heard a wonderful sound, an earsplitting kiyai as Wong Daddy stepped out of the woods, stamping his feet on the asphalt and shaking the trees as he walked up to the huddled bleeding figure of Carl Mandeville and smacked him on the head so hard that Mandeville's head almost came off. His body rolled to the right and out into the parking lot, where it lay very still.

Wong came over to the bench, took a deep breath, and then hand-chopped the board to which Av's arm was tethered. The board shattered and Av was free. He looked up into the big and very pleased moon face above him.

"Took you long enough," Av said, rubbing his wrist. "Who's your sniper?"

"Miz Brown," said a familiar voice. Mau-Mau and Ellen Whiting were approaching. "Told you he had *two* special talents. Uses an old, single-shot Remington model 513T with a sling. Sucker can shoot the eye out of a fly."

As Av absorbed this revelation, two more federal-looking vehicles came down the narrow lane leading in from the parkway. Av eyed them warily, but Ellen was already talking to one of the SUVs on a small radio.

"Them's the white hats," Mau-Mau explained. "Your old buddy Tyree Miller is in one of them."

"Somebody going to explain all this weirdness?" Av asked. His left cheek was a bit swollen after Mandeville's love tap, and a part of him was still ready and willing to take off into the bushes if people became sufficiently distracted. He saw Miz Brown coming down to the parking lot with a stainless-steel scoped rifle held casually across his chest. For once he wasn't talking, but he did wave.

Several FBI agents got out of the two SUVs, including Miller, who walked over to where Mau-Mau and Av were standing. He offered his hand to Av with an apologetic smile. "No hard feelings, I hope," he said. "Anyone told you what's going down here?"

Av took the proffered hand warily. "Not yet," he said.

"Ever heard the term 'stalking horse'?" Miller asked.

"Nope," he said.

Two of the agents had roused Mandeville and had him standing up while a third was opening a first-aid kit. His bloody hands were clenched into quivering fists and his face was one big glare. Not at all like in the movies, Av thought, seeing a flash of exposed bone. Hands do bleed.

Ellen Whiting had been on her radio but now approached. "He's actually coming," she announced. Miller nodded and then walked over to where Mandeville was standing unsteadily, trying not to cry.

"Carl Mandeville, you are under arrest for the murders of Francis McGavin and Hilary Logan. You have the right to remain silent. You—"

"In your dreams," Mandeville spat, wincing as the agent bandaged his ruined hand. "You can't touch me. I am special—"

"We know who you *were,* Mister Mandeville," Miller interrupted. "Right now, however, you are the prime suspect in two murders of senior federal officials. We're still looking for your hatchet man and anyone else he used, but for the first catch, you'll do just fine."

"Never happen," Mandeville said. "No matter what you *think* you know, you have no case. Nor do you have a venue, because everything to do with my job is classified way beyond even the almighty Bureau."

"We can get around all that, Mandeville," Miller said. "We have two people right here who can make a pretty good case that you were the mastermind here. And why."

Mandeville's face contracted as a spasm of pain went up his arms. But then the glare reappeared. "A *good* case?" He snorted. "Bullshit. You have nothing but hearsay. You have no evidence because there is no evidence."

"How would you know that, Carl?" Ellen asked coolly.

"I know lots of things and, even better, lots of important people," Mandeville said. "Tell me something, Mister G-man: you say *I* had a hand in killing those two people? Tell me *how* I did that? Can you do that? Do you know *what* killed them? How they died? No, you do not."

"But *I* do," said a deep voice from just beyond the perimeter of the parked cars. Several of the agents jumped when they caught sight of the towering, gaunt figure walking down toward them. One of the agents started to draw his weapon but then reconsidered.

Av felt the need to sit down. This had been the strangest day of his life, and he suspected it wasn't over yet, as the larger-than-life figure of Hiram Walker stopped in front of the gathered agents.

"What the *fuck* are you?" Mandeville croaked. His heavily bandaged hand looked like a white blob now, but it wasn't completely white anymore.

"I'm the one who handed over some rather exotic materials to your office at the request of a man named Kyle Strang," Hiram said. "Supposedly in support of the War on Terror, as orchestrated by the DMX committee. You, on the other hand, are the man who took those materials and used them to kill two members of that committee because they lost faith in the entire concept of DMX. I can tell any forensic pathologist who wants to know *precisely* what killed those two men."

"Then that makes you part of this, too," Mandeville said, triumphantly.

"In *your* dreams, Mister Mandeville," Miller said. "He's on our side." Then he turned to the other agents. "Get him to the nearest trauma center. Tight custody. No communications allowed. None, got it? When they're done with him, take him to Quantico to the BSU, isolate him under guard, and wait for my instructions."

The agents began to steer Mandeville toward one of the SUVs, but Hiram Walker stepped in front of them. He took the little white carnation out of his boutonniere slit and pinned it into Mandeville's breast pocket. "Just a reminder, Mister Mandeville, in case you think I'd forgotten you. Consider it a memento."

Hiram then turned around and made his way back up the hill toward his waiting vehicle. Av thought he was moving slower than before. Maybe it was the hill.

Mandeville made to brush the white flower out of his pocket, but the agents had a firm grip on both his elbows. They led him over to one of the SUVs and made him take the center seat in the back. One of them handcuffed each of his wrists to a strap running across the back of the front seat, and then put on his seat belt. Av's last sight of him was of that big face grimacing in pain and Olympic anger as one of the agents closed the back door.

"Okay," Miller said. "I think we're done here. Ellen, if you would take your helpers back to town, I'll go ahead to Quantico and set things up with Behavioral Sciences." Then he turned to Av and his partners. "Gentlemen, Special Agent Whiting will explain things to you in due course, and I will personally smooth over any problems this case may have caused for you at MPD. That's a promise. Your Bureau thanks you very, very much."

"*My* Bureau?" Wong said softly as Miller joined the other agents at the second SUV. Mau-Mau snorted.

"Let's go, boys," Ellen said. "The detective sergeant here's had a long night, and I need a drink. Or three."

"Three's good," Wong said. "Four's better. Man! That was nice shooting."

Miz Brown positively beamed.

"Okay, let's start with this stalking horse business," Av said.

The four of them were sitting in his loft apartment; Miz Brown had decided to go home after shooting up Mandeville's hands. He'd said he needed to pray on it. Av had thanked him profusely, but Brown had waved his thanks aside. "Don't like to do that, shooting someone like that," he said. "Had to be done, I know, but I still feel bad about it."

"You hadn't, I wouldn't be feeling anything," Av had reminded him.

"But you would be with the Lord," Brown had said, with a suitably beatific smile.

Ellen had Scotch; Av and his partners were drinking beer. Ellen explained the concept of a stalking horse as something done to draw out someone who would otherwise never show his hand. "Political parties do it in primaries," she said. "Put up some nobody candidate to see what the opposition's going to do, or how strong their own candidate is."

"I get that," Av said. "But why'd you need one to deal with Mandeville?"

"Two reasons," she said. "One, you've heard people talk about the White House as the Bubble. Totally protected. Totally insulated. Secret Service. Building guards. Military snipers and antiaircraft weapons on the roof. Armored transport. Top-flight secure communications. Bunkers. Undisclosed locations, around the city and elsewhere. Jumbo-jet airplanes. Helicopters. No-fly zones—the list just goes on and on."

"But that's all for the President."

"Yeah, but it covers some of the senior staff, too, right? A guy like Mandeville, a senior presidential advisor? He's in that bubble, too. You can *not* get at a guy like that unless you can draw him out of that Kevlar bubble."

"What's the second reason?" Mau-Mau asked.

"The Bureau knew about the dissent within the DMX. It wasn't until I had that lunch with McGavin and then a little recap session with Mandeville that we realized how out-there this was getting. Problem was that Mandeville tricked me into being involved in what happened to McGavin. That gave him a pretty big stick to use on the Bureau if we did do something official."

Bureau involvement, Av thought. Right. Now he understood. "How'd the Bureau even know?"

"I told my boss some of the things Mandeville was saying. He's known to be a crusader for the DMX, so, yes, it was extreme, but no one ever thought he'd start killing people."

Av blew out a long breath. "So: CT equals no rules, then."

Ellen shrugged. "I think," she said, "that they truly believe the CT effort is so important, so vital to the survival of the country, that the everyday laws don't always apply. I mean, for God's sake, look at the DMX."

"And the fact that there are eighty-plus agencies makes it easier for them to do that," Av said. "So why me, and who knew?"

"Second question first—we called Precious in and told her what we were thinking about doing. Let her see a videotape of Mandeville going off on some of his own staff for some mortal sin or other. It was persuasive, right down to the tufts of fire coming out of his temples and the blue light of madness in his eyes. She bought right in. Said you'd be perfect, 'cause you'd never catch on."

"Well, thank you, Precious." Av snorted. "And all those heavy dudes out on the towpath?"

"Those were Mandeville's people, or, rather, Strang's. He's still a loose end. He was the man in charge of the other side of that Chinese wall. We had no frigging idea we had a twenty-six-year Agency CO operative working as a GS-7 in the basement. Or why he was there. We only got onto him because Mandeville had to use one of our ciphers to call in to the headquarters building. If he'd used the White House system, we'd have never known."

"And he was the guy Hiram gave the joy juice to?"

"No," she said. "That was three years ago. Hiram remembered him, because he already knew about the special plants. Strang wanted the plants, actually, but Hiram didn't trust him."

"Okay, okay, wait a minute," Mau-Mau interjected. "All these people knowin' everything, everybody plottin' and schemin', walking right through those Chinese walls and shit—everybody just one step ahead of everybody else: how they doin' that?"

Ellen sipped some of her Scotch. "You read the Snowden revelations?" she asked. "About how the government is listening—hell, not just listening, but *recording*—every phone conversation and e-mail and text and IM and, fuck me, *tweet* in the country, if not the world? Lemme explain something: at every DMX meeting, a rep from the NSA stands up and gives us a briefing. He calls it the nugget brief. He talks about the nuggets of interesting information they glean from all that listening. You know what that rep told me one day? He said: we *are* the Cloud."

"Holy shit," Mau-Mau muttered.

"Well, it's true. You put it out there, someone sees it. Guy like Mandeville? He knew how to get at some of that information, and how to have a funny-looking flower vendor show up in the Bistro Nord and entice me to buy a nice bouquet of flowers, which he placed right under McGavin's nose. A minute later McGavin was dead on the floor, and—*and*—when the cops and the fake EMTs arrived, did anyone mention flowers?"

"So you told Mandeville that I was working the McGavin incident?"

"Nope," she said. "Strang did that. Told Mandeville where the case was being handled. Mandeville told him to see if he could deflect you and the rest of the guys in the Briar Patch. Hence the fake-FPS stunt on the towpath."

"But the FPS actually called our bosses and bitched about that," Mau-Mau said.

"No, they didn't," Ellen said. "We checked—FPS didn't know what we were talking about."

Mau-Mau shook his head. Av suddenly wanted some of Ellen's Scotch.

Wong announced that he was hungry, and did anyone else feel like some Chinese chow. The other three looked at each other and said yes.

"So everything after that, *you* guys were running it?" Av said.

"We were running *you,*" she said. "It was perfect. Mandeville could not believe that some cop in an office known as the Briar Patch was poking his nose into *anything* that was going on at his level. He called the deputy director of the Bureau, Mister Ederington, and told him to have you picked up by a tactical squad and sequestered in the special facility down in Petersburg. Matter of utmost urgency. FISA court warrant to follow. Can't explain it over the phone, even over a secure phone. Presidential interest. DMX related. Just do it."

"And just like that, he did?"

"No, actually," she said. "When he heard 'DMX' he called my boss in and said WTF. We took it from there, called the colonel in charge down there, and then got Wong, here, to spring you out of there and begin the chain of events that, hopefully, would result in Mandeville coming up out of his lair and going for you, personally. That was the only way we figured we could get him."

"Why did I end up at Hiram's?" Av asked.

"I spent some time with Hiram," she said. "He showed me his research facility, explained how he'd helped the government before, and why he'd given Mandeville the materials. It was *his* idea to get you out there, as bait for Mandeville. I think he wanted to see what his little plant arsenal could do."

"It, by God, did the job," Av said.

"And then he set you loose on the river."

"Yeah, where fucking Mandeville's operators were waiting and watching. Jesus, Ellen, they could have just offed me in the helo and thrown my ass into that rotor thing at Little Falls Dam."

She smiled. "That was the FBI's Hostage Rescue Team," she said. "Believe it or not, Mandeville called Strang and told him that he wanted you picked up at Hiram's estate. Strang, God bless him, told Mandeville to call in the HRT—with White House authority, they'd do what he wanted, and bring you to wherever Mandeville said. The HRT boss called my boss to ask who this Mandeville guy was, calling in on a White House phone. My boss called me, and we saw our chance."

"And why did you involve the Briar Patch in the first place?" Av asked. "You got the whole FBI to call on."

She smiled again, with the hint of a blush in it. "My boss said to get you guys to front the operation. That way, if it all turned to shit, the Bureau could say: Who, me?"

The doorbell rang and Wong went to the front door, fumbling with his wallet. He peered through the peephole. White guy, holding up bags. He opened the door.

"So," Av continued. "Did you roll up Strang and whoever he was using?"

"No," she said. "We have no idea where Strang is."

"Oh, I think we do," Wong said, backing into the room, followed by Kyle Strang, carrying an H & K MP5 A2, with which he was casually covering the entire room.

"Aw, shit," Mau-Mau said. "Where's the damn chow?"

"Just outside the door," Strang said. "I paid the delivery guy. Back up, King Kong."

Wong backed away from the door and then went over to the couch, where he sat down next to Ellen and put on his best glare. Strang didn't appear to notice.

"You people need to just relax," Strang said, dropping into one of the living room chairs. "This thing's for my protection, not for you. I need to fill you in on a couple of things, that's all, so don't anybody get stupid on me or we'll have a terrible accident here. Hello, Ellen Whiting."

"One moment," Av said. He'd been sitting in a chair close to the couch. He got up now, put a finger to his lips in Strang's direction, and went over to the couch, where he appropriated what was left of Ellen's Scotch in one gulp. Then he went back to his chair, sat down, and said: "Shoot. So to speak, I mean."

Strang snorted. "Okay," he said. "First things first. I work for the Central Intelligence Agency, and have done so for almost three decades."

"So what are you doing in the audiovisual section of the Bureau?" Av asked.

"I'll get to that," Strang said. "Just as soon as I tell you that I had *nothing* to do with either McGavin or Logan shuffling off this mortal coil."

"Bullshit," Ellen said. "Hiram Walker told me you came to him personally to get your hands on some of his more dangerous plants."

"Yes, I did," Strang said. "And you know what? He said no. Actually, what he said was: 'Let me think about that, Mister Strang. I will need to consult with my colleagues in the society. But, on balance, I think we might be able to help you.' That's what he said."

"And then, later, he turned you down?"

"He did," Strang said. "Which begs the obvious question, doesn't it."

"Absolutely," Ellen said. "If you weren't behind what happened to McGavin and Logan, who the fuck was?"

"You know exactly who, Special Agent," Strang said. "The 'how' is another matter, but we at the Agency have no doubt that Carl Mandeville orchestrated both murders."

"Our sources tell us that *you* were the 'how,' if not personally, then the person who arranged for some operatives from beyond the Chinese wall to come take a hand in saving the DMX," Ellen protested.

"Your sources?" Strang said. "Your sources were told what we wanted them to hear, Special Agent. You're missing the big picture here."

"Me, too," Av said. "So—"

"It's pretty simple, Detective. Before there was a DMX, the only agency that was allowed to go places and kill 'persons of interest' was the Agency. Then, because of all the so-called intelligence failures preceding nine-eleven, the DMX was created. The Agency became just one player among many. It was a signal demotion, both of federal trust, prestige, not to mention budgetary power."

"Wait," Av said. "Are you saying—"

"Exactly, Detective. The Agency was and is in total agreement with the senators who want to kill off the DMX. Not because of some arcane ethical concerns, of course, but for the reason that we want that particular mission back in *our* hands, where it rightly belongs. Once we found out Mandeville was planning to off the entire committee, to purify it, as he said a couple times, then we saw our chance."

"Now *you* sound like Mandeville," Ellen said.

Strang smiled. "Mandeville was told that I could be 'useful' to him, with the idea being that I could watch for an opportunity to unseat him. They gave him my classified bio, and then told him that I'd be hidden in plain sight in the Hoover building. He couldn't resist the irony of that, apparently. They told him I could get things done for him, outside of the usual CT channels. But: Carl Mandeville's not a trusting soul, as you can imagine. So he kept some of his own assets to himself, as you found out, Detective."

"So Hiram gave *him* the magic potions?" Av asked.

"You'll have to take that up with Mister Walker," Strang said. "What I do know is he told me no."

There was a minute's silence in the room as they digested these revelations.

"Mandeville's genius," Strang said, "is that he saw how cluttered the CT world was becoming, with every Tom, Dick, and Harry agency in the government wanting in on the coolest intel action in town—the Kill List. If anybody tumbled to some of the shit he was doing, he could immediately implicate about a dozen different agencies, and then they'd all go after each other."

"You said he was gonna take out the entire committee?" Av said.

Strang hesitated, as if trying to figure out how much more he should reveal. "He had a connection at Fort Detrick, the army's bioweapons defense lab. The CO of that facility called the Agency and asked if they knew why Mandeville was asking for some truly bad shit that could be used to kill instead of warn."

"A biological weapon?" Av asked. "We do that shit these days?"

"No, we don't. But Mandeville had set up a lab within the lab. He covered it by reprogramming a few million into the USAMRIID budget. DMX business. Secret-cubed. The guy was the original loose cannon."

"But now he's in custody," Ellen said.

"For the moment, perhaps," Strang said. "I don't know where you're taking him, but I'll give you one piece of advice: do not, under any circumstances, allow him to communicate with *anyone,* anyone at all, because if he does, you'll never get your hands on him again, *and* you and all your bosses will be wading through a shitstorm for the next year."

"We have him red-handed," Ellen said. "He was about to shoot the detective here."

"No, you don't," Strang said. "For starters, I'm willing to bet you had no federal warrant to even be there at that park. The only help you could muster up were these rather—*interesting* specimens, from the MPD, for God's sake."

"Hey," Wong growled. "You want to see interesting? I'll show you interesting."

Strang rolled his eyes. "You guys did all this on the fly, didn't you, Special Agent. Let me tell you how this will end: my director will come to see your director. I am confident that they will work something out."

"We could subpoena you, then," Ellen said. "You seem to know so much."

Strang laughed a short bark of a laugh. "I keep forgetting—you work for the Bureau. It's all about the airtight case, isn't it? When Mandeville went from éminence grise to personally pointing a gun at a cop? He stepped out of the civilized light and into the same world he thought he owned—the world of ruby-eyed robots coming for you in the night. Besides, I'm going to be—unavailable, for a while."

"Aw, lemme guess," Av asked. "In one of those undisclosed locations, right?"

"Yes, indeed, Detective," Strang said. "One last question, Special Agent—did Hiram Walker make an appearance at your little showdown at Fort Marcy?"

"He did," she said.

Strang smiled broadly at something that obviously pleased him very much and then got up and walked sideways toward the front door.

"You gonna leave the chow?" Wong asked.

"Certainly," he said, as he opened the door. "You just better hope I didn't put something in it, you know, like some, hell, I don't know, seven dragon loose-end sauce?" He gave them a wolfish grin and then left.

Nobody moved for a full thirty seconds after Strang closed the door behind him. Then Wong went to the door, opened it carefully, and retrieved the three white bags of takeout, which were already beginning to show oil stains.

"Seven dragon 'loose-end' sauce?" Av said. "I think I'll pass, guys."

There was general agreement on that strategy. Ellen yawned and said she needed to go home. Av said he would walk her out to her car.

Out on the sidewalk he said he had a couple of questions about their great adventure.

"Shoot," she said.

"First, how'd you guys bug my apartment?"

She smiled. "We discovered that we had some ready-service help right there in your building. By the name of Special Agent Rue Waltham?"

"You're shitting me—*she's* an agent? She said she was a lawyer."

"She is both. We've got lots of lawyers in the Bureau. In fact, back in the day, you had to be either a lawyer or an accountant just to be a special agent. Times have changed; she works in our international operations division."

"You planted her in my building?"

"Nope. She did that rental all by herself. Our surveillance people needed a base of operations near your building, preferably something besides the traditional telephone truck. They scanned all the addresses in your area and hers popped out, right *in* your building. I wish I could tell you that this was all planned, but it was mostly serendipity."

"Okay—one last question: you and Strang—you were a team in this, right? I mean there's no other way it could have worked."

She feigned surprise. "You're suggesting that the Bureau and the Agency might have worked together on this goat-grab?" she said. "What are the chances of that?"

"You didn't answer my question," he said.

She smiled, looked away, but said nothing.

"Okay." He sighed. "But who was the second man working for Mandeville? The guy he sicced on me?"

"We have no fucking idea," she said, quietly. "That's the disturbing truth."

"Disturbing—that's one way of phrasing it," he said. "Because if he's still out there, then *I've* still got a big problem."

"I wouldn't think so," she said. "Whoever he is, he knows the rules of the game. Once Mandeville goes down, his tasking, as it were, goes down with him. What would be the point?"

He sighed again, not entirely sure her logic would hold up. Then asked if he'd see her again.

"Whatever for, Detective Sergeant?" she asked, with a sly smile. "Me being so very scary and everything. You're not about to broach the R-word are you?"

"R-word?"

"As in: relationship?"

"Well, I guess I could make an exception, just this once."

"Uh-huh."

He felt himself blushing just a little. "I mean, well, um—"

"I've got some news," she interrupted gently.

"News?" he said, warily. Oh, God, now what? he thought.

"I've got a date tomorrow, or I guess it's today, now. Dinner, and then a walk in a park, I believe."

"With whom?"

"Can't you guess, you being a detective sergeant and all?"

Av was baffled, and not for the first time, by this high-energy lady. Then he did guess.

"Hiram?" he squeaked. "But—but—"

She was laughing now. "And why not?" she said. "He's head and shoulders the most interesting man I've met in a long, long time."

"Head and shoulders is right," he said.

"We-e-ll, I didn't say it was romance, did I. It's drinks on the terrace, dinner served by the staff, and then a walk in the park. His park. At his mansion on his riverfront estate, where the gardens are alive in more ways than one. Frankly, I was flattered when he asked me. Besides, it's just possible he may have already solved your potentially big problem."

"Wow" was all Av could manage, trying to visualize them as a pair.

She stood on her tiptoes and kissed him on the cheek. "We could always be workout buddies again sometime, Detective Sergeant," she said, her eyes twinkling. "Just keep an eye on your caller ID, okay? Bye, now."

As she drove away, Av looked out into the tiny park by the canal lock. A young couple was walking by, the woman rhapsodizing about the historical canal, the guy looking over at Av, a sympathetic expression on his face when he saw Ellen leaving. Av put up his palms and shrugged. The guy grinned; they do get away, sometimes.

He went back upstairs, where Mau-Mau and Wong were taking beer bottles and glasses out to the kitchen. Wong was still griping about the compromised takeout.

"Gonna see that one again?" Mau-Mau asked him.

"Don't think so," Av said. "You know me."

"Thought I did, till I saw that bra in the bathroom," Mau-Mau said with a grin. "Although it wasn't really your size and all."

Av tried to think of a snappy comeback but all he could do was grin, too. After they'd left, he climbed up to the rooftop and stretched out in the lawn chair.

He thought about Ellen Whiting and her bewildering world of spooks, high-powered secret committees, and scary political games. He conjured up an image of her blasting through D.C. on a Harley with a swarm of feds on her tail—his Harley, now that he thought about it, have to get that back. He wondered if there were warrants out on that bike now. Did he really want to be involved with a woman like her?

Have to think about that, he concluded. Then he heard the house phone ringing. He ran down the stairs and barely beat the voice mail robot.

"Detective Sergeant," Ellen said. "I forgot about your bike."

"Where'd it end up?" he said.

"At the Hoover building. I'll get it back to you tomorrow."

"Take your time," he said. "Bring it when you feel like taking a ride. So to speak."

"Feel?" she said, ignoring his not very subtle suggestion. "As in feelings? *You* talking about feelings? You telling me you felt something that night?"

"It was morning," he said. "And, yes, I did. Feel something. There was something in the bed. Like a rock, maybe. Piece of gravel? A pea?"

She started to laugh. "Careful what you wish for," she said. "And remember, I don't always knock."

"I'll keep the change jar open for you," he said.

TWENTY-FIVE

"You ever seen a guy that big?" the agent driving asked his teammates as he turned the SUV south onto I-395 near the Pentagon and headed for Quantico.

"Looked like fucking Frankenstein," one of the others said.

"Frankenstein was the mad scientist, not the monster," said the third. "But, yeah, that's what I thought of when I first saw him. Had to be what, six-ten, maybe even seven?"

"Had to be. The funeral director from hell. I stopped breathing for a moment. You see Bruno going for his weapon?"

They all laughed at that, except their passenger.

Carl Mandeville was still bound into his personal wiring harness in the middle of the backseat, with a bulky agent on either side. His hands were in his lap, the right one throbbing painfully under bulky bandages and one plaster cast. There was a plastic restraining wire strung between his forearms, supporting a third restraint wire that was clipped to a ring in the floor. His suit-coat sleeves hung empty on either side of his chest. His eyes were closed but he was definitely not asleep.

He was waiting. Wherever they were going, there'd be a phone. Or someone who had a phone, or someone who could *get* to a phone who could be intimidated to make one call, just one call to the White House operator, say a single code word, and then every one of these clowns would be shaking fries at a McDonald's the next day and wondering what had just happened.

Then he would deal with the high-and-mighty leadership at the Bureau, itself. He would smother them under so much superclassified national security bullshit, special task-force inquiries, and maybe even a special prosecutor, that they'd be digging out for years, from the director on down. He would *bury* them for pulling this stunt tonight, and even dumber, claiming they had a case on *him*.

They thought they had a case. Bullshit. Besides, even if they did, it hardly mattered, because what good's a case without a court? There wasn't a court in the land cleared to hear any part of this, not even everyone's pet panel of judges over at FISA. As any real player in the CT business knew, FISA was a judicial fig leaf and nothing more. No agency with any real clout took serious operational cases to FISA—instead, they took the litter-box stuff, the hypotheticals, the borderline targets, the international hairball cases, and so many of them that all those learned judges all thought they were being groomed for the Supreme Court.

Through slitted eyes he watched the exit signs for the northern Virginia suburbs flash by in the darkness. In all his years in Washington, he'd never been able to drive faster than ten miles an hour down this stretch of I-95. No, he wasn't worried about any so-called case the Bureau would try to build against him.

Hiram Walker. There was the real threat. Hiram Nightshade was more like it. Clever bastard had been unwilling to deal with Strang. Oh, no, if he was going to hand over some of his black-widow juice, it was only going to be to the man in charge. And, like a dummy, he, Carl Mandeville, had fallen for it, thus giving Hiram a permanent, stainless-steel fishhook into his guts. He still wondered if Strang had maybe arranged that precondition on purpose.

Smug bastard, Hiram Walker, he thought, looming over everyone out there in that park in his Jack the Ripper frock coat, like some kind of Victorian vampire. He glanced down at the little flower in his buttonhole. Something to remember him by? Hiram Walker would be remembered, all right. Evangelino would see to that, personally. What *he* would do to Hiram Walker would be memorable, indeed.

He tried lifting his arms to see if he could dislodge the annoying flower, but the cast on his four-fingered hand was too heavy and the restraining wire made it impossible. Frustrated, he leaned forward so that his unbandaged hand could just reach his chest and then mashed the flower.

There, he thought. That's what's going to happen to you, you fucking freak.

"Hey, Harry," the agent on his left said. "I think I had too much coffee at the ER—any chance of a pit stop along here?"

"Not until Occoquan," the driver said. "And two of us have to stay with what's-his-name back here."

"He'll be good," the agent said. "Won't you, bud."

"Cold," Mandeville croaked.